W9-CDV-522

RESURRECTION
ROAD

Also by Kathryn R. Wall

In for a Penny

And Not a Penny More

Perdition House

Judas Island

NEW HANOVER COUNTY
PUBLIC LIBRARY
201 CHESTNUT STREET
WILMINGTON, NC 28401

RESURRECTION ROAD

KATHRYN R. WALL

ST. MARTIN'S MINOTAUR NEW YORK

RESURRECTION ROAD. Copyright © 2005 by Kathryn R. Wall. All rights reserved. Printed in the United States of America. No part of this book may be used or reproduced in any manner whatsoever without written permission except in the case of brief quotations embodied in critical articles or reviews. For information, address St. Martin's Press, 175 Fifth Avenue, New York, N.Y. 10010.

www.minotaurbooks.com

Library of Congress Cataloging-in-Publication Data

Wall, Kathryn R.

Resurrection Road: a Bay Tanner mystery / Kathryn R. Wall.—1st ed.

p. cm.

ISBN 0-312-33793-0

EAN 978-0312-33793-3

1. Tanner, Bay (Fictitious character)—Fiction. 2. Women private investigators—South Carolina—Fiction. 3. Hilton Head Island (S.C.)—Fiction. 4. Beaufort County (S.C.)—Fiction. I. Title.

PS3623.A4424R47 2005

813'.6—dc22

2004065354

First Edition: May 2005

10 9 8 7 6 5 4 3 2 1

Once again, this book is for
Norman
husband and friend

Acknowledgments

One of the problems in using real places as fictional settings is that the author must sometimes take liberties with the truth in service to the story. I'd like to state for the record that the Beaufort County Sheriff's Office is one of the finest law enforcement organizations in South Carolina, patrolling a wide and varied geographic area and dealing with an annual influx of more than two million visitors with integrity and dedication. Any implication to the contrary is entirely fictional. Fort Fremont does exist, and its location and history are accurately portrayed to the best of my knowledge.

My gratitude to Jo and Vicky for their continued friendship and support, as well as to Linda, Rachel, Laura, and Amy for their professionalism in bringing the Bay Tanner books to market.

Resurrection
Road

Chapter One

"You're not getting involved with those people again, and that's final!"

I punctuated the shout by ripping the ball cross-court, a stinging backhand that should have left him staring in admiration as it whizzed by. Instead he dived to his left, just managed to get a racket on it, and popped up a lazy floater that nicked the tape and dribbled over to land six inches beyond my side of the net.

"Game!" he shouted, pumping his tanned fist in the air. "And set!"

He dropped to his knees and raised his face and arms skyward, like Pete Sampras at Wimbledon. The group next to us interrupted their doubles game to grin at his antics, and one of the two lanky women waiting for our court applauded.

I flashed him a reluctant smile and trotted over to gather our gear from beside the net post. "I'd be ashamed to take that point if I were you," I said, slinging a towel around my neck and swiping at the strands of sweat-soaked hair escaping from my ponytail.

"Bay Tanner, I would never have expected you to be such a bad loser."

"Alain Darnay, I'd never have expected you to be such a cocky winner."

I was also pretty amazed at how well his recovery was coming along. Less than a year before, I had worked frantically to staunch the blood pouring from a gaping bullet wound in his left side. A scant two months ago he had still looked thin and frail as he glowered from the curb in front of the Paris apartment at the taxi whisking me off to Orly Airport and home. It seemed I had been wrong. Returning to his dangerous work with Interpol hadn't jeopardized his health—it had apparently restored it.

"We'll discuss it, *ma petite,*" he said, mopping his streaming face.

It took me a moment to realize he was referring to my outburst just before the end of the match. LeBrun, his superior at Interpol, had sent another coded fax just that morning, one in a long stream of communications which had kept the international phone lines buzzing for the past week or so. I didn't need to decipher its contents to know Darnay's employers were angling once again to get him back in their deadly game.

"Damn right we will," I said, softening the words with a smile.

We slid our rackets into their carrying cases, and Darnay hefted the double-handled tennis bag. He flung an arm across my shoulder, being careful to avoid the tender area where my own recent wound had still not completely healed.

What a pair we are, I thought. *When we get old, we can sit around and compare battle scars.*

He nodded to the two women who had moved onto the court behind us. "Enjoy your game, ladies," he said in a thick French accent that made even the most mundane comments sound like a lover's caress.

"Quit flirting," I said good-naturedly and received a Gallic shrug from the tall, craggy Frenchman who only that morning had asked me to marry him—for the fourteenth time, if my scorekeeping could be trusted. If he wasn't careful, I thought, I'd begin to take the offers seriously.

"What can I say, my darling? It is the nature of the beast. Bred into the bones, absorbed from the mother's milk, inhaled with the bouquet of the wines . . ."

I punched him playfully in the arm with my free hand.

As we approached the canopy of live oaks under which we'd left the

Thunderbird, Darnay tossed the bag into the rear seat. Turning his back on the parking lot, he leaned casually against the creamy yellow fender of my new convertible. His face had lost its bantering look, and his normally soft eyes had darkened to the steely blue which usually signaled anger.

"Keep smiling," he said, ignoring his own dictum, "and glance over my right shoulder."

I faltered a little, startled by the tone of his voice.

"Smile," he repeated, and I did my best to comply.

"What am I looking at?"

He reached out to slip an errant strand of auburn hair behind my ear. "Black Mercedes sedan at the end of the row. Young man. Dark skin, longish blond hair. Navy blue polo shirt."

I leaned in to kiss him gently on the cheek and whispered, "Got him. So what's the problem?"

Another woman might have asked more questions, been more suspicious of Darnay's sudden change of mood and urgent commands. In the two years since I'd watched my husband's plane explode in a shower of flaming debris and dismembered bodies, I'd experienced enough danger to recognize its reflection in someone else's eyes.

"Do you know him?" Darnay nuzzled my ear, momentarily making me lose track of the conversation.

"Uh, no. No, I don't think so. Why?"

"Give me the keys and get in," he said.

For a moment I balked. Taking orders is absolutely alien to both my nature and inclination. But Darnay's glare didn't waver, so I strolled around to the passenger side and slid into the sun-warmed leather seat. Without turning my head, I managed to get another glimpse of the object of his interest. Definitely young. Expensive-looking wraparound shades. Maybe Latino.

"Smile," I heard again from the other side of the car, so I threw back my head and laughed, a sound so artificial it wouldn't have fooled anyone within hearing distance. Hopefully I looked the picture of carefree, fortyish Southern womanhood: rich and idle, without a problem in the world. I carried on with the charade until Darnay backed the car around and headed us out of the small tennis complex tucked up to one of the three golf courses in Port Royal Plantation.

"What the hell was that all about?" I demanded as we pulled onto Fort Walker Drive. The sweet gums and towering pines cast a welcome shade over the sleek hood of the convertible.

"He's following us." Alain Darnay, Interpol agent and former top investigator for the Sûreté in Paris, barely flicked his eyes to the rearview mirror. "No, don't look!" he barked when I began to turn in my seat.

"You're seriously ticking me off," I said in a voice he should have been all too familiar with. Our on-again, off-again romance had been more off than on recently, due primarily to the demands of his profession. "And so what if he's behind us?" I added, glancing at the firm set of his wide mouth and the slight dimple that bisected his otherwise strong chin.

"This is the third time he's turned up in the last couple of days," Alain remarked, his tone so conversational we might have been discussing last night's Braves game or the time of the next high tide. "I do not like coincidences."

"I don't either. But Hilton Head is an island, after all, and a small one. Even with all the summer tourists here, it wouldn't be that far-fetched to run across the same person a couple of times. Especially if he's staying at the Westin or renting one of the condos at the Barony."

"And you believe he just happened to be at the restaurant last night? And at the bookstore this morning?"

His questions brought me up short. I'd been so intent the previous evening on deflecting Darnay's thirteenth marriage proposal over candlelight and champagne at Conroy's that I'd been pretty much oblivious to my surroundings. He, however, had been captivated by the works of our local literary icon for whom the swanky dining room of the Marriott Hotel had been named. It had been Darnay who insisted on running out the next morning to fill in the gaps in my collection of the works of Pat Conroy. Engrossed in my quest through the aisles of Barnes & Noble, I'd failed to notice a familiar face.

"I'm sorry. I didn't realize."

His smile accepted my apology.

"So what do you think it's all about?" I asked.

It couldn't have anything to do with the fledgling inquiry agency my father and I had established. We had been floundering since the defection of one of our founding members, Erik Whiteside. The last thing remotely resembling a case had been wrapped up months before, its only lingering remnant evidenced by the stiffness that still plagued my injured left shoulder. Having been mangled by the exploding debris of my late husband's plane, then battered again by a through-and-through bullet wound, by rights the shoulder should not have been functioning at all. I applied creams to soothe the shiny skin grafts, exercised the stiff joint every chance I got, and tried not to think about it.

"He was watching us play tennis, then hurried back to his car while we were packing up," Darnay finally answered. "Nice-looking, clean-cut, maybe five-eight or nine. You sure you don't recognize him?"

"Positive," I said as we took a left just before the overpass that led to the security gate.

The road to my beach house skirted one of the golf courses, winding its way to the ocean past sprawling Lowcountry homes nestled among stands of live oaks and screening shrubbery.

"Glance back now and see if he followed us," Darnay commanded.

I turned casually, as if surveying the scenery, just in time to see the black car disappear over the bridge and glide on toward the gate. "Nope, he kept going."

My relief proved short-lived as my companion suddenly whipped the car into a narrow driveway, reversed, and roared back the way we had come. The glint in his eye as he took the sharp turn back onto the main road made me remember that Alain Darnay much preferred the role of hunter to that of quarry.

Just outside the main gate the Mercedes made a right onto the access road to the Westin. We followed more slowly, there being no rush to close the gap since the few turnoffs all led to dead ends. We hung back and watched the young man maneuver his vehicle into a parking space near the entrance to the gleaming resort hotel.

The T-Bird leapt as Darnay gunned the engine and squealed to a halt perpendicular to the black car's rear bumper, effectively blocking it in. He jumped from the driver's seat and in one swift movement had the door of the Mercedes open and a squirming teenager spread-eagled across the trunk.

"Okay, son, I need to hear why you've been following us for two days."

"Screw you!" The voice was garbled since its owner's right cheek was pressed into the hot metal of the Mercedes' deck lid, but there was no mistaking the venom.

"Now, be nice," Darnay replied in his most sarcastic tone. "There's a lady present."

"Lady, my ass!" The boy squirmed under the pressure of Darnay's grip, but he was no match for the older man.

"Don't hurt him," I called from the passenger seat. "He's only a kid."

"Shut up! I don't need you to—" the boy yelled, but the rest was cut off as Darnay twisted his arm up higher on his back.

"Alain! Please!" I was suddenly aware that someone could come along any moment and arrest him for assault and battery. Maybe things were different where he came from, but in Beaufort County, South Carolina, the sheriff didn't take kindly to people roughing up the tourists. Bad for business.

Darnay eased up a little and flipped the young man around, allowing him to stand upright. "I asked you a question, sonny," he growled.

"I don't have to tell you shit, old man." The defiance lasted until Alain pulled off his own sunglasses, and the kid got a good look at his eyes. I could almost feel the fear rising in his throat. "Look, back off, okay? I'm not trying to hurt anybody." He paused a moment, then added, "Okay?"

Darnay glanced at me, and I nodded. He took one step back, giving the boy room to breathe but still guarding against any chance of his bolting. "Let's hear it."

"I . . . I was just curious. About her." His stammering admission made him sound even younger than he obviously was. I was guessing seventeen, maybe a year or two either way. Hard to tell these days.

I stepped out of the car, surveying the surrounding area in the hope we were unobserved. Alain was here on a tourist visa, and I didn't think it would do his reputation any good to get picked up and packed off to France. In these times of heightened terrorist alerts and a rekindled suspicion of foreigners, I was pretty sure no one would be cutting him any slack, Interpol or no.

I moved around the car until I stood facing the kid, his breath coming in short, nervous gulps. Whether they were a result of the tussle with Darnay or from the waves of anger I felt rolling off him, I couldn't tell.

"Here I am," I said softly. "What do you want to know?"

The offer stunned him momentarily, but you had to give the boy credit. He glared past the hulking, six-foot-two Darnay and straight into my eyes. He drew a long, shuddering breath and said, "I want to know why you killed my father."

Chapter Two

I THINK DARNAY WOULD HAVE BLINDFOLDED HIM IF HE thought he could get away with it, but he settled for shoving the boy none too gently into the passenger seat of the Mercedes before sliding behind the wheel.

"We'll take him to the house," he said in that authoritative voice that brooked no opposition, "and get to the bottom of this nonsense. You must drive yourself."

"I'll see if I can manage," I muttered as I slammed the door of the T-Bird and yanked it into gear.

I laid a small strip of rubber, which helped to vent some of my frustration, and led the two-car parade past the covered portico in front of the hotel and back the way we had come. This was a prime example of why I had not succumbed to Darnay's repeated proposals over the few weeks he'd been on the island. Arrogant, domineering, thoroughly maddening, he saw no problem with a virtual kidnapping in broad daylight. The thought I might object to being an accomplice apparently never crossed his mind. On the other hand, he could be irresistibly charming, attentive, seductive . . .

I let those unsettling thoughts drift away on the wind as we pulled into the driveway of my beach cottage. With both motors finally stilled, the muted hiss of the waves, just a few yards away over the dune, was all that broke the somnolent midday silence. Built high off the ground with the garage tucked underneath, the house and its silvered wood siding had withstood battering storms, the relentless assault of a blistering sun, and an explosion whose reverberations were still echoing through my life. The evidence of that could be seen in the person of the young man now extricating himself reluctantly from the car behind me.

I hadn't needed to ask his name. Once I got a close-up look at his face, minus the Serengeti sunglasses, there could be no doubt as to his identity. I didn't know if he belonged to the first or second of his father's wives, but the other half of his parentage was painfully obvious. The hooded blue eyes glowed with the same easy sensuality; the well-muscled arms spoke of athletic prowess, and I could picture him snapping to attention in a perfectly creased military-school uniform.

Only the blond hair threw me until I realized it was a very bad dye job. Probably the boy's idea, along with the wraparounds, of some sort of disguise.

I unfolded my five-foot, ten-inch frame from the bucket seat as Darnay marched the young man toward the house. His struggles were mere formality now. He had apparently realized the futility of trying to break the iron grip encircling his upper arm. That didn't, however, keep his mouth from working overtime.

"You can't do this! It's . . . it's kidnapping! I'll sue your ass, you son of a bitch!"

Darnay ignored the outburst as we mounted the steps to my front door.

"Who the hell do you think you are, some kind of bodyguard? You goddamned people think you can just march in here and take over the freakin' country? My grandfather will kill your miserable—"

Even Darnay had his limits. "Shut up!" he roared in the kid's ear, and the boy fell silent.

I led the way inside, disengaging the alarm system and tossing my bag onto the white sofa in the great room. Darnay dragged the boy across the carpet and shoved him none too gently into one of the wing chairs flanking the fireplace. Thankfully Dolores Santiago, my part-time housekeeper, had the day off. I knew Alain had no intention of actually harming the boy, but additional witnesses would have made his show of outrage and anger more difficult to maintain. Intimidation was obviously his game plan.

Darnay flopped himself down next to me on the sofa and made a dramatic show of consulting his watch. "Okay, sonny, you have exactly three minutes to explain this ridiculous accusation and your harassment of my friend before I call the police." The boy opened his mouth, but Darnay forestalled him with a finger pointed directly at his face. "And watch your language. One more profanity in the presence of Mrs. Tanner, and I shall drag your sorry little butt into the bathroom and scrub out your mouth for you."

From the look in the boy's eyes, I knew he believed it. He drew what I hoped was a calming breath, and some of the anger seemed to seep out of him.

"Look, I didn't mean . . . I just want to talk to her."

"You have no cell phone? You never heard of calling up and asking for an appointment?" Darnay, too, had eased off. His tone now exuded more interest than menace. "And please refrain from referring to Mrs. Tanner as 'her.' She has a name."

The young man hung his head and studied the fingers twisting nervously in his lap. Now that he had the opportunity to confront me, he seemed to be having a hard time finding the words.

I tried to ease the way for him. "I know who you are." I spoke softly, intrigued by the procession of emotions that flitted across the young man's face: surprise, fear, anger. A softening around the eyes I thought might have been sadness. I felt Darnay turn to stare at me, but I ignored him. "What's your first name?"

For a moment I thought he wasn't going to answer. Then, "Carter," he mumbled. "They call me Cart." He raised his head defiantly and really looked at me for the first time, and I gazed sadly across the room into the blazing blue eyes of Geoffrey Anderson's son.

After Carter left, I offered to fix lunch, but Darnay muttered something about an appointment. He grabbed a quick shower, then hurried off in the rental car he'd been using since his arrival a few weeks before. He'd been doing a lot of that lately—disappearing with little notice—and again I wondered if it had something to do with the recent spate of communication from his old employers. I thought I'd made it pretty plain how I felt about his resuming his clandestine life with Interpol, but I'd also come to realize there wasn't a damn thing I could do about it. Either way.

I showered and changed, made myself a tuna sandwich, and puttered around the kitchen, cleaning things Dolores had already left spotless. I needed something to take my mind off the disturbing memories the sudden appearance of Cart Anderson had stirred up, but I found even the pull of the Conroy novel I'd picked up at the bookstore that morning couldn't distract me from reliving the events of that terrible summer . . .

Darnay's return a couple of hours later saved me from plunging into one of my infrequent fits of melancholy. As had become our custom, I didn't ask where he'd been, and he didn't volunteer to enlighten me.

I carried glasses out onto the wide deck which surrounded the house on three sides. We found a shady patch and pulled the cushioned chairs into its welcome coolness. I slid a small glass-topped table between us and settled myself in for the interrogation I had been expecting before Darnay's abrupt departure. But he sipped his wine and occupied himself with gazing out toward the rolling ocean, just visible over the sea oats topping the dune. Beside me the ice melted in my sweating tumbler of sweet tea. Over the cries of the gulls, swooping along the shoreline, the faint squeals of children could be heard on the soft breeze blowing in off the Atlantic. Summer in South Carolina, especially in the beach resorts like Hilton Head Island, means snarled traffic, withering humidity, and a seemingly endless undercurrent of voices with flat northern accents. And it was only the middle of July. Labor Day and the end to this annual madness seemed light-years away.

I stole a glance at my companion, surprised he'd been able to restrain his policeman's curiosity for so long. During the months we'd spent living together in the Paris apartment, I'd told him some of the story of Geoffrey Anderson's duplicity. I knew he'd have questions now. I didn't blame him. I had a few of my own.

"Want to talk about it?" His voice, soft and seductive, nonetheless startled me. When I hesitated, he added, "You didn't exactly tell the truth back there, did you?"

"The boy doesn't need to know the truth," I said.

No one does, I added to myself, although I'd felt more than a little guilty throughout the sanitized version of events I'd related to Cart Anderson. My own childhood had been so warped by secrets . . . by half-truths, evasions, and outright lies.

"Maybe it's not your call." Darnay reached across the space between us to capture my hand.

"I'm the only one who knows the whole story," I said, stung by the implied criticism. "It's mine to tell or not."

Darnay sipped his wine and turned his face again to the sea. "That may be true. You have always been reluctant to share your secrets, even with me. But others know pieces of it: your father, your brother-in-law. Even that . . ." He hesitated, searching for the translation. Despite the idiomatic excellence of his English, he always seemed to think in French. *"Comment est-ce qu'on dit* usé*?"*

"Usé? I have no idea. Who are you talking about?"

"L'avocat. The lawyer."

"Ah, Hadley Bolles. Would 'sleazy' perhaps be the word you're groping for?"

"Oui. C'est ça. The sleazy lawyer. All these people know something about the incident."

Incident. What a nice, innocent euphemism for the nightmare that had been the Grayton's Race development scandal that resulted in the death of Cart Anderson's father. Blackmail, money-laundering, drugs. Murder. For just a moment an image of the bright glare of Rob's plane disintegrating flickered behind my eyelids, and I shook my head. I would not allow the boy's intrusion into my life to revive the grief and pain I'd spent two years laying to rest.

"All he needed to know was that I was not responsible for his father's death, that it was all just a horrible accident. I think he believed me."

Darnay shrugged. "Perhaps. The boy is obviously confused and suffering greatly over the loss of his mother."

I nodded. What a shock it must have been to a seventeen-year-old, to lose both his parents in less than a year. Cart had struggled for control as he'd told us about his mother's death from ovarian cancer barely three weeks before. An only child, he'd been sent to live with his paternal grandmother in Beaufort. He apparently had no inkling he had a half-brother somewhere in south Florida. Unless Geoff Anderson had been lying about that, too. So much of what he'd told me had been untrue: parts of it intentional deception, others his own warped delusion. Why should I tell the kid his dead father had been a liar and a monster? Maybe even a murderer? What purpose would it serve?

"Don't you think the poor kid has been through enough?" I asked.

Darnay gave voice to my earlier thoughts. "You yourself have said many times that secrets only lead to trouble."

I shrugged and rose to lean against the smooth wood railing which encircled the deck. He was a fine one to talk. "This one is better left alone. If he tries to read up on it in the local newspaper coverage, he'll find I've given him the official version, right down to the coroner's verdict."

"But he has doubts." Darnay had risen to drape an arm around my shoulder and pull me close.

"He's distraught. And he's seventeen. After he gets settled in with his grandmother and gets back to school, I think the importance of it will wane. Right now he sees himself as some sort of avenging angel. He'll get past it in time."

Darnay didn't say, "You hope," but I could read it in his eyes.

I was saved the necessity of responding by the faint ringing of the telephone. I disengaged myself from his embrace and trotted inside. Lavinia Smalls, my father's housekeeper and companion and the woman who was primarily responsible for my turning out borderline normal, was inviting us to dinner. My father hadn't seen us in way too long, and our presence was commanded at six. Darnay, wandering in from the porch, nodded in agreement and said we'd bring the wine.

I hung up, half-dreading, half-anticipating an evening spent with retired Judge Talbot Simpson, my formidable father. Perhaps he and Darnay would occupy themselves with war stories of their respective crime-fighting exploits. Perhaps conversation wouldn't deteriorate, as it so often did, into local gossip and reminiscences of the past. *Fat chance,* I thought, especially in a family who could trace their roots back to sixteenth-century French Huguenots fleeing Catholic persecution and who eventually settled in the humid marshes and rich soil of South Carolina. Presqu'isle, the antebellum mansion in which I had grown up, had sheltered generations of my late mother's people—Chases and Tattnalls and Baynards—surviving even the devastation of the War of the Northern Aggression. An evening in my old home with my father without a discussion involving the past. *Fat chance.* Still, a girl could hope . . .

Chapter Three

My fragile expectations were dashed the moment we sat down to dinner in the chill formality of the heavily paneled dining room at Presqu'isle. Even though the leaves had been removed from the sprawling mahogany table, Lavinia's attempts to make it seem more intimate were always doomed to failure. I knew the second-best Royal Doulton china and heavy silver were in honor of Darnay. Had it been just the three of us, we would have been tucked up to the scarred oak table in the much cozier kitchen.

"So, I hear Millicent Anderson's grandson is coming to live with her. Seems his mother just recently passed away in Florida." My father, looking very dapper in a blue oxford cloth dress shirt with the long sleeves folded back over his forearms, watched my face for a reaction.

I stuffed shrimp in my mouth and ignored him.

"Poor boy." Lavinia Smalls shook her head and studied me, too. Her long, brown fingers smoothed the damask napkin in her lap. "And poor Millicent. What with visiting her husband in the home and all her other obligations, she's going to have her hands full. She's not a young woman anymore, and a teenager can be quite a challenge. Especially a boy."

My refusal to be drawn into the conversation forced them to move on to other topics. I ate in silence while my father and Alain debated the relative merits of football versus soccer. I kept my eyes on my plate.

"Let's have coffee on the verandah." Lavinia's words broke the spell, and I jumped to my feet.

I moved to my father's place at the table and gripped the handles of his wheelchair, maneuvering him around onto the heart pine floor, through his study-turned-bedroom, and out onto the wide back porch. A series of strokes had left him unable to walk without assistance, his left arm tucked uselessly in his lap, and the same side of his face drooping slightly. Fortunately his speech and mental processes were almost as sharp as when he dominated local politics throughout a nearly fifty-year career as an attorney and criminal courts judge.

I settled him in his usual spot looking out toward St. Helena Sound. Though dusk had begun to settle over the mainland, there was still enough light to discern a few egrets and herons patrolling the strip of marsh at the edge of the rolling lawn. A pelican perched on one of the pilings supporting the short dock at the foot of the property.

I scurried back inside, ostensibly to help Lavinia with the tea tray, but more truthfully to escape any more talk of Andersons, past or present. Behind me I heard Darnay decline the Judge's offer to join him in an after-dinner cigar.

As I suspected, Lavinia already had everything laid out. She was just pouring hot water from the whistling kettle into the flowered teapot. A carafe of coffee had been settled onto the tray, along with a creamer and a sugar bowl. She looked up as I skidded into the kitchen.

"What's the matter with you, Bay? You've been acting like the hounds of hell were nippin' at your heels all evening."

That made me smile. Throughout the misery of my childhood, Lavinia Smalls had been there to soothe my hurts, both physical and emotional. I still found it difficult to lie to her.

"It's all the talk about the Andersons. Bad memories."

I hoped the brief explanation would hold her. I couldn't have said then why I was so bent on not disclosing my encounter with young Cart Anderson that morning, except I had worked really hard at putting that part of my life behind me. Or maybe it was really all about self-protection, about not stirring up old scandals, old questions. Those dogs had been dozing quietly for the better part of a year, and I couldn't help thinking it wouldn't be a good idea to go kicking them awake.

"Bay? Are you listenin' to a word I'm saying?"

"Sorry!"

"Get the door for me, if you please." Lavinia hefted the tray with an ease belied by her thin narrow body and graying curls.

"Wait, let me . . ." I began.

"Child, I've been doin' this for more years than you've been alive. Just open the door and get out of my way."

"Yes, ma'am," I answered meekly and followed her out to the verandah.

A thin layer of pungent cigar smoke hung in the lifeless air over the Judge's head. After Darnay's wounding, both of us had given up cigarettes, I more reluctantly than he. I inhaled the secondhand smoke with guilty pleasure as Lavinia set the tray on a round, wrought-iron table.

"I was just commenting on the remarkable quality of the light in this part of the world." Darnay smiled and reached for my hand as I settled into my favorite rocker. "I've never seen anything to equal it, not even along the Côte d'Azur."

The contemplative mood seemed to have overtaken all of us, and we drank in the serenity as the mauve and orange streaks gradually faded into silvery black. A shimmering spill of luminescence across the flat water of the Sound gradually expanded into a golden half-circle as the moon rose behind us.

Based on past experience, I almost expected the telephone or the doorbell to disrupt our peaceful evening. But only the rising crescendo of the tree-frog chorus disturbed our quiet appreciation of the stars and the water and each other's company.

My father's nodding head signaled an end to the evening, and Darnay and I said our good-nights.

"You feel like a drive?" he asked as we walked hand in hand down the steps. "Seems like too good a night to waste."

I smiled and slid behind the wheel. "Got someplace in mind?"

He pulled the passenger door closed and reached across the console.

His fingers wrapped themselves in the hair at the nape of my neck, and I leaned into his kiss. When we paused for breath, Darnay said, "What is that delightful word you have for this . . ." With his free hand he caressed my cheek and kissed me again. "And this . . ." The hand traced the line of my throat and trailed almost casually across my breast. "And . . ."

I leaned back and found his eyes locked on mine. "Necking?" I whispered, and he laughed.

"Exactement! Necking." He rested the wandering hand on my knee and smiled wickedly.

I felt sure he couldn't see the warmth rising in my cheeks as I slipped the key into the ignition. "But not here," I said, grinning like the giddy teenager he had conjured up in my memory.

I pulled out of Presqu'isle's drive, a light wind ruffling the gray Spanish moss dripping from the canopy of oaks above our heads as we bumped down the rutted road.

Some time later we made our leisurely way home in the open convertible, soft music flowing from the speakers to drift away on the warm night air. It had been the kind of evening I'd often imagined, the kind of life I'd dreamed of living again one day. Darnay had taken the wheel, and I let my head droop against his shoulder.

A sudden whoop of sirens and the stab of flashing lights surrounded us, shattering my dreams of tranquility like a delicate piece of Waterford crystal dashed against a stone fireplace.

Sergeant Redmond Tanner of the Beaufort County Sheriff's Office strode up toward where Darnay had pulled the car off onto the grass verge. With the light bar still pulsing its rhythmic blue beat, he looked almost like a rock star making his entrance onto the stage. The only thing missing was a sea of screaming fans. The image made me smile, and my brother-in-law grinned back. Somewhat shorter and two years younger than Rob, Red Tanner had more than once tried to parlay his boyish charm and our shared grief into something more intimate. I'd never been sure if it really had anything to do with me—this attraction he kept professing—or whether it said more about the losses in his own life: his brother's murder coming almost on the heels of his painful divorce from Sarah. Maybe, I thought, I was just familiar.

Red's face lost its smile as Alain Darnay turned in the seat to watch his approach. The waves of animosity vibrating between the two men could have been measured on the Richter scale. I sighed and stepped out of the car.

"Hey, Red! How's it going?"

"Bay." He touched his cap in that mock-salute way he had.

"I know we weren't speeding, so what's up?"

His near formality might just have been to impress the newcomer, but something about it was making me uneasy. His eyes never left Darnay's face, though his words were obviously directed at me. "I've been tryin' to track you down. Lavinia told me you set off for home a couple of hours ago."

The alarm bells I'd gotten way too familiar with set up their insistent clamor inside my head. "What's going on?"

Red made a production out of easing the slim notebook from his khaki shirt pocket and thumbing through the pages. He lowered the pad a little to take advantage of the patrol car's headlights still stabbing into the blackness and reflecting off the silent stands of trees guarding the side of the road.

"What the hell's this about, Red?" I tried to keep my voice calm, but I could feel the panic rising in my chest. "Cut the crap and just tell me!"

I heard the click of the driver's side latch, followed immediately by Red's "Stay in the vehicle, sir."

Darnay grunted and slammed the door. I glanced back over my shoulder to see his angry face silhouetted in the glare.

"Red, you've got about three seconds . . ."

"Be quiet, Bay." No hint of our usual bantering disrespect for each other, none of the mocking, feigned annoyance. He glanced up from his notes, and his face was grim. "This is official."

I fixed him with a deep-green glare. "Then just say it. You sound like a bad actor in a third-rate melodrama."

"I want to know about your run-in with the Anderson boy this afternoon."

I slowly exhaled the breath I hadn't been aware I was holding. So that was it. "I wouldn't exactly call it a run-in," I began, only to be interrupted by the slam of the car door and Red's angry voice.

"Sir, I told you to stay in the vehicle." Unbelievably his right hand had come to rest lightly against the butt of his service revolver.

"Red, for God's sake . . ."

"Get back in the car! Now!"

Darnay raised both hands, not entirely mimicking surrender, and slid back behind the wheel. I could feel the heat of his anger from ten feet away.

"Red, stop it! What the hell's the matter with you? Alain's with Interpol. He's been a cop—"

"So what?" he interrupted me. I couldn't remember ever hearing his voice sound so cold. "That and three bucks'll get him a fancy latte at Starbucks. He has no standing in my county. None!"

A vision of Darnay's launching himself across the trunk and slamming Red into the ground whizzed across my inner eye. I didn't think he'd actually be reckless enough to do it, but the thought brought me back to the immediate question and its probable cause. "Someone saw us in the Westin parking lot," I said quietly, hoping to restore some semblance of calm to a situation quickly spiraling out of control.

Red's breathing slowed, and his hand dropped from the gun butt to his side. "One of the kids at the valet stand. Seems he and the missing boy—"

"Missing? What do you mean, missing?" My heart dropped into my feet.

"The witness says you and your . . ." He paused, groping for an appropriate epithet, then decided to maintain his professionalism. "You and your *friend* forced Anderson into his car and drove off with him. The kid hasn't been seen since."

I shook my head and ran a hand through the tangle of my sun-streaked hair. In the year since they'd cut it all off in the emergency room, it had grown back to just past shoulder-length. "Red, you don't seriously believe Alain and I did anything to the boy, do you? He'd been following us—me, actually—for a couple of days. I didn't know who the hell he was until I got a close-up look." I shoved my hands into the pockets of my black linen trousers. "We just wanted to scare him a little. We took him back to my house, I explained about his father's death, which is what he really wanted me for anyway, and that was that. He got back in his Mercedes and drove away. End of story."

An eighteen-wheeler, oblivious to the pulsating light of the cruiser, roared by on its way to Savannah, the slipstream rocking us a little on our feet and drowning out Red's response.

"What?" I asked when the soft night air quieted again around us.

"I said, he was supposed to be at his grandmother's house in Beaufort by noon. He never showed up."

"So? He must have been staying at the Westin. Maybe he decided to have one more night with the beach bunnies before settling in with the old folk. School doesn't start for another couple of weeks."

"He never called," Red responded.

Darnay spoke from the driver's seat, but the sarcasm in his voice carried quite well to where Red and I stood at the side of the road. "A teenager who doesn't show up on time, who would rather party with his friends than spend the evening sitting with his grandmother. I'm shocked."

"Red, this is nonsense. Let me introduce you to Alain . . ."

"I know who he is."

"Yes, and your, uh . . . reputation has preceded you as well, Deputy," Darnay cracked.

"It's Sergeant, Mr. Darnley. Sergeant Redmond Tanner."

"And I am Dar*nay*, officer. Inspector Alain . . ."

"Oh, knock it off, both of you!" I felt like a piece of meat being tugged at by two snarling dogs. "The point is, Alain may have been a little *energetic* in persuading Cart Anderson to explain his actions, but we didn't hurt him. He left my house under his own power, and neither of us has a clue where he went from there." I drew a deep breath and willed myself to speak reasonably. "I'm sure he's out doing what teenaged boys with looks and money and a great car do on a Friday night. He'll turn up." I took advantage of the calm to add, "I could have the Judge call Millicent. Reassure her."

"I think it'll take more than words. She was pretty hysterical when she called it in." Red, too, had lowered the decibels to more normal levels.

"Well, she's elderly, and she's got a lot on her plate right now. She probably just overreacted."

"I don't think so." Red slipped the notebook back into his pocket and straightened his gun belt in a gesture he often used to avoid looking me in the eye. "So where have you and . . ." He gestured in Darnay's direction. "Where've you been for the last couple of hours?"

I forced my face into a nonchalance I was pretty sure didn't fool my brother-in-law for a second. "Just out riding, enjoying the evening. Why?"

He finally looked at me, and his tone held an edge I couldn't quite interpret. "Because we found the boy's car a little while ago, out near Fort Fremont on Land's End." He raised his face and stared pointedly at Darnay. "Doors open, lights on. Nobody around." Red sighed and shook his head. "And traces of blood in the front seat."

Chapter Four

I SLEPT BADLY. AND ALONE.

For the sake of propriety and my housekeeper's strict Catholic sensibilities, Darnay had taken a lease on a tiny furnished condominium just off Mathews Drive. In reality he spent most nights stretched out beside me in the king-sized bed I'd once shared with Rob.

I flipped over, determined not to look at the clock again, but the glowing red numbers drew my eyes. 3:17. Exactly six minutes since the last time I'd checked. I flung back the sheet, fumbled in the dresser for a T-shirt and shorts, and let myself out onto the deck.

The humid night air settled over me like a warm cloud, welcome after the sterile chill of the air-conditioned bedroom. Across the dune the ocean rolled and retreated, its majestic rhythm unaffected by my petty concerns.

"Why now, damn it?" I slammed my fist against the wooden railing, startling a raccoon foraging just below me. The rattle of the palmettos drew my attention to him, barely visible in the thin moonlight. For a moment he studied me, his bright black eyes alert to danger. Then, dismissing me as of no consequence, he lumbered back into the thick shrubbery.

"Why now?" I whispered, but the soft wind carried no reply.

I must have crawled back into bed at some point. I forced open one gummy eye at the tentative knock on my door to find the bedroom bathed in mid-morning light and myself naked, wrapped in a tangle of sweaty sheets.

"*Señora?* You are ill?"

Dolores Santiago slipped quietly into the room. The tiny Guatemalan immigrant, my salvation after the nightmare of Rob's murder and my own agonizing recuperation from the injuries I'd suffered in the blast, came three days a week to cook and clean for me.

I groaned and flung an arm over my face. "I'm fine." I swallowed against the cottony dryness in my mouth. "No, that's not true. I feel like hell. I think I must have slept a total of fifteen minutes last night."

"I make tea," she said and bustled out.

Somewhat restored by a long, hot shower, I dragged myself toward the kitchen just as the front doorbell rang. Detouring into the entryway, I encountered Darnay's beaming face.

"Bonjour, ma petite." He smiled and reached for me, but I spun away out of his grasp. "Bad night?" he asked, following as I headed for the kitchen.

"Miserable." I flopped onto one of the padded chairs pulled up to the glass-topped table and grabbed the steaming mug of Earl Grey Dolores set in front of me. "Ah," I moaned, "that's heaven."

"Nothing for me, thanks," Darnay said.

Dolores sniffed and ignored him.

I was too tired to worry about the thinly veiled hostility which seemed to hover in the air whenever the two of them were in the same room.

"I hope you're not worrying about that boy," he said, turning back to me.

Dolores stepped around him to slide a plate of eggs and bacon onto the place mat in front of me. I opened my mouth to protest, but she cut me off.

"Eat, *Señora*. You feel better."

I watched as Dolores tentatively negotiated the three steps leading down into the great room. Despite two operations and months of physical therapy, the stiffness in her damaged left leg seemed no better.

"It wasn't your fault," Darnay said, reading my thoughts.

"Like hell," I replied and bent my head to my breakfast.

"So are you going to assume responsibility for the disappearance of this young man as well?" When I didn't answer, he went on. "I am truly astounded at the power you wield, Bay Tanner. Can you perhaps alter the tides? Predict lottery numbers? Visit famine and pestilence upon your enemies? *Bon Dieu,* I tremble in your presence."

"Knock it off. I hear you, okay? But there's nothing wrong with accepting responsibility. Answer me this: if Dolores hadn't been working for me, would she have been attacked?"

"No. You're right about that. But did you *cause* her to be injured? Did you plan it? Hope for it? Carry it out?"

I chewed bacon and ignored him.

"Of course not," he answered for me. "So. No more talk of this guilt you seem so determined to assume. And no more talk of being responsible for this boy, either."

"Anything in the paper about it?" I asked, rising to carry my plate and silverware to the dishwasher.

"No. Apparently your brother-in-law has been successful in keeping it . . . how do you say?"

"Under wraps," I supplied.

"Oui. C'est ça."

"I wonder why," I mused, rinsing the bacon grease and egg yolk residue from my plate before stacking it on the bottom rack.

"What do you mean?"

Darnay followed me across the kitchen to the coffeepot Dolores kept going for herself all day long. He pulled down a cup and filled it.

"Well, if the kid is truly missing," I answered, "the more people who know about it, the better, don't you think? I mean, alerting people to be on the lookout for him and all."

"The blood," he replied, returning to his seat at the table where I joined him with a fresh mug of tea.

"What about it?" I blew across the top of the cup before sipping cautiously.

"Is it his or someone else's? It seems to me the only reason to keep this from becoming public knowledge is if they have discovered the blood is not Anderson's."

"In which case he's a suspect and not a potential victim."

"Exactly."

He paused, and I felt his eyes on the side of my face. "What?" I asked, turning to look at him.

"You're thinking about sticking your lovely nose into this disappearance, aren't you? I thought you and your father had given up the idea of becoming private eyes."

I squirmed under his steady gaze, the mocking smile making me more than just a little annoyed. "So what if I am?" I could feel the challenge in my words cause my chin to rise a fraction. "And who said we were giving up the inquiry agency? We've merely hit a . . . a *lull,* a little dry spell, that's all."

"And who will be the client in this new case?" His tone was getting downright snotty.

"I don't see how that is any of your concern. Now, if you'll excuse me, I need to get dressed."

I pushed back from the table and went to dump out the remains of my tea. Before I could turn, I felt Alain's strong arms encircling my waist, his body pressing me up against the edge of the sink.

"Ah, my sweet, I have made you angry. Forgive me."

His lips found the vulnerable spot just below my right ear, and I could feel my knees beginning to wilt when Dolores's prim voice cut across the kitchen.

"Perdone, Señora. I must make the list for the shopping."

I squirmed out of Darnay's embrace and headed for the bedroom.

When I came back, I found both of them gone, Darnay's note propped up against the phone on the desk in the kitchen: "Errands to run. Will call later. *Fais attention. D.*"

Take care. Right.

I tried the sheriff's satellite office on the south end of the island and lucked out. In spite of a late night spent investigating the disappearance of Cart Anderson and harassing Darnay and me on the road back to Hilton Head, Red Tanner was in his office. I declined the dispatcher's offer to put me through. This job would be easier face to face.

Half an hour later I pulled into the parking lot on Lagoon Road and cut the engine. Before I could swing my legs out, the front door of the station opened, and Red strode out into the blistering heat. He stopped short when I hailed him.

"Bay," he said, strolling up to the open car. The look on his face told me he wasn't exactly thrilled to see me, but his eyes had softened from the stubbornness and challenge of the night before.

"Hey, Red. Got a minute?"

"Just about. I'm on my way out to an interview."

Something was missing in his eyes, some spark of the lighthearted way we'd always dealt with each other, that made me hesitate. In the past, we'd have been trading insults by this time, laughing around them in the way of old, familiar friends.

He seriously suspects Darnay and me of being involved in Cart Anderson's disappearance. The words tumbled through my brain and out of my mouth.

"You really think Alain and I had anything to do with the boy?" When he didn't deny it immediately, I exploded. "You can't be serious! Red, for God's sake—"

"Shut up, Bay!" Though he kept his voice low, his tone was stern. "Of course I don't believe it. But I'm not the only one involved here. I know you think I run the sheriff's office, but I do have superiors. The Andersons are high profile, and that makes this case a big deal. They're not going to overlook someone who manhandled the kid and drove off with him just a few hours before his bloody car turned up."

"Was it his?" I asked, relaxing a little. If Red believed me, everything else would work itself out.

"Was what his, the car? Sure. Florida registration in his late mother's name."

"No, I mean the blood."

That stopped him for a moment. "Why would you assume it wasn't?"

"Why would you assume it was? Do you have any confirmation? Match his blood type or whatever?"

Red stood up and hitched his holster around to settle it more comfortably on his hip. "Now why would that be of interest to you? Don't go thinkin' you're gonna butt into this investigation, Bay."

"Butt in? Seems to me a certain police officer pretty much dragged me in last night with that stunt out on the highway. Or were you just getting a kick out of throwing your weight around for Darnay's benefit? I can tell you, he wasn't impressed."

"The hell with your goddamned boyfriend," he growled through clenched teeth. "You tell him to watch his step in my county. You just tell him."

I was surprised the fist he pounded on the top of my door didn't leave a dent in the chrome. He whirled, nearly colliding with a pair of deputies heading for their patrol car, and stomped off, yelling, "And stay out of my business," over his shoulder.

I sat stunned, watching him fling open the door to his cruiser, then slam it viciously before grinding the engine to life and whipping out of the parking lot.

"What the hell was that all about?" I asked the empty seat beside me. I slipped the T-Bird into reverse, backed out, and accelerated into the stream of traffic on Pope Avenue.

An interview, Red Tanner had said before blowing me off in that infuriatingly nasty way. Up ahead I could just see his cruiser stopped at the light at the back entrance to Shipyard Plantation. If Cart Anderson was his case, it probably had something to do with that. I'd just tag along. No law against following a police car, at least not as far as I knew.

And if there was, too bad. What was the point of having a retired judge for a father if you couldn't use it to bend the rules once in a while?

I turned up the volume on the radio and settled in for the chase.

Of course Red knew I was back there. Somehow it always looks so simple in the movies. Keep three or four cars between you and the object of the tail. Change lanes, move up and back occasionally, don't keep your eyes glued on the subject's car. I'd seen so many TV cop shows, I almost felt as if I had been given a tutorial.

The problem is the pursuer isn't supposed to be driving a brand-new yellow convertible. The T-Bird and I were about as inconspicuous as a wart on the end of Red's nose. At one point an SUV which had been providing excellent cover swerved unexpectedly into the passing lane, leaving me only a few feet behind the cruiser. I saw Red glance up to the rearview mirror and could have sworn I caught the flash of his smile in the reflection.

He led me sedately down William Hilton Parkway, past Shelter Cove and its adjacent mall, past the jammed parking lot of Cracker Barrel, and up to the traffic signal at Folly Field Road where he flipped on his right blinker. There were two pickups and a furniture delivery van between us at that point, but they went straight through when the light changed, and I found myself once again riding Red's bumper. When he made a quick turn into the long driveway of Hilton Head Beach & Tennis Resort, I slowed. He stopped at the security gate and, with a casual wave to the guard, pulled through into the property.

Having neither an owner's sticker nor a light bar across the top of my car, I was forced to swing into a parking place in front of the reception center. I scrambled out and trotted down the sidewalk in time to see the cruiser roll to a stop alongside the center of three multistoried buildings. Red exited his car and trotted up a set of steps about halfway down.

I slung my bag over my shoulder and walked purposefully past the guard gate. I'd learned early on that if you acted as if you belonged someplace, few people would have the nerve to challenge you. By the time I'd traversed the sticky asphalt of the parking lot and come up alongside the abandoned cruiser, Red had disappeared. Judging by the number of balconies sprouting out every few yards, I had a snowball's chance in hell of figuring out which apartment he'd gone into.

I stationed myself in between two vans, determined to wait him out, but it took only a couple of minutes for the blistering sun to melt my resolve. The faint strains of music drifted toward me from the direction of the beach, and I followed the sound up a wooden boardwalk, past a huge freshwater swimming pool, and into the shade of an open-air dining area on a deck overlooking the ocean. I collapsed into a white plastic chair right in front of the performer, a bearded young man in Hawaiian shirt, shorts, and sandals whose lively rendition of "Brown-Eyed Girl" had my fellow diners swaying in their seats to his electronically-backed guitar.

As he swung into the national anthem of summer at the beach—Jimmy Buffett's "Margaritaville"—I managed to catch the attention of a harried waiter and order a large iced tea with extra lemon. I slumped back into the chair, not realizing how tense I'd been since my earlier confrontation with Red. I couldn't imagine why I'd let it get to me like that, I thought, as I idly surveyed the chaos of family vacation ebbing and flowing around me.

"Do you mind?" I hadn't realized the singer had quit until his laughing voice startled me. His hand rested on the back of the chair on the opposite side of my table. "It seems to be the only seat in the house," he said with an engaging smile.

"No, of course not." I sat up a little straighter and smiled back. "Please, sit down."

"Thanks," he said, pulling a rumpled handkerchief from his pocket as he sank into the chair. "Man, it gets hot up there. They stick me under the overhang for the shade, but I don't get a breath of breeze." He swiped sweat from his forehead and the back of his neck underneath the short, black ponytail. "Rick," he said, tucking the damp hanky away and extending his hand, "Rick Sanger."

I returned his strong grip. "Bay Tanner."

"Nice to meet you," he said as the waiter trotted up. "Miller Lite for me, Hank. Can I get you anything?"

"Nope, this is mine." Hank slid the iced tea with three lemon wedges perched along the lip of the plastic glass in front of me. "Thanks anyway."

"Put it on my tab," Rick Sanger said, leaning back and stretching out his legs.

"Not necessary," I said, and he shook his head.

"My pleasure. Least I can do for the lady who saved my life. One more minute up there and I think I would have collapsed."

I abandoned the straw, gulping down about half the sweet tea before pausing for breath. "I know what you mean," I said. "Kind of makes you wonder how all these folks can stand to be out in it for hours at a time."

"Yankees," he said with a knowing nod, and we laughed. "I take it you're not on vacation?"

"No, I live here. Over in Port Royal Plantation. What gave me away?"

"You're dressed too nice, and you don't smell like Panama Jack," he said with a grin.

His beer arrived then. Rick Sanger tipped the frosty bottle and drained a third in one long swallow.

"Ahhh," he breathed, "I needed that. Only allow myself one a set, you know. I got a lot of words to a lot of songs to remember. Don't want to make a fool of myself, even if most of them aren't even paying attention to what I'm doin' half the time."

"Is this your full-time job?" I asked, mostly to make conversation rather than from any real interest.

"No, I do a lot of things. I have a gig like this at the Holiday Inn nights during the summer. I also work a couple of shifts parking cars and hauling bags up by your place. At the Westin."

I was just about to open my mouth and remark about the coincidence when a hulking shadow fell across the white plastic table, and I squinted up into the glowering face of my brother-in-law.

"Just what the hell do you think you're doing?" His voice was low, and I could feel the effort it cost him to control his temper.

"Having a tea," I answered sweetly. "Care to join us?"

"What the hell do you think you're doing," he repeated, slowly emphasizing every word, "sittin' here trying to compromise my witness?"

Chapter Five

RICK SANGER GAWKED AT THE TWO OF US, OBVIOUSLY aware of the undercurrents and not quite sure what to make of them. When I failed to respond to Red's outrageous accusation, the young man rose and took a few steps back.

"You lookin' for me, sir?" he asked, indicating Red should take his seat.

"You Richard Sanger?" My brother-in-law ignored the courtesy and remained standing. "Your roommate said you'd be down here."

"Yessir, I am. You wantin' to talk to me about yesterday?"

Red nodded and turned his attention to me. The heat must have been affecting my brain because I was just then beginning to figure out what was going on.

"Is this your witness from the Westin's valet stand?" I asked.

"Like that's a news flash." He finally settled into the empty chair, his eyes never leaving my face, and I could feel myself reddening under his unwavering stare.

"Don't be ridiculous. How could I possibly know that?"

"Same way you always manage to get involved in stuff you have no business meddling in. Are you gonna try to deny you were following me?"

I couldn't quite stifle the smile quivering around my lips. I didn't need Red's glare to tell me I should keep my mouth shut, but his accusation seemed so over the top, so patently ridiculous. "Of course I was following you. And you knew it. So if you didn't want me tagging along, why didn't you just lose me? Don't they teach you guys how to do that in cop school?"

I paused to give him a chance to see the absurdity of the situation, but he remained stubbornly silent. "And if I already knew about Mr. Sanger and his whereabouts, why would I need to follow you?"

I glanced at the young musician, but he merely held up his hands as if to say *leave me out of this*.

"You're not doing yourself or your boyfriend any good, Bay." Red finally spoke, and the snide emphasis he put on the word *boyfriend* wiped the hovering smile from my face.

"You're being a pompous ass, Tanner," I said, unhitching my bag from the back of the chair as I stood. "And I'm getting tired of your innuendos. If you think Darnay and I had something to do with Cart Anderson's disappearance, arrest us. Otherwise, keep in mind, pal, I'm not without connections myself. Continue harassing us and see where it gets you." I turned to the bewildered young musician and held out my hand. "Mr. Sanger, thanks for the tea."

His handshake was a little tentative, but you couldn't really blame him. The poor boy hadn't the slightest idea what he'd gotten himself in the middle of.

"Please cooperate fully with Sergeant Tanner here," I added. "Tell him exactly what you saw. Don't leave out a single, juicy detail."

I spun on my heel and walked quickly back down the boardwalk.

By the time I reached my car, sweat dripped from every inch of exposed skin, and my blood pressure had risen to astronomical proportions. I slammed the door and sat for a moment, my hands gripping the wheel, trying to quell the simmering rage threatening to explode out the top of my head.

The unmitigated nerve of that . . . that bastard! I drew long breaths of scorching midday air into my lungs and tried to force myself to calm down. I knew what this was all about. Oh, yes, I knew full well. Red's attitude, his snide remarks and nasty looks, could all be traced to one source: Darnay.

I turned the key and let the car idle while I cranked the air conditioning up full blast and tipped the vents so they all blew directly at my face. I'd been a fool to think I could keep Alain's presence in my bed a secret for long.

And Red didn't like it. Somehow, over the months since his brother's murder, he'd come to consider me his personal property, the poor little widow-woman who needed his protection. Even after I had proved I could take care of myself, even after I had killed one man and wounded another—even then he wouldn't back off. It was jealousy, pure and simple, and I seethed at the idea of his carrying his personal feelings so far he could seriously let them consider me a suspect in the disappearance of Cart Anderson.

There was only one way to squelch this nonsense before it got completely out of hand. I eased out of the parking space, then drove sedately back out to the highway. Simpson & Tanner, Inquiry Agents, had to gear up and get back into business. And our first priority needed to be to find the missing boy.

One of the first rules I learned about living on Hilton Head Island, especially from June to September, is never to travel outbound between eight and eleven on a Saturday morning and never try returning between two and five in the afternoon. Turn-around day we call it, the time when those whose vacations were ending packed up their vans and headed north, and the newcomers began streaming south to take their places. As I sped toward Beaufort and a powwow with my father, I spared a moment of compassion for those stuck in the lines of bumper-to-bumper traffic inching its way toward the island in the blazing July sun. I could just imagine each carload of cranky kids and exasperated parents wondering why they hadn't just stayed home, turned on the sprinklers, and rented a video instead.

Beaufort, too, suffered from its own version of the Saturday afternoon madness, so it was nearing four o'clock by the time I finally swung into the semicircle of Presqu'isle's drive. After the whipping wind and fumes and cacophony of the thirty-five mile drive in the convertible, the peace of the antebellum mansion's quiet seclusion seemed like a gift. I sat for a moment listening to the silence, broken only by the lonely screech of a solitary gull swooping low over the Sound.

I lifted the cell phone from my canvas bag and checked to make sure I hadn't missed a call from Darnay. I'd left him three messages telling him to meet me at Presqu'isle, but so far he hadn't responded to any of them.

The inside of the house felt almost frigid, the temperature and humidity control system my late mother had installed keeping the air a constant and dry sixty-eight degrees. Protecting her vast collection of antiques and art had always been more important to her than the comfort of her family. But she'd been dead a long time, and I always wondered why my father didn't just sell off the stuff and take a trip around the world or something else equally frivolous. I'd tried over the years to convince him I had no interest in inheriting all the junk and the care and headaches that went along with it, but I had a feeling I hadn't been successful. Not a stick of furniture or piece of crystal had been moved, let alone disposed of, in all that time. Except for the portrait of my mother which used to hang over the fireplace.

"It's me," I called as I passed down the entryway and set my bag at the foot of the sweeping staircase that bisected the wide hall.

"In here," I heard my father reply, and I followed his voice into the study-turned-bedroom he now occupied almost full time. After the strokes, Rob and I had engineered the remodeling of the dark paneled room into a bright sitting and sleeping area with the largest of the closets converted to a wheelchair-accessible bath. With the ramp leading out to the back verandah, it gave my father as much freedom and mobility as he could reasonably expect under the circumstances of his disability.

I found both the Judge and Lavinia engaged in maneuvering him from the recliner in which he took his afternoon nap into the motorized wheelchair where he spent the bulk of his time. Lavinia had already laid out the makings for his pre-dinner drink, so I dropped several cubes from the ice bucket into a tumbler and helped myself to lemonade.

"You look upset," the Judge said in the gruff voice he generally used with me.

I launched into my account of our run-in with Red the night before and of my subsequent encounters with him at the sheriff's office and at the beach. My father sipped at his bourbon and lemon and let me vent. I finally stumbled to a halt, settled back in my chair by the cold fireplace, and waited for his reaction. In the silence, I could hear the sounds of Lavinia's dinner preparations echoing off the paneled walls of the long hallway.

"I fail to see what your complaint is."

"You fail to see . . . ?" I shook my head and slumped down in the chair, my legs splayed out across the faded Aubusson carpet which blanketed the heart pine floor. "You don't find it just a tad annoying to learn your only child is being looked at in the disappearance of a seventeen-year-old boy? That someone high up in local law enforcement seriously considers it possible Darnay and I did away with the annoying little twerp?"

The Judge rolled the accumulation of gray ash off the end of his cigar into a cut-glass bowl and regarded me solemnly. "If you'd take the time to consider the matter dispassionately, you'd see the logic of their conclusions." He raised his good hand and waved the panatela in my direction. "You were seen to argue with the boy. Alain forced him into his car and drove away. Apparently you were not only observed, but overheard to threaten the boy as well."

He paused for breath, but again used the waving cigar to forestall my attempt to interrupt.

"And a scant few hours later, the unfortunate young man goes missing under highly suspicious circumstances. Add to all that the fact that Red finds you attempting to influence his witness, the only one who can positively identify you and your friend, and . . ." He cocked his head, and his clear gray eyes regarded me from under bushy white brows. "Well, I think you might consider yourself fortunate not to be sitting in Shark Morgan's office right this minute."

A dozen reactions fought for voice, but what came out was, "Who the hell is Shark Morgan?"

"Death investigator," my father answered, nodding sagely. "Damn fine one, too. When your old friend Matt Gibson moved down to St. Augustine, the sheriff decided to go with the death investigator concept rather than try to maintain a homicide division. Good move, in my judgment."

"I'm sure he's thrilled by your approbation." Somehow, whenever my father and I got rolling in a conversation like this, the fifty-cent words just tumbled out of my mouth. We had always been fierce competitors on a number of such vague, unnamed levels. Then the import of his words penetrated, and I snapped to attention. "*Death* investigator? Is Cart Anderson dead? Did they find a body?"

A yawning pit of dread opened up in my stomach, and I thought I might be physically ill.

"No, no," the Judge rushed to assure me. "He's still missing. And not even that, officially," he added as I leaned back in my chair, a mixture of relief and anger washing over me. "It has to be forty-eight hours, although considering who his family is they might—"

"Then what the hell are you babbling on about?" I snapped.

"The blood," my father intoned in his best courtroom baritone. "Found on the seat?"

I cringed, knowing what was coming, but needing to hear him say it anyway.

"Preliminary tests point to it being the boy's. Everyone's treating it as a suspicious disappearance, although again that's not official yet. But I have my sources."

I leaned forward, my elbows resting on my knees, and fixed my father with an intense stare. "And what do your sources tell you about possible suspects?"

He locked his eyes on mine and without flinching said, "You and Alain Darnay are at the top of the list." He paused, and his gaze dropped again to his smoldering cigar. "And from what I hear, at this point you're the *only* ones on it."

Chapter Six

When darnay failed to call or appear by six o'clock, I dragged myself to the round oak table in the kitchen and toyed with a plate of what was probably excellent roast beef but could have been old tires for all I tasted of it. Lavinia made a determined attempt to maintain the flow of local gossip we usually chewed on along with our meals in the old antebellum mansion.

"Amelia Merriweather has taken a turn for the worse," she said, shaking her head. Her tight gray curls caught the glint of the fading sun seeping through the mullioned windows. "Mr. Law has hired a woman to come in and see to her more . . ." She floundered for a moment, then continued. "To see to her more intimate needs. Poor woman's hands are so twisted with the arthritis she can't even fasten a button."

"That's too bad," I mumbled, pushing the cold broccoli to the other side of my plate.

"Somethin' wrong with your dinner?" she asked for the third time since we'd sat down to the table. "Meat not bloody enough for you?"

The peal of the doorbell saved me from answering. I hurried through the entry hall and found Darnay leaning casually against the railing of the verandah.

"Where the hell have you been? I've been trying to reach you all afternoon." I turned and stomped back down the hallway.

"Yes, I would love to come in. *Merci bien*."

Behind me I heard the *thud* of the heavy door closing, then the squeak of Darnay's rubber-soled boat shoes on the pine floor as he followed me.

"Ah, I am interrupting your dinner. *Milles pardons*."

"Nonsense," Lavinia replied, sliding another place setting from the cupboard which held the everyday dishes. "Just sit yourself right down there, and I'll fix you a plate."

Even on such short acquaintance, Darnay knew better than to argue with Lavinia, especially in the kitchen.

"Do you know what's going on? Have you heard what my moronic brother-in-law and his pals have come up with this time?" I asked, sliding my chair back out and flopping myself into it.

"No, my darling, but I have the distinct feeling you are about to enlighten me."

Lavinia leaned over to set the heaping dish of roast beef, broccoli, and new potatoes on the place mat in front of him.

"So, *ma petite,* what has you so upset?" Darnay rose slightly in his chair as Lavinia resumed her seat.

In what I felt to have been a succinct and unemotional synopsis, I ran down my day, starting with my trip to the sheriff's office and ending with Red's bizarre performance on the deck of Hilton Head Beach & Tennis. No one was smiling when I finished.

"Surely this is some sort of joke." Darnay paused, the fork midway between his plate and his mouth. "He's just playing with you."

"I think not," my father replied before I had a chance to speak. "Once they decided the blood they found in the front seat was probably the boy's, they had no choice but to treat his disappearance as suspicious." He waited a beat and then added, "You shouldn't have manhandled the boy like that in front of witnesses."

"That's not fair. We didn't touch him." I glanced at Darnay and saw his eyebrows rise in question. "Okay, maybe Alain did rough him up a little. But the kid deserved it, following us all over the island like that, spying on us. I told you we just wanted to scare him, find out what he was up to. And to think I actually felt sorry for him."

"You mean because of his recent losses?"

The Judge's question took the heat out of my anger.

"Yes," I said softly, "because of that. And because of who he is."

"Geoffrey Anderson's son."

"Yes."

Darnay crossed his knife and fork across his empty plate and leaned back against the spindles of the oak chair. "And do you think this is perhaps why the authorities are more interested in us than they would normally be in such circumstances? Because of Bay's involvement with his father's death?"

I gasped, the implications of Darnay's question taking my breath away. How could I not have seen the connection? How could I not have realized how it must look? I waited for my father's denial, for his heated declaration of how ridiculous such a notion must appear to any sane person, to anyone who knew me at all.

"Yes," he said, "that's exactly what I think."

When I'd sped away from Hilton Head that afternoon, my plan had been to hook up with Darnay and explore the scene of the crime, if in fact one had been committed. Fort Fremont, where Cart Anderson's Mercedes had been found, lay at Land's End on the other side of the island from Presqu'isle along a narrow dirt track known as Resurrection Road. A map of St. Helena would have used its official name, but I couldn't even remember what that was. Ever since the reported sighting of a headless Confederate soldier wandering along its dusty track, a lantern swinging jauntily from one hand, it had been Resurrection Road to us locals.

After we finished dinner, I helped Lavinia set the kitchen to rights, watching out the window over the sink as the sun edged toward the horizon, its glow trembling in long, orange ripples across the Sound.

I had to do something to quell the nervous energy which had me pacing from one end of the back verandah to the other. After my father's third admonition to sit down and quit driving everyone crazy, I rifled the old coat closet for the big flashlight, dragged a protesting Darnay from his rocker, and headed the Thunderbird down the rutted lane toward Land's End.

"What do you hope to prove?" he asked, turning to face me from the passenger seat. He tossed his hand in a gesture that encompassed the unlit roadside fading away into dark, rolling lawns and apparently deserted houses. "Even with a light, you may not be able to see your hand in front of your face."

"I don't know what I'm trying to prove," I replied honestly. "I just feel the need to be doing something."

Again I felt his gaze along the side of my face. "You really are worried about this, *n'est-ce pas,* my darling?"

I sighed, and the soft sound drifted away on the night breeze. "Yes."

All evening I'd struggled to push away the thoughts, the images which kept crowding into my consciousness: the sights and sounds of that summer night when Geoffrey Anderson died. I was the only living soul who knew exactly what had happened, the only one who had the proof of the cause of it locked safely away. I'd tried to let the boy down gently, done my best to leave him with a memory of his father he could live with.

"Bay?" Darnay spoke softly, his hand falling to rest on my shoulder.

"Hmmm?"

"You can go now. The way is clear."

"What? Oh, sorry." I shook off the haze of remembering and pulled across the empty intersection.

A stranger to the island would never have located Fort Fremont in the dark. Most people couldn't find it in broad daylight when they were searching for it. Abandoned nearly a century before, the concrete walls and maze of passageways had become so overgrown with the riot of Lowcountry vegetation, it had become almost invisible from the road.

"So how did Cart Anderson find his way out here?" I asked as I allowed the car to coast onto the narrow verge and killed the engine.

When I doused the headlights, the darkness settled over us, silent and oppressive. Sinister.

The atmosphere seemed to invite whispers. "Good question," Darnay murmured quietly. "Eerie," he added to the list of depressing adjectives I already had running around in my head.

I took the flashlight and slipped from the car. My sneakers squished in the dew-damp grass. Behind me I heard Darnay ease the passenger door closed. I flipped on the light and raked it over the few sections of gray wall still visible beneath the curtains of creeping ivy and kudzu. Here and there a patch had been cleared away, and multicolored spray paint memorialized Buck and Tina and someone called The Hulk.

"Is this part of your Civil War?" Darnay asked at my shoulder, and I jumped.

"No, much later. It was originally built in the late 1890s to protect Beaufort from attack by the Spaniards, but the Spanish-American War ended before it was completed. I don't think there were ever more than a few dozen soldiers garrisoned here at any one time."

I aimed the broad beam of the flashlight toward the opening of one of the passageways, and the echoing blackness swallowed it as if it were a candle being snuffed out in a strong wind. In the dead stillness the cicadas and tree frogs sounded like a full symphony orchestra.

Again Darnay's voice startled me. "Do we know where the car was? Exactly?"

I shook my head, then realized he probably couldn't see me. "No," I said, "but there's not much room. It had to be right in here somewhere. You can see there isn't any place across the road."

I turned to graze the light across the almost impenetrable jungle of vines and trees when the beam suddenly caught the reflection of two black, glaring eyes which seemed to float about four feet off the ground. I stifled a scream, and beside me I felt Darnay stiffen, his right hand reaching automatically toward his waistband for the weapon he no longer carried. Then a row of yellow teeth gaped into a crooked smile beneath the shimmering eyes, and a voice as cracked and wispy as the creak of a rusted hinge said, "I declare, Lydia Simpson, you just never did know your place, did ya, girl?" The high-pitched cackle was followed by a dry, raspy cough as the wizened old black woman edged fully into the circle of light. "Lord, chile, I mighta shot y'all." My eyes jumped involuntarily to the ancient shotgun lying in the crook of her sinewy right arm.

"Now why would you want to do a damn-fool thing like that, Miss Minnie Maude?" I asked, laying a hand against Darnay's arm to signal the danger had passed.

Minnie Maude Bleeker, ninety if she was a day, finally pointed the gun toward the ground and studied on my question. "Might maybe jes' for the fun of it," she said. "Or I might could be tryin' to keep another young 'un from gettin' hisself hurt. Yass'um, it might could be dat."

Chapter Seven

THE OLD HOUSE HUNKERED DOWN AMONG A RIOT OF crape myrtle, oleander, and confederate jasmine just at the edge of the narrow beach. The live oak which sheltered its corrugated tin roof had sent out twisted limbs which slithered like giant snakes across the grass. From the glow of the single naked bulb hanging over the stoop in front of the wooden screen door, I could see a newer addition had been tacked on to the two already sprouting from what had once been a one-room cabin. They gave the whole thing the look of something constructed by a capricious child. The new boards had yet to weather into the silvery patina the decades of wind and sun had given the original structure.

The door led directly into a square room which served as both living and sleeping area. A narrow bed with a faded patchwork quilt took up the far corner. A thin circle of light glowed from what looked to be either a genuine Tiffany lamp or an excellent reproduction sitting atop a gate-leg table.

Minnie Maude Bleeker rested the shotgun in a corner next to the empty fireplace, its old stones blackened from use, and waved a bony hand toward a sagging love seat draped in a bright purple afghan.

"Set yo'selfs down," she said, lowering her own thin frame into a rocking chair drawn up by the fireplace.

Darnay and I exchanged a dubious look but managed to squeeze ourselves onto the narrow sofa. What little padding it had once contained had obviously evaporated years before. I tried to settle myself on the edge to avoid the springs I could feel poking up through the thin fabric.

"Miss Minnie," I began, but the old woman waved me off.

"You never could stand for folks tellin' you no, could ya, chile?" Again her cackle of laughter took any sting from her words. "Keep Out signs made you no never mind. You and dat little blond-haired one. What was her name? Somethin' foreign, as I recollect."

I smiled at the memory. My best friend Bitsy and I had taken over the fort every summer since we were old enough to keep a bicycle upright for longer than thirty seconds. The abandoned pile of concrete became our castle, our dungeon, our secret hideaway. From the moment school let out, our days revolved around evading Lavinia and Bitsy's overprotective mother to sneak off to our refuge behind the curtains of creeper guarding the passageways.

"Elizabeth," I said. "Elizabeth Quintard."

Miss Minnie nodded. "Thass right. Called her Teeny or somethin' like dat."

"Bitsy."

She smiled. "Bitsy. Dat be it. Pretty little thing. Mostly scared of her own shadow, I recollect. What ever become of her?"

"She's married. Lives over on Hilton Head. She has three children now."

The old woman shook her head, her smile revealing gaps where most of her back teeth had once been. "Three chilruns. Imagine that." She paused and fixed me with a quizzical look as if trying to remember something that wouldn't quite come to mind. "You ain't gots none. Chilruns."

"No, ma'am," I said.

"Terrible thing a woman goes through life with no babies. I allus meant to have me a brood, but . . ." Some memory, bittersweet by the look which passed across the sagging, wrinkled mouth and sunken eyes, occupied her for a long moment before she returned to the dim room and her unexpected visitors. "Now, what for you wanna be traipsin' around in the dark over to dat old ruin next door? Bad things happ'nin' over there. Bad things."

I glanced at Darnay who hadn't spoken a word since we'd followed the old woman back to her cottage. I couldn't tell if he was intimidated or enthralled by Miss Minnie Maude Bleeker and the soft cadence of her Gullah dialect, the stark evidence of her genteel poverty.

"That's what we've come about, Miss Minnie Maude," I said, leaning forward a little more so she could read my face. "Did you know about the trouble last night?"

"*Po*-lice come."

"I know. A young man . . . disappeared. They found his car abandoned along the road. Did the policemen ask you about that?"

Her head bobbed on her scrawny neck, and I noticed her eyes had gone closed as if she were watching the scene unfold in her mind.

"Miss Minnie?" I prodded.

"Aksed," she said as her eyes suddenly popped open to fix me with a defiant stare. "Didn't get no answers."

"You withheld information from the authorities?"

Darnay's voice startled me as did the tone in which he delivered the question. Getting high-handed with Miss Minnie would do nothing to serve our purposes. I reached over to take his hand and tried to convey my disapproval with a gentle pinch of the tender flesh between his thumb and forefinger.

"Don't have no truck with no *po*-lice," she said, her rheumy black eyes still locked on mine. "I may be older 'n grits, but I gots a long memory. I 'member back in forty-six, right after my Rufus come back from the war, *po*-lice come bangin' on our door, sayin' Rufus stole some lumber from Mr. John Marcum's place over to Lady's Island. Said he was usin' it to build dat kitchen right over yonder there where I'm pointin'."

The gnarled black finger wavered in the direction of one of the added-on rooms behind us. "And Rufus says, he says he ain't stole no lumber from nobody. Bought it, he did. And they say, ain't no nigger got enough money to buy no lumber. And Rufus he show 'em the bill, marked paid all proper-like, by Mr. Thomas B. Carter hisself down to the yard." She sat back, her thin body trembling from the indignation of it, still vibrant in her mind after more than fifty years.

"I'm sure things were hard back then," I said, immediately embarrassed because of course I had no idea how difficult her life must have been. Not the slightest idea whatsoever. "But about last night," I went on, leaning toward the proud old woman. "Even if you didn't tell the sheriff's deputies about it, did you see anything? Do you know what happened to the boy?"

We held each other's eyes for a moment before hers slid away as she braced her twisted hands on the arms of the rocker and pushed herself to her feet.

"I'm needin' my bed now," she said, shuffling toward the door.

I glanced at my watch, surprised to find it only a little past ten. It seemed as if we'd been sitting there for hours. "Of course, Miss Minnie," I said, rising and pulling on Darnay's sleeve when he failed to follow suit. "I'm sorry we've kept you up so late."

She pushed open the screen door and moved cautiously down the two steps leading from the stoop to the overgrown yard. "Good to see you agin, chile," she said, reaching up to grasp my face between her bony fingers. "You best be tendin' to your own bidness now," she whispered, giving my cheek a pat before stepping back. "Folks's best served when they tend to their own bidness."

"Goodnight, Miss Minnie," I said and squeezed her hands between my own in a gesture I hoped gave her some reassurance. "We'll come visit again, if we may."

"You give Miz Smalls my kind regards," she said. "And your daddy."

"Yes, ma'am, I sure will."

I flipped on the flashlight. We were almost at the road when she called, "And marry that good-lookin' young man there, you hear me, Lydia Simpson? Marry him and make you some babies 'fore it's too late."

Her girlish laughter followed us down the yard and into the dark.

"Surely you don't intend to let it go at that," Darnay said as I slid behind the wheel. It should have been a question, but the words came out more like a command.

"You don't understand." I wiped the accumulated dew from the steering wheel and dried my hands on the legs of my slacks.

"What don't I understand? This . . . this *vieille sorcière* is a witness. She may be our best hope of disproving this idiotic notion we are somehow involved in the Anderson boy's disappearance."

"I don't know what you just called Miss Minnie, but I have a feeling it wasn't nice." I turned to stare coldly at him in the darkness. I hoped he could hear the anger in my voice even if he couldn't see my face. "You have to start remembering you're not in Kansas anymore, Toto."

After a long moment, he said, "I have no idea what that means."

"Then we're even." I twisted the key in the ignition, and the powerful engine roared to life. The sound bounced off the concrete walls of the abandoned fort and echoed around us. I took a long breath and laid my head against the back of the seat. From the clutter of stars visible through a gap in the towering trees, I tried to pick out Cassiopeia while I gathered my thoughts.

"Look, Alain, all I'm trying to say is this isn't France. This isn't your territory. I know these people, the people like Miss Minnie. She's lived here her entire life. Her grandmother was a slave on Tombee."

"Tombee?" Darnay echoed.

"It's one of the plantations that used to thrive here a hundred and fifty years ago. Anyway, she's known me since I was born, like all the native black folks on the island know all the white folks, and vice versa. We've been coexisting and doing a pretty damn good job of it for a long, long time, despite what outsiders may think."

The anger, so quick to overtake my better judgment these days, had ebbed, and I turned to smile at Darnay. "There's a protocol that needs to be observed. You can't just barge into Miss Minnie's house and grill her as if she were some sort of criminal. She's an old woman, and she's had way too many white people try to take advantage of her, to bully her and her friends just because they're poor. And black."

"You make me sound like a *fanatique*. A bigot."

"Of course I don't think any such thing. I'm just telling you we need to be patient. She'll tell us what she knows in her own good time." I backed around and headed us out down the rutted lane toward the Judge's house. "I'll get Lavinia to make up a basket, and I'll come back tomorrow. I think maybe she'll be less intimidated if I don't have my beau tagging along."

"So we will stay the night at Presqu'isle?" he asked in that warm, liquid voice that melted my bones. "*Très bien.* I have entertained a few interesting fantasies about making love in that big four-poster bed of yours."

I pushed his hand away from my thigh and shook my head. "You can stay if you like, but you'll be sleeping in a guest room."

"Do you think for a minute that will keep me from creeping down the hallway in the dead of night?" His finger traced the line of my jaw in a soft, languorous caress.

I smiled, happy for the time being to put away thoughts of blood and suspicion and missing teenagers. "If you think for a minute that little routine will work, you have sadly underestimated our Lavinia."

In spite of Darnay's promises, I slept undisturbed. The hands of the round alarm clock, which had stood on my bedside table all through my childhood, pointed at just after seven when I hauled myself down the hall to the bathroom I'd taken over as my own. By seven forty-five I sat at the table sipping Irish Breakfast tea and salivating over the smell of baking powder biscuits rising in the oven.

"So you had a sit-down with Minnie Maude Bleeker last night," Lavinia said, pulling a carton of eggs from the refrigerator. "You should be flattered. I hear tell she's picky about who she lets inside that old cottage."

From the looks of the preparations, we were in for one of Lavinia's famous down-home breakfasts. I hoped she had redskin potatoes for home fries. Blasphemy though it was, I'd never really developed a liking for grits. I wasn't sure how Darnay felt about them.

"Surely she doesn't stay out there all by herself," I said.

"Mostly. The ladies from the church pick her up and take her where she needs to go. Shopping, the bank, Wednesday night prayer meeting. She's only comin' out of that ramshackle old place feet first, or so she says."

I smiled. "You mentioned relatives. Something she said last night made me think she doesn't have any children. I sure don't remember any when I was growing up."

Lavinia opened the oven door to check the biscuits, and my stomach growled in anticipation. "Not surprisin'. Her children would be close to my age. Seems to me there was a boy, maybe two, but I have no idea where they might be. Never heard of any grandchildren, though I imagine there probably are some. Maybe even some greats. She had a niece used to come in and help out, but she passed more than ten years ago, right after Rufus did, as I recall." She sighed and began cracking shells against the same blue pottery bowl she'd used for mixing up scrambled eggs for as long as I could remember.

"It must be hard to outlive everyone you care about," she murmured as she set the big cast-iron skillet on the range top.

I swallowed hard against the memory of the gravesite Erik Whiteside, my former partner, and I had uncovered just a few months before. But at least Lavinia had Thaddeus and her grandson, Isaiah, getting ready to head off to college in a couple of weeks.

"I think she may know something about what happened to Cart Anderson." I rose and opened the cupboard holding the everyday dishes and began distributing them around the table.

"Why?"

"Well, she dropped a lot of hints about bad things happening around the old fort. She showed up toting a shotgun almost as soon as we were out of the car. I asked her about the boy, and she said the deputies had been there the night it happened, but she wouldn't tell them anything. She had that look, you know what I mean? Like she had secrets?"

"Could be she's just angling to get you to come back. Must be lonely for the poor old thing stuck out there in the middle of nowhere."

Lavinia dropped a glob of butter into the hot skillet. Over the sizzling and popping, she added, "I'm long overdue for a visit myself."

"I was thinking of putting together a basket." She turned from the stove, one eyebrow raised in question. "Okay, I was thinking of asking *you* to put together a basket. Think she'd be insulted?"

Lavinia poured the egg mixture into the skillet and began working it with her spatula. "I think it would be a nice gesture. I'll fix one up as soon as we finish breakfast. And speaking of which, go rouse out the menfolk. Tell 'em they don't get themselves movin', we're gonna start without 'em."

Lavinia left for church after settling my father on the back verandah, and I cleaned up the kitchen. Darnay, staggering under the weight of eggs, bacon, home fries, and nearly half a dozen biscuits, headed back toward Hilton Head just before ten. We made a date to meet at my house later in the day. His goodbye kiss held a little more insistence than usual, and I sensed a suppressed excitement in him I suspected had nothing to do with my body pulled tightly against his.

More secrets, I thought.

In tribute to the glorious summer morning, I let down the top on the T-Bird and stowed the heaping basket in the back seat. Lavinia had outdone herself, adding a few still-warm biscuits and three strips of bacon to an assortment of goodies culled from the freezers and pantries of Presqu'isle. Without digging around I could see a small ham, several Mason jars of vegetables she'd canned from last fall's garden, and even one container of her green tomato relish.

"Feeling very generous indeed," I said to no one, sliding behind the wheel.

Lavinia guarded her relish like a new mama cat does her kittens.

One of the nice things about traveling down bumpy, rutted dirt roads is it forces you to go slowly. I was hailed by a couple of my father's neighbors, backsliders working in their flower beds and yards instead of hauling themselves off to church. I meandered down the long avenue of oaks which had once constituted the approach to Presqu'isle. As soon as my mother had inherited the property, she'd promptly sold off much of the land in order to finance her restoration of the house.

One of Bitsy's and my favorite fantasies had been to imagine ourselves back in those days of antebellum splendor. Arrayed in a castoff dress and purloined hat, an umbrella-turned-parasol protecting her delicate skin, one of us would perch in splendor on a box upended in the old wagon. The other, usually me, played the parts of the horse, the driver, and whoever else we required. The scenario usually involved the arrival of a daughter from a neighboring plantation come to pay a call on her dearest friend, some elegant Chase or Tattnall or Baynard of Presqu'isle.

As I moved across the highway and on into the poorer section of the island, I sobered, remembering how naïve we had been about the "glory" of those days.

I was surprised to find a fairly new Buick pulled up on the barren yard in front of Minnie Maude Bleeker's cottage. Its black finish sparkled in the shafts of sunlight angling between the branches of the live oak. I eased in behind, careful to leave enough room for whoever it was to maneuver their way out, and lifted the basket from the seat.

Although the temperature had already climbed well into the eighties, the inside door was closed, and I knew Miss Minnie had no air conditioning. I rapped tentatively and waited, then knocked again. The stoop was too narrow for me to see into the windows on either side even if wilted white curtains hadn't been pulled across them against the heat. I stepped back into the yard, uncertain about what to do next.

Lavinia had said Miss Minnie didn't usually go to church on Sunday mornings because it was too hard for her to get up and moving about so early. She preferred the livelier Wednesday night prayer meetings, which usually included a meal before the service and lots of the handclapping music the old woman loved.

I'd just about decided to check out the back of the house and had taken a step in that direction when the door swung open. The woman who filled the doorway was obviously on her way to or from morning services. A soft peach-colored suit strained against her thick hips and massive bosom, and a wide-brimmed hat complete with veil and long, sweeping feather matched it perfectly. Her steel blue hair clung to her head in tight curls.

"He'p you?" the woman asked.

"I'm sorry," I said, raising the basket. "I came to call on Miss Minnie. Is she here?" When she didn't reply, I said, "I'm Bay Tanner. Lydia, that is. Judge Talbot Simpson's daughter?" Still no reaction. "Lavinia Smalls sent these things over."

That seemed to break the tension. The woman's face crumpled, and she brought a pristine white handkerchief to her lips, her stubby brown fingers trembling.

"What's happened?" The fear struck me like a slap.

"She's gone home to be with the Lord," the woman said, and I felt my knees wobble.

I set the basket on the ground and approached the door. "What happened?" I repeated.

The woman pushed open the screen and stepped aside for me to enter. It took a moment for my eyes to adjust to the dim interior, but the cause of the swaying woman's tears was immediately evident.

Minnie Maude Bleeker lay sprawled across the floor, the faded housedress and old gray cardigan sweater she'd worn the night before now stiff and stained with blood. Another pool of it darkened the threadbare carpet beneath her head. Bright red splotches mingled with the soot-darkened stones of the fireplace. The floor around her was littered with sparkling shards of glass from the ruin of the Tiffany lamp which lay just beyond her outstretched arm.

"Are you sure . . . ?" My voice came out in a hoarse croak, but the woman understood me all the same.

"Yes'm, she's dead. My daughter Helen was with me, and she's a nurse over at the hospital. She checked." As if on cue, we both turned away from the pitiful sight of Miss Minnie in her final indignity. "I'm Annie Chaplin, Miz Tanner. My daughter and me, we come to bring Miz Bleeker some lunch between Sunday school and church." She nodded toward a white Styrofoam container on the table next to the old sofa. "Greens and cornbread. Miz Bleeker sure did love her greens and cornbread."

"What do you think happened?" I asked, tactfully studying the floor while Annie Chaplin sniffled into her hanky.

"Fell, poor thing," she replied promptly, nodding her head in agreement with herself. "Not surprisin'. She wasn't real steady on her feet. Musta hit her head on the fireplace. And broke her lamp on the way down. Such a pity. Miss Minnie set such store by that old lamp."

I took a quick check around the room. Nothing else seemed to have been disturbed, although a rag rug lay bunched up near the old woman's feet. "Was the door open when you got here?" I asked.

"Closed, not locked," Annie Chaplin replied.

"Is that unusual? For her not to keep the door locked?"

When she didn't reply, I glanced up to see a closed look sliding across her puffy brown eyes. "I couldn't say. My Helen's gone down to see if she can find a phone to use. That little cell thing o' hers only works in certain places out here." She paused and moved toward the door. "I'm thinkin' we should maybe wait outside. For the sheriff."

And with those words, the precariousness of my situation suddenly struck me. Darnay and I were right in the middle of another suspicious death. Not that Cart Anderson's disappearance had been officially declared a murder, I assured myself, but once again we were in the proximity of some sort of violence.

Without conscious thought, I scanned the room as Annie Chaplin urged me toward the door. *What had we touched?* I forced myself to conjure up our previous night's visit.

Miss Minnie Maude had opened the door, both coming and going. We'd sat on the afghan-draped sofa. No chance for prints there. We'd drunk nothing, hadn't even been offered anything, come to think of it. No, I couldn't see a single object which might betray our presence.

How then to explain my visit on this tragic Sunday morning?

Stepping outside behind the now silent Annie, I spotted the napkin-covered basket where I had left it next to one of the creeping limbs of the live oak. Lavinia. She would be my excuse. I needed to get back to Presqu'isle and make certain she and my father were prepared to back up my story. And Darnay! I'd have to alert him as soon as I got home.

We stood awkwardly in the front yard, the well-dressed black woman and I in my casual polo shirt and shorts, our eyes carefully avoiding each other as we waited. I took in the serenity of the isolated cottage, the still air occasionally pierced by the sweet call of a mourning dove or the sharp screech of a sea gull. The light breeze drifting in off the water behind the house carried the scent of pine and dead fish.

"Have you known her a long time?" I asked to break the silence. I didn't recognize her, although the Chaplin name was an old and respected one.

She unbent enough to reply in a conversational tone. "Mostly all my life, off and on. We just come back to the island a couple years ago. We were cousins, in some sorta twisted way I never did understand. Her mama and my granddaddy were some kinda kin."

"I'm sorry for your loss," I said.

"Can't think what's takin' so long." The woman's feet were stuffed into white pumps which looked to be cutting off her circulation as she fidgeted on the soft, sandy ground.

"It might be difficult finding anyone home on a Sunday morning," I offered, realizing for the first time how strange it was Helen hadn't taken the car. That thought set off another jolt of panic ricocheting around in my head.

The car! Tire tracks!

I looked over my shoulder to the tangle of undergrowth which hid Miss Minnie's cottage from the ruins of Fort Fremont. I dug my keys out of my pocket and turned to Annie. "I'm going to move my car," I said, edging in that direction as I spoke. "To make room for the emergency vehicles."

Without waiting for a reply, I scooped up the basket and strode toward the Thunderbird. I backed up and pulled around the Buick, easing onto the shoulder in what I hoped was the same spot I'd parked the night before. I reversed and maneuvered the car back and forth, making certain to pass over the entire area at least several times. If anyone was able to lift my tire imprints from the grass and sand in front of the old fort, I'd have a plausible explanation for their presence. And Annie would be forced to back me up.

I left the car pointing back toward Presqu'isle and rejoined Miss Minnie's cousin just as the first flashing light bar bounced into view. No sirens. There was obviously no need for haste. I felt Annie Chaplin move closer to me as the sheriff's cruiser slid into the yard, and I nearly jumped a foot when her pudgy brown hand slipped clumsily into my own.

Battle lines had been drawn. Us against them. I needn't have worried about Annie Chaplin. She managed a watery smile as we watched the first officer haul himself out and direct the rescue unit to pull up close to the cottage.

I squeezed her hand and thanked the gods Red Tanner had not been assigned to the call. I took a deep breath and prepared to lie like a trooper.

Chapter Eight

"*Merde!* WHAT ON EARTH POSSESSED YOU TO LIE TO the police?" Alain Darnay ran his hand through his thick brown hair and whirled to face me.

I fondled the unlit cigarette, twirling it around in my fingers, packing the loose tobacco at the end more tightly into the paper.

"And put that damned thing away!"

I'd stopped at the convenience store attached to the gas station at Gumtree Road on my way back from St. Helena to fill up the T-Bird. The pack of Marlboros had been an impulse buy, the very reason they put them at eye level right behind the cash register.

"You're treading very close to the edge," I said in as reasonable a tone as I could manage considering the verbal assault I'd been enduring for nearly half an hour. Reluctantly I tossed the cigarette onto the coffee table and settled back into the cushions of the sofa.

"And what does that mean?" He wasn't exactly snarling, but it was close.

"It means I've spent the better part of the day being harangued by one man after another, and I'm not taking too much more. If you'd quit playing the outraged policeman for a minute or two, you might come to the same conclusion I did."

"And that would be?"

"That we could be having this conversation in an interrogation room at the Beaufort County Jail instead of in the comfort of my living room. In case it's slipped your mind, we're already in it up to our eyeballs with the local cops because of Cart Anderson. Admitting to having been the next-to-last people to see Miss Minnie alive probably would have cinched it." I pulled my legs up under me and drew a deep breath to calm myself. "If you were in their shoes, wouldn't you be looking at us as the prime suspects in her death?"

Darnay pushed himself away from the mantel and dropped onto the sofa beside me. "Of course, but that's just the problem. I *am* a policeman, and I do know how they think. The moment they find out we have been lying to them about being at the old woman's house, their suspicions will multiply tenfold."

"You and my father keep forgetting I didn't lie. No one asked me if I'd been there the night before. I just didn't volunteer the information. And besides, you're working on the assumption they'll find out. We didn't touch anything they can lift our prints from, no one saw us coming or going . . ."

"Now you are assuming."

I nodded. "Yes, I suppose I am. But I think it's a safe bet. The only person—or persons—who might possibly have seen us are the ones who killed Miss Minnie, and they're not about to come forward."

I reached for the cigarette, and Darnay slapped my hand.

"Okay, okay," I said.

He twined his fingers through mine and pulled me into the circle of his arm. "You're convinced the poor woman was murdered, that it has something to do with the young man who's disappeared. And that it resulted from our visiting with her last night."

I sighed and relaxed into the comfort of his embrace. "Yes. I know you and the Judge are having a hard time with the idea, but my gut says I'm right." I fought hard against the wave of guilt and sadness welling up in my chest.

"Ma pauvre petite," he whispered against my hair. "The other woman—

this Annie. She could be right, no? Perhaps your Miss Minnie tripped on the rug and hit her head. So sad, but many old people die in such accidents."

"No," I said, pulling away from him so he could see the conviction in my eyes. "I saw the inside of the house. You didn't. The lamp? The one Annie Chaplin said Miss Minnie set such store by? That will prove to have been the murder weapon. I saw blood along the edge of the base. And the splatters on the fireplace. Blood doesn't fly like that just from a fall. Someone hit her in the head. And hard." I swallowed around the bile rising in my throat and forced the image out of my mind. "Damn it, we need inside information. Red's out, at least as far as I'm concerned, and the Judge didn't seem to be making much progress with his other sources either."

After I'd received the first of my tongue-lashings, my father had set to work trying to find out exactly what the deputies had discovered and which way they were leaning regarding the cause of death of Minnie Maude Bleeker. I hoped it was only the fact it was a Sunday and many of his former colleagues were away from their offices that was preventing him from cracking the ominous silence.

"And we have to find out what's going on with the search for Cart Anderson. If Red weren't being such a bastard . . ."

"Enough. This is not something we will resolve here and now." Darnay stood and pulled me to my feet. "And my 'little gray cells' need food. Red meat, I think, very thick and very rare. Do you know of a place that can provide such sustenance?"

Before I could reply he covered my mouth with his own, his strong hands pressing me to him. In a brief, coherent moment I marveled at how neatly our bodies molded together. A long time later I disengaged my lips and leaned back to smile up into his face.

"I do," I said, then colored when I realized how it must have sounded.

"Hold that thought," Darnay said, grinning.

We beat the tourist crowds to a local steakhouse where Alain demolished the biggest T-bone I'd ever seen. We lingered over dessert, purposely avoiding any talk of our troubles, then window-shopped along the narrow stretch of stores beside the restaurant. I still sensed some unspoken tension in him, as if he were a child bursting with an untold secret, but I didn't pry. There'd been little enough peace in the past few days, and I wanted to hold on to it as long as I could. By the time we pulled back into my driveway, the sky had melted into the soft lavender-gray which precedes sunset in the Lowcountry.

I heard the shrill of the telephone as I pulled my key from the lock. I tapped in the code, disengaged the alarm, and still managed to grab the handset before the answering machine kicked in. My "hello" came out in a breathless rush.

"Mrs. Tanner?"

The voice was a deep, rich baritone I didn't recognize. "Yes, this is she."

"Mrs. Tanner, this is Henry Chaplin. The Reverend Henry Chaplin. I believe you met my mother and sister this morning under some trying circumstances."

"Annie. Yes, of course. And . . ." I groped for the other name. "And Helen."

Darnay had followed me into the kitchen and had set about brewing a pot of coffee for himself. I smiled at how readily he'd made himself at home. He tossed a quizzical look over his shoulder and mouthed, *Who?* I shrugged my shoulders.

"Yes, that's right," the reverend continued. "Tragic, the loss of Mrs. Bleeker. She was a fine woman, a fine woman. Our consolation must be that she was right with the Lord when she was called home."

I hitched one hip onto the built-in desk and let the Birkenstock sandal dangle from my foot. I had no idea where the call could be leading, but I didn't think it had much to do with the state of Miss Minnie's soul.

"Indeed." One of the first lessons I'd learned from the Judge was that the best way to get people to talk is to shut up yourself. Something in the human psyche just can't tolerate extended periods of silence. Especially on the telephone.

The Reverend Chaplin didn't prove me wrong. "The thing is, Mrs. Tanner, some of us here, some of the deacons and myself, are not quite satisfied with the . . ." He paused as if searching for the proper word. "With the conclusions the authorities may have drawn."

Darnay crossed the kitchen and stood next to me, his face still wearing that questioning look. I hopped off the desk, pulled a pen from the coffee cup I used as a holder, and scribbled *Miss Minnie's pastor* on the notepad. His eyebrows rose as he leaned back against the counter and folded his arms across his chest.

"Reverend Chaplin," I said in my brisk, former accountant's voice, "I'm confused as to the purpose of your call. I share your congregation's grief at the loss of Miss Minnie, but I'd appreciate it if you would tell me exactly what it is I can do for you."

He got the point. "We'd like to engage your services to investigate the circumstances of Mrs. Bleeker's death. I wondered if we might meet to discuss it."

I stood speechless. This was the last thing I'd expected to hear, and I had no idea how to respond. "Reverend, don't you think that's just a bit premature? I don't believe the coroner has yet ruled on the cause of her death."

At least not that the Judge could pry out of anyone, I thought. I glanced up at Darnay whose mouth dropped open in astonishment as I scribbled *hire me re MM's death* on the pad.

"I have my sources, Mrs. Tanner," Henry Chaplin replied, a little smugly it seemed to me. "They tell me the sheriff has already decided it was an accident."

I ignored the possibility his "sources" might not be the most reliable, and instead asked, "And you have reason to believe they're wrong?"

"I'd really prefer to discuss it with you in person. Are you perhaps available tomorrow? I'd be happy to meet you somewhere halfway."

I needed to talk this over with the Judge and Darnay, so I stalled. "I'll have to see if I can reschedule a few things, Reverend. Can I get back to you later this evening?"

"Of course." He gave me his numbers—church, home, cell—and said he looked forward to my call.

I hung up, suddenly realizing I hadn't flat-out told him no.

I warmed milk in the microwave and mixed myself a mug of Chai tea latte, guaranteed to soothe jangled nerves. We carried our cups to the deck off the bedroom and settled into lounge chairs. Darnay must have been paying attention over the few weeks he'd been with me, because he didn't open the discussion by telling me I had completely lost my mind. I could sense he wanted to, but he mastered the impulse.

"I thought you were out of the sleuthing game," he said in a deceptively calm voice. "Your partner gave it up after that business with Judas Island, did he not?"

I nodded, remembering Erik Whiteside's pained face as he told me he'd had enough of guns and danger. He'd originally signed on to Simpson & Tanner, Inquiry Agents as our computer expert, and he'd certainly proved himself in that area. Outside of a few military and government systems, I didn't think there was any machine he couldn't get into if he set his mind to it. The problem was his involvement had escalated over the past year into an active participation which had placed him in harm's way—twice. He'd decided not to press his luck a third time.

I'd been sad but entirely understanding. Erik still wanted to be a part of the organization, but from a safe distance. Since his defection, S&T had been pretty much defunct. The Reverend Chaplin had just given us a reason to resurrect it. The question was, did I want to? I'd toyed with the idea the day before. In my anger at Red Tanner and his implied accusations regarding the disappearance of Cart Anderson, I'd vowed to get the business up and running again, if for no other reason than to put to rest the ridiculous notion of Darnay's and my involvement. Henry Chaplin and his deacons seemed to be providing me with an added incentive.

"Bay?"

I realized I hadn't answered. "Yes, Erik's pretty much out of it, although I know he'd be happy to help. That is, if we had any computer work which needed done. Right now, this doesn't look as if it has anything to do with technology."

"What do you think it's about then?"

I felt the comfort of his hand close around mine. Despite having my own cop sitting just a few feet away, I couldn't quite muster up the courage to voice my feelings. I wasn't even certain I could have put them into words. A nebulous fear had been lurking in the back of my mind, a sort of free-floating anxiety that there was a link between my past and the current trouble.

I shook off the paranoia and smiled over at Darnay. "I haven't a clue," I said, "but I intend to find out."

Chapter Nine

THE IMPERIAL DRAGON FEATURED A WONDERFUL CHInese buffet at lunchtime, so Henry Chaplin and I met at the Bluffton location in Sheridan Park just after twelve-thirty the next day. Although it was farther from Beaufort in miles, I had calculated our travel time to be about the same when you factored in that I had to fight the traffic going off Hilton Head.

I had no trouble recognizing the pastor as I stepped into the noisy restaurant. Though by no means the only black man in the place, he still stood out among the crowd of casually dressed diners. Not quite as tall as I, he held himself erect with an easy assurance which came perhaps from the instant respect accorded his well-cut black suit and pristine white collar. He was also strikingly handsome, his close-cropped black hair accentuating finely wrought features.

Denzel Washington as Father Flanagan, I thought and smiled.

The Reverend Henry Chaplin approached with a welcoming grin and enveloped my extended hand in a surprisingly gentle grip. "Mrs. Tanner. I can't tell you what a pleasure it is to meet you."

"Thank you, Reverend. Shall we find a seat?"

An Oriental man in white dress shirt and black trousers bowed slightly and led us to a small table at the rear of the main dining area. We ordered a pot of green tea to share and proceeded to the long buffet table to fill our plates. They had my favorite, General Tso's chicken, so I loaded up on that with a little steamed rice on the side. I carefully avoided the long, deceptively innocuous-looking red peppers I knew could take the lining off the inside of your mouth in a heartbeat. Henry Chaplin chose small bits of a variety of dishes and joined me at the table.

"You're probably wondering why we've asked you to help us with this problem," he said just as I stuffed my mouth full of rice and chicken. I was surprised he wanted to jump right into business before we'd had a chance to feel each other out. "Actually, it was Mrs. Smalls who first suggested it."

Luckily I had just swallowed, so I was saved the ignominy of spitting food across the table. "Lavinia?" I managed to croak out before gulping down a large swig of ice water. "My Lavinia?"

If he took offense at the possessive, it didn't register on his face. "She's a parishioner of mine, as I'm sure you're already aware," he said, ignoring the stunned look on my face.

Truth to tell, I wasn't aware, but I suppose I should have been. Not that there were dozens of churches on St. Helena, but Lavinia's familiarity with Minnie Maude Bleeker and her situation should have given me some clue. Every now and then an incident such as this, in which I was forced to admit to an incredible ignorance of things I should have known about, reminded me I was not a real private investigator and probably never would be.

The minister seemed puzzled by my discomfort. I straightened out my face and said more calmly, "I didn't know Lavinia attended your church."

"I've only recently taken over the pulpit."

"I spoke to my father last evening, after your call, and he didn't see fit to mention it either."

He smiled. "Perhaps they didn't want to influence your decision."

"Perhaps."

I didn't at all like the turn the conversation was taking. After I'd finished giving my statement to the officers at Miss Minnie's cottage, I'd hightailed it back to Presqu'isle to get my story straight with

Lavinia and the Judge. Though both reluctantly agreed with my reasons for keeping quiet about Darnay's and my Saturday night visit with the dead woman, I could tell neither was happy about being drafted as accomplices in my deception. I didn't know whether to feel angry or betrayed that my father's housekeeper had apparently hot-footed it right over to the church to discuss my private business with her pastor.

We ate in silence for a few more minutes, although I'd pretty much lost my appetite. I refilled our dainty, handle-less cups while Reverend Chaplin piled a dessert plate with deep-fried doughnut holes rolled in sugar and a few peach slices. Before resuming his seat, he dropped two fortune cookies wrapped in cellophane onto the table between us.

"Go ahead," he said, "you choose. Ladies first."

I toyed with them for a moment, then selected the one which hadn't already been partially crushed. Someone somewhere had once told me not to take a broken fortune cookie because all the luck would have leaked out. I peeled away the wrapper and cracked it open. I glanced at my companion as I unrolled the thin strip of white paper.

"What does it say?" he asked, wiping a dusting of sugar from his fingers.

I pulled my reading glasses from my purse and studied the message before bursting into laughter.

"What?" the minister asked, his smile matching my own.

" 'You will meet a dark stranger who will change your life,' " I read, dropping the scrap of nonsense onto the table.

When I looked up, Reverend Chaplin was no longer smiling.

I found the house empty. The place smelled like furniture polish and the sharp, salty tang of the ocean. Despite the scorching heat shimmering just outside the French doors, Dolores must have had the windows open at some point. She was a firm believer in the benefits of fresh air.

I checked the machine and found it devoid of messages, so I poured myself a glass of tea and headed for the office. Since the conclusion of the nasty business on Judas Island, I hadn't been in the room except to dash off a few how's-it-going e-mails to Erik Whiteside and to my friend Jordan von Brandt, still in Europe battling her ex-husband's family for full custody of her daughters. I fired up the computer, opened a blank Word document, and spent the next few minutes making notes on everything that had happened over the past few days, beginning with our confrontation with Carter Anderson in the parking lot of the Westin.

I hadn't made the reverend any promises, only that I'd look into a few things and let him know if I thought he had reason to question the way the sheriff's office was handling Miss Minnie's death. I would have to rely on the Judge to get me accurate information on that front. I hoped his sources were proving as quick and reliable as they usually did, despite the previous day's lack of success.

As I typed, a number of questions occurred to me, and I noted them as well. First and most important was the cause of Minnie Maude Bleeker's death. If she had died from a fall, then the sad occurrence had no connection to the boy's disappearance and was none of my business. I could write off the Reverend Henry Chaplin and concentrate on Cart. That definitely deserved my time and energy, if for no other reason than to keep Darnay and me out of jail.

As ludicrous as the idea sounded, I knew that more than a few people, most of them affiliated with the sheriff's office, had latched on to us as viable suspects. In spite of Red's blustering about our having manhandled the kid, my connection to the boy's father had to be the motivating factor. Geoffrey Anderson's death had been ruled accidental, and I'd actually come out of the whole thing as something of a local heroine for enabling those who'd been swindled by Geoff to recoup some of their losses. Everyone had taken my word as the only living witness that the entire thing had been a horrible accident. I'd been so relieved at the time I hadn't seriously questioned how easy it had all been. Perhaps it was time to re-examine my good fortune.

While the printer whirred and spat out pages, I pulled a file folder from the deep right-hand drawer of the desk and labeled it. After placing the printout into the folder, I carried a yellow legal pad and my Waterford pen back out to the great room and settled onto the sofa. Typing may have been neat and efficient, but my old accounting days had given me a preference for the scratch of pen on paper. Something about it stimulated my brain in a way tapping on keys never could. I'd have preferred to sit out on the deck with the soft *shush* of the Atlantic rollers and the screeching cries of the gulls for company, but the outdoor thermometer registered just below one hundred degrees.

I ran back over the events of the past few days, drawing boxes around the names of the principal players and doodling notes beneath each one, connecting some with solid lines and others with squiggly ones, as if I were working out a genealogy chart. Everyone was so frustratingly interwoven, as was so much of life in this former bastion of the Confederacy. Although we liked to think we had moved on from the bonds of the past, they tied us to each other in ways few outsiders could understand. Magnificent plantation houses like Tombee and Presqu'isle had been built and maintained by the sweat and misery of Miss Minnie's and Lavinia's people. And yet, there was a connection, a shared past not always bound by hate . . .

I felt my eyes closing. Though I had tried to erase the image of the old black woman's shriveled body curled on the floor in a pool of blood, I watched the scene drifting through the haze of my half-dreamy doze. Something scratched at the back of my subconscious as my inner eye surveyed the ramshackle cottage—the bright Sunday morning sun seeping through a crack in the curtains . . . falling across the pine boards and one pitiful foot thrust into a tattered old carpet slipper . . . dappling the blackened stones of the fireplace and . . .

I shot upright, sending the pad and pen tumbling to the floor. It wasn't what I'd *seen* yesterday morning that had been tugging at my memory. It was what I hadn't. I shook myself fully awake and crossed to stand in front of my own cold hearth, staring into the bookcases but seeing the corner in Minnie Maude Bleeker's sparse living quarters, the corner next to her fireplace. *Empty.*

Where the hell was her shotgun?

I finally tracked down Darnay on his cell phone somewhere on the road. He seemed strangely reluctant to tell me exactly where he was but promised to be at the house within the hour. I took him at his word. In the kitchen I dumped a couple of dozen frozen shrimp into a colander and ran cold water over them. I wondered if my supply of fresh local seafood would dry up now Lavinia's grandson was heading off to college. I rarely left Presqu'isle without enough for a couple of meals and excess to freeze up for later use. I set water for pasta on to boil and began assembling dried herbs. Unlike my father's housekeeper, I had no talent for growing them myself.

I was just transferring the drained penne into wide bowls when I heard the front door close and Darnay's voice call, "Ah, you are truly an angel! I could smell *l'estragon* all the way out in the driveway."

He bounded up the steps into the kitchen and planted a loud kiss on the side of my neck.

"Do you mean tarragon?" I asked, turning so his next kiss landed squarely on my lips.

"Oui, c'est ça," he replied when we came up for air.

"Your nose is correct. Shrimp in tarragon butter. Sit. Everything's ready."

I spooned sauce over the pasta, ladled on the shrimp, and joined him at the table where he was already dishing up salad.

"What?" I asked in response to his grin. "You've got that I-have-a-secret look on your face again."

"All in good time, my darling. All in good time."

And I had to be content with that until we'd polished off every bite of food and settled onto the cushioned love seat in the screened-in area of the deck. The temperature outside still hovered around ninety, so I left the inside door open. The air conditioning pouring out of the house provided a little relief from the stifling humidity.

"Okay, buster, spill it," I said, setting my glass of iced tea on the wicker table in front of us.

I turned to face him, and he reached for my hand. He studied my eyes, his own so intense, so devoid of their usual playfulness, I had a sudden vision of his dropping to one knee right there on my porch. Panic washed over me, and I tried to pull my hand free, but his grip only tightened.

"Alain, please don't," I pleaded, squirming in my effort to escape. "Really, I mean it. You know I'm not ready to . . ."

"Tais-toi!"

I jumped at his tone, the command flipping my mood from apprehension to anger.

"Don't tell me to shut up!"

His smile silenced my outburst, and I settled back against the cushions as he shook his head in that way he sometimes had of making me feel like a naughty child. "You are hopping to conclusions again," he said.

"Jumping."

"Eh?" He raised my hand and carried it to his lips.

"It's *jumping* to conclusions, not hopping."

"If you say so."

He nibbled on my fingers for a while, and I had to force myself back to our original topic of conversation.

"So what have you been looking so smug about then?" I asked.

"I have a new home."

It was the last thing I'd expected him to say, and I spluttered out my questions without giving him a chance to reply. "Why? How? I mean, when did you . . . Where? Does this mean you're staying?"

"Come," he said as he rose and pulled me to my feet. "All will be revealed."

I shoved aside the need to discuss my revelation about the missing shotgun and my meeting with the Reverend Henry Chaplin and threw myself fully into sharing Darnay's excitement. We stood on the upper deck of his new condominium, our arms resting side by side on the railing, as the sun slipped behind the mainland in a magnificent, fiery orange blaze reflecting off the waters of Broad Creek and turning the swaying marsh grass a soft, translucent gold.

"It's wonderful," I said, smiling up at him. The two-bedroom, two-and-a-half-bath townhouse nestled on the south end of the island would provide just enough room to feel like a home without requiring constant attention. "What are you going to do about furniture?"

"I was hoping to have the benefit of your excellent taste and sound advice," he replied, pulling me close to his side. *"Est-ce possible?"*

"Shopping with someone else's money is every woman's fantasy," I said with a smile. "Can we start now?"

"We have time," he replied softly, and the full meaning of his words settled over me.

On the brief drive from Port Royal, Darnay had finally explained his sudden absences and the tidal wave of faxes and phone calls from Europe over the past week or so. The announcement would be made public shortly: the next G-8 economic summit, the annual meeting of the world's richest, most powerful nations, would be held in nearby Savannah the following spring. In anticipation of the kinds of violent protests which had marred these gatherings in other cities across the globe, Interpol had agreed to provide a presence, a liaison with the appropriate agencies of the participating countries to coordinate security for the conference.

Darnay would be a consultant, his vast experience in undercover work and infiltration a valuable resource to be tapped by his colleagues. There would be endless meetings, reconnaissance, and vetting of the sites, interviews, research. He would need a base of operations, and he had chosen Hilton Head. Interpol wanted him badly and had agreed to foot the bill.

I'd sat silently beside him when he'd finished dropping this bombshell, unsure of how to reply because I had no idea yet how I felt about it. Part of me rejoiced. Part of me recoiled in dismay at the thought that decisions I was unprepared to make might be forced on me by the mere fact of his daily presence in my life.

As the last of the fierce July sun gilded the palms at the edge of Bram's Point across the narrow creek, Darnay lifted my chin with a gentle finger and turned my face to his. "I make you this promise, *ma petite,* so your mind may be at rest, at least on this one issue. We have both enjoyed the game, have we not? The crazy Frenchman, mad to marry his reluctant lover?"

I nodded, his steely blue eyes holding mine in an unwavering gaze.

"But the next time I ask, I will expect an honest answer. And no matter your decision, I will not ask again. *Comprends?*"

I stepped back away from his touch, my eyes locked on his. "I understand," I said, and he smiled.

Chapter Ten

Darnay spent the next two days in Savannah helping establish an office and all it entailed, so we postponed our shopping trip. By unspoken mutual consent, we'd also deferred any more discussion of the mess his manhandling of Cart Anderson had landed us in. He had enough to worry about with gearing up a team to handle a horde of international protestors. I decided to handle the local stuff myself.

The story in the *Island Packet* didn't offer many details, so I ran out to the drugstore and grabbed a copy of the Beaufort paper. The tourists appeared to be spending the morning at the beach instead of mobbing the local stores and roadways, so I carried the paper across to Starbucks and scanned it over a cup of Chai.

The *Gazette* didn't provide much additional information except for a brief obituary. It seemed Miss Minnie did indeed have children, although two of the three had predeceased her. Her surviving daughter was listed as MaeRose Bleeker Jones of Clarksville, Tennessee, and the several grandchildren and greats were scattered all over the country. None of Miss Minnie's close relatives seemed to have stuck around Beaufort County.

The funeral was slated for Saturday, with viewings on Thursday afternoon and Friday evening. Services would be conducted at Reverend Chaplin's AME church.

I folded the paper and wondered if the fact that everything had already been scheduled meant the body had been released. If so, the coroner must have ruled out suspicious circumstances in her death and passed on having an autopsy performed. I pulled the cell phone from my bag and called the Judge.

I caught Lavinia just on her way out to do the marketing. She seemed reluctant to talk to me and quickly handed the receiver over to my father. I wondered if she was having second thoughts about siccing her minister on me, but she didn't give me the opportunity to ask.

The Judge's gruff voice rattled in my ear. "What the hell kind of mess have you gotten us into this time?"

"And a pleasant good morning to you as well," I said, shifting around so I could prop my feet up on the seat of the chair tucked in to the other side of the table.

"I've had three calls already this morning, the last one from Charlie asking me what you were up to. You're becoming a considerable embarrassment, are you aware of that, daughter?"

"Get over it," I said. "What did he hear?"

The former county solicitor, Charlie Seldon, had an information network almost as formidable as my father's.

"Well, you're still on the hook about the Anderson boy. It's become an official missing person's case as of last night, and I don't mind telling you the sheriff's boys don't have the first thing in the way of a lead. So, until something else jumps up, they're holding out hope you and Darnay can be tagged with it. Charlie wants to know if he should start soliciting donations for a legal defense fund."

"You're actually finding this amusing, aren't you?" I shook my head and slurped the last of the latte from the bottom of the Styrofoam cup. "I hope it's really as ridiculous as you're making it sound."

I heard the muffled noise as his hand slipped over the mouth of the receiver followed by a series of muted but very audible coughs and a deep honking sound as he blew his nose.

"What's the matter?" I asked, my heart beating a little faster. "Are you sick?"

It took a moment for him to come back on the line. "No, I'm not sick. Don't fuss."

"Well that didn't sound real good. How long have you been hacking like that?"

"Ever since Vinnie made me give up my morning cigar. Can't get her to understand my poor old lungs need the smoke." His raspy laugh was interrupted by another cough. "All I need's a good Havana, and I'll be right as rain. Problem is I can't find where the damn fool woman hid 'em."

I knew there was no point in arguing with him. I understood Lavinia's concern, one I generally shared. But I also tended to be of the opinion that a man pushing eighty should enjoy life in whatever ways he could and not worry too much about the consequences.

Still, I didn't like the sound of his cough. Or the honking. "Maybe you should call Harley."

Harley Coffin, whose name had subjected the poor man to endless harassment since the day he'd chosen medicine as a profession, had looked after my father for the past twenty-plus years.

"Maybe you should mind your own business. Harley Coffin is an old woman. First thing he'll do is want to cart me off to the damn hospital for 'tests.' Sometimes I wonder if the old fool doesn't get a kickback or something."

I surrendered. "Okay, okay. Have it your own way. Just don't let yourself get really sick just because you're too damned stubborn to ask for help." I sighed and pulled the stirrer out of my empty cup. Chewing on the tasteless plastic didn't give the same satisfaction as cigarettes, but it would have to do. "So what exactly did Charlie Seldon have to say? Did he hear anything about Mrs. Bleeker? I read in the paper just now they're having her funeral on Saturday, so they must have released the body already."

My father cleared his throat loudly. "Charlie says they think she fell, poor old thing. Hit her head on the fireplace. It's probably gonna be ruled accidental, so there'll be no point in holdin' on to the remains."

A young couple with a screaming toddler in tow stepped up to the counter. I turned my back on them and lowered my voice. "I have some questions. Who's likely to talk to me? I think we can pretty much rule Red out of the picture. He's leading the charge to lock us up."

"I think you're being unfair, but I agree it's best if we work behind the scenes as much as possible. There's some new blood in local law enforcement. Out-of-towners. Folks who don't understand our traditions here."

Translation: these carpetbaggers haven't gotten the word yet about who actually runs things in Beaufort County.

I smiled. "So whose brain can we pick? I've got some questions about Miss Minnie's death, and getting answers to them is going to force me to give up the truth about being there the night before she died. Who can we trust to keep that to themselves for the time being?"

"Let me check with Charlie." The Judge paused. "Am I guessin' you and Alain don't think this was an accident?"

I hesitated as well before answering. "Two things," I said, lowering my voice even more. "The base of the broken lamp appeared to have blood on it, but it wasn't anywhere near the pool around the body. How the hell could they have missed that? Don't they send a crime scene unit in on a case like this? I mean, if I noticed the blood on the lamp from fifteen feet away, why didn't the pros?"

"Good point." I could hear the slight hum my father sometimes made, unconsciously and low in his throat, when he was deep in thought. "Charlie didn't say they'd *absolutely* ruled it an accident, just that it looked likely. I'll check further. What's the other one?"

"The other what?"

"You said you had two things."

"Oh, right. Miss Minnie's shotgun was missing from the corner by the fireplace. I saw her put it there on Saturday night, but it was gone on Sunday morning."

"And you think that means what—exactly?"

"I don't know—exactly," I replied, mocking his sarcastic tone. "There's no reason Annie Chaplin or her daughter would have moved it, at least none I can think of."

"This for your own knowin' or because Vinnie's preacher-man wants to pay you?"

I tried not to take offense at the implication and failed. "Both. Do you want in on this, or has Simpson & Tanner been reduced to a sole proprietorship?"

I waited a long time for my father's response. "I'll make some calls and get back to you."

Although I itched to be doing something constructive in regard to Cart Anderson's disappearance and the questionable circumstances surrounding Miss Minnie's death, I knew I needed more information. No sense running off half-cocked, as the Judge was fond of saying. Back home in my office I pulled out the file and scanned all my notes again. I'd added the fact of the missing shotgun, but something else had been bothering me.

I found my reconstruction of our meeting on Saturday night. I'd summarized our conversation with Miss Minnie, which hadn't amounted to a whole hell of a lot except hints and innuendos. But I hadn't given much ink to our initial encounter when she'd scared the living hell out of me by appearing suddenly out of the tangle of bushes and trees beside the ruined fort.

I closed my eyes and tried to conjure it up: the eerie silence, my flashlight playing across the brush along the side of the road. The heart-stopping sight of those knowing black eyes peering at us in the narrow beam of light. She'd leveled the shotgun at us, challenging our presence before recognizing me. And what was it she'd said? Something about keeping another "young 'un" from getting hurt?

I opened my eyes and scribbled it all down on the legal pad. Had other kids been injured while swilling beer and testing sexual boundaries in the dank cement corridors beneath Fort Fremont? Miss Minnie's words, now I'd recalled them, seemed to suggest it. Was that what she'd been reluctant to talk about on Saturday night? Her face had told me she knew things. What had kept her from telling me right then and there? Did someone think she'd eventually spill her secrets? Was that why she was dead? The idea seemed preposterous, and yet . . .

I glanced down to find I'd let my thoughts find expression in the margins of the ruled paper: a stick figure lay sprawled on the ground while another stood over it, one stick-arm holding a replica of Miss Minnie's Tiffany lamp.

Two courses of action seemed open to me. I chose the most expedient and signed on to AOL.

The *Beaufort Gazette* had much of its content archived online, but a search using "Fort Fremont" yielded only a couple of feature articles about the history of the property in the last century and its abandonment by the military almost before the walls had been completed. Another told the tale of the headless apparition with the lantern, but I was fairly certain our problems lay with inhabitants of this more earthly plane. I tried a couple of other permutations of the name with similar results.

Next I typed in references to drug raids, disturbance calls, other crimes involving the Land's End area, but my parameters were too wide. I had no idea of names or dates, nothing concrete to give the search engine something to lock on to. What I really needed was access to police reports. I wondered if ordinary citizens could just walk in and check out arrest records. Maybe Erik Whiteside could give me some direction. I dialed the Charlotte electronics store he managed and waited while his receptionist tracked him down.

"Erik Whiteside."

"Bay Tanner," I said, mimicking his businesslike tone.

"Well, hey there! How the hell are you?" His soft, Southern drawl held just a trace of apprehension.

"I'm fine," I lied. "How about you?"

"Keepin' busy. How's Alain?"

"Fine." I wasn't certain if Darnay's extended presence in the States and the reasons for it were ready for public dissemination yet, so I left it there. "And Mercer?"

Erik and my half fifth cousin, Mercer Mary Prescott, had become an item shortly after we nearly got ourselves killed trying to keep her out of trouble. Though an unlikely liaison, at least in my judgment, the pair seemed to be heading toward a serious relationship. Or at least they had the last time I'd been in their company.

"Mercer's okay, I guess. She keeps pretty busy down at the farm."

His reference was to the tumble-down place my cousin and her mother had originally rented, then purchased when they came into an unexpected infusion of cash. Even though they could now afford much better, the two of them seemed happy there. Catherine, Mercer's mother, suffered from recurring bouts of mental illness, and she felt safe in the old farmhouse.

Erik didn't seem inclined to be more forthcoming about Mercer, and I wondered if there was trouble in paradise. Then I shrugged. *None of my business.* I hesitated, unsure how to broach the reason for my call. Erik had made it plain he'd lost his stomach for the danger and misadventure he'd encountered as an active member of Simpson & Tanner, Inquiry Agents. I wasn't certain how he'd react to my trying to drag him back in, even peripherally.

"Listen," I began, "I have a computer question for you." That seemed innocuous enough.

"I'm your guy. Shoot."

"I'm trying to track down a story, or maybe several, in the local paper. Not the *Packet*, but the *Beaufort Gazette.* I'm having a hell of a time getting close to what I want. Anything you can suggest about phrasing the search parameters, maybe narrowing them down?"

"What kind of stories are you looking for?" When I didn't immediately reply, he prodded, "Maybe something to do with a crime?"

"Lucky guess," I said and allowed myself a small smile.

Unlike our previous discussions on this topic, he didn't ask for specifics. *Happier in his ignorance,* I thought.

"Problem with small-town papers is they don't have the gigs—

gigabytes to you cyber-challenged folks," he joked. "Not enough storage space on the servers to keep whole issues over long periods of time. Don't they have their own archives? Maybe microfilm or something equally antiquated?"

I laughed. "The library does, but I don't have any dates to work with. Barring that, I'd have to sit for maybe the next ten years and go through them page by page."

"Bummer. That's no good."

He paused, and I could almost hear the internal monologue going on about whether or not he should get involved. I left him to work it out, embellishing my crude drawing of the crime scene in Miss Minnie's cottage while I waited.

Finally he said, "Give me some details, and I'll see what I can do."

I mumbled my thanks and rattled off the information before he could change his mind.

After hanging up, I prowled the house, tense and edgy for no particular reason I could put my finger on, although finding myself a suspect in a serious crime might have done for starters. A check of the outside thermometer yielded the depressing information that the heat wave continued unabated. The best thing to shake me out of this kind of floating anxiety had always been a long, pounding run on the beach, but I didn't think setting out at high noon in ninety-six degree temperatures would probably be the smartest decision I could make.

I sighed and trotted up the steps into the kitchen. I shredded some romaine into a bowl, cut up a hard cooked egg, and drowned the whole thing in Caesar dressing. Eventually we'd have a cooler day, and I could run off the accumulated fat grams. I carried my salad and a glass of sweet tea over to the kitchen table and settled in to finish reading the morning's *Island Packet.*

When I'd been at college, up at Northwestern near Chicago, I'd been too busy earning my finance and accounting degrees to pay much attention to how politics operated on the enemy side of the Mason-

Dixon Line. Still, I wondered if they experienced the same in-fighting and backroom bickering which seemed to dominate every one of our governmental agencies from the school board to the various local councils. The paper was always full of their self-righteous letters to the editor and long-winded speeches on the floors of meeting rooms. Since the explosion of development on Hilton Head and along the Route 278 corridor out through Bluffton to Sun City, Beaufort County seemed to have divided itself into two almost distinct entities, with the more rural areas north of the Broad River struggling to keep from being swallowed up in the rolling tide of progress.

St. Helena Island was one such area which fought hard to maintain its peaceful, agrarian heritage. Huge tracts of savannah and marshland lay undisturbed along its narrow side roads. Black families, many of them having worked the small truck farms and fields for generations, tried to hold on to the legacy of their freed ancestors. And yet every time I made the trip out to Presqu'isle, it seemed I noticed another sign, another placard nailed to an ancient tree announcing acreage for sale and development.

Minnie Maude Bleeker's place would be available now. I shoved away the soggy remains of the salad and gazed unseeing out the bay window toward the road. I wondered if her daughter would sell. I had no idea if Miss Minnie's holdings included the back land which rolled down to the narrow white beach behind the fort, but that water access would definitely jack up the price. I hoped MaeRose had an interest in holding on to the property. The Judge had often said it wouldn't take too many of the old landowners to knuckle under to the temptation to make a fast buck, and the pristine beauty of the whole island would collapse in a domino effect that could lead to disaster.

I folded the paper and carried my dishes to the counter. The shrill of the phone made me jump, and the fork clattered noisily against the stainless steel sink. I thought immediately of Erik and grabbed up the receiver before the third ring.

"Bay, it's Red."

The unexpectedness of it made me pause. We hadn't parted on the best of terms, but time and distance had pretty much softened my anger at him. I tried to put that into my voice.

"Hey, Red. What's up?"

"I shouldn't be calling you, but there's no way . . . Listen, this isn't official. I mean, I'm not on duty. I'm calling on my cell, so you have to consider this as coming from your brother-in-law and not . . ."

"Red, hold it! You're not making any sense. Slow down and just tell me."

"Right. You're right. I just want to be clear that I could get my ass fired for this, okay?"

"Got it." My heart rate skipped up a level, but I tried to keep it light. "What's the deal? Are they coming to haul me away?" When he didn't respond, I swallowed hard and forced myself to speak calmly. "Are you calling to tell me I'm going to be arrested?"

"Not exactly." He sighed, and I could envision his hand running distractedly through his short brown hair. "They just got the definitive results back from the blood we found in the Anderson kid's car."

"The Judge already told me it was his. Cart's, I mean."

"Yeah, they're pretty sure. But there were two. Two different blood types, I mean. They want you and Darnay to come down to the office to give a sample. Along with a DNA swab. A couple of deputies are on their way over with a warrant."

The last sentence came out in a rush. I looked around and found myself sitting in my chair at the kitchen table with no memory of having crossed the room. *This is crazy!* I heard the words inside my head. This was no longer an intellectual exercise, a what-if scenario. They actually wanted to check our blood against what they'd found in Cart Anderson's abandoned car.

"Wait!" I said aloud. "Wait. This is a good thing. Because we weren't there, Red. You know damn well we weren't there. This will clear us."

"I hope to God you're right," he said.

"Of course I'm right!"

"Well, think about it. Somebody came up with enough probable cause to convince a judge to issue a warrant. And considering who you are, and the international connections your boyfriend's got, they either had to have some solid evidence or a hell of a lot of juice."

I let that thought simmer as I watched the white Beaufort County sheriff's cruiser turn sharply off the road and roll down the driveway toward my house.

Chapter Eleven

THE SWABBING OF THE INSIDE OF MY LEFT CHEEK TOOK only a matter of seconds, and while I hate the thought of needles, let alone the reality of them, the blood draw went about as well as could be expected. Everyone treated me with courtesy and respect. I was also grateful they'd let me drive myself down to the satellite sheriff's office and not forced me to endure the indignity of being hauled away in the back seat of the cruiser.

Under the guise of changing clothes, I'd also bought time to make some hurried phone calls. I got Darnay's voice mail and left an urgent message detailing our predicament. The Judge had been adamant I fight the warrant, but Lawton Merriweather had counseled me to cooperate and just get it over with. Apparently he had more belief in my innocence than my own father. Hard as I tried, I couldn't see a downside to eliminating myself as a suspect in whatever had happened to Cart Anderson.

Outside the sheriff's office I sucked in a lungful of heavy, humid air, and the sharp, insistent craving for a cigarette struck me like a slap. I stuck my hand in my tote bag and fondled the illicit pack of Marlboros I'd told Alain I'd pitched in the trash. What could it hurt to have one? It had taken me years to become addicted. Surely one wouldn't send me skidding down that slippery slope again. And hadn't I quit fairly easily?

Maybe I wasn't hooked on nicotine after all. Maybe it was just a habit, like biting my nails when I was little.

Gazing off toward the low shopping center across the street, I battled the devil Temptation. The sharp blare of a horn startled me back to reality, and I jerked my hand guiltily out of my bag.

"Do you mind?" A glowering deputy in a sharply pressed khaki shirt, one tanned arm resting on the ledge of the open window, leaned out of his patrol car.

"Excuse me?" I said, then looked around and realized I had been daydreaming in the middle of the last remaining parking space in front of the building. "Oh, sorry!" I stepped back up onto the sidewalk.

"You're Bay Tanner, right?"

I turned back at the sound of my name and watched the stocky young officer heave himself out of the cruiser. He adjusted his gun belt in the same way Red always did, his hand running over the holster, nightstick, and handcuffs as if taking inventory before venturing out to face a hostile world. The tenor of his voice made me wary. I shaded my eyes against the glare of the late afternoon sun as he marched up to join me on the walkway.

"I'm sorry, do we know each other?" I asked.

"Only by reputation," he said.

He hadn't removed his wraparound sunglasses, so I had no opportunity to study his eyes, but there was something in his tone that sent me into defense mode. I took a step backwards. Although I topped him by a couple of inches, the breadth of his chest and the ripple of biceps visible under his short sleeves said this was a man who could take care of himself in any kind of physical confrontation.

"Was there something you wanted? I'm in a bit of a rush." I took another step away, my hand again sliding into my tote bag. This time I bypassed the cigarettes and firmly grasped the car keys.

"Oh, I just bet you are." Again that tone, slightly disrespectful, mocking, but not anything I could have complained about to his superiors. He planted his feet a little wider apart and let his right hand fall to rest on the butt of his service gun. "So how'd it go in there?"

"Excuse me?"

Suddenly he leaned forward until our faces were only inches apart. "We gonna be able to nail your ass this time?" he whispered.

The glare from his reflective sunglasses seemed to be stabbing directly into my brain. I had a vision of those beefy hands wrapped around my throat, and I could feel my knees starting to quiver. If I could see his eyes, I knew they would be burning with anger. The moment passed as two deputies erupted from the station door and trotted toward the parking lot.

"Hey, Lonnie! Let's go! Big pileup out on 278 by the outlet mall. Half a dozen vehicles and injuries."

"I'm right behind you," he called, then whirled back toward me. "We ain't finished here, lady."

"Who the hell are you?" I demanded. I grabbed at his arm as he spun away from me, but he shrugged it off.

"Name's Daggett. Maybe you remember my brother, Tommy? Used to be a deputy, too, until you and your damned friends got him kicked off the force."

I stared after Lonnie Daggett as he marched to his patrol car and yanked the door open. "Remember what I said. We ain't through yet. You're gonna wish you'd been a little nicer to the cops, lady. Count on it." The door slammed, and he flung the cruiser into reverse, laying rubber as he shifted into drive and sped away toward the accident.

I watched the flashing blue lights disappear onto Pope Avenue, and the sharp wail of his siren faded into the still, heavy air.

I checked my voice mail on the cell and dialed into the answering machine at home, but neither yielded a message from Darnay. I drove on past the entrance to Port Royal Plantation, pulled into Burger King, and ordered a Whopper and fries at the drive-thru. A short block up the highway, I turned into Jarvis Park. The soccer field and small playground lay deserted in the lingering heat of early evening. The whine of a few insects and a steady hum of traffic from the Cross Island Parkway were the only sounds to intrude as I settled myself on a bench beneath an overhanging oak.

I tried to empty my mind as I automatically fed French fries into my mouth. I could feel myself losing control of the events of the past few days, and I didn't like it. Not one bit.

I stuffed the last bite of burger in my mouth and wiped the remnants of grease from my fingers with a paper napkin. A ripple off to my left disturbed the smooth tranquility of the lake, and I watched the scaly back of a small alligator slide in graceful S-turns just beneath the surface. A gentle breeze ruffled the leaves above me, and I settled back into the welcome shade.

I felt a genuine sense of relief now I'd been given the opportunity to eliminate myself as a suspect in the disappearance of Carter Anderson. Once they caught up with Darnay and stuck the little cotton swab in his mouth and the needle in his arm, we could both move beyond the cloud of suspicion which had risen so quickly to hover over us like the remnants of a bad dream.

It surprised me how easily some people had accepted the notion of our guilt. I'd always enjoyed a spotless reputation, both personally and in my accounting practice. Funny how all that could change in the blink of an eye. Maybe it had more to do with Darnay than with me, I thought, stretching my arms over my head and tucking one leg up under me on the bench. Guilt by association. Anyone who hadn't spent the last hundred and fifty years in the county tended to be looked at with suspicion.

The word brought another ugly thought to my mind. What on earth had that encounter with Tommy Daggett's brother been about? I remembered the tall, gangly deputy from a couple of run-ins we'd had the previous year. He'd been the responding officer on a couple of my recent brushes with bad guys, and I'd found him surly and offensive.

Must run in the family, I thought as I swatted at an annoying fly dive-bombing my empty food bag. Why Lonnie thought I'd had anything to do with getting Tommy bounced off the force, I couldn't imagine. I shrugged. *Both of them could go to hell.*

I stood and walked to the end of the metal dock. Signs encouraged visitors to fish but requested they throw their catches back in an effort to keep the small lake stocked. I hadn't been fishing in years. A sudden vision popped into my head: the Judge, strong and vigorous, squatting beside a coffee can of loamy dirt, patiently demonstrating to a six-year-old me the proper method for threading a squiggly nightcrawler onto the hook . . .

The sound of an engine made me turn toward the parking area. I sighed in resignation when I recognized the long frame of my brother-in-law jumping down from his lovingly restored Ford Bronco. I listened to the crunch of his shoes on the gravel as he crossed the playground area.

"If you've come to demand bodily fluids, I already gave at the office," I said, as he moved up beside me. "Your office." His laugh carried some of the old Red in it, and I turned to face him. "Did you follow me, or was this just a lucky shot?"

"I tailed you from the station. I'm much better at it than you are."

"Not much of a feat." I eyed his yellow polo shirt and khaki shorts. "You're in civvies. Can I take it this isn't an official visit?"

"You can." He glanced back toward the crumpled Burger King bag on the bench. "Leave me any fries?"

"Nope. I ate every last damn one of them."

"Glutton." His tentative smile turned a little brighter. "Want to take a turn around the lake?"

"It's still over ninety out here in the sun. Sure you're up to it?"

"If you want to put some money on it, I'll kick your butt in any kind of race you care to name."

"Let's just walk. I wouldn't want to take your last buck so close to payday."

We set off to our left following the paved pathway, meandering in and out of the dappled shade. Occasionally a fish broke from the confines of the lake in a glorious burst of freedom, its scales shimmering iridescent silver in the slanted rays of the fading sun, before slapping back to glide beneath the surface once more.

"Thanks for the heads-up about the warrant," I said. "I know that could have cost you big-time if anyone higher up found out." He nodded without speaking, so I went on. "Did they locate Alain?"

A cloud passed briefly over his face at the mention of Darnay. "I don't think so. They've left messages for him to call in, but so far no luck."

"I haven't heard from him all day myself," I said. "He's in Savannah on business."

"Interpol business?"

"Not for me to say."

"He needs to surrender himself pretty soon. Doesn't look good if they have to go out hunting for him."

I jumped on the word. "Surrender? What the hell is that supposed to mean?"

"You know exactly what it means." Red sighed and shook his head. "Is it my imagination or are you gettin' more prickly in your old age?"

I stopped and swiped at a rivulet of sweat running down the side of my face. "You try having everyone thinking you're some kind of child kidnapper or murderer and see how agreeable you feel after a couple of days."

We walked on for a few steps before he replied. "You can't go around dragging people away against their will. Especially not in front of witnesses."

I kicked a pine cone out of the path, and it bounced off the trunk of a stately old oak. "And we were getting along so nicely," I said, anger rising in my throat.

"All I'm saying is, we . . . they had good cause to look at you for it. That kid at the valet stand—"

"Doesn't know his ass from third base. Do you realize I sat there at Beach & Tennis with him for ten minutes, as close as you and I are right now, and he had no idea who I was? I even introduced myself by name, and he never flinched. Yeah, great witness."

Red waited a beat before saying, "He described your car right down to the last three digits of the plate number."

We passed the overflow lock at the near end of the lake and headed back toward the parking lot. "Anyway, it doesn't matter now," I said. "The DNA sample will eliminate me. And Darnay, too, as soon as he checks in." I glanced at Red when he didn't reply. His face had gone pink, and I didn't think it was from the short bursts of sunlight that fell between the tangled limbs of the trees.

"Hold on," I said, grabbing his arm and forcing him to stop. "That unidentified blood in Cart Anderson's front seat is not mine, and it's not Darnay's. The test will prove it." His eyes refused to meet mine, and I heard my voice rising on a tide of anger. "What? Goddamn it, Red, what is it now?"

"The results of the DNA tests won't be back for at least a week," he mumbled, "maybe two."

"So? I don't care if it takes a month. We were not there. We did not harm that boy. And no wishful thinking on the part of whatever idiot is conducting this so-called investigation will prove otherwise."

We stopped at the rear of the Bronco. "That may be so," Red said softly. "But mistakes have been known to happen. Contamination, mis-labeling, whatever. Don't put all your faith in the science."

"But—" I began, and he cut me off.

"That's not what concerns me right now."

"Then what?"

He shook his head. "What in the hell were you two doin' at Mrs. Bleeker's place the night before she died?"

Chapter Twelve

I TOSSED MY KEYS IN THE SWEETGRASS BASKET ON THE console table and reached back to punch in the alarm code. Another circuit in the extensive security system had turned on the lights, both inside and out, as soon as dusk had spread its fingers across the ocean just over the dune. I had two messages on the answering machine, neither of which was from Darnay. My last check of the voice-mail inbox had yielded the same lack of result.

I nuked a cup of Earl Grey and carried it with me into the office. I logged on to the Internet, but the only e-mails were from the usual cyber-idiots, one offering to increase the size of an appendage I didn't have and another from the son of a Nigerian diplomat wanting to deposit millions of dollars of his country's treasury in my bank if only I'd send him my account number and password. I reported them to the spam-blocker site and signed off.

I shed the sleeveless white dress and sandals I'd chosen for my date with the forensic tech and slipped on a cotton nightgown. Even though I had drawers full of sexy French lingerie selected in chic little shops along the Rue du Faubourg St. Honoré, Lavinia had given me this one on my birthday the previous month. The softness, the just-laundered smell and feel of the white cotton sprigged with blue forget-me-nots reminded me of the nighties she'd pulled over my head before tucking me into the big four-poster in my room at Presqu'isle. I needed the comfort of those memories.

I settled myself onto the sofa in the great room and flipped on the television, more for company than for entertainment. My own thoughts would certainly keep me busy if I allowed myself that indulgence. I'd promised myself to put Red's startling question out of my head until I had a chance to discuss it with Darnay. If he didn't show up soon, I decided, I'd get in the car and go hunting for him on my own.

I lost myself in a tight baseball game between the Giants and the Braves being broadcast from the West Coast. Barry Bonds was tearing up the league again, already at twenty-one home runs and the season just three months old. As always Atlanta tried to rely on pitching, but the old days of Glavine and Maddux and Smoltz were long gone.

Funny how ingrained the things we learn as children become, I thought, stretching out on the soft cushions of the sofa. My father had painstakingly taught me the fundamentals of the game before I was even old enough to hold a bat. When the Milwaukee Braves moved to Atlanta, they became the closest thing we had to a home team, but my father had little time to travel to actual games. My indoctrination had been conducted in front of the small television set in the study, curled up in the Judge's lap while he pointed out the beauty of a well-turned double play or the nuances of the battle between pitcher and hitter. I smiled, remembering the joy I'd felt nestled there next to him, cheering when Hank Aaron added another home run in his pursuit of the Babe's once unassailable 715.

The good guys were trailing 4–2 when I nodded off . . .

I awoke to an infomercial for some sort of rotisserie cooker and Darnay's soft breath against the side of my neck.

"Mmmm, what time is it?" I asked, leaning away from him and stretching. I'd fallen asleep with my head resting in the palm of my hand, and knots had settled into my damaged left shoulder.

"A little after midnight." He plopped down beside me on the sofa and pulled his loosened tie out of the wilted collar of his white dress shirt. "Now I remember why I hate administration," he added as he worked his feet out of his black wingtips. "I fail to understand why business cannot be conducted just as efficiently in shorts and a T-shirt."

"No argument here." I snuggled up closer, and he slipped an arm around me. "You can't really complain, though, until you've gone eight hours in pantyhose and stiletto heels."

"Not my style," he answered. He let his head flop onto the back of the sofa. "*Je suis complètement fatigué*. How was your day?"

All the anxiety came flooding in, and I had to force myself to reply calmly. "Pretty interesting, all things considered. Didn't you get my messages?"

"No. I allowed the damn cell battery to run down and forgot to bring the charger with me. Was it something important?"

I warred with myself about whether to let him have a good night's sleep before bombarding him with our recent troubles or just to spit it all out and get it over with. I decided against taking the coward's way out.

"I guess you could say that. The cops have a warrant out for you. Me, too, actually. I had to go down and give them blood and a DNA sample. They want one from you, too."

He sat up, eyeing me as if I'd lost my mind. "For what?"

"To compare with the second blood sample they found in Carter Anderson's car. I had mine taken this afternoon down at the satellite station. No big deal."

"No big deal? You mean you went? Just like that?"

"Why not? It's not my blood. Or yours either for that matter. It seemed like the perfect chance to clear ourselves of any complicity in his disappearance."

Darnay pulled his arm from around my shoulders and ran a hand through his thick hair. "What did the Judge have to say about it?"

I stood and moved toward the kitchen to avoid the underlying tone of accusation in his voice. "Want something to drink? I'm going to have some tea."

"*Non, merci*. Well? What did he advise?"

I rattled a glass out of the cupboard, then added ice and poured from the pitcher Dolores always kept chilled in the refrigerator. When I walked back down into the great room, Darnay had stretched himself out full-length on the sofa, his hands tucked behind his head.

"He told me not to do it."

"So why . . . ?"

"Jesus, Mary, and Joseph! I don't get you people. What is so difficult to understand? They had a warrant, Alain. It's not as if they knocked politely on the door and asked if I'd mind dropping in at my convenience. Law Merriweather, who is *my* attorney, advised me to cooperate. So I did. Not only did I have no choice, I also thought it was a damn good idea. The test will prove I did not leave a blood trail in the victim's car. I see this as a good thing. I don't have a clue why you and my father don't. Enlighten me. Please." When he didn't immediately respond, I added, "And they also have a pretty good idea we were at Miss Minnie's on Saturday night."

I dropped onto the raised hearth and waited.

Darnay swung his legs around and pushed himself upright. "One of the things I love about you is this wonderful belief you have in the integrity of those in positions of power. I fail to understand how you could have grown up with a lawyer-judge for a father and still retain such naïveté, but I do find it charming."

"Don't patronize me, Darnay," I snapped from across the room. "I'm not naïve. I'm about as pragmatic a woman as you're ever likely to find." I drew a deep breath and tried to kick it down a notch. "What does the poor, sappy little American girl not understand that the wise old French policeman needs to explain?"

That brought a smile to both our faces. Then his clouded over. "Your eagerness to cooperate makes you look as if you have something to hide."

I studied his face for a long moment. "That's about as illogical a statement as I've ever heard."

"That is because you do not understand how we think. *Attendez*. A man commits a burglary. He picks a house well screened from the street with no near neighbors and whose occupants are out of town. He wears gloves from the moment he approaches. He knows with absolute certainty he has not been observed, that he has left not one clue behind. But the police pick him up and ask for his fingerprints. What does he do?"

I set the glass of tea next to me and leaned forward, trying to keep the annoyance out of my voice. "Well, that's a ridiculous example. He agrees. Why not? If he knows he didn't leave any prints behind, what does he have to lose?"

"*Précisément!* But if he is entirely innocent? Ah! Then our accused, he storms and shouts about the incompetent police, the infringement of his rights, the lawsuit he will bring for attacking his character. You see? The innocent are generally incensed even to have been considered as guilty."

"And that's how you think?" I shook my head and walked toward the kitchen. "God help us all," I muttered.

Darnay followed me up the steps. As I slid the dirty glass into the dishwasher, I felt his arms encircle my waist. "Do not worry, *ma petite*. I will give your *gendarmes* their sample. But I will make certain they pay a heavy price for my cooperation." I turned and leaned back to stare into his face. "I am more concerned about this business of the old lady's death," he added.

"Me, too," I replied, easing myself out of his embrace. "Red didn't know how they found out about it, but I'd be willing to bet we're going to have a visit from somebody higher up the law enforcement food chain before too long."

"We will deal with that tomorrow." Darnay clasped my hand in his firm, comforting grip and urged me toward the bedroom.

With only a slight hesitation, I followed.

He was already gone when I rolled over and checked the clock at a little after seven the next morning. I let my hand wander to the indentation he'd left in the rumpled sheet. It took me a couple of minutes to locate my nightgown tangled in the duvet we'd managed to kick onto the floor at some point during the previous night's activities.

I smiled as I pulled the gown over my head and padded into the kitchen. For some reason I was absolutely ravenous. I poached three eggs and slid them onto the halves of a toasted English muffin. Seconds later the kettle whistled its readiness. With a steaming mug of tea, I set my breakfast out on the table and flipped open the paper Darnay had so thoughtfully brought in before departing for Savannah.

The sobering news from the Middle East dashed my good mood and sent all the depressing happenings of the past few days flooding back into my head. I used the last sliver of muffin to mop up the remaining egg yolk and settled back into the chair with a sigh. Everything had become a jumble, a kaleidoscope of bits and pieces of information, accusation, and trouble which so far I had been unable to force into any coherent pattern. I sipped tea and watched a huge grackle strut along the apron of the driveway, rooting with his long beak among the scattered piles of pine straw for any edible tidbits.

I set the mug down on the glass-topped table and straightened my shoulders. I needed to quit this mental whining and get off my butt. Action would keep the fear from eating away at me. Too much of what had happened in the past week seemed calculated, almost choreographed. Who wanted me embroiled in this mess, and why?

I carried my plate and silverware to the sink and rinsed off the sticky egg residue before dropping them into the dishwasher. As I turned, I heard the front door open, followed by the series of beeps which indicated the security system had been disarmed.

"Hey, Dolores," I called, "I'm up here. In the kitchen."

"*Aiy, señora!* You frighten me. *Hola*. You are awake so early?"

"Things to do," I replied. "I've already had breakfast."

My diminutive housekeeper climbed up to join me, and I cringed as I did most days lately at the stiffness in her gait.

"Leg bothering you?" I asked as she set her worn black handbag and a Tupperware container on the granite counter.

"*Está bien,*" she answered, avoiding my eyes. "I bring the lunch today. Hector and Alejandro, they catch the beautiful fish *ayer*. I make for you the *sopa*."

It took me a minute. "Soup. Yes. Great. I'm hitting the shower."

Dolores halted me with a sharp, "*Señora!*"

I paused at the foot of the steps. "Yes?"

"Must I put on the clean sheets today?" Her voice seemed normal enough, but there was no mistaking the disapproval on her face.

"Yes, please do. And yes, Darnay slept here last night." I moved up onto the first riser so we were nearly eye-to-eye. "Why don't you like him, Dolores? He's a policeman. He saved my life last year in Grand Cayman. He's really a wonderful person, if you'd just give him a chance."

"Is no my place to like or no like, *Señora*." She had folded her tiny hands in front of her, and her stern look held none of the sweet affection I usually found in her eyes.

"You're right," I said, startling us both as I turned on my heel and strode barefoot toward the bedroom. "It's not."

Showered and dressed in cotton shorts and a tank top, I pulled out the chair of the desk in the bedroom-turned-office and fired up my computer. I had resisted everyone's urging to haul myself into the twenty-first century and finally invest in a cell phone, but now I had one I couldn't imagine how I had managed without it. I could sign on to the Internet and put in a call to Erik Whiteside in Charlotte all at the same time. Maybe I should investigate a cable modem, too.

Feeling very high-tech this morning, are we? I asked myself, a little of my natural good humor returning now that I was actively engaged in problem-solving.

The e-mail from Erik popped up on my screen at almost the exact moment I heard his receptionist's nearly incomprehensible drawl. I asked for her boss and clicked open the message, scanning its meager contents while a string quartet poured soothing hold music into my ear. By the time she managed to track him down, I'd read the scanty information my former partner had been able to cull from his online searching.

I tried to hide my disappointment. "Hey, Erik! Good morning."

"Hey, yourself. Get my message?"

"I'm looking at it now. I guess there wasn't a whole lot out there, huh?"

I could see his blond head shaking. "Nope. I'm really sorry to let you down like this. I did find a couple of references to Fort Fremont in the police report section, but as you can see they were pretty short on details."

Erik had located two items in the archived newspaper files in which the old ruins were mentioned as the site of a disturbance, but there were no identities or other pertinent information provided.

"You didn't let me down," I hurried to assure him. "If it's not there, it's not there."

"Thanks. Not much consolation for you, though. Anything else I can help with?"

I thought for a moment. "Do you know if police reports—the ones they actually have on file at the sheriff's office—are available to the public? Maybe through the Freedom of Information Act or something similar?"

He pondered my question for a moment. "I'm not sure, but I could try to find out." Again he paused. "You know, I used to date a reporter for the *Charlotte Observer,* and it seems to me she used to have to go down to police headquarters and get the information for that part of the paper. I could ask her. Or do you know any reporters down there?"

A name popped immediately into my head, and I wondered why it hadn't occurred to me before. "Yes, actually I do. That's a great suggestion, Erik. Thanks. I'll give her a call."

"Sorry I couldn't be more help." He managed to sound both embarrassed and relieved at the same time.

"No problem. I appreciate the effort. Give my best to Mercer and Catherine."

"Sure. And the same to Alain and your family."

I hung up, disappointed with Erik's lack of results, but buoyed by the new idea he'd planted in my head. I walked back out to the kitchen and retrieved the *Island Packet* from the stack of papers Dolores had collected to take to the trash. I thumbed to the contact section and found the name immediately.

I had met Gabby Henson twenty years before at Northwestern where she'd attended the school of journalism. She'd grown up in a little town just a few miles from Beaufort, but we hadn't been acquainted until we stumbled across each other at some sorority rush party we'd both been badgered into attending. Though our paths rarely crossed on the vast campus on the shores of Lake Michigan, I had noticed her byline two decades later when she'd apparently come home from wherever her career had taken her to become a reporter for the hometown newspaper.

I tapped the number into my cell phone and prepared to renew old acquaintance.

Gabby was out on assignment, so I left a message on her voice mail inviting her for lunch or a drink or whatever at her earliest convenience. I hinted at a story she might find of interest just in case the old-school-tie thing didn't resonate with her. As Dolores bustled around stripping the sheets from my king-sized bed and carrying them out to the washer, I settled in to make some sense of the Chinese fire drill which had become my life in recent days.

At the top of the pristine sheet of yellow legal paper, I wrote CHRONOLOGY and underlined it. For the next half hour I worked on a timeline of all the events of the past few days, beginning with Darnay's and my first and only encounter with Cart Anderson and culminating in Red's revelation that someone higher up in the law enforcement community knew about our visit to Miss Minnie's cottage the night before she died. Less than a week, and I had somehow become embroiled in one death and a suspicious disappearance, and I didn't even have a client. Unless you counted Reverend Henry Chaplin. I found it strange I hadn't heard from him again, especially since I hadn't yet kept my promise to get back to him with a decision.

I flipped the page and began a new list, this one of questions: Who knew about Cart Anderson's relocation to Beaufort, and did he know anyone here besides his grandparents? Why would he have gone out to the old ruins on St. Helena on Friday night instead of to his grandmother's where he was expected? How did he even know how to find Fort Fremont? Had he ever visited there while his parents were alive? What, if anything, did his disappearance have to do with Minnie Maude Bleeker's death? What had she meant to imply when she told me about "bad" things happening at the fort? What, if anything, did she know about Cart's disappearance? Who had seen us at her house and ratted us out to someone in Beaufort? Whose blood was it in the boy's car?

The steady march of question marks blurred in front of my eyes, and I slipped off my reading glasses just as Dolores stuck her head into the office.

"*Señora?* Someone to see you."

"Who is it?" I asked, massaging my eyelids with the tips of my fingers. When she didn't immediately reply, I turned in my chair toward the doorway. It seemed as if all the color had drained from her face, and she clutched the hem of the smock she always wore as if it were a lifeline. "Well?" I demanded, more sharply than I'd intended, and she jumped. "Who is it?"

"*Policía, Señora*. They say . . . They have a paper. They say you must come."

"Come where? What paper?" I rose and crossed the room just as three men, two in uniform and one in plain clothes, filled the doorway behind the trembling Dolores.

"Mrs. Tanner?" The one in the beautifully cut gray suit spoke in a clipped, staccato voice that labeled him immediately as a displaced Yankee. "We have a warrant."

He thrust the piece of paper over Dolores's shoulder and waved it at me.

"A warrant for what?" I reached to take the folded sheet from his hand, easing Dolores into the room and away from the towering policemen. She retreated to the farthest corner, continuing to twist the cloth gripped in her fingers.

"To search the premises," the plainclothesman replied. "I think you'll find it all in order."

I'd be damned if I'd let them sense the turmoil bubbling up inside me. Then I remembered Darnay's dissertation of the night before about how policemen expected innocent citizens to react to such court-sanctioned invasions of privacy.

"This is ridiculous! What do you think you're going to find? You're not touching a thing until I have a chance to consult my attorney."

I whirled and snatched up the cell phone, my fingers automatically tapping in the Judge's number.

"You certainly have the right, Mrs. Tanner," the suit replied in his condescending, let's-just-humor-her voice, "but it doesn't negate the validity of the warrant. If you and your maid will just move out to the kitchen, we'll start in here. Officer Tate, you take the guest room across the hall. Daggett, you've got the master."

I barely heard Lavinia's voice on the other end of the line, demanding to know who was there, as I stared into the sneering face of Lonnie Daggett. The thought of his blunt-fingered hands fondling my silky French underwear nearly made me gag.

"Get the Judge on the phone," I snapped at Lavinia as I ushered Dolores past the hulking forms of the three policemen.

Lonnie Daggett's low, nasty chuckle followed us down the hallway.

Chapter Thirteen

I DECIDED THAT IF THEY ASKED ABOUT THE PRESENCE of a man's clothes in my closets and dressers, I'd refuse to answer. Detective Ben Wyler, he of the gray suit, asked a lot of questions, but that one never came up. Besides, the Judge had told me to keep my mouth shut, offer no assistance, and stay out of their way. He'd also promised to get Law Merriweather speeding toward Hilton Head as soon as he could reach him, but the cops were pretty much finished destroying my home by the time my attorney finally arrived.

Dolores escorted the slightly stooped, white-haired bastion of old Beaufort aristocracy up the steps and into the kitchen where I sat nursing a glass of sweet tea and drumming my fingernails on the glass-topped table. I resisted the urge to throw myself into his arms.

"Bay, darlin', I came as soon as I could."

I did allow him to wrap me in a brief fatherly hug of reassurance before offering him a chair and refreshment.

"Nothing for me right now, thank you," he told Dolores, bestowing on her one of his soothing smiles.

With a nod, she returned to straightening the mess the young black deputy named Tate had made of the drawers and cupboards. Gray, chalky fingerprint powder drifted across every conceivable surface and stubbornly resisted her attempts to remove it. I'd tried to get her to go home, knowing how much the presence of armed, uniformed men in the house had to be frightening her. In the part of the world Dolores came from, such intrusions were commonplace and usually unaccompanied by such niceties as warrants and probable cause. Such visits often meant the removal of a loved one who never returned.

"Let me see the warrant," Law said in the calm, reasonable voice I'd known and trusted since childhood.

I handed over the paper, crumpled and sweat-stained from being gripped in my fist for more than an hour. Although I'd read every word, I still had no idea what had prompted a judge to send these oafs rifling through every corner of my house. The forensic tech who lifted fingerprints from counters, furniture, and doorknobs had followed close on the heels of the deputies, adding his mess to that of his buddies.

I watched Law straighten out the warrant and study it through the bottom half of his wire-rimmed bifocals. "They're authorized to lift prints, look for blood-stained clothing, and any weapons that might show evidence of recent use."

"What kind of weapons?" I asked, my mind darting to the hidden floor safe and its contents. I had carry permits for both the Glock and the little Seecamp the Judge had presented me with just before Erik Whiteside and I had set off for Judas Island the past spring, but I didn't think they'd stand up to much scrutiny. My father had obtained the permits without any active participation from me.

"It doesn't specify, which is somewhat unusual." Lawton Merriweather leaned back in the kitchen chair and smoothed the document out in front of him.

"How so?"

"Usually the authorities are looking for a specific weapon they believe was used in the commission of a particular crime. In other words, they have a victim with a knife or bullet wound, and they want to see if the suspect is concealing such an instrument. If they find something likely, they can test it for blood residue and to see if the blade matches the pattern in the wound or if the bullet came from that particular gun."

Across the room I heard Dolores's tiny gasp as she clattered some cutlery into the drawer. "Forgive me, ma'am," Law said, inclining his head in her direction. "I don't mean to be indelicate."

"Dolores, why don't you leave that and go on home? There's no reason for you to be subjected to this"—I groped for a way to describe the sense of violation I felt—"this invasion. I'll finish cleaning up after these goons are out of here."

"The goons are just leaving." The voice with its harsh New York accent nonetheless carried a note of humor.

Detective Ben Wyler stood at the bottom of the steps leading up to the kitchen. No one would have called him a handsome man. His nose had obviously been broken more than once, and the other parts of his face seemed to have been arranged just slightly off center. He was fighting the onset of baldness by wearing his hair longer than I thought was probably regulation. The dark brown waves hung over his ears and curled against the collar of his pale gray shirt. Nevertheless, his height and build gave him a certain presence, an air of authority that made one stop and take notice. The six-hundred-dollar Brooks Brothers suit didn't hurt, either.

I expected him to take his little plastic evidence bags filled with the fingerprint lifts and a couple of my good stainless knives and leave, but he stood planted on my creamy carpet looking expectantly up at me.

"What?" I turned in the chair and stared into his expressionless eyes. "Am I supposed to thank you? Offer my hand? If you're done, just get the hell out of my house."

"Bay, I really don't think . . ." Law began.

"That's okay, counselor," Wyler interrupted. "I assume you're the lawyer?"

Lawton Merriweather nodded.

"I understand how Mrs. Tanner feels. I left a receipt for what we've taken on the desk in your office. We just need to get your prints and your maid's for comparison, and we'll be on our way."

He signaled to the forensic tech hovering near the entryway, but Law's quiet voice stopped him. "I don't think so, Detective. There's nothing in the warrant which requires Mrs. Tanner to submit to being printed and certainly nothing which includes Mrs. Santiago."

"Now hold on," Wyler spluttered, but this time it was Law who cut him off.

"No, Detective. Absolutely not. The fact that your warrant is sloppily drawn is no concern of ours. You're finished here, so I suggest you and your cohorts thank my client for her cooperation and be about your business. I'm certain there must be some genuine criminals in Beaufort County who require your attention."

Wyler nodded and headed toward the entryway, herding his minions in front of him. I jumped from the chair and followed to make certain they all left. At the door, the detective turned.

"Appreciate your hospitality, ma'am," he said in a snide imitation of Law's soft drawl. "I'm sure we'll be seein' each other again."

"Don't count on it," I snapped.

"Oh, and tell your boyfriend he needs to get his . . . get himself down to the station by six o'clock tonight, or there'll be an arrest warrant out for him."

I smiled, remembering Darnay's face when I'd told him about the DNA sample. "You really don't want to tangle with him," I said. "He's got connections someone like you only dreams about."

His deadly serious tone sent a shiver of dread rippling across my shoulders as he parroted my own words back at me: "Don't count on it."

I finally convinced Dolores to leave the mess until the next morning by the simple expedient of telling her I wanted to be alone with my attorney. At the door she paused and turned back to hug me in an uncharacteristic show of emotion.

"*Mañana, Señora*. I fix everything *mañana*."

"It'll be okay," I said, patting her back. "Really."

A tremulous smile quivered, and she nodded. "*Sí, Señora*." As she limped her way down the steps to the driveway, I heard her mutter something like, "*Ilegitmos!*"

I thought a rough translation might have been "bastards," and the rare profanity from the mouth of the very Catholic Dolores made me smile.

Law had moved to one of the wing chairs in the great room, so I poured him a glass of tea and carried it to him.

"Thank you, my dear." He sipped, then set the tumbler on the raised stone hearth.

"So now what?" I flopped down onto the sofa and pulled my bare feet up under me. "Do you have any idea what's going on?"

"Frankly, no, I don't. But there is definitely a hand at work here." Law straightened the creases in the pants of his lightweight summer suit and studied his loafered feet.

"What do you mean?"

"I haven't practiced criminal law in over twenty years," he began in what seemed like a change of subject. "I have a few clients, old friends for whom I prepare the occasional will or other document, assist with estate planning, that sort of thing. And probate." He shook his head, and I watched a deep sadness settle over his lined face. "Way too many probate matters." He lifted his eyes to mine and forced a smile. "Our generation—the Judge's and mine—is disappearing all too quickly. I don't think a week goes by we don't lose a friend or colleague, someone it seems we've known forever. I suppose that's what comes from living your whole life in the same small town. So many folks become like family."

I didn't know how to respond to this wave of melancholy which appeared to have gripped my father's old friend. I waited a moment before saying, "I understand, Law. Really, I do. Can you recommend someone who might be willing . . . ?"

"Heavens, child, I didn't mean to imply I didn't want to help you. No, not at all. It's just that I want you to understand I'm an old workhorse who's rightly been put out to pasture. I'm not certain I'm a match for the kind of men I believe you're up against here."

"Are you implying this is being orchestrated by someone?"

He nodded. "I do, though I'm damned if I can see who or why. How did it go yesterday? With the DNA test?"

"They were very polite. I mean, everyone said 'please' and 'thank you' like good little girls and boys." Law smiled, and I joined him, then sobered as another thought occurred to me. "Except for one. In fact, he was one of the deputies who just spent two hours rifling through my clothes."

"Who is that?"

"Young guy named Daggett. He accosted me out in front of the satellite office yesterday after I gave them the sample. He accused me—or rather, me and my 'friends'—of getting his brother, Tommy, fired from the force. I have no idea what he was talking about, but it kind of freaked me out when he showed up here today as part of the search party."

Law nodded. "Yes, that does seem like too much of a coincidence. Did the young man say why he thought you might have had a hand in his brother's dismissal? Or who your partners in crime supposedly were?"

"Nope. He got called out to an accident before he had a chance to enlighten me on that score. I remember the brother. He and I had a couple of run-ins last year. He didn't strike me as being the brightest bulb in the chandelier, so maybe he got canned just because he's an idiot. Whatever the reason, I'm damned sure I had nothing to do with it, and I can't imagine anyone I know did either."

"Curious." He reached into his inside coat pocket and retrieved a small spiral notebook and a gold fountain pen. "Let me have those names again."

He asked a few more questions, taking notes as I talked. The one that most intrigued me was one for which I had no answer: Had the signatures on both warrants been the same? I left him there for a few moments while I searched the desk in my office, certain I'd tossed the summons for the DNA sample in the center drawer, but I came up empty.

Law didn't like it. "I can find out down at the courthouse, but it concerns me an officer of the law might have removed a document not included in his warrant. Was it on the receipt for the items they removed?"

I shook my head. "Nope. Just two knives and a T-shirt."

"A piece of *your* clothing?"

The sharpness in his voice snapped me to attention. "Yes, I suppose so." I glanced down at the scribble on the paper I'd carried in from the office. "It just says 'one T-shirt, white.' "

"So you don't know if it belongs to you or to . . ."

He left the thought dangling, perhaps embarrassed to be calling attention to my sinful cohabitation with Darnay. Sometimes the hypocrisy of his generation is more than I can take, but I bit back the sharp reminder that I hadn't invented sex outside of marriage and replied calmly. "It doesn't say, and I don't think I could tell if one shirt was missing from either my own or Darnay's collection even if I took an inventory."

"I'll inquire," was all he said.

I tossed the receipt onto the table and tried to steer the conversation away from my sex life and back to Law's original question. "Okay, so they took the first paper with them for some unknown reason. But why are you so interested in the signature on it?"

He opened the copy of Wyler's search warrant and waved it in my direction. "This was signed by Judge Virginia Newhall, one of the newer members of the bench. If she also authorized the previous document, it would give me a place to start." He paused and returned his notes and the warrant to his suit pocket. "I must admit I'm not very well acquainted with Judge Newhall. I believe she's only been in the area a short time."

For men like my father and Law Merriweather that could mean anything from a couple of months to fewer than fifty years. In our little corner of the South, "newcomer" has a whole different connotation from what it has in most other parts of the country. It might also explain why the Judge was having less than his usual stellar success at gathering inside information.

"Who is this guy Wyler?" I asked.

"New on the force, or so I believe," Law answered. "I heard he's recently moved into the area from New York City. Rumor has it he had a somewhat checkered career there."

"Checkered?" I asked. "You mean he was in some sort of trouble? On the take? A dirty cop?" I stopped, suddenly realizing I sounded like someone out of a *Law & Order* rerun.

"I don't have the details, but rest assured I'll get them." Law nodded emphatically.

"So what is he? I mean, what department does he work out of? Missing persons?"

Lawton Merriweather shot his cuffs and adjusted the gleaming gold links. "I believe it's homicide," he replied softly.

"Homicide? I thought the Judge told me some guy named Morgan took that over after Matt Gibson went to Florida."

"He did, but Detective Morgan is on temporary reassignment while he takes some courses offered by the FBI. He's up in Quantico, Virginia, if I'm not mistaken. And his partner is off on maternity leave. I hear Detective Wyler was coaxed out of retirement to fill in."

"Great. So we've got a new cop and a new judge, and they both seem to have their sights set on me." I rose and crossed to the small table in the entryway and carried my purse back into the great room. "Think that's a coincidence?" I asked as I tossed things out onto the sofa. My fingers finally closed around the illicit pack of Marlboros and disposable lighter I'd bought at the gas station. Without giving myself time to reconsider my actions, I flipped out a cigarette and snapped the lighter to flame.

I watched Law's shaggy white eyebrows lift in mute question, but he refrained from jumping on me. I figured the Judge had probably informed him of my decision to quit, but it would be tough for those two old cigar-smokers to mount any kind of defensible objection. What Alain would have to say didn't bear thinking about at the moment.

I exhaled and waited a minute for the dizziness to clear from my head before repeating my question. "Do *you* think it's a coincidence?"

"Right at the moment, I don't know what to believe." He stood and shrugged back his shoulders to straighten the line of his coat. "I need to get back to town and begin my inquiries. You'll be all right?"

I smiled and linked my free arm in his as we moved toward the door. "Of course I'll be okay. Don't worry. And please don't get my father's spleen all in an uproar. The less he knows about the details, the less grief I'll get."

Law Merriweather shook his head. "Now, you know I can't keep this from Tally. You know that, Bay, darlin'."

"I suppose." We stepped onto the porch, and I flicked the half-smoked cigarette out into the yard. It didn't taste quite as good as I'd anticipated, and the knot of nerves in the pit of my stomach hadn't actually gotten any smaller. "Any idea where to start? With your inquiries, I mean?"

"A few." He hugged me gently and tossed my own words back at me. "Don't worry. There may be some new players in town, but don't count out the old guard just yet. You know what they say."

I looked up into his faded eyes, sparkling now with suppressed laughter, and blessed the kindness and loyalty of old friends. "No, what do they say?"

"'Old age and treachery will overcome youth and skill.'" He winked and patted me gently on the cheek before making his way down the steps and out to his black Lincoln Town Car.

I hope to hell you're right, I thought as I turned back inside to find the cell phone and track down Darnay.

Chapter Fourteen

I ended up having to leave an extended voice-mail message. I hung up hoping I'd been able to convey forcefully enough how important it was for Darnay either to get himself to the sheriff's office before six o'clock or give them a damn good reason why he couldn't. I'd meant to ask Law Merriweather if warrants issued by local authorities had legal standing against citizens of other countries, but I'd forgotten. I toyed with the idea of calling the Judge for his opinion but decided against it when I realized I'd never be able to keep him from wheedling the whole story out of me before it was all over.

I stepped up into the kitchen, amazed to see the clock over the sink registering only a little after two. It seemed as if an eternity had passed since the deputies had arrived to disrupt my life and desecrate my home. Still, the rumbling in my stomach told me it had been a long time since breakfast.

Dolores had managed to scrub the worst of the fingerprint powder off the counters and drawer fronts, but the whole place felt dirty somehow. I shuddered at the thought of those alien hands fingering my dishes and glasses, not to mention my clothes.

I turned and trotted down the steps, then grabbed up my tote. My hips really didn't need another application of hamburger and fries, but at least Wendy's or McDonald's or Burger King wouldn't carry the feeling of violation I couldn't seem to shake. If Dolores and I had to wash every single piece of clothing I owned, run every plate and fork through the dishwasher twice, so be it. We'd clean and launder everything in sight until I managed to bleach Detective Ben Wyler and Deputy Lonnie Daggett out of my house, if not out of my head.

I forced myself to stay away until late afternoon by the simple expedient of blowing the better part of five hundred dollars.

I'd wolfed down the fast-food meal, which lay like a lump in the bottom of my stomach, then pulled into the vast parking lot of the Mall at Shelter Cove. The place was crawling with tourists who seemed to have a frenzied need to leave large chunks of their vacation money in the hands of local merchants. As a taxpayer, I silently applauded their decision.

I began at Saks and worked my way down to Belk's, wandering into every store along the way. In Williams-Sonoma I selected a set of knives to replace those carted off by the deputies. Even if I got them back, there was no way I'd ever touch them again. In another of my favorite shops, I picked up a great little monogrammed handbag which I'd probably never use, then spent a considerable amount of time choosing new underwear at Victoria's Secret.

Still, when I pulled into my empty driveway at a little past five-thirty, even the joys of conspicuous consumption hadn't loosened the knot in the center of my chest. I carried my booty inside, dropped it in the entryway, and sprinted up the steps into the kitchen. The cell phone had remained mute throughout my shopping spree, and my shoulders drooped at the sight of the empty answering machine on the desktop.

I dialed Darnay's mobile number and tucked the phone between cheek and shoulder as I poured myself a glass of tea. Again his heavily accented voice gave me terse instructions on how to leave a message.

"Damn!" I said aloud into the yawning silence. "Alain, I need to hear from you. Now. At least let me know you got my previous message." I swallowed a gulp of tea and nearly choked on the rising panic constricting my throat. "Listen, I know you think these guys are just a bunch of yokels, but they're serious about throwing your ass in jail if you don't show up at the station by six o'clock. I swear I'll let you rot in there if you get yourself arrested. Call me!"

I slammed the portable phone back into its cradle and stalked off to the bathroom. I peeled off my clothes and cranked the shower up full blast. *The hell with him!* I told myself, but I dropped the lid on the toilet and set my cell phone within easy reach before stepping into the rising cloud of steam.

The call, when it came, wasn't from Darnay.

By that time I'd managed to choke down a few forkfuls of salad and a couple of sweet potato biscuits Dolores had left for me, paced about a hundred miles from one end of my house to the other, and smoked three cigarettes in rapid succession before tossing the pack into a drawer and resolutely slamming it shut. At the rate I was going, I'd be completely hooked again before the night was over.

When the phone rang, I was in the process of filling my tea glass for the third or fourth time, and the sharp sound in the otherwise silent house sent my hand jerking and the tumbler crashing to pieces against the stainless steel sink. A jagged edge had nicked my right thumb, and I sucked at the trickle of blood as I snatched up the handset.

"Darnay?"

The pause lasted only a couple of seconds, but the soft sigh that followed carried a volume of meaning. "No, it's me. Red. Sorry to disappoint you."

I pulled the chair out from beneath the built-in desk and dropped into it. "I'm sorry, too," I said, cradling the phone against my shoulder as I pulled a tissue from the box on the counter and wrapped it around my bleeding thumb. "It's just I've been sort of waiting . . . Well, never mind about that." I forced as much cheerfulness into my voice as I could muster. "What's up?"

"So you haven't heard from him, either," my brother-in-law responded.

I drew a long breath and let it out slowly. "I take it he didn't show up by six."

A glance at the clock over the sink told me he'd missed his deadline by more than two hours.

"Nope. Didn't show up at all." Red hesitated. "I hear they're issuing a bench warrant for his arrest. Newhall has already signed it. I just thought you'd want to know."

I watched my bright red blood seep through the makeshift bandage and shook my head. What did he want me to do about it? Did he think I was harboring Darnay, maybe had him stashed in a closet or under my bed? An incredible wave of fatigue, born of the anxiety of the past few days, washed over me, and I slumped against the back of the chair.

"I don't know what you want me to say," I mumbled into the phone. "I left him several messages. It's out of my hands now."

"Out of mine, too," Red snapped.

His tone stiffened my spine, and I sat up straighter. "Did I ask for your help? I believe you called me, or am I missing something?"

"Look, Bay, I just wanted to let you know what was going on. I tried to talk them out of it, but they seem hell-bent on tagging you and your boyfriend with whatever happened to Carter Anderson." Red paused, and I heard genuine concern in his next words. "Somebody's put out the word you and Darnay aren't to be given any special treatment. Scuttlebutt is you're both at the top of the hit parade on this case and likely to stay at number one until something breaks." Again he hesitated before adding, "I'm on your side, you know. Always have been."

My anger seeped away in the soft warmth of Red's assurances.

"I know that. Really. And I'm grateful." I drew another long breath. "So now what? I mean, what's going to happen next?"

"We'll have to see how the DNA test turns out."

"You already know the answer to that."

He paused for only a second before answering, but it was enough to send alarms clanging through my head. "Bay, things don't always turn out the way they're supposed to." Before that enigmatic remark had a chance to settle in, he added, "I'll keep you posted. If you hear from Darnay, tell him to get his butt in here. Pronto."

"Red, I don't . . ." I began, but he cut me off.

"Sorry, gotta run. I'll be in touch." And with that he was gone.

I sat for a long time staring at the blood-soaked tissue wrapped around my thumb, Red's not-so-subtle message echoing in my head, then forced myself down the steps and into the bathroom. With little awareness of what I was doing, I poured hydrogen peroxide over the still oozing cut and wrapped two Band-Aids tightly around it. Back in the kitchen I gingerly retrieved the hunks of broken glass from the sink and dropped them into the wastebasket. I cleaned up the rest of the mess I'd made and tried to ignore the siren song of the Marlboros lurking in the bottom drawer beneath the desk.

Maybe I should take up drinking, I told myself as I resumed my measured pacing: from the dining area, across the great room, down the hallway to the bedrooms and back again, pausing each time I approached the windows over the driveway to scan the darkness for any sweep of headlights turning in toward the house.

By ten I had worked myself into something approaching panic. In spite of the withering humidity outside, goose bumps raced up and down my arms, and I pulled open the door to my walk-in closet in search of a sweater. I flipped on the light and stopped dead, my fingers still gripping the switch. For a moment I couldn't understand what my eyes were telling me. I tried to conjure up the memory of the last time I'd been in there.

Surely today? When I dressed this morning?

Then I remembered grabbing a tank top and shorts out of the drawer of the bureau before settling in to work in the office. And the same when I'd stepped from the shower after my shopping trip. But the deputies had been through it, as evidenced by several skirts and a couple of blouses lying in heaps on the floor and by the crazy angle of some of the hangers where a careless hand had pawed through my clothes. My eye went immediately to the clever panel which concealed the floor safe and my stash of illegally permitted guns, but it appeared undisturbed.

What sent the pain coursing through my body so that I felt my knees quiver with the intensity of it was the gaping void where Darnay's European suits, custom-tailored slacks, and crisply laundered dress shirts had hung in the space I'd cleared for him just a few weeks before. A glance told me his shoes were also gone from the rack I'd bought especially to accommodate them.

I whirled and dashed across the bedroom, flinging open the bureau drawers I'd assigned him amid much laughter over his having brought his entire wardrobe with him from Paris. The pristine white liner, only slightly rumpled by the clumsy hands of the police, stared back at me.

"But when?" I heard myself say out loud. "When could he have done it?" I collapsed onto the bed. "Wait a second," I said, again speaking aloud to the empty room, "just wait." I ran a hand through the tangle of my hair, snagging a few strands on the adhesive of the bandage around my thumb.

He had to have come while I was out squandering time and money at the mall. There was no other window of opportunity. While I was trying to choose between lavender and pale pink underwear, Darnay had sneaked back into the house, thrown his belongings into . . .

Although I already knew the answer, I forced myself out to the entryway and the door that led to the attic. It seemed as if each of my feet weighed fifty pounds as I dragged them up the steps. I paused at the top and surveyed the neat arrangement of all the things I'd discarded from my everyday life, things I'd once cherished but which had eventually outlived their usefulness or appeal.

The space where Darnay's two massive suitcases once stood sat empty.

Chapter Fifteen

I don't remember how long I sat on the rough floor of the attic, sweat trickling between my breasts and sliding down my cheeks to mingle with the tears. Once I thought I heard the phone ringing, but I made no move to answer.

So that's it, a small voice whispered inside my head. *Game over, end of story. When the going gets tough, the tough take a powder.*

Another part of my brain kept trying to introduce logic. Perhaps he'd been called back to Europe by Interpol, or his sister Madeleine might have fallen ill or met with an accident. There could be a hundred valid reasons for this sudden defection, all perfectly legitimate.

So why did I feel this overwhelming sense of abandonment? Of betrayal? And why hadn't he left some word?

I wiped my eyes on the hem of my T-shirt and dragged myself to my feet. I moved woodenly down the steps, out of the stifling heat of the attic, and set about a systematic search of the house, straightening some of the mess left by the deputies as I went. I began in the office, first checking the computer to see if he had e-mailed me. Nothing. I straightened the edges of the folders and tucked the legal pad I'd been working with back into the desk. I wondered if Detective Ben Wyler had gotten a laugh out of the notes about the case I'd been scribbling when he and his storm troopers invaded my house.

It took me the better part of an hour, but I finally found the note buried in my lingerie drawer, tucked in between the shimmering layers of satin, silk, and lace. I sat on the edge of the bed, slowly turning the single folded sheet over and over in my hands, afraid somehow to see in black-and-white the evidence of Darnay's desertion. I drew a long, shuddering breath and flipped it open.

I don't know how long I stared at the few, meaningless words scrawled across the top of the page:

Forgive me, my darling.
D.

I awoke with the blazing July sun beating through the open drapes and my head pounding as if someone had taken a baseball bat to it. I rolled over on the duvet and realized I still wore the same shorts and T-shirt from the day before. I forced myself to sit up, one hand gripping my sweaty forehead, and found small pieces of paper stuck to my bare arms and thighs.

Sometime in the night I had ripped Darnay's note into tiny pieces and scattered them around me on the bed.

I dragged myself to the bathroom, peeled off the sticky clothes, and climbed gratefully into a steaming shower. As the water cascaded through my hair and soothed my aching body, I tried to recapture the anger of the night before. I was all too familiar with despair and loneliness and my inability to handle those twin monsters. Anger I could deal with. I promised myself to hold on to it through the long weeks and months to come.

As I toweled myself dry, I heard the faint *beep* as Dolores let herself in the front door and disengaged the alarm. I followed her progress into the kitchen, her damaged leg making her gait slow and awkward. I dropped the towel across the edge of the tub and padded quietly into my bedroom, gathering the evidence of Darnay's perfidy and dumping the pieces into the wastebasket. I drew my ratty chenille bathrobe around me and straightened the creases in the duvet.

By the time I'd given up trying to force a brush through the tangle of my hair and slipped my feet into my worn Birkenstock sandals, I heard Dolores's tentative rap on the door.

"*Señora?* You are awake?"

"Yes," I answered in a clear, confident voice. "I'll be out in a minute."

"You wish the breakfast?"

I ignored her and leaned in to study my image in the mirror over the bureau. I didn't look like a woman who had just been devastated, whose life had once again been ripped apart by the loss of a man. The familiar leaf green eyes stared back unwaveringly. I even managed the semblance of a smile. The bricks and mortar of my defenses would take time to reconstruct, but I'd done it before, and I'd just damn well have to do it again.

Maybe there's even a learning curve, I thought, turning from my reflection. I'd had so much practice I should be a lot more efficient at the process this time. I stepped into the closet and pushed an armful of my clothes down the rod, filling in the space where Darnay's had once hung.

"*Señora?*"

I slammed the closet door shut, pulled open the one into the hallway, and smiled down at my old friend. "Yes, breakfast it is. And make it a big one." Dolores stared, her face not quite able to hide her dismay at the sight of my disheveled hair and manic grin. "Actually, make it a *huge* breakfast."

"For one, *Señora?*"

I watched her eyes dart around me to the neatly made bed before she stepped back at the determination in my voice. "Yes. Absolutely. From now on. Only for one."

Gabby Henson, the reporter from the *Packet,* saved me from spiraling into a depression by the simple act of finally returning my call. We made a date for Starbucks around two that afternoon.

Dolores did her part as well. After stuffing myself with French toast and sausage, I pulled on my rattiest pair of cut-offs and a paint-spattered T-shirt and joined her in a cleaning frenzy that lasted until well past noon. We polished and vacuumed and dusted, pausing only long enough to transfer clothes from the washer to the dryer. By the time we collapsed onto kitchen chairs, we'd managed to erase almost every trace left by the police search of the day before.

"That ought to hold us for a while," I said, after draining half a glass of sweet tea in one long, icy swallow. "We won't have to do it again for at least a year."

Dolores smiled. "*Sí, Señora.* Is good to work, no? Good for the body, good for the . . ." She groped for the word, then shrugged and tapped her chest.

"For the soul," I said, and she nodded.

The intense physical activity had kept me occupied throughout the morning, allowing the pain of Darnay's desertion to settle into a dull ache somewhere behind my breastbone. I knew from past experience that in time it would dwindle to more manageable proportions. In time . . .

I wouldn't have recognized Gabby Henson if she hadn't been the only person inside the coffee house when I arrived and hadn't also been waving her arm wildly in my direction.

"Bay! Over here!"

I waved back and approached the table in the farthest corner of the small seating area. "Hey, Gabby. Good to see you. Thanks for coming."

I tried to keep the total dismay I felt from being reflected on my face, but it was tough duty. The girl I remembered—short, painfully thin, with beautiful brown eyes and a pixie face—had somehow morphed into this doughy, unkempt, middle-aged woman whose stringy hair looked as if it had been hacked off with a dull knife. As she rose for the obligatory hug, I found my arms reluctantly encircling a body that seemed to have doubled in size over the past twenty years.

But her smile held the same candor, and her eyes, seeming smaller now sunk deep in folds of skin, still stared back at the world with intelligence and a burning curiosity that no doubt had contributed to her choice of profession.

"You look fabulous!" she gushed, dropping back into her chair with a thud. "You've hardly changed at all! If I didn't like you so much, I'd hate you!"

I smiled. "Thanks. And thanks again for agreeing to meet me."

"You were pretty cryptic on the phone this morning. Got the old reporter's nose twitching." She paused to slurp up the last of whatever she was drinking. "I'm ready for a refill. What'll you have?"

"Let me get it," I said as we both headed for the counter.

"Sure. Great."

I paid, and we stepped aside while a bored teenager set about preparing our respective iced lattes. While we waited, we chatted about the usual things which need to be addressed between two people who have lost track of each other's lives over a period of years. Gabby told me she'd graduated from Northwestern the year after I did, landed a plum intern job with the *Chicago Tribune,* and launched a career which had garnered her numerous awards.

"I was even short-listed for a Pulitzer once for a series I did on corruption in the federal housing program in the Chicago slums," she said as we carried our drinks back to the table.

"Wow! A Pulitzer! I'm impressed."

"Don't be. The world only cares about the winners, not the also-rans. Still, it looks good on my résumé."

"So what brought you back to Beaufort?" I asked. "It must be quite a letdown after the big-city life."

The sparkle left her eyes, and she hunched over her Styrofoam cup. "Divorce," she said simply, "and money. Or rather, the lack of it."

I waited for her to fill in the blanks, but she simply shrugged.

"Water over the old dam. We had some good years, some lousy ones. The more he cheated the more weight I gained. I guess it's a good thing I finally threw his worthless ass out or I might have exploded."

The laugh was good-natured, so I felt safe in joining in.

"Kids?" I asked.

"Three boys, but I won't bore you with the photo thing. My oldest is hiking the Appalachian Trail with a group from his school, and the other two are spending the summer with their father. Part of the agreement when we split. I make them call me every day to make sure the bastard hasn't dumped them somewhere and run off to Mexico with his latest bimbo-of-the-month."

I wondered if Gabby Henson's nonchalance hid a deeper pain or if she really didn't give a damn. Maybe she could give me pointers on how to deal with treacherous men.

"Sorry to hear about your husband," she said, her tone sobering. "That must have been rough."

I nodded, determined not to get into any explanations.

"So. What can I do for you? Your message said you had questions about the sheriff's logs. I cover that once in a while, to fill in, although it's not my regular beat. But I know a lot of the guys over there."

I squared my shoulders and launched into my prepared story. "A friend of mine is worried about her son. She's heard the crowd he runs with congregates at Land's End out on St. Helena, and she wants to know if there's been any trouble out there, anything that might have involved the cops. You know, gangs or drugs. Stuff like that."

I'd toyed with the idea of leveling with the reporter. Miss Minnie's vague hints about kids getting hurt at the abandoned fort next to her property had set me thinking about why Carter Anderson might have been out there. I also couldn't shake the idea her talking to Darnay and me about it might have had something to do with her sudden death just hours later, although I couldn't figure out what the connection might be. I was simply looking to rattle a few cages and see what fell out.

Now the whole helping-out-a-friend thing sounded more than lame, but I had no choice. Once you start lying, you have to keep on shoveling, no matter how deep the hole gets.

"She asked me to find out, and I thought the sheriff's logs might be the best bet. I don't think they're available to the public, and I thought you might be able to get copies for me. Or maybe just check them out. Or something."

Gabby Henson stared at me as I stumbled to the conclusion of my pathetic story. She hadn't asked a single question or interrupted once, but her eyes had never left my face. It was unnerving, having someone locked unblinkingly on to your eyes for that long a time.

"So," I said into the uncomfortable silence, "what do you think?"

"I think you're feeding me a pile of bullshit a foot deep, and I'm wondering why."

"What's that supposed to mean?" I felt the defensiveness bunching in my shoulders and forced myself to relax.

"Well, for openers, you left out a few parts. Like how you and your boyfriend are the prime suspects in the disappearance of a seventeen-year-old kid whose car just happened to be found out at Land's End. And the part where they demanded DNA and blood samples from you, executed a search warrant yesterday looking for a possible murder weapon, and are just waiting for the forensics to come back before hauling you in for questioning."

I sipped at my icy drink and tried to still my whirling brain. How much did Gabby Henson really know and how much was just fishing, a seasoned reporter's technique I'd actually used myself on occasion: claim to have more information than you actually do, drop a line in the water, and see who rises to the bait.

Two can play at this, I thought, leaning back in the chair and mimicking my companion's easy nonchalance.

"I think you've gotten bad information," I said. "It's true we're cooperating with the sheriff's office in their investigation. Because my . . . friend and I had a conversation with the kid earlier in the day, we volunteered a blood sample. The DNA will be negative because we weren't anywhere near Cart Anderson's car."

And the moment the words were out of my mouth I knew Darnay's disappearance would have more momentous consequences than just leaving me alone and hurt. He *had* been in the boy's car. His fingerprints would be all over the damn thing. Hopefully that could be explained away. What couldn't were the missing two hours between the time we'd left the Judge's that night and when Red had pulled us over on the highway back to Hilton Head.

Darnay had been my alibi, and I his. He didn't need one anymore because he'd skipped out before the cops ever got around to questioning him. And I had no doubt he'd put an ocean between himself and any possibility one of Interpol's top undercover men might become the target of a local murder investigation.

Which left me hung out to dry.

Bastard! I screamed inside my head and jumped at the cool touch of a hand on my arm.

"Bay, let me help you."

I looked up into Gabby Henson's liquid brown eyes, expecting to see the gleam of ambition, a reporter's hunger for the inside track on a story which could send headlines screaming across the state. Instead I found a sympathy I wanted desperately to believe in.

"I don't understand," I lied, stalling as I slid my arm from under her pudgy fingers.

"Stop acting dumb. Look, I know people. I have sources even your father may not have access to. I can help you get to the bottom of this."

"The bottom of what?"

She shrugged, and some of the light faded out of her eyes. "Okay, if that's the way you want to play it."

"What makes you think I'm not guilty?" I had no idea what prompted me to blurt out the question, but I knew I desperately needed to hear her answer.

"Because I've checked you out, and I can't believe you'd be anything but an unwitting party to harming some kid." She paused. "And because I've known you for a long time."

"You don't know me at all," I said, anger rising from somewhere deep within me. I leaned in and whispered, "We haven't seen each other in twenty years, Gabby. And I did kill a man. Once."

To my complete amazement, she laughed. "I know that. But he was someone who needed killing, wasn't he?"

I felt about fifty pounds of pressure ease from my chest. I smiled back. "Definitely," I said.

"So let me be the one to request the incident logs. No one will give it a second thought if I go snooping around. It's what I do."

I was tempted beyond all reason to tell her everything, to let someone else lift this terrible blanket of suspicion off my shoulders.

"What's in it for you?" I asked.

"Helping out an old college pal," she replied immediately, then paused once more to stare straight into my eyes. "And the exclusive on a story that could get me out of this podunk town and back to civilization. Ain't no such thing as a free lunch, Bay, darlin'."

I sipped the last of my latte and hesitated.

"Hey, gotta run." Gabby rose abruptly and pulled at the cheap cotton blouse hanging over her bulging hips before snatching up a battered briefcase. "Weight Watchers meeting at four. This time next year I expect to be so damned gorgeous my ex will kick himself all the way to Atlanta for lettin' me get away."

"But . . ." I began as she tossed a crinkled business card on the tabletop in front of me.

"Think about it. Check me out. If you think we can work together, give me a call. *Ciao!*"

I swiveled in my chair and watched her plod out into the shimmering afternoon.

I sat a long time absently swirling the foamy cream and melted ice around in the bottom of the tall cup before tossing it in the trash and following Gabby Henson out into the brutal July heat. Although I'd left the Thunderbird under the shade of a crape myrtle, the leather upholstery felt like a griddle. I sat gingerly on the edge of the seat as I put the top up and cranked the air conditioning to max.

As I waited for the steamy interior to cool, debating what my next move should be, I thought about how my life had changed in the past few months, how easily I'd slipped back into the routine of having someone to answer to, someone whose feelings and desires had to be considered at least as much as my own. It occurred to me how much Alain Darnay had come to dominate my life. I was either with him or waiting for him or on my way to meet him every waking—and sleeping—moment of the day. Now all that was gone, and my interior compass spun wildly.

I sat there trying to think of where to go, what to do next, and the decision, when it came, was one of default rather than deliberate choice. Only one place offered unequivocal welcome, although seeking refuge there would have a price. So be it. I pulled out into the first trickle of rush hour traffic and headed for Presqu'isle.

Chapter Sixteen

As I climbed out of my car, I heard the old mansion's door creak open on the verandah above me. Climbing the steps, I encountered Lavinia stationed in the entryway like a guardian at the gates. I had no idea what had precipitated the stony look on her creased brown face, but I knew it couldn't be good news.

"Is Daddy okay?" I asked, sidling by her and into the house.

"He'll be fine. He's just havin' his bourbon."

"What do you mean, he'll *be* fine?"

I turned toward the door to his room, but Lavinia caught me by the arm. "Let him be," she said and motioned with her head for me to follow her into the kitchen.

I dumped my bag on the floor and collapsed onto one of the sturdy chairs pulled up to the old wooden table. Without asking, Lavinia poured a tumbler of iced tea and set it in front of me before dropping into the chair opposite.

"Your father's been on the phone all day, and Mr. Merriweather stopped by right after lunch. They were in there arguin' and fussin' for the better part of an hour. The man is flat worn out. And I don't like his color. All this worrying isn't good for him."

Now that I had an opportunity to study her up close, Lavinia looked pretty careworn herself. "What's he worried about?"

Lavinia looked directly into my eyes. "You," she said simply.

I had the feeling she expected me to apologize, to offer atonement for being the cause of my father's distress. But wasn't that what parents did, worry about their children? Although I had none—and recent events seemed to have sealed my fate in that arena—I had no doubt Lavinia herself still spent sleepless nights over the problems of her son and his family. Did she blame *him* for causing her grief, or did this mantle of responsibility only fall on my shoulders?

We sat staring at each other, neither of us willing to be the first to blink, an unspoken contest whose rules I knew all too well.

"I don't suppose it will do any good to tell him I can handle things myself?"

It wasn't exactly an apology, but it worked. Blame had been apportioned, assigned, and accepted. We could move on.

"None whatsoever," Lavinia answered. "After Mr. Merriweather left, I heard him in there muttering to himself and trying to reach you at home. I figured you were probably on your way here."

"Why would you assume that?"

"Because you got trouble, child, big trouble. And this is where you belong." She rose and crossed to the refrigerator where she began hauling packages from the freezer and stacking them on the counter. "I think I'll do up some fried chicken for tonight. And maybe a macaroni salad. Doesn't that sound good on such a scorcher of a day?"

I couldn't fathom what was generating these sudden shifts in temperament in this usually placid and stable woman. I wondered if she was losing her grip, and a terrible fear punched me in the gut. What would I do if something happened to Lavinia? Who would care for my father? In a split second a vision flashed across my mind: I saw myself held hostage at Presqu'isle, turning into a lonely, middle-aged woman at the unending beck and call of a withering, cantankerous old man.

I didn't realize Lavinia had returned to the table until I felt her knobby fingers patting my back. "Don't fret so, child. Nothin' so bad it can't be overcome."

I gazed up into her brown eyes, relieved to see again the wisdom and courage I'd always found there.

"Go on in and talk to him, will you do that for me?" she asked. I smiled and nodded. "Good girl. Get him calmed down enough to take a nap before dinner. He'll feel better just knowin' you're here and safe."

I left Lavinia humming softly to herself in that way which always signaled she felt right with the world. As I turned the knob on the door into my father's study, I hoped the next few hours would somehow grant me the same feelings of peace.

By eight o'clock the sun hung low in the western sky, but the oppressive heat hadn't abated. I leaned my elbows on the railing along the back verandah, my eyes straining through the lowering twilight in an effort to make out the bare limbs of the dead tree at the edge of the narrow marsh. I thought about running indoors to retrieve the compact binoculars the Judge kept in his room, but I couldn't bring myself to disrupt the fleeting moment of serenity.

Instead I squinted toward the collection of twigs and branches assembled over time in the crotch of the old sycamore. For years a family of ospreys—magnificent birds of prey reminiscent of the bald eagles we spotted only rarely in the Carolinas—had made their home in the nest they enlarged and fortified every season. The books said the same pair returned to their home nest each year. I had no way of proving or disproving this theory. I only knew each spring found the huge black and white birds with their hooked beaks and deadly talons guarding their eggs with fierce determination. Even our mild winter had been reluctant to give up its grip this year, and everything was running a few weeks behind schedule. The Judge reported the hatchlings had been trying their wings over the past few days, and I was eager to catch a glimpse of their fluttering attempts at flight. As I watched, one of the parents glided in from the Sound, a silvery fish squirming in its beak. The still night air carried the faint squealing of the youngsters eagerly awaiting the delivery of their dinner.

If I'd expected this moment of respite to wipe the events of the day from my mind, I had sadly miscalculated. Parents feeding and caring for their offspring. It seemed I couldn't escape the recurring theme.

After I'd left Lavinia in the throes of preparing dinner that afternoon, I'd found my father slumped in his wheelchair, his head nodding against his chest. Though I'd tiptoed around him to my favorite spot in the bay window, my presence had somehow disturbed him enough to jerk him out of his nap.

Without preamble, he'd said, "Law was here today."

"I know."

"They're going to bring you in for questioning, maybe as early as tomorrow." He had studied my face then, anticipating some outburst, but I simply nodded. "Of course, they'll want Alain as well. Is he with you?"

I drew a long, shuddering breath and said as calmly as I could manage, "No, he's not. Actually, he's gone."

It took a moment for my words to register. "Gone? What do you mean, gone?"

I straightened my shoulders. "Flown the coop. Over the wall. AWOL."

"Don't be flip," the Judge barked. "Explain yourself."

"He's left me. Packed up his things and split. The note just said he was sorry." I watched the incredulity wash over his face. "Yes, your protégé, your fair-haired boy, has taken the coward's way out and left me here to deal with this crap on my own. Sort of makes you question your own judgment, doesn't it?"

I watched the barb strike home. Strange how proximity and time make it so easy to know exactly how to wound, exactly which way to twist the knife, especially when it's stuck in someone you're supposed to love.

The Judge recovered quickly. "No doubt he's been recalled to France."

"Believe whatever you like. It doesn't make a damned bit of difference to me *why* he left. The fact remains he's gone and taken my only alibi along with him."

That brought him up short, and I saw his next rejoinder die on his lips. "What are you talking about?"

"My alibi. Darnay was with me Friday night after we left here, and we didn't see anyone else until Red pulled us over on the way back to Hilton Head. And we were together at Miss Minnie's on Saturday. Again, no one can vouch for me except him." I had paused then and drawn another deep breath. "By the way, which one of these crimes am I being charged with? Or is it both?"

"You're not being *charged* with anything, at least not so far as Law could ascertain. The detective merely wants to question you concerning your knowledge of . . ." He stumbled for a moment, seeking the right words, ". . . recent events."

My bark of laughter deepened his scowl. "Yeah, right." I leaned forward in the chair, elbows resting on my knees, and stared directly into his face. "Well, explain this to me, Your Honor. I didn't pay a whole lot of attention in those boring pre-law classes you badgered me into taking at USC, but don't they have to have probable cause to justify hauling me in for questioning?"

He nodded, and I realized the smile was that of a professor pleased with the performance of a promising student.

So much for his being worried to death about me. Maybe he and Lavinia were both losing their marbles.

I watched the pleasure fade from his eyes before he added, "We understand Detective Wyler is going to request your cooperation. Law thinks you should comply."

I remembered Lavinia's talk of fussing and arguing during the afternoon. "I take it you don't agree?"

"Why should you help the bastards weave the rope to hang you with?"

I hadn't been crazy about the analogy, but I got his drift. The silence deepened, and I could hear the strong, measured beat of the grandfather clock in the hallway. "So what should I do?" I asked.

We had both looked up then, startled, at the sound of Lavinia's voice from the doorway. "You can let this nonsense rest for a bit and get yourselves in to dinner. I haven't spent the last hour hanging over a kettle of hot grease and chicken parts so I could sit out there all by myself."

The buzzing of a persistent mosquito somewhere in the vicinity of my right ear snapped me out of my reverie, and I waved my hand in its general direction without result. The sun had entirely disappeared while I'd stood lost in thought on the verandah, the dead tree and its nest of ospreys barely visible in the soft pink haze which presaged full darkness.

I made another ineffectual swipe at the maddening mosquito and turned back toward the furniture clustered beneath the overhang of the hipped roof. I picked up the box of matches from the wrought-iron table and lit a citronella candle, then flopped into my favorite rocker.

I had decisions to make, important ones which could affect my future for years to come. And I had so little information. Nothing but two old warriors, Law Merriweather and my father, each counseling diametrically opposed courses of action. Before I decided whether or not to stick my head in the lion's mouth, I needed to know exactly what the cops thought they had on me, and so far neither one of my champions had been able to come up with the goods.

I reached into my pocket and retrieved the crumpled business card Gabby Henson had tossed on the table at Starbucks earlier that afternoon. Maybe she did have better connections in this new Beaufort County than the Judge and his old cronies. It couldn't hurt. And besides, I had to start trusting someone.

I blew out the candle and slipped inside to use the phone.

Chapter Seventeen

I left messages at the reporter's home and office numbers and waited through eight rings for her cell phone to switch over to voice mail. I didn't know who else might have access to her various answering systems, so I simply asked her to contact me in the morning. I didn't want to be explaining to the Judge about the nature of any late-night phone calls disturbing the stillness of Presqu'isle.

When I ducked into the study to say goodnight, I found my father already tucked into his bed like a wizened child, one pajama-clad arm flung outside the light blanket, his snores bubbling softly over the hum of the air conditioning. I tiptoed back out, checked the locks, and carried my bag upstairs to the bedroom I'd occupied since I'd moved out of the nursery. After Rob's death I'd taken to spending the night occasionally, so I had plenty of toiletries and nightwear stockpiled along with a few casual changes of clothes.

I paused, my hand resting on the polished brass knob, when I noticed light seeping under the door to my mother's old room. While she and my father had to have occupied the same bed at least once, my childhood memories were of separate suites, each with its own bath, connected by a dressing room they rarely used. Lavinia had her own setup at the back of the house: a bedroom she shared with her son until he got old enough to be on his own, a sitting room, and a bath, all adjacent to my mother's. I suppose Emmaline Baynard Simpson needed her "help" nearby. On those occasions when the jewels came out of the bank vault and the furs were retrieved from their temperature-controlled storage, Lavinia became lady's maid as well as cook, housekeeper, and surrogate mother to me.

I stepped into my room, tossed my tote bag on the ruffled white counterpane spread across the four-poster, and moved quietly down the hall. I couldn't have said why I felt the need for stealth, but I moved as quietly as I could along the narrow carpet runner which stretched the length of the hallway bisecting the house. The childhood memory of how to avoid the noisiest creaking boards guided my steps. Strange, though, I found myself thinking, it had never been *this* door I'd listened outside of after sneaking out of my own room. It had always been Lavinia's.

Inside I heard the murmur of a TV or radio, its volume set low, and a sharp clacking that brought a smile of remembrance to my face. I tapped lightly and waited for permission to enter.

"Come in, child," I heard her call and pushed open the heavy door. "Everything all right? Your father isn't . . ."

"He's fine," I said, stepping into the room. "Snoring like a trooper."

Lavinia sat in an old rocker, the one I remembered from her own parlor down the hall, a mound of soft white yarn and a pair of knitting needles resting in her lap. If she was surprised by my late visit, she didn't let on.

"Something I can get you? Are you hungry?"

"No, I'm fine." I hesitated, unsure of exactly why I had disturbed Lavinia's privacy. I crossed in front of her to stretch myself out on the chaise my mother had always referred to as her fainting couch.

Upholstered in a soft yellow silk, the back and single arm were edged in a deep, rich mahogany, ornately carved with birds and flowers. It had been salvaged from one of the Chase or Tattnall or Baynard plantations up the river sometime before the hated Sherman had destroyed the old houses along with their doomed way of life. I'd always wondered how the times before the Civil War could have been so predictably strenuous that ladies felt the need of a specific piece of furniture on which to swoon.

"Are you okay with this? Me bein' in her room?" Lavinia's eyes never left her knitting.

"Of course. I told you that a long time ago."

"Your father insisted, you know." Her fingers stilled. "Never made me any nevermind where I slept, but he wanted me to have more space. I held out for quite a while, but he finally wore me down."

I didn't give a damn where she slept, either. Besides, if anyone had earned the right to enjoy the comforts and luxury of Presqu'isle, it was certainly Lavinia.

"I'm glad," I said, tucking my legs up under me on the chaise.

"Shoes," Lavinia said, and I kicked off my sandals.

"Yes, ma'am." I paused to survey the dark, heavy furniture my mother had always favored and realized, except for the addition of the rocking chair, nothing seemed to have been moved. It had been years since I'd set foot inside Emmaline's sanctuary, and yet I had the feeling she could appear at any minute, sweeping through the door in one of the flowing dresses she loved, her rich auburn hair streaming behind her.

I shivered, and Lavinia caught the movement.

"Cold? There's a throw over there on the cedar chest."

I shook my head. "Ghosts," I replied, and she nodded.

"Used to take me that way sometimes, right after I moved in here. Felt sure I could see those flashin' green eyes of your mama's demanding to know just what I thought I was doin' in her room."

"I used to sneak in here after they'd gone out for the night, to some party or something, and try on the discarded jewelry she'd leave heaped up on the dressing table. I got really good at putting everything back exactly like I'd found it so she wouldn't know."

The muted glow cast by the floor lamp behind Lavinia's chair bathed her in a warm light, softening the lines crisscrossing her face and burnishing her skin to a rich, golden brown. "I knew," she said with an indulgent smile, "especially since you could never resist dousing yourself with three or four different kinds of her perfume. I'd come in to get you up for school in the morning, and you'd smell . . ." She hesitated, and I thought I saw the beginnings of a blush on her thin cheeks.

"Like a whorehouse on a Saturday night?" I finished for her, completing one of the Judge's pithier expressions, the kind that used to drive my puritanical mother up the wall.

She laughed. "Exactly. Sometimes I'd have to scrub your neck for twenty minutes to get all the evidence washed away. Thank goodness your mama rarely came down to breakfast."

Lavinia picked up her knitting, and I let my eyes wander around the forbidden room. It had always been stuffy, overdecorated and pretentious, much like my late mother herself. Appearances had ruled her world, and no wonder. She had been an incredibly beautiful woman. The portrait of her that used to hang over the mantel in the main parlor downstairs had always inspired me with awe and envy and a touch of sadness that I'd failed to inherit any of the ethereal charm and grace which had been the essence of Emmaline Baynard Simpson. Only the bright green of my eyes testified to my maternal heritage.

"You have the look of her sometimes," Lavinia said, startling me out of my trance by once again reading my mind.

"No, I don't. I'm the Judge with boobs."

"Don't be crude, Bay. It doesn't become you." The reproof delivered, her voice softened. "It's not that you have her face or even her mannerisms. It's the way you hold your head sometimes. Or a smile you don't want anyone to see that sort of sneaks up on you anyway. We didn't get to see it much, but Miss Emmaline had a sweet smile."

I spoke without thinking, the words tumbling out of me in a rush, but the thoughts were ones I'd been harboring for most of my adult life. "Why did she ever have me? It was plain she never wanted a child, that I was an accident. Why didn't she just . . . you know." I stumbled to a halt, shocked at my own temerity.

Lavinia set her knitting wool back in her lap and looked directly into my eyes. I think she wanted me to see there was no evasion in her answer, no attempt to soften the truth. "I won't lie to you, Bay. She thought about it. She even asked me if I knew anyone who could . . .

perform the procedure." Her face darkened, remembering. "As if just because I was a servant I'd know how to go about finding an abortionist."

The word hung between us, ugly and frightening, but honest at least. That's what I'd always wanted from my mother and never gotten: the truth.

Lavinia reached across the space between us and patted my hand. "I would never have told you if you hadn't asked, child," she said, and I nodded. "Truth is always best," she added, echoing my own thoughts. "Anyway, I told your mama I had no idea who could do that sort of thing, and besides it was wrong. 'Thou shalt not kill,' the Bible says, and it doesn't matter to the Lord whether it's someone old and used up or the first spark of life in the womb." She straightened her shoulders. "I looked her square in the eye and told her I'd take my boy and be outta this house by sundown if she did such an evil thing. Besides which, your daddy would probably have killed her himself if he knew she was even thinkin' about it. We never spoke of it again."

Hearing the words had a strange effect on me. I suppose I should have been shocked and appalled to learn my mother had seriously considered aborting me, but a part of me had known it all along. Having my fears confirmed somehow robbed them of their power.

"Did she always drink?" I asked. Cocooned in this temple to the past, it seemed the perfect time and place to launder all the family's dirty linen.

"Some. It got worse as she got older." The needles resumed their clicking, and the strands of wool glided through her fingers. "Aging takes some women that way, especially the pretty ones. Miss Emmaline always had a delicate constitution. Headaches, pain in her joints, a finicky stomach. She used to call it her 'medicine.' "

"She didn't fool anyone. Even the kids I went to school with knew she was a drunk."

Lavinia paused in her work to fix me with that stare. "She fooled herself, and that's all she needed to do. I tried not to judge." She reached behind her to retrieve a canvas bag and stuffed her yarn and needles into it. "I'm tired," she said, and I knew the rest of the secrets would remain buried. At least for the time being.

I rose and slid my feet back into my sandals. Lavinia reached for my hand, and I clasped her warm, brown fingers. Yielding to an overwhelming temptation, I let my legs fold under me until I knelt on the floor at her feet. A sweet longing for the simpler days of my past swept over me, and I dropped my head into her lap. With the same soft hands of my memory, she stroked my hair away from my temples with a feather-light touch, murmuring all the while in the sing-song voice of her Gullah ancestors.

"Everything's gonna be all right, baby girl," she whispered. "The Lord is watchin' over us, don't you forget. If we're strong in the Lord, nothing can harm us."

I might have dozed, my head and shoulders swaying rhythmically with the gentle rocking of the chair, the strong, sure fingers caressing my brow. Some time later I felt the motion cease and looked up to find Lavinia's eyes closed and a smile of contentment playing across her lips.

I slid myself out from under her hands and draped the throw across her thin arms, then slipped quietly from the room.

So peaceful was my rest that night I nearly slept through breakfast. I awoke to the sounds of pots clanging below me and scurried to brush my teeth and pull on clean shorts and T-shirt. I bounded down the stairs and into the sunny kitchen just steps behind my father's wheelchair.

"Good morning, all." I beamed at the Judge and settled into my assigned seat. "I'm starving. I hope you've got lots of whatever it is you're cooking."

My father snorted, and Lavinia glanced back over her shoulder. Her smile told me she, too, had slept well after our late-night conversation.

"French toast and sausage," she said. "How many you good for?"

"Three and three," I answered. I seemed destined lately to repeat the patterns of my childhood.

"So I figured." Lavinia set the plate with three slices of golden French bread and three sausage links in front of me. She turned back to the stove, then carried plates for herself and the Judge to the table. "I never did understand how you manage to stuff more food in your mouth than a farmhand and still stay so skinny."

"Genes." I drowned my breakfast in maple syrup and grinned across at my father.

"What the hell do you have to be so damned cheerful about?" He gestured empirically with his good hand, and I passed the syrup pitcher across to him. His scowl only accentuated the droop left by the strokes. "You, too, Vinnie. I swear the two of you are enough to put a man off his feed."

"Oh, hush," Lavinia replied. To my amazement, he did.

It took me only a few minutes to demolish my food. I longed for a cigarette as I leaned back in my chair and decided it was probably a good thing I'd left them at home. In spite of all my self-assurances that I could handle an occasional puff or two, my body was telling me differently. Even after only half a pack, smoked over the course of a couple of days, I could feel the pull of the addiction.

My father sopped up the last of the syrup on his plate and set his fork down with a clatter. "So what's the decision?" He wiped his mouth and tossed his napkin on the table.

"About what?"

"You know damn well about what. Are you going to fight this New York bully boy of a detective or not?"

"I don't know." He took a breath preparatory to launching another salvo, but I cut him off. "Hey! Just listen a minute, okay? I need to talk to Law, and I've got a couple of other feelers out." I didn't, really, until I had a chance to connect with Gabby Henson, but he didn't need to know that. "We're not even sure what this Wyler's going to do yet. I'm thinking it's better to wait until we see what they're up to before we formulate a game plan."

The Judge snorted and turned his chair so he faced me. "That's not how it's done, daughter. 'The first blow is half the battle.' "

"I hate to break this to you, Daddy, but this isn't a war. You yourself said they have good reason to look at me. And Darnay. But we all know neither of us had anything to do with these crimes. I don't see anything wrong with holding tight until we have more information about what sort of evidence they think they have. Am I wrong, or was that you last night going on about not helping them weave the rope to hang me with?"

"Stumped you, eh?" His smile seemed out of all proportion to the unpleasant topic.

"What are you talking about?"

"The quotation! 'The first blow is half the battle.' You don't know it, do you?"

This hardly seemed the time or place for our childhood game, except the last few hours seemed to have been dedicated to dredging up the past. "Oliver Goldsmith," I said wearily. "*The Vicar of Wakefield,* I think."

"Aha! Incorrect! *She Stoops to Conquer.*"

"Whatever," I said and saw the light go out of his face.

I'd stuck my cell phone in the pocket of my shorts on my way down to breakfast, and its raucous little tune saved me from more verbal sparring with my father. I excused myself and hurried down the hallway and outside onto the front verandah.

Gabby Henson seemed delighted at my decision to enlist her help, and we made a date for lunch at the Fig Tree. Gabby had to cover a county council meeting later in the afternoon, so the trip to Beaufort would dovetail nicely with her plans. I showered and changed into a cotton skirt and sleeveless blouse, then put in a call to Law Merriweather.

"Bay, honey, I was just about to phone Presqu'isle when I didn't get you at home."

"So what's the word? Are they coming to haul me away?" I tried to keep it light, but I couldn't quite conceal the underlying anxiety, at least not from someone who knew me as well as Law did.

"Now, darlin', don't you worry. I'm meetin' with Detective Wyler this afternoon to discuss exactly what it is he wants to talk to you about, so nothing's going to be happening today. Once I know what direction they're headed in, we can decide how to respond."

"You really think he's going to reveal the extent of his evidence to you? Why would he do that?"

Law Merriweather's low chuckle gave me hope. "As you know, Mr. Wyler is a recent transplant, and I don't think anyone has yet taken the time to instruct him as to how things are done in our little corner of the world. I believe he's operatin' as if he were still stalking the mean streets of the big city." He paused, and I heard the hint of steel underlying his familiar drawl. "I intend to enlighten him."

I knew my father's old friend firmly believed he could manipulate the New York detective just as he and the Judge had been doing to others in the local establishment for decades, but I had serious doubts. Gabby Henson's assertion that times had changed had struck a chord, and I wondered if the old guard had become nothing more than charming anachronisms, as much footnotes to a faded past as debutante balls and afternoon tea.

Law must have sensed my doubts because he rushed to fill the silence. "I don't want you fussin' about this, you hear? You just relax and leave everything to your father and me. Everyone knows you and Mr. Darnay had nothing to do with the boy's disappearance or with Mrs. Bleeker's unfortunate accident, either. I'll be in touch as soon as I have news."

I would have loved to be able to take the old man's advice, but the niggling fear refused to allow me to sit idly on the verandah like some nineteenth-century belle content to wait patiently while the menfolk did the dirty work.

"I have a couple of appointments, so let me give you my cell phone number," I said and rattled it off before hanging up.

I had a couple of hours to kill before meeting the reporter and I didn't want to get into another debate with my father. I told Lavinia I had errands to run and wouldn't be home for lunch, then slipped out the front door. I had no plan as I started the car and let down the windows to allow some of the trapped heat to dissipate, but I wasn't surprised when I found myself ignoring the main highway and bouncing down Resurrection Road to Fort Fremont.

The sun beat down relentlessly from a wide dome of blue sky, and dust rose in smoky clouds to coat the car's yellow finish with an ashy film. We desperately needed rain, and July usually provided us with a large percentage of our annual allotment, generally in the form of fierce thunderstorms which pelted the parched fields before moving on as quickly as they'd appeared. This year it seemed as if the weather gods had deserted us. The local papers were full of dire predictions from area farmers about widespread crop failures and warnings from the Department of Natural Resources about the danger of open fires.

I slowed nearly to a crawl as I approached Miss Minnie's place. The old cottage with its hodgepodge of added-on rooms lay deserted and forlorn in the late morning heat, a slight breeze off Port Royal Sound ruffling the drooping leaves on the twisted oaks. The place looked abandoned, as if it had stood empty for months rather than just a few short days.

I was surprised not to see a bright yellow sash of crime-scene tape draped across the screen door. Did that mean anything? I wondered and made a mental note to find out. It didn't make any sense half my informants insisted the old woman's death had been ruled an accident while the others claimed I was about to be charged with her murder.

I pulled on past the ramshackle old place and into the turnaround which a constant stream of trespassers had worn in front of the abandoned fort. The graffiti-covered concrete slabs looked much less ominous than they had with only a thin moon and a weak flashlight beam for illumination. I maneuvered the car around until it was facing back toward Miss Minnie's and killed the engine. The old woman's sudden appearance had cut short my previous visit. I pushed away the tide of anxiety those thoughts brought welling up in my chest and stepped out of the car.

The massive walls of Fort Fremont blocked any breath of breeze. Through the underlying hum of insects I heard the tapping of a woodpecker high up and off to my right. A snatch of music drifted from one of the houses on the other side of the impenetrable tangle of vines and brush which separated them from this rutted lane. I moved past the front of the car, and a faded sign tacked to the trunk of one of the towering pines caught my eye.

PRIVATE PROPERTY

KEEP OUT

The cluster of crumpled beer cans littering the dirt in front of me bore mute testimony to the ineffectiveness of the warning. As I negotiated my way around the mess, I paused to wonder who actually owned the deserted fort and when it had passed from government hands into private ones. I determined to add that question to the growing list I had for Gabby Henson.

A wave of nostalgia washed over me as I approached one of the cavernous openings which gaped like giant eyes in the façade of the structure. Bitsy Quintard and I had been fearless explorers of this pile of concrete, scrambling over its ramparts and abandoned gun emplacements, sure-footed as mountain goats. I ran my hand along the rusted rungs of a metal ladder still attached firmly to one of the walls and marveled at our elementary-school bravado. Or stupidity. If Lavinia or Bitsy's mother had ever had an inkling of how we spent our summer vacations, we would have been sent to our rooms for life.

I peered inside one of the doorways, its stout wooden door long ago rotted away, and smiled as more memories came tumbling back . . .

Two little girls, one too tall for her age, the other with the fragile beauty of a Dresden doll, hover in just this spot, heavy flashlights stolen from kitchen cupboards clutched in quaking hands.

"You go," whispers the smaller one, her fine blond hair pulled up in two neat ponytails on either side of her head. "It was your idea."

"Why, because you're chicken? I dare you!" The taller, gangly girl with the ever-present smudges of dirt streaking her face fires off the challenge.

"Double-dare!" comes the squeaky reply.

"Double-dog-dare!" The silence of the tomblike emptiness seems almost alive. The chestnut-haired tomboy relents. "Okay then, let's go together."

Each clasps the other's hand and switches on the flashlights. Their grins trembling with equal parts fear and excitement, they step tentatively into the yawning darkness . . .

The cry of a jay high up in the rustling pines brought me crashing back to the present in time to realize I had been about to mimic my ten-year-old self and step into the dank corridor. I jumped back as if someone had jerked me by the collar and stumbled out into the dappled sunlight. I gasped at a flash of movement in the dirt at my feet. A scream erupted as I watched the snake slither past me and disappear into the gloom.

Chapter Eighteen

I darted into the restroom at the Fig Tree and used several paper towels to clean the dust of Fort Fremont from my sandaled feet and to compose myself after my close encounter of the serpent kind. Gilly Falconer, her long gray-and-black braid swinging in time to her determined walk, intercepted me as I emerged into the hallway.

"Lydia! Hold up!"

The longtime owner of the local hangout could never seem to bring herself to use my preferred name, the one everyone else had gotten used to over the past thirty years. Fists placed firmly on her generous hips, she planted her chunky body directly in my path.

"Hey, Gilly. How you been?"

"Tolerable. Listen. You might not want to go in there." She tossed her head in the direction of the long corridor leading to the combination bar/dining room.

"Why not? I'm meeting someone."

"Who? Not that sneaky reporter, I hope." She snorted in contempt and took my arm to ease us both to the side as a family of sweaty tourists erupted through the front door. "Hi, folks. Just go on back, and Dana'll seat you."

The automatic smile clicked off as soon as her customers had moved away.

"Sneaky?" I asked, lowering my voice.

"Wrote an article last year about underage drinkin'. Didn't exactly say we let kids in here, but she hinted pretty good." The glowering look softened a little, and something approaching a smile played around her mouth. "You know better 'n most that ain't never happened in my place."

I answered her smile, remembering her chasing my teenaged friends and me out the door when we'd tried to pull the fake ID bit on her.

"Look, Gilly, I've got an appointment, and I'm already late. I'm a big girl now, you know. I can take care of myself."

Again that infamous grunt. "Ain't seen much evidence of that lately."

I bit back my annoyance. "Thanks for the warning." I patted her shoulder and moved toward the bar.

"Hold up." She placed a restraining hand on my arm. "Ain't that one I'm worried about. Your archenemy's in there, too."

I raised an eyebrow. "Archenemy? I didn't know I had one."

Gilly Falconer nodded sagely. "That cop. The one from New York."

"Wyler?"

Again she nodded. "Yup. Sittin' there by himself readin' some book or other." She sniffed. "Looks like not even his new cop pals can stand him."

I decided to take Gilly's warning in the spirit in which I was certain it had been intended. While I often chafed at the way everyone in the county seemed intimately involved in my personal business, I had to admit it felt reassuring to know so many people had my back.

"Thanks for the heads-up. I'll be on my best behavior."

This time I moved out away from her grasp and walked down the hallway into the low-ceilinged room. A thin haze of smoke hung just over the bar whose stools were packed with the usual lunch crowd, swelled by our summer visitors. I saw the reporter gesturing to me from the table in the farthest corner and threaded my way to her. A quick look told me Detective Ben Wyler had selected the other side of the room. His eyes never strayed from the thick book spread out in front of him as I pulled out the chair across from Gabby Henson.

"Sorry," I said, dropping my bag onto the floor and sparing a quick glance out the window, past the porch filled with diners, to the sparkling river beyond. "I took a little detour and lost track of time."

"No problem. I had some prep work to do for the council meeting." She closed the leather-bound notebook and tucked it into her bulging briefcase. "Ready to order?"

I felt the presence of the waitress at my shoulder and turned to smile up at her. I hadn't looked at the plastic-coated menu in front of me because my selection at the Fig Tree alternated between two choices: burgers in winter, crab cakes in the summer. I added a sweet tea.

"Make it two of everything." Gabby settled her elbows on the table and rested her chin on her open palms, "So, what can I do for you?"

"Do you know that's Ben Wyler over there?" I asked, tilting my head in his direction.

"Sure. I've run across him a couple of times. Why?"

I darted a quick look over my shoulder and caught my "archenemy" flipping the page, his attention apparently riveted on the book. I turned back to the reporter and leaned in closer.

"Did he come in before or after you?"

"After. Just before you showed up. What's the big deal? It's a small town. Not that many places to have lunch."

"He's not eating," I said, and saw Gabby Henson raise one eyebrow. "I checked the table on my way by. He doesn't even have a drink in front of him."

I watched the expression of mild amusement fade from her face, and my internal radar sensed the problem a moment before he spoke over my shoulder.

"Mrs. Tanner? Sorry to interrupt."

I turned my head to meet the strangely arresting face of Detective Ben Wyler. I felt the flush rising up my neck despite every effort of will I could exert to prevent it.

Gabby saved me from saying anything stupid. "Hey, Detective! How's it going?" She jabbed her pen in the general direction of the brightly jacketed book tucked under his left arm. "Reading something good?"

Ben Wyler smiled, an act which transformed his normally saturnine expression into something almost pleasant. "Mystery novel," he said, directing his words toward me. "Cops and robbers stuff. I hear the Judge enjoys them, too."

"Sort of a busman's holiday, don't you think?" Gabby asked before I had a chance to reply.

"Oh, I think the ordinary police officer could learn a thing or two from some of these writers, at least the good ones. Although, the bad guys always seem to get caught in crime fiction. Not very realistic, don't you agree, Mrs. Tanner?"

The challenge couldn't have been more clear if he'd slapped me across the face with a glove. I fixed a grisly smile on my face and for once found the wisdom to keep my mouth shut. My silence had the desired effect, and I watched his smugness melt into annoyance.

"Well, you ladies have a pleasant day." He turned and strode back up the corridor toward the front door.

"Ciao!" Gabby called sweetly to his retreating back.

"Bastard!" I muttered, and she laughed.

"I think he might be an okay guy, but he still thinks he's in New York. That kind of intimidation doesn't work down here, at least not with folks like you. There's something to be said for having history in a place. Gives you sort of a feeling of invincibility, doesn't it?"

I shrugged and forced my taut muscles to relax. I longed for a cigarette with a deep, visceral need.

She laughed. "You should have seen your face! I was afraid you were gonna jump up and deck him one, right here in front of half the town. Wouldn't have been your best move, under the circumstances."

"What circumstances?"

The reporter leaned back as the waitress set plates in front of us. After she'd moved away, Gabby said, "Cut the bullshit, okay? I offered to help, and I meant it, but you've got to be up front with me, or the whole thing's pointless. If you play it straight, I'll be the best friend you've got. I'm assuming we both want the truth."

When I didn't respond, she picked up her fork and waved it in my direction.

"The truth, Bay. Yeah, maybe for different reasons, but that doesn't matter. Between the two of us we could crack this thing wide open." She paused, the fork poised over her food. "But you have to trust me."

Then, like an osprey diving into an unsuspecting school of fish, Gabby swooped down on her plate and didn't rest until her prey had been vanquished.

I finished one crab cake, picked at the slaw, and left the French fries untouched. Too much breakfast or too many nervous knots in my stomach, I couldn't tell which. I jumped as Gilly popped into view.

"Somethin' wrong with the food?"

"No, of course not. My stomach's a little twitchy today."

"No wonder," she said, whisking the plate away, "company you keep." She and my half-finished lunch disappeared behind the swinging door to the kitchen.

Gabby laughed. "Not my biggest fan," she said as she wiped her lips and settled back with a satisfied sigh. "Too bad. I love her food." She reached down to retrieve her notebook and flipped it open on the table between us. "Okay," she said, her mood sobering, "let's get started."

I stalled, my gaze following two businessmen as they moved out the back door and across the porch to the wide promenade skirting the river. Even in the midday heat, the benches and swings scattered along its length looked inviting, the quivering branches of dozens of trees giving evidence of a welcome breeze off the water. Out of the corner of my eye I could see the reporter fidgeting in her seat.

Back at Presqu'isle the night before, I'd decided I needed an ally, someone who hadn't lived every second of her life in our insular, Lowcountry community. Someone with a fresh perspective. Now that the moment had arrived, the doubts had begun to seep in. Could I really trust a reporter, even one who seemed so firmly planted on my side?

"Having second thoughts?"

Gabby Henson's ability to read my mind—or maybe my face—didn't help.

"I can understand that, I guess," she said, leaning back in her chair. "Look, Bay, you're right to be a little suspicious. I would be, too, in your shoes." She tapped her pen against the laminated top of the table. "Tell you what. I'll show you mine first. Maybe you'll feel a little more comfortable when you realize I already know most of your secrets."

If she meant her smile to be reassuring, she didn't succeed. "What do you mean?"

"Your predicament has pretty much been the topic of conversation around town for the last few days. Talk in the newsroom has been pretty evenly divided. Some of them think you've been singled out for special attention by the sheriff's office, and there's a lot of speculation as to why that should be."

Some of them. I tried not to let the implication of it distract me. "What are they saying?"

Gabby shrugged. "Oh, you know. There's some who aren't exactly the biggest fans of you and your father, that whole 'we-were-here-first' attitude you high-society types seem to wear like battle armor. A couple actually think you might have done it. You and your boyfriend."

"Done what?"

The amiable smile slipped from her chubby face. "Come on, Bay. I thought we were going to level with each other. You know damn well what I'm talking about. That you knocked off that kid your pal had the wrestling match with in the parking lot of the Westin."

"And which camp are you in?"

"I told you yesterday, kiddo. I'm on your side."

"I'd like to believe that," I said.

"Fair enough. Here's the scenario the cops are working on," she said.

It was past three by the time Gabby tilted her empty tea glass in the general direction of the bar and waited until we had both been served our fourth or fifth refills. She rolled her head around on her neck and flexed the fingers on her writing hand.

In exchange for her rundown on why Wyler and the sheriff were so convinced I had murdered Cart Anderson—much of which the Judge, Law Merriweather, and I had already deduced—I had given her a recap of our encounter with the boy the day he disappeared. I'd watched her scribbling frantically in her notebook as she took me back over it again and again.

I kept Darnay's desertion to myself.

"I'll tell you what, girlfriend, this is a hell of a story. I could run it right now and get some serious attention."

"But . . ." I stuttered, and she waved her hand.

"No, no, I told you I won't do that. I'm just saying you've got yourself into a real tangled-up mess here. I think we need to set a strategy and get started on some digging." Her gaze locked on to mine, and grim determination had replaced her usual careless grin. "That is, if you're in."

Gabby Henson had spent the past couple of hours amazing me with her knowledge of the old Grayton's Race scandal and my part in it. No one alive except me and perhaps Hadley Bolles, the crooked lawyer who had fronted for the drug cartel, knew all the details, but Gabby had come pretty damn close. She seemed convinced the two incidents were somehow related. Yet despite knowing the suspicious circumstances surrounding the death of Geoffrey Anderson, she still believed me innocent in the disappearance of his son. And she wanted to help me prove it. Her belief had almost brought me to unaccustomed tears.

I'd decided to trust her.

"Okay," I said, relaxing back into my chair, "I'm in. What's next?"

Gabby flipped through a few pages and jotted a couple more notes. "I'm going to concentrate on finding out exactly what the cops have on you besides a cockamamie theory. It could be a little tougher since the big kahuna there saw us together, but I've got other sources I can tap. I'll also get hold of the incident logs and see what kind of reports have been filed about disturbances out at the old fort. If Mrs. Bleeker was right about there being funny business going on at Land's End, it could have a lot to do with what happened to the kid. And maybe to her as well."

"You think Miss Minnie was murdered?"

"Doesn't matter what I think. Word around town is they're leaning that way."

"And I suppose I'm the chief suspect in that, too?" I tried to make it sound like a throwaway line, but Gabby already knew me better than that.

"Wouldn't surprise me. You have to quit showing up in the vicinity of dead people."

I knew she was referring to my appearance at Minnie Maude Bleeker's cottage on Sunday morning just about the time her body was being discovered. Despite Red's hints to the contrary, no one but Darnay and my family knew for certain I'd been there the night before. I had decided to trust Gabby Henson, but not with everything.

"Here's what I think you should do," she went on. "Dig up everything you can find about this Cart Anderson kid. Your family probably runs in the same circles as his, right?"

I smiled at the memory of my mother and her chief rival, Millicent Anderson, as they'd vied for top dog honors among the local aristocracy. The contest had never been officially decided until my mother's death had taken her out of the running.

I flipped back to the present as Gabby finished. "You'd probably have a better idea of where to start poking around than I would."

"What am I looking for?" I asked.

"Talk to the grandmother. Find out what arrangements she made with the kid. See if she has any idea what took him out to the fort that night, if he'd ever been there before, stuff like that."

I felt vindicated to a certain extent when I remembered these were almost the exact questions I'd jotted down on the legal pad at home just minutes before Wyler and his goons had burst in on me.

"Okay, I'll talk to Millicent. What else?"

"Something you said about the boy struck me as kind of strange."

She shuffled the pages of her notebook. "Wait a sec, here it is. When you and this Interpol guy of yours first hijacked the kid back to your place, you said he was mouthing off pretty good. Making threats."

"Yes. Darnay finally put the fear of God into him, and he shut up."

"But at one point he said, 'My grandfather will kill you,' or something similar."

"Right. Those were almost his exact words."

"Well, he couldn't have been talking about his namesake, Carter Anderson. I hear he's been in a nursing home for a couple of years."

"You're right. I never gave it any thought." I shivered. "He must have been referring to his mother's father."

"Yeah. Kind of makes you wonder who the guy is that his grandson would use him to threaten people with."

"I'll get on it," I said, reaching for my bag and wondering if I could con Erik Whiteside into doing some checking for me. I glanced at my watch. "Hey, you better get a move on. Doesn't the council meeting start at four?"

With a little squeal, the reporter shoved everything into her briefcase and pushed back her chair. "Right! My editor will have my butt if I miss one boring little morsel of bureaucratic doubletalk, and I want to look up a couple things while I'm at the courthouse."

We'd long since settled up the bill, and I followed Gabby out to the front where we'd parked our cars. Neither of us had given a thought to feeding a parking meter, and a bright blue ticket adorned the windshield of her ancient Mustang convertible.

"Shit! I think I'm running out of people to fix these for me," she said with a laugh and tossed the ticket into the front seat of her car before turning to face me. "I'm off tomorrow and Sunday, so let's see what we can each dig up and rendezvous at your place Monday. You think you'll be back on the island by then?"

I thought of my refuge at Presqu'isle and Lavinia's tender ministrations of the night before. Better not get used to it. "I'll try to see Millicent Anderson while I'm here and be home by Sunday night. Call me there, and we'll see where we stand."

"Cool!" Gabby clutched my hand in both of hers and beamed up into my face. "We're gonna get to the bottom of this thing, Bay. All we have to do is stick together."

She would have hugged me if I hadn't stepped back. I covered the awkward moment by feigning a cough. "See you," I called and headed up the street.

I knew without turning around that the woman's basset hound eyes followed me until I turned the corner.

Gabby Henson might be my only chance to clear my name, but I had a terrible feeling the price might turn out to be more than I was willing to pay.

Chapter Nineteen

I PLUCKED MY OWN PARKING TICKET FROM UNDER THE wipers of the T-Bird, then wandered down to the waterfront. A few tourists still lingered along the shaded walkways, and squealing children chased each other around a sandy area filled with swings and slides. The withering heat shimmered across the placid surface of the river.

I stood for a while at the water's edge. The high, arched bridge which connected the mainland to Lady's Island was just swinging closed, and a long line of idling cars stretched out of sight in both directions. The elegant, tall-masted sailboat whose passage had necessitated the delay glided serenely toward the tiny marina just up the waterway as I pondered my assignment from Gabby Henson.

I had avoided thinking about Millicent Anderson for the better part of a year. A conversation with my mother's old rival would force me to examine things I'd hoped never to have to face again. I stepped back into the shade and settled myself on a deserted bench. I drew a long breath and tried to empty my mind, but the memories I'd buried for so many months kept struggling to break free . . .

The Grayton's Race investment scheme for which Millicent's son had died had been a scam, although the shadowy men behind it had never been prosecuted. Geoffrey Anderson had been their front man, the local boy turned advisor and attorney to some of the more questionable members of the south Florida power elite. I had stumbled into the mess quite by accident. Approached by family friends because of my financial expertise, I had set out to assure the viability of their considerable investments in the project supposedly designed to reclaim the old Grayton mansion and turn its grounds into an upscale housing development.

Despite the blistering sun, I shivered. Blinded by the memory of a girlhood crush on the dashing Geoff Anderson, I had let myself be seduced by his easy charm and lying heart. I rubbed my arms, remembering the touch of his hands on my skin . . .

I closed my eyes, but the images of that horrible night shimmered before me in vivid color: flashing blue lights against the black August sky, the flickering reds and yellows, the overpowering heat. And the *smell* . . .

Stop it! I swiped at the tears I couldn't control and rose abruptly from the bench.

I'd done all I could, I told myself. I'd confronted one of Geoff's cronies, a sleazy local lawyer named Hadley Bolles, and blackmailed him into returning my friends' investments. I'd never told anyone, not even my own father, of my former lover's involvement. Or of his admissions about the bomb which had killed my anti-drug-crusading husband the year before. I'd done my best to keep my surviving family safe and tried to get on with my life.

I drew a tissue from my purse as I approached the car. I slipped inside, blew my nose, and ordered myself to get a grip. I had made my deal with the devil. I had traded justice for Rob for the assurance there would be no reprisals against the rest of the people I loved. I had cost the Miami drug machine a couple of million dollars and one of their hired hands. They probably thought it a cheap price to pay for my assurances the evidence I held would not be used against them so long as they left me and mine alone.

I turned over the engine and eased out into the late afternoon stream of traffic.

Like my own family, Millicent Anderson's had occupied the same piece of Lowcountry real estate for the better part of two hundred years. Hers, however, rose majestically on a sprawling lot in the historic district of downtown Beaufort known locally as the Point. Bordered on two sides by a sharp bend of the Beaufort River, the stately antebellum homes had originally provided summer retreats for the plantation owners of the outlying islands.

A few die-hard tourists still strolled the narrow streets, while the less venturesome crawled along, gawking at the magnificent houses from the air-conditioned comfort of their vans and SUVs. I'd always been grateful Presqu'isle lay tucked away down a rutted lane at the end of St. Helena Island, too far off the beaten path for all but the most determined of visitors to find us.

I pulled up on the sandy shoulder in front of the Anderson mansion and got out of the car. I pushed open the intricate wrought-iron gate and forced myself to move with confidence up the old brick walkway. *Riverdell* rose, white and pristine, its dual, balustraded porches and slender white columns so typical of what gave Lowcountry architecture its grace and distinction. Twin chimneys bracketed either side of the red shingled roof, and black plantation shutters provided a wonderful symmetry. The lawn was, as always, perfectly manicured, the azalea bushes flanking the wide front steps trimmed to a thick hedge.

I used the brass knocker, admiring the delicate fanlight above the door as I waited nervously. Millicent Anderson would no doubt be home, resting before dinner after her visit to the skilled nursing facility where her husband now resided. Though still strong enough in body, Carter Anderson's mind had long since wandered off to a place no one else could follow.

I knocked again, this time with my knuckles, and almost immediately the gleaming black door swung open. The young woman who confronted me, tall and impressive in dark trousers and a starched white shirt, smiled warmly. Her face beneath the rows of tightly woven braids gleamed a deep, rich ebony in the late afternoon sun.

"Yes, ma'am? May I help you?" Her voice was as smooth as her skin.

I tried to mask my confusion at not finding the venerable Ardelia standing in her place. "Hi! I wonder if I could see Miss Millicent for a moment. I'm Bay Tanner. An old friend of the family."

Friend. A slight exaggeration, perhaps, but I'd been unprepared to have to explain myself. Ardelia had been with the Andersons since I was a teenager and would have welcomed me with a bone-crushing hug and no questions.

The smile never left the young woman's lovely face, but the warmth had definitely faded from her eyes. She stood resolutely blocking the doorway. "I'm sorry. Mrs. Anderson is resting right now."

We stared at each other for a long moment, our expressions amiable enough, but I could sense a current of animosity building in the heavy air between us.

"I just need a few minutes. Perhaps if you'd tell her I'm here." I could see the refusal rising to her lips, so I quickly added, "It's about her grandson."

"Janice, who is it?" The querulous voice echoed down the long center hallway.

With resignation, the young woman moved aside. "Come in," she said grudgingly, then called over her shoulder, "A visitor for you, ma'am."

I stepped into the cool dimness beneath the magnificent crystal chandelier Millicent Anderson had been bragging about for as long as I could remember. Her great-grandfather had bought it on a trip to Italy just before the War of the Northern Aggression. He'd been able to secrete it in its shipping crate in an old pump house on the property before the entire family fled the Yankee invasion. The occupiers had never found it, and the treasure had been resurrected when the Bowdoins returned to reclaim their home.

I had heard the story so often I could have recited it, chapter and verse, from memory.

"Answer me, girl!" The quavering voice, still firm with command, preceded the tap of a cane on the polished wood floor as Millicent Anderson shuffled from the front parlor to the right of the hall.

"It's me, Miss Millicent," I said. "Bay . . . Lydia Tanner. Emmaline's daughter."

Though I hadn't seen her in years, I could never have mistaken the haughty carriage and steely blue eyes. Dressed as impeccably as I remembered in a soft lavender dress with the ever-present Bowdoin pearls draped around her crepey neck, Millicent Anderson paused in the doorway to fix me with a look of astonishment.

"Lydia! Whatever . . . ? Do you have news of Carter?"

The gnarled hand clutching the cane trembled, and I moved quickly to her side. "No, ma'am, nothing new. I'm sorry."

She allowed me to cup her elbow and lead her back into the parlor, the new girl trailing along behind us. I lowered the old woman into the straight-backed chair covered in fiery Chinese red silk and took the cane from her hand.

"Are you all right?" I turned toward the hovering Janice. "Maybe some water?"

She glared at me and flounced from the room.

"I'm fine, Lydia," the old woman said, some of the vigor returning to her voice. "Don't fuss, child." She drew a shallow breath. "Go sit down." She waved me away with a bony hand weighted down by a magnificent square-cut emerald.

I crossed to the matching divan and perched primly on the edge of the seat. The girl Janice bustled in with a tumbler of water and set it on a coaster on the cherry drum table at her employer's right. I noticed the remains of tea spread out on the butler's tray, a few crumbs of some sort of yellow cake on the fine white china.

Millicent Anderson sipped from the glass, then handed it back. "Bring us some fresh tea and another cup." Her face softened, and she smiled. "Thank you, Janice. You're a good girl."

The young woman nodded and hurried out, never once looking in my direction, and the deep silence which followed her exit made me edgy. I wanted to get this over with. "I'm sorry if my just showing up like this upset you," I said. "I should have called."

My hostess eyed me with less hostility than I had any right to expect. "Nonsense! You know you're always welcome at *Riverdell*. Just because your mama and I didn't always get on doesn't mean I hold any grudge against you. Besides," she added with a telling sigh, "it was all so long ago."

I saw no point in beating about the bush. "Miss Millicent, I want to assure you I had nothing to do with your grandson's disappearance."

Her answer was forestalled by the return of Janice with a flowered china pot of tea and a delicate cup and saucer. Without a word she set both on the tray and left us alone.

"I know that, Lydia. Will you pour?"

I moved across and performed the ritual as if I had been doing it every day of my life. Perhaps somewhere the spirit of my mother looked down and smiled, content that all her endless efforts to housebreak me had not been in vain. Somehow I even remembered Millicent took hers with a little milk. I passed her the fragile cup, then used the silver tongs to add one cube of sugar and a slice of lemon to my own cup, and resumed my seat.

"Very nicely done. Emmaline quite despaired of you, although I expect you already know that." Her smile warmed me as much as the tea.

"Yes, ma'am. She never took much trouble to hide it."

I sipped and rested the saucer on my knee. I knew how entangled we'd get if we let ourselves drift back into the past. I took a deep breath and plunged in.

"Miss Millicent, I know the police have some crazy idea that my friend and I had something . . ."

"I've told them what utter nonsense that is." Her vehement interruption brought a spot of color to her powdered cheeks. "I don't want to speak about their wild theories. I want Carter found! The poor child! Losing both his parents . . ."

I felt my hand tightening around the edge of the saucer and consciously relaxed my grip. Now was the time. If Geoffrey Anderson's mother had any inkling of the true circumstances of his death, of the kind of monster her son had been . . . I waited, prepared to defend myself if necessary against her accusations, her hatred . . .

But the moment passed, and I felt a wave of relief so profound it almost made me dizzy. In spite of her ingrained snobbery and pride of ancestry which had so infuriated my mother, Millicent Anderson was simply a tired old woman who deserved to spend the rest of her life in as much peace as she could find. Let her remember her son as she wanted him to be. I breathed an unaccustomed prayer of thanks and promised whatever gods might be paying attention that I'd do whatever I could to keep her from ever finding out the truth.

"Can you tell me about that day?" I asked. "Last Friday? What arrangements had you made with Cart?"

She looked up from her Meissen cup and seemed not to understand the question.

"I know the detectives told you I saw him. Around noon," I went on. "We had a little . . . misunderstanding, and my friend and I persuaded him to come back to my house. We talked for a while, and he left. Was he supposed to come directly here? Had you talked to him at all on Friday?"

"He always comes straight home after school. Such a good boy. We often have tea together."

I gave myself a mental shake, certain I had misunderstood. "Miss Millicent? We're talking about your grandson. From Florida? The one who's missing?"

"Oh, Emmaline," she said with a tinkling, girlish laugh that sent goose bumps crawling up my arms, "Geoffrey's not missing! He's probably off with some of his friends. He's a very popular boy, you know. Especially with the girls. I swear, you read way too many of those gothic romances. Haven't I always told you? One should read uplifting things, biographies and histories. Food for the soul as well as the mind." The old woman lifted the cup to her lips and regarded me over the rim. "Maybe if you set a better example, your only child wouldn't be such a trial to you."

"Miss Millicent, it's me, Lydia."

It was as if the room were empty except for the ghost of my mother only Millicent could see. "More cake? Oh, dear, we seem to have finished it. I'll ring for Ardelia to bring us another slice." She reached for the little silver bell beside her on the drum table as I watched in horrified fascination.

Janice hurried into the room as the notes died away. "Yes, ma'am?"

"Ardelia, will you bring us some more of your wonderful pound cake? Mrs. Simpson and I seem to have been a little excessive in our appreciation of it."

The young woman glared at me as if her employer's drift back to earlier times was somehow my fault.

"Now, Mrs. Anderson, we don't want to go spoilin' that fine figure of yours, now do we? And besides it's time for your rest." Gently she took the saucer from the trembling hand and set it on the tray. "Come on now. I'm sure your guest will excuse us."

She looked pointedly at me. "Of course," I said. "I have to be going anyway."

Janice helped her to rise and supported her across the brilliant blue Persian carpet toward the stairs. "Thank you, Emmaline. I know you need to get home yourself. Why it takes us ladies so long to get ready, I have no idea, but we mustn't keep the menfolk waiting. My Carter gets so agitated if we don't arrive precisely on time for these galas. I'm sure Tally feels the same."

I stood and followed them out into the hall. Janice tenderly urged Millicent Anderson up the sweeping staircase, her low voice murmuring encouragement. A few steps from the top the regal old woman paused and looked down at me, the deterioration of her mind heartbreakingly evident in her pinched face.

"Lydia?" she called, her voice cracked and frail. "Find him for me. Please." A single tear slid down her hollow cheek. "He's all I have left."

Chapter Twenty

I WAITED NEARLY TWENTY MINUTES, THINKING PERhaps Janice could answer my questions about Cart Anderson, but she never returned. Finally I gave up and let myself out the front door. Back in the car, I nosed into the homebound traffic and crawled back to Presqu'isle.

I'd been hoping for a quiet tête-à-tête with Lavinia, but the presence of two vehicles pulled up in the semicircular drive in front of the house put an end to that notion. I had one foot on the bottom step when the front door swung open, and Reverend Henry Chaplin stepped onto the verandah.

"Thank you, Lavinia. See you tomorrow," I heard him say.

The door closed, and he turned in my direction before hesitating, his deep brown eyes registering surprise as he saw me climbing the steps.

"Reverend," I said when I finally reached him. "Good to see you."

"You, too, Mrs. Tanner." He pulled a crumpled white handkerchief from the pocket of his slacks and mopped his face. "Not coolin' off much, is it?"

"Did you want to see me?" I asked, moving farther back into the shade of the verandah roof.

"I . . . I needed to have a word with the Judge."

I couldn't figure out why he seemed so uncomfortable. "Well, nice to see you again," I said, my hand on the doorknob, when I heard him clear his throat.

"I told them . . . I told them you had nothing to do with it."

I turned back toward him. "Nothing to do with what?"

"With Miz Bleeker's death." He edged closer to me, as if fearing we might be overheard. "Detective Wyler came to see us, to question my mother and sister, since they were the ones who discovered the poor woman's body. He wanted to know what you were doing there, and if we had any information about whether or not you might have been at her house the day before."

My heart skipped a couple of beats. "Did Wyler say why he thought I might have been there on Saturday?"

Reverend Chaplin shook his head. "No, he didn't. And since none of us could shed any light on the matter, he left soon after."

"And you felt the need to come running to my father with this news?" I knew my voice sounded sharp and accusatory, but I didn't care.

Henry Chaplin took no offense, at least not outwardly. "I did try to reach you, Mrs. Tanner. When I couldn't, I felt it best to let someone close to you know. I'm sorry if I crossed a line."

He stuffed the damp handkerchief back in his pocket and turned toward the stairs.

"Wait!" I called, and he hesitated. "I'm the one who's sorry, Reverend Chaplin. Forgive me."

A sad smile settled onto his face. "No need to apologize. When Lavinia first suggested you might be willing to help us with keeping the sheriff's department from simply writing off Miz Bleeker's death, I'm sure no one ever thought they'd be insinuating you had anything to do with it. Nor do I believe it now. I can't imagine how upsetting it must be for you."

I felt myself relax a little. "Thank you. Do you still need my help in any way? I haven't meant to ignore . . ."

The minister cut me off. "No, but thank you for askin'." He paused. "I think things will play out as they were meant to. Keep your hope in the Lord, Mrs. Tanner," he added and headed down the steps.

I pondered the minister's cryptic remark as I pushed open the door, deposited my bag on the floor, and tiptoed toward the kitchen.

"Bay, is that you?" my father's voice thundered down the hallway from the study.

With a shrug of resignation, I reversed my steps. "Yes, Your Honor, guilty as charged."

I stepped into his room, flooded with light in the late afternoon, to find Lawton Merriweather ensconced in the wing chair by the dead fireplace.

"Come in, daughter. We've been discussing your options," my father said in his most pompous voice.

"How nice. I don't suppose it occurred to anyone I might like to be in on the conversation?"

Law ducked his head. "You're right, of course, Bay darlin', but there was a certain . . . urgency, and we didn't know when you'd be back."

"So?" I said as I crossed to the window seat. "What conclusions have you reached?" I swiveled my eyes from one to the other, but no one spoke. "Come on, gentlemen. I'm a big girl. I can take it."

My father cleared his throat. "Law met with that detective this afternoon."

"Wyler," I said. So he had gone running from the Fig Tree straight to my attorney. More silence. "And? Am I going to be arrested?"

"Not yet. But they do want you to come in for questioning. We think you need to cooperate."

"What changed your mind?" I asked the Judge.

"Preliminary tests show one of the blood types in the missing boy's car is a match with yours." Law hung his head as if it were all somehow his fault.

"No! That's impossible!"

"It's not as bad as it sounds, sweetheart," my father rushed to reassure me. "All they're saying is it's the same type as yours. They can't prove it's definitively your blood until the DNA results come back."

"They can't prove it's definitively my blood, period, because it's not!" I drew a calming breath and lowered my voice. "How do they know I'm not a match with Carter?" I asked.

"What do you mean?" my father asked.

"I mean, do they know which blood type is Carter's and which belongs to the unidentified donor?"

Law answered. "Although they don't have the boy to do a comparison with, they've somehow determined he's type O. Detective Wyler didn't feel inclined to enlighten me on how they had come to that conclusion." He paused and glanced at the Judge. "The other sample is B. Same as yours." He lowered his eyes and shook his head. "I had no idea it would come to this when I counseled you to submit to the test. I'm truly sorry, Bay."

"Child didn't have much choice." In one of his typical reversals, my father now absolved his old friend from all responsibility. "At any rate," he added, turning again to me, "they have it. It gives them enough probable cause to invite you in for questioning."

His calm recital suddenly hit home, but before I had time to let the fear and anger get a good grip on me, Law spoke softly. "Do you happen to know what blood type Mr. Darnay is?"

I stared at him for a long moment. "No. Why?"

My attorney ducked his head. "Although Wyler wouldn't confirm it, my sources tell me they also found blood on the shirt they removed from your house." Slowly Law lifted his eyes to mine. "Type O. Same as the boy's."

"And several million other people," my father offered. "And you told me my daughter had no idea which one of them the shirt belonged to."

"Could you please quit talking about me as if I weren't here?" I surprised myself with the calm assurance of my own voice. "Unless I can see the T-shirt, I obviously have no way of knowing."

Law cleared his throat. "I understand Mr. Darnay is . . . no longer in the area."

I smiled to show him I appreciated his delicacy. "I don't have a clue. All I can say for sure is his things are gone from my closet."

An uncomfortable silence settled over the room. I kicked off my shoes and pulled my legs up under me.

"What about Miss Minnie?" I asked, watching closely for their reactions. "I saw Reverend Chaplin just now as he was leaving."

My father and my attorney exchanged a look.

"I know they're probably ruling it a homicide," I said, unwilling yet to name Gabby Henson as my primary source of information. I could just imagine the Judge's tirade against the stupidity of trusting a reporter. "Am I on the hook with Wyler for that one as well?"

"He thinks her death is tied to the boy's disappearance." My father made the assertion as if he'd been privy to the workings of the New York detective's mind. "He thinks Mrs. Bleeker saw something incriminating the night before, and you and Darnay had to silence her. It's the only thing that makes sense."

"None of it makes sense." I stood and paced the worn boards of the heart pine floor, my gaze wandering out over the Sound where the waning sun cast long shafts of light across the flat sheet of water. Without thinking about it, I walked toward the door, stopping to turn back at my father's stern voice.

"Bay, come back here. We have things to discuss."

I watched him bring his clean white handkerchief to his nose and hold it there while his eyes bored into mine.

"I'm thirsty," I said, ignoring his blazing look and heading toward the kitchen.

I also ignored Lavinia, who looked up from her cutting board as I poured myself a glass of ice water and leaned against the refrigerator. Neither of us spoke for a few moments, and she resumed her attack on a pile of pungent herbs.

"You saw Reverend Chaplin on his way out," she said into the silence. When I didn't correct her assumption, she went on. "I know you didn't like me goin' behind your back to him, but we needed someone we could trust, and naturally I thought of you."

I carried my glass across the room and sank into one of the oak chairs. This wasn't the topic of conversation I'd wanted to raise, but I figured we might as well get it over with.

"Why did all of you jump to the conclusion the authorities wouldn't handle it fairly?"

Again she spoke without turning to face me. "Experience. History. Call it what you will. Helen Chaplin is a nurse. She's seen a lot of injuries in the emergency room where she works, and she knew right off someone had struck that poor old woman with the lamp. A body couldn't get that kind of gash in the head just by fallin' down."

"But you didn't even give the deputies a chance to finish their investigation before you sent the reverend running to me. I still don't get it."

This time she did turn, and the look on her face said more than her words. "I told you once before, Bay, back when my grandson Isaiah was in trouble with the law. I've lived here all my life. I know how things happen." She paused and resumed her chopping. "And how they don't."

I wanted to protest those days were gone, that the new South had no place for the kind of attitude she feared, but I couldn't. I, too, had witnessed the subtle forms modern-day racism could take, and we'd certainly had a recent and stunning example of the legacy of that hatred in the events surrounding Judas Island.

"Well, this may fall under the category of be careful what you wish for," I said. "I hope when y'all set out to make sure Miss Minnie's death got treated like a homicide you weren't planning on my being tagged for it."

I saw her shoulders slump and cursed myself for being so flip about something so serious.

"Don't fret about it," I said, carrying my empty glass to the sink. "The fact this new hotshot detective is on my case has nothing to do with you."

"I don't understand." She laid the knife aside and stared into my eyes. "I know as sure as I'm standin' here you'd never hurt anyone. Not Minnie Maude Bleeker and not that Anderson boy. What's goin' on here, Bay? What in heaven's name is goin' on?"

I gave her shoulders a quick squeeze and shook my head. "I'm damned if I know. And it's way past time I was finding out."

Law Merriweather refused our invitation to stay to dinner and took his leave shortly after my return to the study. He instructed me to sit tight until he worked out the details with Detective Ben Wyler but added I should be prepared to appear at the Hilton Head satellite sheriff's office sometime on Monday to answer questions about the disappearance of Cart Anderson and the death of Minnie Maude Bleeker. We spent a few minutes kicking around whether or not I had to volunteer the information that Darnay and I had been at her house the night before she died, but we reached no conclusion. Law would be with me throughout the interrogation, which we could stop at any time. Both he and the Judge kept reminding me I was not under arrest, that I would be voluntarily submitting to questioning.

I tried hard to imagine what the hell difference it made what you called it.

Back in the kitchen I helped my father settle his wheelchair at the table while Lavinia carved slices from a plump pork tenderloin glazed in sage and honey. I cut my father's portion into manageable pieces and held the bowl while he served himself creamed corn and whipped potatoes. We ate in silence for a few minutes before I mustered up the courage to broach the subject I'd been waiting to introduce.

"I stopped by to see Millicent Anderson this afternoon." The words dropped like rocks into a pool. Neither of my dinner companions responded.

"Get me some ketchup, will you, Bay?" my father asked.

I sat back down with a thump when Lavinia snapped, "No! Don't you go ruinin' my good pork roast with ketchup, Tally Simpson."

My father grumbled but resumed picking at his dinner.

"Ardelia isn't there anymore," I said. "There's a young woman named Janice."

Again I waited for a reply. The Judge and Lavinia ignored me.

"So what's the deal?" I demanded in exasperation, my voice rising on every word. "What happened to Ardelia? And why didn't anyone tell me Millicent is nutty as a fruitcake?"

Lavinia laid her fork across the top of her plate and folded her worn brown hands in her lap. "Ardelia retired sometime last year. Those stairs just got too much for her arthritis. Janice is her niece, her brother Charles's girl. She's attending USC-Beaufort and works to pay for her schooling by lookin' after Mrs. Anderson. She's studying to be a nurse, I believe. She's twenty years old, an excellent student, has a steady boyfriend, and pretty much stays around the house when she's not in class." Lavinia paused for breath and charged ahead. "As for Miss Millicent, she has what Ardelia used to call her 'spells' now and again, but most of the time she's quite coherent. Anything else?"

If it hadn't been so important, I would have laughed. Trust Lavinia to have the lowdown.

"Thanks," I said, "that's exactly what I wanted to know." I turned to my father. "Didn't anyone check her out before they awarded her custody of a teenaged boy?"

"I understand it was spelled out in her daughter-in-law's will. Anyway, what makes you think she's not capable of being an adequate guardian?"

I dabbed at the corner of my mouth with the heavy napkin. "She thought I was my mother."

That got their attention, and I proceeded to recite the gist of my strange conversation with Millicent Anderson. When I finished, my father shook his head.

"Poor woman. I had no idea she'd deteriorated to such an extent." He slumped against the backrest of his wheelchair. "We're all getting so damned old!"

"Well, nobody's getting young," I quipped and earned myself a stern look. "All I'm trying to say is, even if they find the missing boy, he can't possibly stay in that house. Once he sees how dotty his grandmother . . ." I broke off, the idea materializing from out of nowhere. "What if he already knows? What if that's why he's disappeared?"

"What are you getting at?" The Judge leaned forward. "Are you suggesting he may have staged . . ."

"Exactly!" I said, the possibilities expanding by the second. "Think about it! He stops in to visit Millicent, needs about five minutes to see what his life with her is probably going to be like, and gets the hell out as fast as he can go."

"Did Millicent say she'd seen him? Talked to him?"

"No. Just as I began questioning her about Cart she went off into her memory drift, thinking I was talking about Geoff. I really don't know if she ever saw the boy or not. Even if she did, she might not remember." I glanced at Lavinia who had risen and begun to remove the empty plates. "What do you think?" I asked.

"I haven't seen Mrs. Anderson in years," she said, turning toward the sink. "Last time I talked to Ardelia was right before she went to live with her daughter up near Florence. She never mentioned any problems. Still, it wouldn't be surprisin'. Millicent always was high-strung."

"Must be something in the water," I said half under my breath, remembering the similar excuses Lavinia had made for my mother during our soul-baring of the night before. "Anyway," I continued in a normal voice, "I think this scenario has possibilities the cops haven't even considered."

My father checked my rising enthusiasm with a claw-like grip on my arm. "Hold on, though, daughter. How does that explain the two different kinds of blood they found in his car? Matter of fact, how does it explain there being any blood at all? Or that he left his car behind?"

I gave his questions serious thought while I helped Lavinia finish clearing the table. I held the dessert plates while she plopped on huge slabs of chocolate cake. I set my father's portion in front of him, surprised when he didn't dig in immediately.

"How about this?" I asked as I resumed my seat. "Cart Anderson leaves my house and heads up to Beaufort. He checks in at granny's house, sees the lay of the land, and decides he needs to get out of there. He's visited before, with his parents, and he's aware of Fort Fremont. It's probably one of the most desolate spots around here, and he might have thought he could leave his car where it wouldn't be found for a while and split."

"But I keep coming back to the blood," my father said.

"Maybe he got in a fight out there," I said, warming to my theory as I talked. "Miss Minnie hinted there were strange goings-on in the neighborhood. I assumed drugs, but it could be anything. Maybe gangs. He could have had something as simple as a bloody nose. And, if he got in a few licks himself, that would account for the secondary sample."

"But why would he leave his car behind?" Lavinia asked.

"I don't know! I haven't had a chance to work it all out yet."

My father shook his head. "I know you want to believe this is what happened, Bay, but your theory has serious flaws. It's been almost a week since he disappeared, and there's not been one sighting. I'm beginning to agree with the sheriff that he must have met with foul play." I opened my mouth to protest, but he forestalled me. "But just for the sake of argument, let's say the boy did run away. How would he expect to live? Where would he go?"

For a moment I felt deflated. It had seemed such a perfect solution. Then a snippet of my conversation with Gabby Henson flashed into my head, and I snapped my fingers. "I know exactly where he'd go," I said, unable to suppress the excitement in my voice. "Back to Florida. Back to his other grandfather." I turned again to Lavinia. "What do you know about Geoff's widow? Cart's mother, I mean."

Lavinia shrugged. "Not much. Ardelia said she and Millicent didn't get on too well, but then she never did approve of any woman her son brought home." She paused. "I think I remember something about her bein' foreign."

"I need to get back to the house," I said, tossing my napkin on the table.

"Bay! Wait! What are you running off for?"

"I need to get on my computer and do some serious digging into Cart Anderson's family tree," I called over my shoulder as I bolted from the room.

Chapter Twenty-one

I slipped into the pew beside Lavinia with a couple of minutes to spare. I'd dropped her off while I hunted for a parking place in the overflowing lot next to the church. She set her handbag on her lap and patted my knee.

The hush of the sultry Saturday morning was underlain by the somber strains of an organ prelude designed to put the mourners in the proper frame of mind. I glanced around the crowded sanctuary, pleased to find mine was not the only white face in the congregation. I spotted Gabby Henson a few rows behind us on the other side of the aisle. Apparently she had been watching me, because she immediately waved in my direction. I supposed her presence had to do with the newsworthiness of the manner of Miss Minnie's death.

My eyes traveled on across the rows of dark shoulders and funereal black hats until another flash of white made my breath catch in my throat. Detective Ben Wyler sat almost in the back of the church, and he, too, had me in his sights. He raised a shaggy eyebrow as my gaze paused for a moment on his stony face before I whipped my head back around to the front.

Damn! What the hell was he doing there? I wondered, before the obvious solution presented itself. Cops always went to victims' funerals, at least in crime novels and TV shows. Probably hoping to catch the perpetrator admiring his handiwork, or some such nonsense. Beside me I felt Lavinia stir, almost as if my uneasiness had transmitted itself to her, and again she patted the modest skirt of my navy blue suit where it draped over my knees.

The organ fell silent as Reverend Henry Chaplin stepped onto the altar and positioned himself in front of the closed, plain wood coffin draped in white lilies. Without benefit of a microphone, his voice reached to the farthest corners of the old building. "Let us pray."

A hundred or more heads dropped in unison, and I let the words drift over and around me. There was no order of service printed out in church-bulletin format as there would have been at an Episcopal service. I rose to share the hymnal with Lavinia and actually joined in on a couple of the songs I remembered from my childhood. Strange how many of the beautiful old melodies and lyrics transcended sects and race and all the other barriers we erect to separate ourselves from each other, I thought, and tried to lose myself in the calm dignity of the proceedings.

Several people spoke of Miss Minnie's strength and generosity. In the front pew I could hear someone, probably the daughter, sniffling loudly, and I wondered if any of the old woman's other relatives had bothered to turn up. I snapped my mind back to the present as Reverend Chaplin invited us to bow our heads for the benediction, and six large black men in dark suits marched up the aisle and hefted the coffin onto their shoulders.

The choir, resplendent in bright red robes, rose and followed the organist into the haunting chorus of "Amazing Grace." At first they sang it slowly, deeply, almost like a dirge, and I thought I had never heard anything quite so moving. I felt tears rise unbidden and cascade down my cheeks. Lavinia handed me a tissue. As the somber recessional moved past us, the voices rose in volume and tempo until the entire building reverberated with the pure hand-clapping joy of the gospel beat.

Chatter erupted as the music ended, and mourners gathered their belongings and prepared to join the crowd flowing outside. A woman I assumed to be Miss Minnie's daughter MaeRose, small and frail like her mother had been, shuffled along on the arm of Henry Chaplin, pausing to acknowledge the extended hands and murmured condolences of the congregation as she passed.

I eased around Lavinia, who had stopped to speak to several people, slipped into the side aisle, and made my way to the exit. I bypassed the chatting knots of regular churchgoers gathered on the steps and headed for my car. A hand on my shoulder made me spin around in fright.

Ben Wyler dropped his arm and tried for something that fell just short of a smile. "Mrs. Tanner. Nice service, don't you think?"

"What do you want?" I took a step backwards and fumbled with the keys on my chain until I had the one to the Thunderbird firmly between my fingers.

"Just paying my respects. Same as you." As had been my experience when he'd invaded my house, I couldn't tell if his words held a hidden meaning.

"Don't give me that crap. You didn't even know her. You wanted to see who showed up. Well," I added, throwing my arms out wide, "here I am. And here I go."

I turned my back and crossed the narrow driveway to the row of pines where I'd parked the car, but I could tell by the crunch of gravel under his shoes that he was right behind me. I unlocked the door and whirled to face him.

"Look, Detective, don't read anything sinister into my presence here this morning. Lavinia—Mrs. Smalls—asked me to drive her, and I did. Besides, I've known Miss Minnie almost all my life. Down here, we honor those relationships. I'm sure it's an alien concept to someone like you, but—"

"The arrogance of you people never ceases to amaze me," the big detective interrupted me, his tone gruff and nasty. "You think we don't have friends in New York? You think we don't go to their funerals when they die?"

"Frankly, Detective," I said, "we don't give a damn what you do in New York. And if it's acceptable behavior where you come from to accost people practically on the steps of a church, I strongly suggest you haul your ass back up there and leave us the hell alone!"

I didn't realize my voice had risen to quite such a level until I noticed heads turning in our direction. I lowered my eyes, embarrassed to have contributed as much to disrupting this solemn morning as Wyler had been. Lavinia saved me by approaching us in a firm stride.

"I'm ready, Bay," she said.

"Let me get that." Wyler moved as if to open the passenger door for her, but she brushed by him and yanked it open herself. Seat belt fastened across the deep purple jacket of her suit, she folded her hands primly in her lap, completely ignoring the detective's annoyed glare.

I slid into my own seat, turned the key in the ignition, and flipped on the air conditioning. Wyler's hand on the top of my door prevented me from closing it. I looked up into his craggy face. "Do you mind?" I pulled on the handle, but he held it fast.

"I'm looking forward to our little get-together on Monday," he said with a sneer. "Eleven o'clock. Don't be late."

I held his gaze, my own never wavering, until I felt the pressure on the door ease slightly. I jerked it toward me, catching him off guard, and he had to snatch his hand out of the way to avoid losing a couple of fingers. I jammed the car into reverse, and he jumped back, stumbling slightly and banging his elbow on the fender of the van parked to my left. I straightened the wheel and shot past him, my eyes straight ahead. As we approached the road, I had to slow for those forming into the procession to follow the hearse to the cemetery, and I risked a glance into my rearview mirror.

Detective Ben Wyler stood gazing after us, and his expression was not pleasant.

"Probably not the brightest thing to do, Bay Tanner," Lavinia said beside me, shaking her head in dismay.

"I know," I replied, trying unsuccessfully to stifle a grin, "but it sure as hell felt good!"

Lavinia hadn't wanted to leave my father alone for too long, so we turned away from the line of cars with the purple funeral pennants flapping in the stiff breeze and followed the winding road back to

Presqu'isle. I declined lunch, eager to get back to my investigation of Cart Anderson's family. I left her standing at the top of the steps gazing after me as I drove away, the look on her face one I couldn't quite read. Concern? Apprehension? Whatever it was, I knew I'd feel better out from under it.

As I waited for the light at the foot of the bridge at Bay Street, a car pulled out from the parking lot near the waterfront, its driver leaning on the horn. It took me a moment to recognize the open Mustang convertible and its driver, Gabby Henson. I had no idea what she was trying to tell me until I saw her gesture to our left. I flipped on my turn signal as the light changed and waited for traffic to pass before swinging onto the main drag, the Mustang right on my tail. Saturday morning in July is not the best time to find even one empty parking space along Beaufort's main street, so I crawled behind the line of vans with out-of-state plates until we reached the big parking lot by the marina. I pulled into the first space I came to, and Gabby wheeled in beside me. I let down the window and leaned out.

"Hey, partner!" she called, jumping out of her battered car.

Partner? Where the hell had that come from? I remembered my misgivings of the day before as the reporter moved around to approach me. She leaned her considerable bulk against the passenger door of the Mustang and grinned.

"Saw you at the funeral. Nice turnout."

"Were you covering it for the paper?" I asked, easing my head back into the car. Again I had the feeling of being crowded by Gabby Henson.

"Not officially. Thought I might get some stuff for a background piece, maybe a feature, depending on how things shake out. We'll see. What did Wyler want?"

I stiffened, embarrassed for some reason I couldn't name that she had been a witness to that little scene. "Just being a jerk," I said.

"I never understood why they think the perp will show up at the funeral of the vic," she replied, her whole demeanor one of amused contempt, which made the hackles rise on the back of my neck. I wondered if she'd picked up the cop jargon on the streets of Chicago, or if, like me, she watched way too much television.

"I don't know," I said and glanced purposefully at my watch. "Was there something specific you wanted?"

Her body stiffened, and I felt some of the chummy atmosphere evaporate. "I picked up some info yesterday," she said, turning to shuffle through a sheaf of papers on the seat behind her. "Here. Thought you might find these interesting."

She shoved a fistful of photocopies at me. They appeared to be entries in some sort of book, and I threw her a surprised glance.

"Are these the sheriff's logs? They let you duplicate them?"

She shrugged one pudgy shoulder, but the smug expression on her face told me all I needed to know. "*Let* might not be the exact term I'd use." The self-satisfied smile faded, and she slapped one meaty thigh. "Believe it or not, underneath all this flab there's still a woman capable of exuding considerable Southern charm and persuasion."

"I'm impressed," I said, meaning it. I looked down at the half-dozen sheets of paper. "Find anything of interest?"

"Let's get out of this heat, okay?"

Before I had a chance to reply, she had tottered around on her high-heeled sandals and stood waiting for me to pop the lock on the passenger door. With a sigh, I hit the release, punched the air conditioning up a couple of notches, and slid my window all the way closed. I tried to conceal the feeling of annoyance I couldn't quite explain, even to myself, and watched my new "partner" drop heavily into the narrow bucket seat.

"Okay," she said, leaning across the console and taking the copies from my hand. "I didn't get all of them, of course, but these are the ones that show the most serious crimes investigated out at Fort Fremont in the past few months." She stabbed a finger at an entry about halfway down the first page, leaving a damp smudge next to the date. "See this one? Some kind of fight involving a bunch of teenagers. Doesn't look like there were any serious injuries, but it's kind of hard to tell from this."

"There aren't any names on this one," I said as she handed the papers back to me. I scanned through the other notations on the page. They listed traffic accidents, burglaries, and bar fights, all of which included not only the identities of the complaining parties but addresses as well.

"Musta been underage. Juvie offenders get their names withheld from public record."

"Then what good—" I began, but Gabby interrupted.

"I know, but keep going. It gets better."

I continued to read while icy air, pumped from the dashboard vents, created a welcome oasis from the blistering heat bouncing in waves off the long yellow expanse of the hood. I found a couple of disturbing-the-peace entries, one recovery of a stolen car, and a defacing private property which no doubt stemmed from the coat of graffiti covering the walls of the old fort. Beside me I could feel Gabby squirming around in her seat. Finally she reached across and again snatched the papers out of my hand.

"Here. Let me show you." She flipped to the next-to-last page and jabbed at an entry. "This one. Look at the date."

I leaned over to see where she was pointing and did a little mental math. "A week ago Wednesday. Two days before Cart disappeared."

"Bingo! See? It must have been a good-sized drug bust. Kids again mostly, I'd guess, but there must have been one or two grown-ups involved because we've got names."

"Anyone you recognize?" I asked.

Gabby shook her head. "I checked the morgue at the paper and found squat, so apparently they weren't big enough fish to warrant anything more than the usual couple of lines in the daily sheriff's report."

"So what good is any of this doing toward finding out what happened to Cart Anderson?"

"Nothing specific, I'll grant you. Not yet, anyway." The reporter wriggled around in the seat, settling herself more comfortably. "It's what we call 'background' in my biz." She hurried on, eager to prove the results had been worth her efforts. "We've established that Fort Fremont is a drug hangout, among other things. It gives you another theory of the crime."

"And you think the cops haven't already looked at this and discarded it in favor of nailing my hide to the tree?" I shook my head. "I think we probably could have pulled anyone of high school age off the street and gotten pretty much the same information."

I didn't realize how condescending and ungrateful my words had been until I turned to see Gabby's fierce brown eyes blazing at me from across the console.

"Look, toots, you came to me for help, as I recall. You don't like the quality of the answers you're getting, just remember how much you're paying for them."

"I'm sorry. I didn't mean for that to come out sounding so snotty."

She shrugged, and some of the anger left her face. Her stiffened shoulders relaxed, and she tucked a wayward strand of dull, straight hair behind one ear. "Don't worry about it. I guess with half the cops in the county breathin' down your neck, you're entitled to get a little cranky."

I smiled. She was right. I didn't have a lot of friends right at the moment. It didn't make sense to alienate the few who still clung to a belief in my innocence, no matter how improbable.

"So where do we go from here?" I asked.

"I had a little chat with the regular crime reporter," Gabby said. "Seems the cops have had their eye on the fort for some time. Used to be kids just hung out there and drank beer and had sex. Last few months the activity has picked up to the point where it was more than just neighbors complaining about noise. My guy says there was talk of their bringing in a couple of fresh faces from out of the area to go undercover, but he hasn't heard whether or not they ever got it off the ground."

"But how does that help us?" I repeated. "The last bust went down before Cart Anderson ever got to town."

Her voice carried a note of exasperation that made me feel like a complete moron. "The last one we know about. If they were working some kind of sting, they wouldn't exactly send out engraved invitations to the local media."

"So you think Cart wandered into this somehow? And what?"

"Who knows? Maybe he went out there to make a buy. Maybe some of the locals figured him for a narc, him bein' the new kid and all, and decided to take him out. Or at least beat the crap out of him."

I winced at her casual dismissal of the boy's possible fate. "Why do you assume Cart Anderson is into drugs?"

Her shrug spoke volumes about her experience with the seamier side of life she'd no doubt spent years investigating in the back alleys and projects of Chicago. "He's what—seventeen? Grew up around Miami? Hell, it'd be a miracle if he wasn't involved with the stuff on some level."

She had a point. In fact it dovetailed nicely with my own half-formed idea, the one which had popped into my head the day before. If the boy had gotten wind of what his life was going to be like with his dotty old grandmother and had decided to cut and run, he might have needed a hit of something while he worked out his plan. Maybe he'd run into someone out at Land's End who offered to help. He could have hitched a ride with one of them and headed back to Florida. He could even have offered to pay. I had a lot riding on my search for Cart's maternal grandfather. Maybe . . .

Only the soft purring of the T-Bird's big engine broke the silence for a couple of minutes while I considered whether or not to share my thoughts, mindful of my recent misgivings about how much of my fate I had placed in the hands of this woman I barely knew. But although I found her incredibly pushy and annoying at times, perhaps these were exactly the qualities I needed in an ally right at the moment.

In for a penny, a reedy little voice whispered inside my head.

"I have another theory," I said before I could change my mind.

Back home I stripped off the jacket of my suit and worked my way out of the silk tank I'd worn underneath. A wave of dizziness washed over me as I reached down to pull off my pumps, and I told myself it was because I hadn't eaten anything all day. I crossed to the refrigerator and studied its contents, lifting the lid on a covered casserole Dolores must have left for me. I couldn't deal with any more seafood, so I pulled the peanut butter from the cupboard, took a spoon from the silverware drawer, and dug out a scoop of extra-chunky. *Protein,* I told myself, and carried the jar into the bedroom and its empty drawers and closets.

Half an hour later I laced up my running shoes and trotted down the steps of the deck. I walked briskly across the wooden bridge which spanned the rippling dunes and paused in the soft sand to run through my preprogrammed series of stretches before heading off away from the Westin. I had pulled my hair into a ponytail and settled my old Braves baseball cap on my head, but I could still feel the power of the late-afternoon sun beating against my scalp in spite of a strong onshore wind. The beach was packed with tourists, their kids, and their dogs, and I had to zigzag around blankets, umbrellas, and coolers for the first few hundred yards. Finally, open sand stretched out in front of me. I kicked up the pace, my damaged left shoulder settling into its accustomed ache as my arms pumped in rhythm with my stride.

Running has always been my refuge. In punishing my body, pushing it to its limits and sometimes beyond, I've always been able to clear my mind of its frequent clutter of doubt and confusion. As I pounded down the beach on sand packed hard by the retreating tide, I found the magic formula had failed me. Though I had successfully shoved my legal problems into their proper mental storage compartment, images of Darnay pushed their way through the haze of sweat fogging my wraparound sunglasses.

How could he desert me like this? I had taken his sudden appearance the past spring, just at the moment I needed him most, as a promise, an unspoken commitment to the life we'd begun to build together in Paris. While I had laughingly rejected his half-hearted proposals of marriage, he'd told me one day he'd ask in earnest. I had almost made up my mind to accept. I'd thought at long last I'd be able to conquer the devastating loss of my husband and find some peace.

I rounded the point where a long finger of sand reached out across the Sound toward St. Helena and increased my pace. Tiny bursts of multicolored light danced in front of my eyes, and I shook my head to clear them away. Darnay had buried his note in a drawer in order to give himself maximum time to make his getaway. I could feel a growl of anger building in my chest at the arrogance of the man. Did he think I'd go trailing after him, weeping and begging him to come back? After all we'd been through, after all we'd shared, did he really know so little about me?

I had run through the burn, and the muscles in my legs trembled with the rubbery feeling which told me I had pushed my body too far. I forced myself to slow gradually, dropping into a lope, then a trot, and finally a brisk walk before kicking off my shoes and tossing my hat onto the sand. I turned and plunged into the sparkling surf.

The hell with him, I told myself as I surfaced, spluttering in the bath-warm ocean. *The hell with all of them.*

" 'He travels the fastest who travels alone,' " I shouted to a solitary pelican cruising low over the water. "Rudyard Kipling. 'The Winners.' " I swallowed the sob of despair trying to force its way from my lungs. "Two points," I whispered as I dived deep into the welcoming darkness of the sea.

As I jogged back to the house, showered and changed, and heated the casserole, I exchanged thoughts of Darnay for those of the recent events surrounding the disappearance of Cart Anderson. There were so many disparate threads, and I was trying to weave them into some sort of pattern which could explain the sea of trouble I found myself floundering in. By the time I settled onto the chaise on the screened porch, I felt as if I had at least a glimmer of understanding about the underlying currents which had been carrying me along since Darnay first spotted Cart Anderson tailing us.

Around me, twilight settled over the silent oaks. In the still night air, heavy with the remembrance of the day's punishing heat, the flare of the lighter stabbed into the darkness. Only three left in the pack, I'd noticed, as I carried my one rationed cigarette out to the porch. Decision time soon. In more ways than one. I picked up my cell phone from the wicker table next to me, speed-dialed Erik Whiteside, and leaned back to wait.

His "Hey, Hilton Head, what's up?" brought the usual smile to my lips.

"Hey, yourself. How's business?"

He didn't answer right away, and I wondered if I'd somehow struck a nerve. "It's been a little slow the past month." He sounded down.

"If this is a bad time, I can call you back." I savored the last lungful of smoke and stubbed out the cigarette.

"No problem. How's everyone down there?"

Fine. The conversational lie hovered on my lips, but I didn't voice it. Truth time. "I'm in some serious trouble, Erik, and I could use your help."

I knew my statement would tap into my former partner's conflicting loyalties: his friendship with me vying with his determination to stay out of harm's way. I had no right to put him in this position, but Alain Darnay's defection had left me little choice.

His firm response, however, carried no hint of doubt or equivocation. "Of course. Anything you need. What can I do?"

I exhaled the breath I'd been holding and smiled into the darkness.

Chapter Twenty-Two

THE RELIEF I FELT AT HAVING ERIK WHITESIDE BACK ON the job lasted until early the next afternoon.

I'd scrambled myself a couple of eggs and spent the morning lazing on the porch, the bulky Sunday edition of the *Island Packet* spread out around me. I'd promised myself a day of quiet solitude, a respite from the anxiety of the past week. On Monday I'd have to run the gauntlet of the sheriff's station and Detective Ben Wyler. For one day I wanted to put it all on hold. I'd just about decided to take myself off to the beach for a swim, tourists be damned, when the sound of a car pulling into the driveway sent me scurrying back inside.

I gazed down from the bay window in the kitchen as Red Tanner unwound his long legs from the patrol car, hitched his gun belt around on his narrow hips, and marched up the walkway to the front entrance. I met him there, the inside door standing open as I watched him through the screen.

"Good afternoon," I said, startling him so that he paused one step from the top.

"Geez," he said, "you scared the hell out of me." Despite the withering heat, the creases in his khaki-and-army-green uniform held their knife-edge crispness, and his boyish face betrayed no trickle of sweat.

"Business or pleasure?" I asked, swinging the screen door open and standing aside for him to enter.

He didn't reply, moving quickly down the hallway and up the steps into the kitchen. "Got a beer?" He swung the refrigerator door open and stooped to peer inside.

Off duty then. "Nope. Sorry." It was on the tip of my tongue to declare Darnay's preference for wine, but I managed to bite it back. "How about a tea?"

"Sure," he said, "thanks."

As I pulled out the pitcher, he crossed back down into the great room. I watched him unhook his belt laden with cuffs, nightstick, and the ever-present sidearm and drape it across the back of my white sofa. I carried his glass to the table in the breakfast alcove and turned to see him loosen the top button on his shirt.

"Make yourself at home, why don't you."

Red smiled, acknowledging the sarcasm, and rejoined me in the kitchen. He took a long swallow of tea and flopped down in one of the chairs. I settled in across from him.

"You ought to know, though," I continued in the same bantering tone, "I'm drawing the line at your taking off your shoes."

"I always knew you were a woman with standards." He drank again and set the glass back on its coaster.

"You didn't answer my question." I stifled the urge to cross to the drawer under the desk and retrieve one of my two remaining cigarettes. I had allowed myself only one after breakfast.

"You mean the 'business or pleasure' one?" He shrugged. "Both. Neither." He glanced across at my raised eyebrows. "I just wanted to see you. See how you were doing."

A dozen smart-ass remarks leapt into my head, but what I actually said was, "I'm scared." I avoided Red's eyes as I picked at a loose thread on the edge of the place mat in front of me. "Everything's falling apart, and I don't know how to stop it."

I could feel the treacherous tears rising in my throat a moment before my brother-in-law's hands settled over mine, stilling my trembling fingers.

"I want to help you," he said, so softly it was almost a whisper.

I forced myself to raise my head and look directly into his face. "But you can't."

He didn't deny it, but his voice when he spoke was calm. "Listen, this Wyler is a loose cannon, and everybody knows it. He came struttin' in here as if he owned the damn place. Big city cop. Gonna show the rednecks how it's done." He smiled, and I felt some of the fear settle. "No one's got any idea why the sheriff put him on when Morgan took his leave of absence, but he's not here to stay, I can guarantee you that."

I slipped my hands out from under his and dabbed at the single tear which had managed to leak out of the corner of my eye. "If no one trusts him, then how has he managed to jam me up like this? Half your buddies and half the town are convinced I murdered Cart Anderson and Miss Minnie Maude, either alone or in cahoots with Darnay."

The name wiped the smile from Red's face. "Is it true he's . . . ?"

I sat up straighter, anger once again rescuing me from turning into a weak-kneed, slobbering mess. "You mean, is it true he's gone? Hit the bricks? Taken a powder? Flown the—"

"Okay, okay," he said, again laying a restraining hand on my arm. "I didn't mean to get you all riled up." He paused long enough for me to get control of myself. "His taking off doesn't help your situation any. You can see how it looks to . . . outsiders."

"Of course I see how it looks," I snapped. "I'm not a moron. But the fact remains your hotshot detective doesn't have one damn shred of proof." I watched his lips crease into their familiar smile. "And what are you grinning about? You find something about this amusing?"

Red leaned back in his chair and shook his head. "Nope. I'm just enjoyin' the return of the real Bay Tanner. I wasn't quite sure how to deal with that weepy little Southern belle who popped up a few minutes ago."

I tried to resist the charm he and his brother had both inherited in spades, but it was no use. I knew what he was trying to do, and it was working. I drew a long breath and rose to cross to the desk. I whipped out my next-to-the-last cigarette and flicked the lighter. I turned back to the table and pointed the glowing tip at Red.

"And not a damn word about this, you hear? I'm entitled to a little something to take the edge off, and this beats the hell out of Prozac or a bottle of gin."

He held up his hands. "Hey, fine by me. It's your lungs." He picked up his empty glass and waggled it at me. "Refill?"

I poured us both tea and sat back down. "Okay, here's the deal. I have to go in there tomorrow and get grilled by this Wyler guy. If you really want to help, give me some tips about how to deal with him. Tell me exactly what evidence they have and how worried I have to be."

For a long moment he didn't speak. "I can't do that," he finally said, his eyes locked on to mine.

"Why not?"

"Because if I get booted out of the department I won't be able to help you at all. And that's what will sure as hell happen if anyone finds out I've been coaching you before an interrogation."

I sighed and crushed out my cigarette in the ashtray I'd carried over from the desk. "Okay, I understand what you're saying. But how about if I tell you exactly what happened, from the time I first encountered Cart Anderson until the morning they found Miss Minnie's body, and you can . . ."

"No!" He nearly shouted the word and reinforced it by jumping up from the table. "You can't tell me anything. I've already compromised the investigation by warning you about the DNA warrant and giving you a heads-up about the tip on your being at the old woman's house the night before she died."

"I'm not asking you to tell me anything," I began, but he was already shaking his head.

"If you reveal any details to me that might help Wyler, I'm bound to report them."

"Then what's the point of waltzing in here, all supportive and wanting to help? What the hell good are you?" I yelled, immediately sorry as I saw the cop mask slip back over his strong, familiar features.

"I'm your brother-in-law, your family. I'm offering you my moral support, my belief in your innocence." He sighed, and the anger slipped out of his voice. "I wish I could do more, but I can't. I just can't."

This time it was my hand reaching out to offer reassurance. "I know, Red. I understand. Really, I do."

He nodded, and the old teasing smile worked its way across his face. "You hungry?"

I corralled the fear which seemed to have been hovering somewhere near the center of my chest forever and shoved it viciously back into its hole. "Is the Pope Catholic? Does a bear . . ."

"Okay," he laughed, "I get the picture. How about Jump & Phil's?"

I could almost feel the soothing atmosphere of our favorite local pub, smell a giant burger with my name on it sizzling on the grill. "Let me get my shoes," I said, turning for the hallway.

We had lucked into an early afternoon lull as we settled ourselves at one of the outdoor tables and scooted around until we'd found the shade. The after-church brunch crowd had already retreated, and the tourists hadn't yet gotten hungry enough to drag themselves off the beach. I tossed my bag onto the opposite chair and propped my feet up. Red had left all his cop paraphernalia locked in his cruiser and looked almost casual, even in his uniform.

After we'd ordered the food and had sipped gratefully at our drinks, my brother-in-law hitched his chair closer to mine. He looked as if he was about to reveal something he really didn't want to, and I felt the now-familiar catch in my chest.

"What?"

He sipped from his mug of beer and sighed. "I hear you had a run-in with Lonnie Daggett out in front of the station the other day."

So much had happened in the meantime, I'd almost forgotten about that enigmatic encounter. "Yeah. He thinks I had something to do with getting his obnoxious brother bounced off the force."

"Did he threaten you?"

I tried to dredge up the conversation. "I guess you could call it that. He said something about hoping they nailed my ass this time. And that you guys weren't through with me. Which certainly proved to be prophetic, as things turned out." I leaned back as the waitress set our burgers in front of us. "Oh, and one day I'd wish I'd been a little nicer to the cops."

"Bastard," Red muttered.

"Hey, don't worry about it. His brother was an idiot. It doesn't surprise me he got himself canned."

Red bit into his cheeseburger, then wiped his fingers on his napkin. "Lonnie isn't entirely off-base about his brother."

"What the hell does that mean?"

"Tommy did get fired, and it was all done sort of under the table. One day he's here, next day he's history. Lot of speculation flyin' around."

"Speculation about what? I sure as hell didn't have anything to do with it!"

"Settle down." Red reached across and patted my arm, but I flung his hand away.

"Don't tell me to settle down. Every time I turn around the last couple of weeks, someone is accusing me of lying or double-dealing or . . ." I spluttered and lowered my voice, ". . . or of *killing* someone. I'm getting pretty damn sick of it!" I finished in a tight whisper which might as well have been a shout. Around me I could hear conversation drop to nothing at a couple of nearby tables.

"Bay, get a grip."

I stabbed a French fry into the little cup of mayonnaise on my plate and stared at my brother-in-law.

"Look, I'm sorry I brought it up, okay?" he said, the exasperation plain in his voice. "It's just there's been a lot of talk around about the Daggetts. I thought maybe you might know something I didn't."

"I don't know a damn thing other than they're both obnoxious, male chauvinist rednecks." I exhaled slowly and eased back in my chair. "If you want to know about Lonnie, why don't you ask Wyler? The two of them seemed attached at the hip the other day. I couldn't tell which one of them was enjoying ransacking my place more."

"Wait a minute! Are you telling me Lonnie Daggett helped Wyler execute the search warrant?"

His question puzzled me. "Sure. Grinning all the while. I think he gets off on pawing through women's underwear. Why? Is there some reason he shouldn't have been there?"

Red ignored my question. "Who else?"

"The fingerprint guy, but he came later." I tried to reconstruct the humiliating afternoon in my mind. "And a black deputy. I don't remember his name. I'm not sure anyone ever told me."

Red smiled absently at the waitress as she handed him the check. He reached back to pull his wallet from his hip pocket.

"Wait, I'll get it," I began, but he waved me off and dropped a twenty on the plastic-coated tablecloth.

"Was it Tate?" he said when we were once again alone.

"It could have been. I told you, I don't remember." I reached for my bag, thanking the gods when my rummaging fingers wrapped themselves around an unused packet of nicotine lozenges. I peeled off the foil and popped one gratefully into my mouth. "What difference does it make who searched my house?"

Red stood abruptly and slipped his sunglasses down over his eyes. "Because Lonnie's just a traffic cop. There's no way he should have been assigned to something as sensitive as that."

I trotted along behind him as he hurried toward the parking lot where we had left both cars. "Hey! Hold up!" I yelled at his retreating back. I increased my pace and caught up with him just as he yanked open the door of his cruiser. "Red, stop, damn it!" Even without being able to see his eyes behind the reflective glasses I could tell he was angry. "What's going on?"

"I'll let you know," he said, turning to slide behind the wheel.

I watched helplessly as he reversed the big Ford and sped off toward the Sea Pines Circle, leaving me standing alone in the driveway staring after him in utter frustration. If there'd been a rock handy, I would have pitched it at his retreating taillights.

I stomped back to the Thunderbird and tossed in my bag just as the opening strains of Beethoven's Ninth began to drift out of its depths. I fumbled for the cell phone.

"Yes," I snapped.

"Bay? It's Gabby. Where are you?" Her words came in excited whispers.

"I'm at Jump & Phil's. On the south end. Why?"

"Great! How long will it take you to get to the shopping plaza at Moss Creek?"

"About fifteen minutes. Why?"

"Meet me there. Hurry!" she said, and I was listening to silence.

My first instinct had been to tell both Red and Gabby Henson to go to hell, drive straight home, and bury my head under the covers. As appealing as that sounded, I found myself drifting down off the second of the two bridges that connect Hilton Head to the mainland and easing into the turnoff for the small cluster of businesses tucked in next to the entrance to Moss Creek Plantation. I spotted the nose of the reporter's disreputable Mustang convertible bracketed by two SUVs at the far end of the parking lot and swung in behind her.

Gabby climbed immediately out of her car, the billowing sleeves of some sort of flowing caftan making her look like an exotic bird about to take flight. "Don't park here! He knows your car."

I turned down the volume on the radio and leaned out. "What? Who knows my car?"

"Wyler!" she hissed in what she obviously thought might be something resembling a whisper.

I shot a quick glance over my shoulder. "Wyler? What's he got to do with anything?"

"That's why I called you." She moved around and dropped her huge handbag onto the floor, then let herself into the car. "Move around over by Gold's Gym. There's a lot of cars over there. Make sure you find a spot where we can keep an eye on the parking lot."

I gave serious thought to asking if she'd completely lost her mind, then shrugged and did as she instructed. I squeezed into a spot on the far side of the workout palace and cut the engine.

"Okay, that's it. I'm not moving another inch until you tell me what the hell is going on." I shoved the sunglasses up onto the top of my head and turned in the seat to confront her.

"Okay, okay. See, I was on my way back to the *Island Packet* office in Bluffton to check on some stuff with one of the guys I know over there, when this big-ass Lincoln blows by me on 170. I glance over, like you do sometimes, you know? And there's Detective Ben Wyler, big as life, tooling along, hot in conversation with some woman. So I dropped back and let him get ahead and followed them here. They were so deep into whatever they were talking about they never noticed me. They've been inside Do Si Do's ever since."

I glanced at the western-themed bar and restaurant and drew a long breath, making a concerted effort not to lose my temper. *She's only trying to help,* I told myself, but I wasn't sure that would be enough to keep me from decking her one if she didn't get to the point of this cloak-and-dagger nonsense, and soon.

"Why would you follow a man on his way to lunch? And what does it have to do with me?"

Gabby shook her head in exasperation. "Let me finish, okay? I had a hunch I knew who the babe was, but I had to make a couple of calls to confirm. The description fits her perfectly."

"Fits who? Gabby, I swear if you don't quit jerking me around . . ."

"Don't get your panties all in a twist, girlfriend. It's gonna be worth waiting for." The smug smile raised my blood pressure even higher, and I suppose my exasperation must have registered on my face. She held up a placating hand. "Okay, I'll spill it, although I hate you making me spoil the surprise. Your arch nemesis is having a cozy little tête-à-tête with none other than Judge Virginia Newhall."

I grappled with the name, and the significance of it hit just as Gabby Henson nodded and smiled.

"Yup, that's right, good ol' Judge Ginny, the obliging lady who signed all those warrants for him." She paused and added, "Now what do you suppose the two of them have to discuss that's so private they had to come all the way over here to talk about it?"

Chapter Twenty-Three

I don't remember how long we sat, the sun beating down on the open convertible, before Gabby finally broke the silence. "Do you mind puttin' the lid on this thing and turning up the air? I'm about to fry here."

Without acknowledging her request, I turned the car back on and raised the saddle-tan top, instructing Gabby to help me secure the latches. I punched buttons, and soon mist was forming on the closed windows as the vents pumped frigid air into the passenger compartment. Again the quiet settled over us as we stared straight ahead toward the empty Lincoln parked across the way.

"You calmed down some?" Gabby asked, her voice soft and measured, as if she were soothing a skittish horse.

"Yeah," I said, "I am. Sorry for the outburst."

"No problem. Ready to hear the rest?"

"There's more?" I managed a smile as I turned to face her. "I can hardly wait."

"Good girl." She wriggled around in her seat and tucked one pudgy leg up under her. "I've been doing some digging since we last talked, and the results have been quite interesting."

I marveled at how she could move from sounding like an uneducated country hick to a veteran city reporter in the blink of an eye.

Maybe it was part of her success that she could adopt a persona for every occasion. "How so?" I prompted.

"First off, there's a lot of head-scratching going on around the upper echelons of power around here. Lot of folks can't figure out how you went from fair-haired girl to murder suspect in such a short period of time."

"We should start a club," I said with a wry smile.

"Newhall and Wyler are both new around here, so some put it down to their bein' eager to make names for themselves."

"And they think they can do that by railroading me for crimes I had nothing to do with?" I shook my head. "You know what I don't get? Where are all my friends? And the Judge's? I know some of them were just parasites who sucked up to him and rode his coattails all those years, but what about the rest? We have real roots here, ties. People we've known our whole lives, family connections going back for generations." I blinked back the tears of frustration and betrayal I felt welling in my eyes. "Why isn't anyone jumping to my defense?"

Gabby reached across the console and patted my arm. "They're out there, kiddo, believe me. It's just everyone's so damned confused." She shook her head. "The minute they think they've got an answer figured out, another bombshell drops. You have to admit the evidence against you has been piling up pretty fast."

I shook my head even before she finished speaking. "No, don't you see? That's just it. There is no evidence, nothing concrete. Everything is circumstantial, full of *might haves* and *could haves* and *maybes*. Anonymous tips, hints, innuendoes. Why won't anyone give me the benefit of the doubt? As soon as they get the damned DNA results back from Columbia they're going to know I had nothing to do with it. Why the rush to judgment?"

"Here they come." Her sharp fingernails dug into my arm, then she reached for her bag on the floor. A moment later a series of clicks made me turn my eyes away from the couple who had paused for a moment just under the canvas roof of the covered patio. Gabby Henson had a 35mm camera with a huge telephoto lens pointed directly at them.

"What—?" I began, but she cut me off.

"Evidence. Insurance. Call it whatever you like."

I watched Detective Ben Wyler and a tall, angular woman step out of the shadows and cross the parking lot toward the dark blue Lincoln. Beside me, the constant whirring of the camera told me the reporter knew how to use it. I concentrated on the judge, although not much could be seen of her face at that distance. She had long blond hair wound into some sort of coil at the back of her head and the kind of posture which spoke of a desk job and little exercise. Painfully thin arms without the hint of a tan stuck out from the flowered, sleeveless blouse, and equally spindly legs flashed from beneath a hideous green cotton skirt. It looked as if her feet were shoved into white tennis shoes.

"Not exactly a fashion plate, is she?" Gabby read my mind with an ease I was becoming increasingly uncomfortable with as the camera continued to click away.

I studied Wyler as he opened the driver's door for the judge, then walked around to the passenger side and let himself in. "They don't exactly look like a pair of lovers, do they?" I mused, and my companion chuckled.

"That's not what I thought they were up to, although it's not a bad scenario. Still," she went on in the same amused voice, "it's not impossible. Sometimes there's no accounting for taste."

Neither of us spoke as the big car pulled off toward Route 278 and eased into the light traffic flowing toward Beaufort. I settled back in the seat, not realizing how many knots had been bunched in my shoulders until I felt them slump.

"So now what?" I asked.

Beside me, Gabby fiddled with the lens on the camera before dropping it into the bag at her feet. "Now we really start digging."

"What does that mean?"

She squirmed around and repositioned herself in the bucket seat before answering. "Up until now, this has been an intriguing little mystery, maybe the first thing that's really set my reporter's nose twitching since I came back here from Chicago, you know?"

I bit my lip and kept silent. The fact that her "intriguing little mystery" might land me in jail for the rest of my life apparently didn't qualify for concern.

"But this," she went on, enthusiasm lighting her eyes, "this could turn into a first-rate political scandal. The lead detective on a murder-kidnapping sneaking off to a clandestine meeting with the sitting judge on the case . . ." Her voice trailed off. I watched a hungry, almost rapacious look settle onto her face.

"Right up your alley, eh?"

"Yeah."

Despite her so-called reporter's instincts, she'd missed the sarcasm. "So do you think you'd have a better chance at a Pulitzer if they fry me or if I beat the rap? I don't want to stand in the way of your rising career path."

That one registered. "What? Oh, Jesus, Bay, don't be ridiculous! This is good, don't you see? There's definitely a conspiracy afoot, and we've got the proof." She nudged the bag at her feet. "Almost a whole roll of proof."

I shook my head. "Gabby, what you have are pictures of a man and woman out to lunch on a Sunday afternoon in broad daylight. Is there some law against a cop and a judge sharing a meal?"

"Actually there is. Well, maybe not a law exactly, but it's probably a breach of the canon of ethics. For both of them."

"No way. My husband worked for the state attorney general's office, and his brother is a cop. All of us socialized with my father and most of his political cronies at one time or another. You can't convict someone of corruption just for having friends."

"Maybe there's nothing in writing." Gabby wasn't about to let go of her theory quite so easily. "But what's the old saying about avoiding the appearance of evil? And the one about where there's smoke there's fire? This was *not* just an innocent lunch between friends." She laid her finger against the side of her nose. "Trust me."

I could feel the knots of frustration creeping back into the muscles of my neck. "I have to go," I said abruptly as I pulled my seat belt harness across my shoulder and clicked it into place.

For a moment Gabby didn't move. Then she shrugged and reached for the door handle. "Think about this," she said, her eyes fixed straight ahead. "You're cruising along, mindin' your own business, and suddenly you find yourself suspected of multiple crimes that could land you in Leath Correctional up at Greenwood for the rest of your life. Folks you thought you could trust find themselves thinking you might be guilty. Circumstantial evidence piles up pointing to you and your foreign boyfriend, and he takes off. The chief players in the case are meeting in secret, and you're about to be dragged in for official questioning." She snorted loudly and finally turned to stare squarely into my eyes. "If that doesn't spell conspiracy, I sure as hell don't know what does."

She pushed open the door and hauled herself to her feet, then leaned back into the car. "You can pretend I'm crazy if it makes you feel better, but I'm not lettin' this go. I said before that I'm looking for a ticket out of this dead-end job, and my gut tells me this is the story that could do it."

I tried to hold my tongue against the anger I felt rising in my throat, but it was no use. "Does it make a damned bit of difference to this little scenario of yours that I'm innocent?" I asked through clenched teeth.

"Probably not at first. The corruption's the real story. But it'll make a hell of a follow-up piece when we blow the bastards out of the water and you get off."

"I can't tell you how relieved I am."

"Good. See ya!" Gabby Henson hefted her bag onto her shoulder and slammed the door shut.

I watched her pick her way through the low shrubbery which divided the two parking areas and climb into her battered old Mustang. With a wave and the rattling roar of her worn-out muffler, she was gone.

Chapter Twenty-Four

I TOSSED ASIDE MY READING GLASSES AND THE OLD REX Stout mystery I'd mistakenly thought might take my mind off things and reached for the remote control. The Braves were down by three runs to the Cleveland Indians in the bottom of the eighth. I could just hear the Judge ranting about how they'd destroyed the sanctity of the game with interleague play, and I had to smile. You didn't want to get him started on the blasphemy of the designated hitter rule.

I rose from the white sofa, stretched, and wandered to stare out over the deck toward the ocean. The sun had lost some of its fierce, blinding power as evening encroached, and the light wind which had been rattling the palmettos had stilled. I pulled open one of the French doors and breathed deeply of the heavy, salt-laden air. Over the rolling dunes bathed in a soft, shimmering light I could hear the muted shouts of children still romping on the beach.

The sound of their laughter brought an old, familiar stab of pain to my chest. For months I had allowed myself to dream again of a family of my own, of a sturdy little boy with steel blue eyes, and an auburn-haired girl who would never have to worry about the proper way to pour tea or grow up thinking her mother didn't love her. After Rob's murder I had buried those fantasies so deeply in my soul I felt certain nothing—or no one—would ever stir that desire again.

Darnay had allowed me to hope, and for that I could never forgive him.

The sound of the doorbell cut through the stillness and straight into my gut.

I whirled, fear rising like a tide into my chest. My eyes shot to the pistol lying next to the remote on the sofa, and I hurried across the room to tuck it hastily behind one of the cushions. I couldn't explain exactly what my purpose had been in retrieving the gun from the hidden safe in my bedroom closet, except the sight of it within easy reach gave me comfort.

The bell rang again. I stepped into the entryway and pushed the button on the intercom.

"Yes?" I hoped the quaver in my voice hadn't registered with whoever stood outside my front door.

"Bay? It's me Erik."

"Erik? What are you . . . ?" I fumbled with the latch and yanked the door open.

"Hey!" he said, his grin bringing the first ray of hope I'd felt in almost a week.

"Hey, yourself! Come on in."

Erik Whiteside sidled past me into the house, stopping on the way to drop a comforting hand on my shoulder. "How are you holding up?"

His quiet voice and genuine concern almost unnerved me, and I had to swallow hard to keep myself from bursting into tears of relief.

"I'm okay," I said, meaning it for the first time in days.

"I would have called," he said, setting his small overnight bag and his ever-present laptop down on the floor, "but I thought you might tell me not to come."

When we'd all been convinced our fledgling inquiry agency might actually blossom into something full time, I'd gotten Erik a permanent decal to allow him past the guard gates and into Port Royal Plantation.

"I might have." I grinned up into his face and found an answering smile. "But I wouldn't have meant it." I led the way up the steps and into the kitchen. "Can I get you something? I'm afraid I'm out of beer."

"Tea's fine." He lowered his six-foot-plus frame onto one of the chairs at the glass-topped kitchen table and rested his elbows on the blue linen place mat. "So what's been happening? Bring me up to date."

I turned and set two glasses on the table, trying hard to recall when it was we'd last spoken. It startled me to realize it had been only the day before.

"Well, not much, really." I told him about my conversation with Red over lunch and his strange reaction when I'd mentioned the names of the deputies who'd searched my house.

"No idea why that might have set him off?" Erik slugged back iced tea and waited.

"He just seemed surprised. The fact that I had a run-in with Daggett and then he turned up with Wyler didn't strike me as all that odd, although it certainly pissed me off. But it's a small force. I just assumed everybody probably has to do double-duty a lot of the time."

"Still," Erik said, and the significance of that one word wasn't lost on me.

"I know. Red must have some suspicions about something, but he didn't share them with me." I paused to sip from my glass. "And then I got this call from Gabby Henson, the reporter I told you about? Apparently she thinks Wyler's having lunch with the lady judge who signed the warrants they served on me constitutes another Watergate or something."

Erik pressed me for details, and I gave him as close to a verbatim account as I could. I'd never have the skill of the fictional Archie Goodwin who could rattle off lengthy conversations word for word in his reports to his boss, the elephantine but brilliant Nero Wolfe, but my memory's pretty good.

"I think she may be onto something there," Erik said when I'd finished.

"Really? You know I'm the farthest thing from naïve and trusting, but I have a hard time believing in all this conspiracy stuff. Do you have any idea how many people would have to be involved to pull off something like that?"

Erik stood and crossed to the refrigerator where he refilled his glass from the pitcher. He leaned against the counter, his usually kind, open face puckered in a frown. He looked good, tanned and healthy, the navy blue shorts exposing his long, muscled legs. He seemed to be studying his feet encased in worn Topsiders before he finally looked up.

"Sometimes it isn't paranoia. Sometimes they really are out to get you."

I tried to think of a witty reply and failed. "You haven't said why you're here." I hoped it didn't sound like an accusation.

Erik rejoined me at the table, although it seemed he had a hard time meeting my eyes. "I spent most of the night online tracking down some of the information you asked me for." He sighed and shook his head. "I didn't much like what I found."

The relief I'd felt at my former partner's arrival seeped away like sand through a child's fingers. I cast a glance at the desk drawer which held the last of my pack of cigarettes and folded my hands primly in front of me to quell the urge. I drew in a calming breath and exhaled slowly.

"Tell me," I said.

We talked and argued through most of the evening. I grilled tuna steaks and tossed a salad, a simple dinner which allowed me to keep my mind firmly fixed on the conversation. Cleanup took about five minutes, and we carried our after-dinner drinks out to the relative coolness of the screened area of the deck. The wind had kicked up again, and the coppery smell of an approaching storm drifted to us from the ocean. I set my cup of Earl Grey down on the wicker table and settled onto the cushioned love seat, pulling my legs up under me.

"So you're saying this was planned right from the very beginning, that's your theory?"

Erik blew across his steaming mug of coffee and nodded. "That about sums it up."

"You're saying Cart Anderson deliberately let us spot him, let us manhandle him in front of witnesses. That's what got the whole thing started, and you think it was intentional."

"If you'd get off the idea this kind of stuff only happens in the movies, I would think you of all people would see the logic of it. You're the bean-counter, the obsessive-compulsive." He lowered his voice and grinned. "And I mean that in the nicest possible way."

I loved how Erik could always defuse a situation with some light, offhand remark like that. "Of course you do. So the kid set me up right from the jump? Staged his own disappearance and planted blood in the car to implicate Darnay and me?"

I flinched inwardly at the mention of his name but forced myself to keep my face from showing it. Up to that point we had somehow managed to avoid any mention of my vanished lover. Even in our phone conversations following Alain's desertion, Erik hadn't pressed me for details. I wasn't sure if it was because he didn't want to make things tougher for me or he just really didn't want to know.

I forced my mind back to the discussion at hand. While I had arrived at much the same conclusion as Erik only a couple of days before, my assessment of Cart's motives had been entirely different from his.

"Once I found out who his other grandfather is, it all fell into place. They couldn't get you one way, so they're trying something else."

My head was shaking even before he finished the sentence. "No, Erik, that's the part I can't get past. What good does it do them to get me convicted of a crime? I'd still have control of my box at the bank in the Caymans. I could still expose them any time I wanted to."

"But you couldn't, don't you see? First off, you have to be there in person. Bring the key, give the password, submit to that retinal-image-scan thing. You can't do that if you're locked in a state prison."

In my phone conversation of the day before I'd spilled the whole thing to Erik: the papers I'd stolen from the Grayton's Race office that last horrible summer, my trip to Grand Cayman, and how the security system at the bank worked. All of it. Almost.

"Besides," he went on, "you'd be totally discredited. Even if you did figure out you'd been railroaded and somehow managed to get to the papers you'd stashed, who'd believe you? You'd be a convicted felon, your credibility shot to hell."

It had the ring of truth to it, and yet something in me refused to accept the possibility that the men who had engineered the Grayton's

Race scam, the men who had been the architects of my husband's murder, could reach out after so much time to weave such a complicated web to insure my silence.

"They can't just . . . kill you." Erik avoided my eyes and concentrated instead on the high tops of the loblolly pines whipping in the rising wind of the approaching storm. "You told their lawyer, that Hadley Bolles guy, you'd made arrangements for it all to be revealed if anything ever happened to you. This way, nothing ever triggers that fail-safe."

Thunder rumbled in the distance, and a sharp streak of lightning lit up the sky out over the ocean. I sipped tea and pondered his scenario.

"It sounds way too convoluted," I finally said. As I downed the last of the tea, the first dime-sized drops plopped onto the dusty deck. "I'm just not buying it. There has to be some other explanation."

I didn't hear Erik's reply over the continuous roll of thunder and the pounding sheets of rain blown sideways by the screaming wind. It felt as if the temperature had dropped ten degrees in a matter of seconds. Though the slant of the roof protected us from the worst of the weather, I soon found myself shivering in my T-shirt and cotton shorts.

"Let's go in," I said, untangling my legs from the love seat. "I'm freezing."

Erik followed me into the great room and closed the door, shutting out the noise of the storm. I crossed to the fireplace and touched a long match to the wood I kept laid out on the grate for just such chilly evenings. The dry kindling caught immediately, and I sat down on the raised hearth trying to capture the first flicker of warmth. My partner settled himself on the sofa.

"More coffee?" I asked, but he shook his head. "Then tell me about Cart's grandfather." I rubbed my arms and moved down to the floor, propping two cushions behind me so I could stay close to the fire.

Erik sighed and leaned forward, his elbows resting on his knees. "Cuban. Came as part of the Mariel boat lift back in the late seventies."

"I remember something about that. Some cockamamie idea of the Carter administration, wasn't it?"

"Right. They wanted to get people out of Cuba and negotiated some sort of deal with Castro. Everyone in the Cuban expatriate community was thrilled until it became apparent they'd been tricked. All he'd done was empty out his prisons and asylums and send every murderer, drug dealer, and rapist on an all-expenses paid, one-way trip to America."

"And we just took them in."

"Didn't have much choice. They tried to process them through the naval base at Key West and weed out the really dangerous ones, but a lot slipped through the net. I had to dig really deep to come up with the connection to the Anderson kid, but I'm pretty confident in my information. Juan Luis Hermano. Ring any bells?"

"Nope."

Though I'd gone through most of the contracts and deeds I'd stolen from the office at Grayton's Race and eventually stashed in the Gellenschaft Bank of Grand Cayman, I hadn't studied each and every piece of paper. The name wasn't one I recalled, but that didn't mean it hadn't been there. Or been concealed behind one of the dozens of dummy corporations connected with the project.

"The guy owns huge chunks of Dade County real estate and lots of other legitimate businesses. He's been targeted by the feds a couple of times for connections to organized crime and drug trafficking, but nothing sticks." Erik kicked off his shoes and swung his legs up onto the sofa, then leaned back and tucked his hands behind his head. "He has lots of partners, many of whom share his shadowy past. It's not a very original story, I guess."

"So Geoff Anderson married Hermano's daughter?"

"Right. Juan managed to bribe enough people to get his wife and kids brought over from Havana sometime in the eighties. But the poor guy couldn't get himself a son to carry on the family business, so he had to rely on his three daughters' husbands. All his grandchildren are girls, too, except for Geoff's son, this Carter kid." He rolled onto his side and propped himself up on one elbow. "At least as far as I could track the records."

I closed my eyes and tried to conjure up an image of Geoffrey Anderson as I'd known him in my childhood: tall and devastatingly handsome in his Citadel uniform as he escorted his mother, Millicent, up the steps to Presqu'isle's verandah. My childish heart had been his for the taking from the first moment I saw him. I had yet to forgive myself for allowing that girlhood silliness to cloud my judgment so disastrously more than twenty years later.

Suddenly that idyllic scene dissolved into the terrifying picture of the last time I'd seen him, fire spewing from the collapsed welcome center at the Grayton's Race site, his blackened hands clawing at the narrow window too tiny to allow his escape. I gasped at the memory, and Erik jerked himself upright.

"Bay? What is it?"

I didn't trust myself to speak, shaking my head and swallowing hard to regain control. I knew I'd done all I could to save Geoff that horrible summer night, despite his revelations about his involvement in Rob's murder. I studied the tiny burn scars on my hands, proof I hadn't just let him die.

Eventually Erik settled back onto the sofa, and we sat in silence, the rain easing off to a few splatters against the windows of the French doors, then stopping altogether. The crackle of the wood in the fireplace had also settled into a soft hiss, and the room grew warm as the wind subsided. I reached up and slid the glass fire doors closed.

"So what does all this prove?" I asked, pulling myself into a modified lotus position. "I mean, it's amazing how much information you managed to find, but I still don't see how it's going to get me out of this mess I'm in."

" 'Knowledge is power.' "

I watched Erik's lips twitch, then burst into a wide smile.

"Oh no, not you, too!" I shook my head in mock despair.

"Come on, let's have the citation." He swung his bare feet back onto the carpet and regarded me expectantly.

"Francis Bacon, but I don't remember the work. What brought this on?"

His smile dimmed. "I figured if I was going to be hanging out with you and the Judge for an extended period of time I'd better be prepared to play the games. All of them."

"Hanging out . . . ?" I began before the full meaning of his words struck home. "You mean . . . ?"

"Yup. I'm here for the duration."

"But what about your job? And Mercer?" I couldn't quite grasp this sudden change in my former partner. Or maybe *former* wasn't any longer the right word.

"Look, I know I should have talked to you about this, but it all happened kind of fast. The owners of the store are retiring, and they sold it to some jackass kid with lots of daddy's money and not a brain in his head. I stuck it out for a couple of weeks, but this jerk wants to change direction, undo everything I've worked at to make the place as successful as it is." Erik shook his head. "Wants to concentrate on selling MP3 players and PDAs and plasma screen TVs, get out of the computer business altogether. Even if he hadn't decided to turn the whole thing on its head, I couldn't work for the little weasel."

"So . . . what? You quit?"

"Yeah. Yesterday was my last day."

"Why didn't you tell me? When I called." I reached across to pat his arm. "God, Erik, I'm really sorry."

His wonderful smile lit his face again as he said, "You don't know the half of it. You may end up being a lot sorrier in a few minutes."

"What does that mean?"

His eyes roamed around the room, refusing to meet my own. "Well, see, I hadn't really made any firm plans about what to do next, you know? I had a lot of paid vacation days coming, part of my severance package, so I figured I'd just hang around, sleep in, maybe play a little tennis." He paused and studied his hands, clasped tightly in front of him. "But then when you called last night, it all came together. Especially after I realized how much trouble you could really be in. So I just thought, I mean, I was hoping . . ." He swallowed and hunched his shoulders. "I wondered . . ."

"If the job as the resident computer whiz of Simpson & Tanner, Inquiry Agents, was still open?"

He nodded.

"What about Mercer? What does she think about all this?"

"We sort of had a parting of the ways. Nothing serious. We just don't seem to be on the same wavelength anymore. We still talk once in a while, but it's not, you know, like it was before."

I didn't know whether to be sad or happy. I'd never envisioned Erik and my half fifth cousin, so different in temperament and outlook, as having what it took to sustain any kind of permanent relationship. I smiled to take any criticism, implied or otherwise, out of my next words.

"I think that's probably a good thing. In the long run, anyway." I straightened my shoulders and smiled. "So now what? You know the agency isn't exactly raking in money. In fact, we haven't had a case since Gray Palmer, and that didn't really qualify."

Erik winced at the memory of the death of his old college drinking buddy and the bloody aftermath of our investigation. "I know. But I can get a job down here, something in computers, until we really get this thing cranking." He looked squarely into my face. "That's if you still want me."

Just in case the wide grin on my face didn't adequately convey my feelings, I scooted across the white carpet and threw my arms around his neck.

I rose and walked toward the kitchen, pausing next to Erik's slim overnight bag where it still rested on the floor of the entryway. "Is this all you brought?" I asked.

"I have another suitcase in the car," he said, following me up the three steps into the kitchen. "The rest of my stuff is still at the apartment. My lease isn't up until the end of next month, so I've got time to find a place. And a job."

"You'll stay here until then," I said in a statement I hoped would get no argument and smiled when Erik simply said, "Okay. Thanks."

I pulled the iced tea pitcher from the refrigerator and filled two glasses. "Not much in the way of a celebratory drink, but it's all I've got. Here's to beginnings." We clinked rims and drank.

"Thank you, Bay," Erik said in a somber voice, and I waved him to silence.

I didn't want anything to squelch the mood of euphoria that had settled over me. Darnay had deserted me, but Erik had come back. *One door closes and another one opens,* I thought, not giving a damn who'd said it or where. As he clattered down the front steps to retrieve his suitcase and I carried the smaller bag toward the guest room, I felt a lightness of spirit I hadn't experienced in a long time.

I hummed as I made up the bed and set out towels in the adjoining bath. The glorious bubble of hope lasted until I'd said goodnight to Erik and settled myself into my own king-sized bed, as relaxed and ready for sleep as I'd been in days. As I lay there, feeling comforted by his presence just down the hall, I heard the rumble of thunder boom again out over the ocean. By the time the sheets of rain had begun pounding the weathered boards of the beach house, I had already slipped into what would prove to be the last untroubled sleep I would know for quite some time.

Chapter Twenty-Five

"The body washed up on the beach just a few houses down from Mrs. Bleeker's place. Some early morning fishermen found it just before sunrise."

Though I heard my father's voice clearly enough, the words failed to register in my sleep-fogged brain. "I don't understand," I said for the second or third time as I rubbed at my gritty eyes and squinted toward the numbers on the clock beside the bed.

The phone had jerked me awake while only a feeble, watery light seeped through the crack in the heavy drapes hanging across the French doors of my bedroom. I finally managed to bring the time into focus: 6:27. I swung my feet onto the floor and padded to the closet to pull on a robe.

"Slow down, Daddy," I said, stifling a yawn. "And take it easy. You sound all out of breath."

"Wake yourself up, girl, and pay attention! This is the body of a young man, do you understand me? Most likely a teenager."

"Carter Anderson?" The question seemed no more than a vague whisper to my own ears, but the Judge must have heard it.

"No way to tell, not just yet. But if you don't think that bastard, Wyler, isn't all over this like ticks on a coonhound, you're sadly mistaken."

"Hang on a minute."

I carried the phone with me into my bathroom and laid it on the marble counter while I splashed cold water over my face. I grabbed two aspirin from the medicine cabinet and downed them in a preemptive strike against the pain I could feel building at the base of my neck.

I picked up the phone and moved back into the bedroom. I flung open the drapes and stared out over the dune to the beach littered with driftwood and debris tossed up by the storms which had rumbled through the night before. I shuddered at the mental image of a waterlogged body, long strands of dripping seaweed plastered against its face . . .

"Damn it, girl, where are you?" I heard my father's booming voice blare from the handset I had been holding close to my chest.

"Sorry," I said. "I'm here. What do you want me to do?"

I seemed to have lost all ability to think rationally, to assess the situation and decide on a course of action. For the first time since I'd convinced myself I'd come to grips with Rob's murder, I felt completely lost. I looked longingly at the bed, remembering those days right after his death when it had been my refuge from the unthinkable pain, both physical and emotional.

The Judge's tone softened. "Get hold of yourself, Bay. We don't know for certain it's the Anderson boy, although the coincidence would be too much to credit. Red's on the scene and will keep me informed. I'll know as soon as they do."

I turned from the window and tried to focus. What day was it? I closed my eyes and concentrated. *Monday!* The realization sent a wave of panic washing over me.

"I'm supposed to meet Wyler at the sheriff's office today," I blurted out, and I knew my father heard the fear in my voice. "What am I going to do?"

"The first thing you need to do is calm down, sweetheart. I'm going to wait a little bit and get in touch with Law. We'll put our heads together and decide what's best to do. Don't worry."

Don't worry! I almost laughed at the absurdity of it.

"I mean it, daughter. Get yourself together and wait until you hear from me. Bay? Are you listening to me?"

Across the hall I heard the rush of water in the guest bath. "Erik's here," I said into the phone.

"Erik? Whiteside? What on earth is . . . ?"

"He quit his job. He's moving down here and coming back to the agency. I told him it was okay."

The silence stretched out for several long seconds before my father finally said, "Good! I'm glad you're not alone in this. Let me talk to him."

"He's in the shower. I'll have him call." I paused, a small part of my brain finally kicking into gear. "Why can't they identify the body right now? They've had pictures of Cart plastered all over the state ever since he went missing." This time the pause lasted so long I thought we might have been cut off. "Daddy?"

His heavy sigh sent shivers of fear racing along my arms. "There's no good way to say this, honey. Most of the face is gone."

My legs no longer felt able to hold me, and I dropped onto the bed. "From being in the water?" A picture of Erik's friend, Gray Palmer, flashed into my mind. He, too, had died horribly in the ocean just a few miles away.

Again the Judge's hesitation threatened to overwhelm me. "No. He died from a shotgun blast to the head."

I made tea and carried it back into my bedroom, slid open the French door, and stepped out onto the deck. Perhaps it was the caffeine or the quiet normality of early morning joggers pounding along the beach in the distance, but it took only a few minutes for me to regain control of my senses. I set the mug on the railing and reached into the pocket of my robe. I pulled out the last Marlboro and sighed contentedly as the lighter flame ignited the tobacco. A thin thread of smoke spiraled lazily upward toward the overhanging limbs of the stately live oak that guarded the house.

I don't know how long I stood there locked in thought before the sound of Erik's voice drifted over to me from the other end of the porch. "Bay? Is the house on fire or have you taken up smoking again?" He approached tentatively as if I might cut and run.

"Guilty," I said, exhaling in the direction of the dunes.

His hair was still wet from the shower, and I could smell the citrusy scent of his aftershave. "Did I hear the phone earlier? Around six-thirty?" he asked.

I knew I'd have to tell him sooner or later, but I'd hoped to have more time to get my own thoughts in order. "My father." I inhaled deeply on the cigarette and reached down to cinch the belt of my robe a little tighter. I'd forgotten I was completely naked underneath, and I used my free hand to gather the lapels across my chest.

"Trouble?" He turned to lean his elbows on the railing and gaze out over the ocean.

His reaction when I told him surprised me, or else he was getting really good at hiding his feelings. Only a few months before, Erik had been eager to sever his connection with the grisly, often dangerous business we'd begun together. On that still, perfect, July morning he seemed unmoved by the horror of a young man's murder. I took a moment to mourn his loss of innocence before I spoke.

"I've been trying to decide what to do. About this meeting I'm supposed to have with the detective this morning."

"What did the Judge advise?"

"To wait until he talks to Law Merriweather. And see if Red reports in with anything conclusive."

Erik turned and leaned his back against the rail. "I don't remember you bein' real good at waiting."

His grin forced an answering smile to my lips, and I felt some of the tension ease from my neck and shoulders. I dropped the remains of the cigarette into the cold tea at the bottom of my mug and searched his eyes as I spoke.

"Right. I'm thinking I need to disappear for a while."

I expected shocked outrage, some sort of outcry against my trying to elude the authorities. Instead, Erik nodded slowly. "Maybe that's not such a bad idea." He paused before adding, "Worked for Darnay."

I opened my mouth to protest, but what could I have said? He was absolutely right, and I had no defense against the implied accusation. Alain had vanished back into the shadowy netherworld of his undercover life and left me as the sole available suspect for the cops to focus on. Whether it had been out of fear or necessity—or guilt—hardly mattered any more.

"Where would you go?" Erik asked when I failed to respond.

"I haven't thought that far ahead. I just think it would make sense for me to be out of touch, at least until this . . . latest thing gets sorted out."

"How long before the DNA results get back from Columbia?"

The question caught me off guard. "I don't know. Let me think." I did a quick mental recap of the events of the past week, shocked at how much had happened to me in such a short amount of time. "Tuesday," I finally said. "They took the swab from me last Tuesday. I think Red told me it would take at least a week or two depending on how backed up they were at the testing lab."

"Well, let's assume they're going to kick it up to the top of the priority list if the body turns out to be Carter Anderson. That means it could be as early as tomorrow."

"You're right, and it can't be too damned soon for me. The test is going to exonerate me." I watched the frown crease Erik's face. "What? You have a problem with that?"

He shook his head. "Geez, Bay, get serious. What if I'm right about who's behind all this? You think they can't buy someone off to alter the lab results?"

I stared at him in disbelief. The idea had never once occurred to me. I had placed all my hope on the scientific infallibility of the DNA process. "That's not possible! How would they . . . how could they find out . . . ?" I stumbled to a halt.

I slumped against the railing. Why did I resist believing the bastards who had murdered my husband, engineered the biggest money-laundering scheme in the history of the state, and corrupted a man I had once idolized were above bribing whoever they needed to in order to guarantee my silence?

I rubbed my hand across my forehead. "Wait a minute, though," I said, a new thought leaping into my mind. "If your Juan Hermano is behind all this, he wouldn't kill his own grandson. I can believe a lot of things about these people, but I won't buy in to that. Cart Anderson is his grandfather's future. No. That scenario won't wash."

Erik sighed. "I agree. I don't know how to get around that. Unless the body isn't Cart's?"

"But if this is a setup to get me, it doesn't make any sense for them to kill some stranger. If they're trying to bury me with the fight in the parking lot and the blood in his car, it only works if the body is Carter Anderson."

Erik ran a hand through his short blond hair. "I know. It doesn't make a whole lot of sense. We don't have enough critical data to operate with here." He sighed. "But I still think it would be a good idea for you to take a powder for a while. At least until they get a positive ID."

"The Judge will have a fit."

Erik smiled. "I can sell him on it. I'll tell him it all got to be too much, and you took off to clear your head. Sort of a modern-day fit of the vapors. You've got your cell, right? I can keep you up-to-date with what's going on. And if your dad and Mr. Merriweather decide you need to show up for this interview with the detective, you can hightail it back." He paused. "I'm assuming you're not going far."

I opened my mouth to answer, but he waved me off.

"Wait! Don't tell me. That way I won't have to lie about it when they ask me."

"Good plan, since you're such a lousy liar anyway." I smiled, and Erik nodded. "Can I borrow the Expedition? My convertible is pretty recognizable around here."

"No problem." He glanced at his watch. "It's almost seven-thirty. Why don't you get dressed, and I'll rustle up some breakfast. I think the sooner you get on the road the better."

"Right." I turned and stepped back into the bedroom. If I'd had more clothes on, I probably would have hugged him in gratitude for his calm strength and unwavering belief in me. Instead I pushed the door closed and headed for the shower.

I decided I liked the view from high above the fray in Erik Whiteside's mammoth vehicle. *I could get used to this,* I thought as I whizzed past the off-ramp for 170 and the turn toward Beaufort. Besides, the unfamiliar controls forced me to concentrate on my driving and kept my mind off more unpleasant topics.

Past the sprawl of Sun City, a gaping hole in the otherwise solid phalanx of pine trees revealed the faux-antebellum buildings of the New River campus, the University of South Carolina's most recent expansion. On the right I could see, next to the Wal-Mart Superstore, construction underway for another auto dealership joining the half dozen already hunkered down along the highway. Progress. I shook my head and pushed on toward the interstate.

I didn't remember making the decision to seek refuge with my old college roommate, Neddie Halloran, Savannah's most sought-after child psychologist. The flamboyant, Boston-Irish redhead would be in her office in an old converted Victorian fronting one of the city's picturesque squares. Maybe I could help her receptionist occupy the kids and anxious parents in the waiting room. Or perhaps I'd just wander the tree-lined streets or take a horse-and-carriage tour. Whatever I found to occupy my time, I'd be out of reach of Detective Ben Wyler, at least for a while. Erik would let me know if anything needed my attention.

I lucked into a parking space on the street in front of Neddie's office. I stepped down onto the sidewalk and reached in my bag for the pack of cigarettes I'd picked up at the gas station on my way off the island. I told myself I was entitled to some comfort, but I knew my old friend would pitch a fit. Even I was beginning to doubt my own assurances I could quit again whenever I wanted to. Resting my back against the expansive fender of the Expedition, I tried to force myself to relax.

Twenty minutes and another Marlboro later, I smiled as Neddie whipped her pearl gray Mercedes into the driveway of the old house and pulled around to the back. I wasn't sure she'd spotted me until I saw her march down the concrete, her bright hair catching the dappled rays of early morning sun filtering through the branches of the live oaks. The deep fuchsia of her linen suit nearly matched the tumbling sprays of bougainvillea that lined the narrow drive.

"Where in the hell did you get that monster?" Neddie asked by way of greeting. "Please don't tell me you gave up your wonderful little T-Bird for this gas-guzzling environmental disaster on wheels." Before I had a chance to defend myself, she wrapped me in an exuberant hug and stepped back. "And you're smoking again. You reek of it. Good God, woman! Do we have to have another session about addictive personality? I know you get my insightful commentaries for free, but—"

"Neddie, shut up for a second, will you?" Her mouth snapped shut, and I laughed. "Whatever happened to, 'Hi, how's it going, nice to see you'?"

The woman I loved like a sister hugged me again. "Hi! How's it going? Nice to see you." She paused at my smile. "You look like hell."

"Not exactly what I had in mind, but close."

"Come on in, and I'll fix you some tea." Neddie linked her arm with mine and dragged me toward the front steps. "I don't have any patients until eleven, so I'm free to shrink your head for an hour or so. Think that'll be enough time?"

I stepped back while she unlocked the massive oak front door and led me through her cluttered waiting room to the back of the house. Modernized without destroying its turn-of-the-century details, Neddie's office with its large bay window and pitted wood floors reflected her own special blend of brash New England practicality and the warmth and charm of her adopted South.

"Sit," she ordered, tossing her briefcase onto the desk and disappearing into the closet she'd converted to a multitude of uses, including a coffee room.

I dropped into one of only two chairs designed to hold an adult and settled back. For the first time since the Judge's call had awakened me, I felt safe. I relaxed into the silence, my face turned toward the soft sunlight falling through the tall windows as I listened to Neddie running water and rattling cups out of the cupboard. I felt my eyes drifting closed in lazy contentment when Beethoven jerked me back to reality.

With a hand trembling just slightly, I pulled my cell phone from my bag. The readout told me the call was originating from my house. I cleared my throat.

"Hey, Erik, what's up?" For a moment I thought we might be in one of those dead zones where the signal is too weak, because he didn't reply. "Erik? Can you hear me?"

His voice, tight with fear, boomed in my ear. "We've got a problem."

"What's the matter?" I swallowed hard and closed my eyes as if anticipating a blow. It came almost immediately.

"I went hunting for the beach chairs you keep under the deck."

I had no idea where this was going, but the quaver in his voice told me I wasn't going to like the destination.

"And?"

"And I tripped over what looked like a bundle of old rags under there, wrapped around something heavy."

To this day I don't know why it hadn't occurred to me to search for it. Even after the Judge's predawn revelations, I didn't want to believe Erik's theory. But I should have. And I should have anticipated this as their next move. Even then I didn't want to say it out loud, didn't want to make it real by putting it into words. I made Erik do it.

"What is it?" I asked calmly.

He paused for only a moment. "An old shotgun," he said. "Wrapped up in a bloody towel."

Chapter Twenty-Six

Erik's second call came as I was barreling back up I-95, the cruise control on the Expedition set at eighty, and smaller, slower vehicles scattering before me like a flock of birds fleeing a charging cat.

I'd set the cell phone on the seat beside me, and I fumbled with the buttons while trying to keep the hurtling SUV under control with just one hand. I managed a fleeting thought of absolution for all those drivers I'd cursed out over the years for talking while their cars were in motion. Sometimes, I realized, it couldn't be helped.

"Hey, where are you?" Erik's voice sounded tinny, and there was a slight echo after every word.

"I'm on 95 just passing the Eighth Air Force museum. What's the matter?" A crackling sound made the next part unintelligible. "Say again. You're breaking up."

"I said I just spoke to the Judge. He and Mr. Merriweather want you to go straight to Presqu'isle."

"Why?"

"Detective Wyler's called off your meeting for today. Your father thinks he wants to wait until after they identify the body."

I blew past a silver BMW sports car, top down, and spared a moment of nostalgia for my own lost Z3. I'd loved that car. *Maybe I should think about trading in the T-Bird for one of these babies,* I thought, patting the steering wheel of the Expedition. *No one would dare mess with me in a tank like this. Or maybe a Hummer . . .*

Then the memory of the narrow road between Charleston and Beaufort flashed before me, and I realized it didn't really matter what kind of car you drove or how many guns you carried or how careful or smart you were. If they wanted to get to you, they could. Directly or in some hideously devious way . . .

"Bay? Did you hear me?"

I forced myself to focus. "Yes, I heard you. What do they want?"

"For all of us to put our heads together on this thing, I guess. Have a plan in place when . . . in case . . ."

"The body is Cart Anderson's, and Wyler comes to arrest me this afternoon," I finished for him.

"Something like that. You sure you don't want to stay disappeared? I told them I wasn't sure if I could reach you."

"No, but thanks." I sighed and pulled around a lumbering eighteen-wheeler. "I should be there in about an hour."

"Your call. I'll head out then myself in a couple of minutes. See you there."

"Fine. Thanks."

I managed to punch the disconnect button with my thumbnail and tossed the phone back onto the seat beside me. So I'd been granted a reprieve. Temporary at best, I told myself. Sooner or later Detective Ben Wyler and I would be eyeing each other across a table in an interrogation room at the sheriff's office. I just hoped I wouldn't be in handcuffs and an orange jumpsuit.

The picture of him and the lady judge popped into my mind as the three northbound lanes narrowed to two, and I sailed across the Savannah River and back into South Carolina. If Erik was right . . . And if Gabby Henson was right . . . I pulled a cigarette from my bag and lowered the window. That would mean both Wyler and Newhall had been bought and paid for by Cart Anderson's drug-dealing grandfather. The scenario made perfectly good sense, and again I asked myself why I had such a hard time buying into it. Hadn't Law told me Wyler had been kicked off the force in New York? Or at least left under some cloud of suspicion? A perfect tool for men who had millions to lose if their operation got compromised by the papers I had stashed in an offshore bank. Not to mention their freedom. I tried to remember if Florida had the death penalty . . . I cut the wheel hard to the right as I nearly sped past the 278 off-ramp. The big vehicle swayed a little but held its ground.

You shouldn't be driving if you can't keep your mind on what you're doing, I admonished myself and hoped the old guy in the little pickup truck behind me hadn't been scared into a coronary.

I thought back to my conversation that morning in Neddie's office. Though I hadn't gone there to spill my guts about my troubles, she'd managed to worm most of it out of me by the time I finished my first cup of tea. Especially the part about Darnay.

"The incredible bastard! Although I can't say I'm surprised."

"What is that supposed to mean?" I'd demanded. I asked myself why I felt compelled to defend him and couldn't come up with anything remotely resembling a good reason. "You don't even know him."

"Don't have to. I know the type."

"That is such incredible bullshit, Neddie, even for you."

Her smoky green eyes narrowed, and I realized I might have gone too far.

"That's your one free shot," she said evenly, and I could see the effort she was making to control her anger. "Next one comes right back at you."

"I'm sorry. Really. This whole thing has got me completely . . ." I groped for an appropriate adjective and came up empty. "I can't seem to think straight anymore."

"Are you sleeping?" Neddie asked, her shoulders relaxing as our voices dropped back to conversational levels.

I shrugged. "Sometimes."

I'd stood up then and walked to the windows overlooking her well-tended garden and the bright sunlight bathing the square of staid, old houses.

"Well, you know I'm not an M.D., so I can't prescribe anything. But I could teach you some relaxation techniques."

I smiled ruefully at her. "I recite 'The Highwayman' to put myself to sleep."

"What?"

"You know, the poem? I had to memorize it in high school."

Neddie cocked an eyebrow at me. "I can't say I'm familiar with it."

" 'The wind was a torrent of darkness among the gusty trees. The moon was a ghostly galleon tossed upon cloudy seas.' It's very visual."

"Whatever floats your boat." She had removed her glasses then and flipped them onto the desk. "Do you want to talk about Darnay?"

I turned and shook my head. "What's the point?"

"The point is it might make you feel better." When I didn't respond, she said, "I know I never met the man, but I meant what I said about not being surprised. There's a reason those types of guys get to be forty years old and have never married. Believe me, I've met more than my share of them. Bedded quite a few of them, too, now that I think about it."

She waggled her eyebrows and forced the laugh out of me.

"Sorry, pal, but I'm not going to satisfy your prurient curiosity."

"A girl can but try. Hey! What do you say I blow off my patients for the rest of the day, and we go do the town? There's a great restaurant down by the river I've been meaning to try, then we could go spend obscene amounts of money on totally frivolous stuff."

I was shaking my head before she'd finished. "You wouldn't blow off your patients, and you know it." In the reception area outside her office I could hear the sounds of people speaking in low tones. "Besides, I think the first ones are already here."

"You're welcome to go hang out at my place," she said. "Use the pool and the sauna. Or go get a massage. Do you good to relax a little."

"No, I need to get back. Hiding out was just a fantasy, although a pleasant one, at least for a little while."

Neddie reached out and pulled me into a hug. "Maybe it'll just go away, honey. Maybe it'll all just go away . . ."

From your lips to God's ear, I thought as I braked to a stop at the angled intersection where the narrow side road met Route 170.

I pulled out into traffic and tried to give my mind something else to do. I flipped on the radio and punched buttons until I caught the familiar voice of the local newscaster in the middle of his noon report.

"A spokesman for the Israeli government told reporters the attack is still under investigation, but added that those responsible will be dealt with swiftly and decisively.

"Closer to home, former Beaufort attorney Hadley Bolles was found dead in his home on Cypress Key . . ."

I gasped and reached for the volume control.

". . . last night, the victim of an apparent robbery-homicide. Authorities speculate the flamboyant Bolles may have interrupted a burglary at his estate on the tiny island north of Key West. Bolles practiced law and held a number of political offices in Beaufort area government spanning a nearly forty-year career before his retirement last fall. Police have no suspects at this time, but say the investigation into his death will be ongoing. Hadley Bolles was sixty-eight.

"Turning now to weather, abundant sunshine will continue to dominate . . ."

I switched off the radio, my mind awhirl with stunned disbelief. It couldn't be a coincidence. Hadley Bolles, the man I'd blackmailed into returning the investors' money, had worked with Geoffrey Anderson and his scumbag clients. One of the two remaining people who knew the details of the Grayton's Race money-laundering scheme was now dead. And the other one was in danger of being sent to jail for murder.

I slammed on the brakes just inches from the rear bumper of a Palmetto Electric service truck and let my head drop onto my hands.

"This has to end. Now," I said aloud.

I reached for the phone and punched in Red's number.

My father rolled his wheelchair up to his usual place at the head of the table, and I took Lavinia's—and before her, my mother's—accustomed place at the foot. By unspoken, mutual consent we'd postponed our council of war. Although I'd professed myself not hungry when the call to lunch had come, I spooned up the thick, creamy she-crab soup and demolished more than my share of warm rolls before sitting back in my chair.

On my right, Erik Whiteside and Law Merriweather ate in silence.

Across from them, my brother-in-law glanced repeatedly at me out of the corner of his eye as if he thought I might be on the verge of bolting. Or having a nervous breakdown. I tried to smile my reassurance, but I could tell he wasn't convinced.

My father toyed with his lunch and said nothing.

I let the quiet hover until the last spoon had clattered against the side of an empty bowl. "Does anyone want coffee?" I saw nods all around and rose to head for the kitchen.

"I'll bring it," Lavinia said from the doorway, stopping me in midstride.

"Thank you, Vinnie." My father toggled the controls on his motorized wheelchair and led the parade down the long hallway.

We settled ourselves around the Judge's study, the arrangement seeming haphazard until I realized I had been maneuvered into the center of the room, the cynosure of the four men ranged around me. I had promised them the story—the *whole* story—and my mind groped for a way to begin. The only option seemed to be to start at the beginning, on that terrible day when I watched my husband die . . .

The decision to spill my guts had been a fairly easy one after I'd had a chance to absorb the shock of Hadley Bolles's murder. My intention the previous summer had been to do whatever it took to safeguard the lives of my family—and myself. Recent events had made it fairly obvious I'd drastically underestimated the patience and the ruthlessness of my opponents. Hadley, their former associate, had been as naturally wary and self-serving a man as I'd ever encountered. If they could get to him with such apparent ease, what chance did any of us have? I'd sought to protect us by threatening them with exposure. I'd had no idea the lengths to which they'd go to put the final period to their failed enterprise in Beaufort County.

Or perhaps I had. Deep down, I'd always known these were the same men who had planted the bomb on Rob's plane, even before an enraged Geoffrey Anderson had admitted it to me in the tiny office at the development site. They had blown my husband and his pilot and bodyguard out of the sky with no more thought than it took to crush an annoying insect. His sin had been heading up the task force created to rid the state of drug-dealing slime like Geoff and his cohorts. How much more they must want me—someone who had thwarted their money-laundering scheme, cost them a painstakingly constructed network, and forced them to retreat from an area they deemed ripe for the picking. I'd been a fool to think a few incriminating documents in an offshore bank vault would deter them from having their revenge.

I drew a long breath and looked directly into my father's faded gray eyes.

Half an hour later I slumped back in my seat, drained. No one had interrupted me during my recitation of the events of the past two years, beginning with the explosion of Rob's plane and ending with Erik's stumbling across the shotgun wrapped in its bloody shroud beneath my deck. The ice had melted in the glass of sweet tea Lavinia had carried in along with the coffee service, but I gulped it down anyway.

For a long while, no one spoke.

I knew my father would be a long time forgiving me for keeping him and everyone else in that room in the dark about the specifics of Geoffrey Anderson's death. I'd tried to make him see that I'd had no choice. In my mind, holding the details close had seemed the only prudent course of action. No danger could attach to the ignorant, I'd told myself. I'd been protecting my family in the only way I knew how. And besides, there'd been Millicent Anderson. And the boy . . .

Finally, my father raised his head and looked across the room at me. "Who would have thought a woman could be so good at keeping secrets?" he asked, and much of the coiled tension in the air evaporated.

"You poor child," Law Merriweather added, his patrician face reflecting more sadness than shock. "Why didn't you let us help you?"

I glanced at Red, but I couldn't read his expression.

Erik summed it up for all of us. "That's over and done with. What do we have to do now to get these bastards?" His quiet voice seemed more menacing for its very softness.

His question dropped into the silence and hung there, unanswered, until Red finally shook himself and met my eyes. "You have no proof," he said matter-of-factly. He raised his hand and stopped my attempt to interrupt. "I know what you've told us, Bay, about the papers you have in the bank in Grand Cayman, but what will they prove?"

"That these . . . these scumbags murdered Rob, set up the scheme to wash their filthy money by running an investment scam on my friends and family, and are trying to eliminate anyone who might be able to nail their miserable hides for all of it. They knocked off Hadley in some faked burglary attempt and cooked up this whole scenario with Cart Anderson to get my ass thrown in jail. And you're just pissed because it looks like they used some of your pals to make it work."

He held my gaze and slowly shook his head. "Are you sure?"

"What do you mean, am I sure? I was there, for God's sake! I watched Geoffrey Anderson die!" I could hear the anger in my voice, feel the tightness in my chest that signaled I was losing control, but I didn't care. "What are you suggesting, Red? That I made the whole damn thing up?"

He answered me in that same maddeningly quiet voice. "Of course I don't think you made it up. My question is, how incriminating are those documents you stole? Do they name names? Is there a confession conveniently tucked away in one of the envelopes?" Again he forestalled my words with a hand. "Hold on. Just hear me out."

I slumped back into my chair and pulled the pack of cigarettes out of my purse. No one said a word as I flicked the lighter and exhaled smoke into the crowded room.

Red frowned at me but continued. "You say you have proof, and maybe you do. At least enough to satisfy yourself these are the men who killed my brother. Don't you think I want that to be true? Don't you think I'd like to see someone strapped in a chair with electrodes taped to his head? Hell, I'd throw the switch myself."

He paused long enough to run a hand through his light brown hair leaving several clumps standing straight up on end. I felt the anger ebb out of me at the endearing gesture, so reminiscent of my dead husband.

"I'm just trying to point out that what you think you have may not be the kind of thing that can be used in court. I think the Judge and Law will back me up on this. You may have satisfied yourself it's enough, but it could be worthless in a trial. And that's the only way we're ever going to bring this to an end, by nailing them legally." This time the pause brought the ghost of a smile to his face. "Unless you think we should just go take them out."

I nodded. "The thought has occasionally crossed my mind."

"Mine, too," he said, sobering.

"Red is absolutely correct." My father spoke quietly, but forcefully. "There's no point in our speculating." He stared at me for a long moment before continuing. "Did you keep copies?"

I shook my head. "I told Hadley Bolles I did, but that was just a bluff. I didn't want to take the chance. I was afraid if they found out who had them, those people would become targets, too."

"Probably just as well." The Judge let his eyes wander around the room, his gaze lingering on every face before settling on mine. "We need to see those documents."

It seemed as if we all held our collective breath while the import of his statement sank in.

Erik finally broke the stillness. He reached across and laid his hand on my arm. "I'm going, too," he said.

Chapter Twenty-Seven

The sense of déjà vu lasted through the bumpy landing and sharp application of both the huge plane's brakes and reversed engines on the short, narrow runway. I'd let Erik have the window seat, content to lose myself in the pretense of reading the mystery I'd picked up at the Savannah Airport gift shop. In reality, my eyes had been fastened on the same page for hours, my mind replaying my last visit to Grand Cayman over and over, like a videotape in a continuous loop.

"This is so cool."

I turned at Erik's voice and had to smile at the grin of excitement on his handsome face.

"You've never been out of the country before?" I asked.

"Oh, sure, but not far. You know, Mexico for spring break, a couple of times to Canada. Stuff like that."

"You're lucky you had a valid passport, or I would have had to leave you behind."

A quick call to his mother in Charlotte had produced the document, and thanks to overnight delivery it had arrived just minutes before we had to leave for the airport. We were counting on that same efficiency to get the Grayton's Race documents out of our possession as quickly as possible after reclaiming them from the bank. I pulled my oversized tote bag onto my lap, patting it to reassure myself the preaddressed and prepaid FedEx shipping envelope was still inside. As we rose to join the debarkation bustle I could feel the warm metal of the key to the safe deposit box nestled tightly against my left breast.

With no luggage and a return ticket for later that evening, we cleared the formalities in record time and stepped out into the brilliant sunshine. The overpowering fragrance of gardenia, camellia, and a dozen other exotic flowers was so strong it might almost have been artificial. I glanced around at the waiting line of vehicles at the curb. I half-expected Jenkins, the hired chauffeur in his shorts and knee socks, to be standing beside the idling black London taxi ready to whisk us off to the docks as he had on my previous visit. Instead we selected the third cab in line and ordered the grizzled black driver to take us directly to the bank.

This time my reception was a bit more cordial, especially after my identification card and passport had been inspected and my thumbprint compared to the satisfaction of the silent gentleman with the starched French cuffs who'd opened the door to us. Erik sat fidgeting on one of the ornate, gilded love seats in the hushed lobby, having been admonished by the gatekeeper not to move from that spot unless accompanied by one of the staff. After passing through all the rigors of proving my identity, I joined him.

"I thought these places only existed in spy movies," he whispered, then gestured with a slight tilt of his head. "See that guy over there? He's carrying a gun about the size of a cannon. And not doing much to disguise the fact, either."

I followed his eyes. "They mean it when they say they guarantee the safety and privacy of their clients."

I broke off as the small, balding figure in the perfectly tailored Saville Row suit bustled across the blood-red carpet. "Frau Tanner! How lovely to see you again! How may we be of service to you?"

His impeccable European manners and bank policy forbade him from inquiring about my companion, so I quickly executed introductions. "A pleasure, young man," Herr Helmut Wagner bubbled and extended his tiny, well-manicured hand. His beaming smile bounced from one to the other of us.

"I need to access my box, Herr Wagner," I said, and he nodded.

"And how is my dear friend Harry?"

Harry Drayton, my former client and an expert in international banking, had been my liaison the previous fall when I'd decided to get the Grayton's Race papers stashed somewhere out of the reach of Geoff Anderson's cronies.

"We haven't spoken in some time, but I assume he's well."

"Excellent."

I glanced at my watch, hoping the protocol and formalities had been properly dispensed with. "I hate to appear rude, sir, but we're in something of a rush."

"Of course, of course. Forgive me! Chattering here like an old woman when we have business to conduct. Won't you follow me, Frau Tanner?"

I signaled Erik to stay put and trailed along behind the fussy little banker. In a matter of minutes I had submitted to the retinal scan device, passed muster, and been ushered into the vault by one of Wagner's coolly efficient assistants. I reached into the tight sweater I'd chosen deliberately to make someone's relieving me of the key as difficult as possible and pulled it from the cup of my bra. If the cold-eyed woman who stood in front of the box thought anything about my hiding place, she gave no sign. We inserted our separate keys in the lock, and when it had clicked open, she turned on her heel and slipped silently from the room.

With trembling fingers I emptied the contents into the FedEx envelope, resisting the urge to leaf through the papers on the spot. We'd have plenty of time once they were delivered safely into the hands of my brother-in-law. Addressing the package to Red Tanner in care of the Sheriff's Office in Beaufort had seemed the least risky when we'd discussed it the previous afternoon. Not an ideal solution, but we'd all come to the conclusion it was the best one we had. With no return address to alert anyone to its contents, the package wouldn't arouse any suspicions. Sending it to Red would also provide less chance for it to be intercepted or tampered with. At least that was the plan.

I sealed the envelope and returned it to my bag. I tucked the key back into my bra and pushed the button on the wall as I'd been instructed, signaling one of the staff that I had completed my business and was ready to return to the lobby. I found Erik still seated on the narrow antique sofa, his legs bunched under him as if prepared for flight. He jumped up at my entrance, the obvious relief I saw on his face no doubt reflected on my own. Herr Wagner appeared from his office to shake hands and send us on our way with his best wishes for our safe journey and his fond hope we would honor him with our presence again soon.

We paused just inside the door while I pulled a wide floppy hat and oversized sunglasses from my bag. I handed Erik a tattered baseball cap, and he shrugged out of his bright tropical shirt to reveal a disreputable-looking T-shirt underneath. I added a long flowered jacket to my ensemble and stuffed the discarded clothes back into the tote. They weren't much in the way of disguises, but at least we looked superficially different from the two well-dressed tourists who had stepped out of a cab a half hour before.

Out on the stoop, we wasted no time but turned sharply left. I had memorized the location of the nearest Federal Express office two blocks over, and we walked briskly in that direction. I kept the bag firmly on my shoulder, both hands tight on the straps, and the comforting solidity of Erik's body between me and the steady stream of traffic rushing by beside us. I wanted no repeat of my last trip away from the Gellenschaft Bank when I had found myself suddenly sprawled in the street with a lumbering produce truck bearing down on me. The memory brought a sharp flash of pain as Darnay's face swam before me in the late afternoon heat, but I pushed it away with a forceful shake of my head.

Concentrate! I ordered myself. This short walk was the only time in which we would be vulnerable, and I had no intention of letting anything—or anyone—interfere with our reaching our destination. My eyes scanned the jostling crowds who filled the sidewalk around us, but five minutes later we stepped into the cool oasis of the FedEx office having encountered no trouble whatsoever.

With a sigh of profound relief I handed over the package to a seemingly bored but pleasant young woman who inspected the label, pronounced it adequate, and tossed the envelope through a slot marked *International Overnight—United States*. Erik and I grinned and thanked her, barely restraining ourselves from an undignified high-five as we stepped back out the door.

"Now what?" my companion asked.

I checked my watch. We had nearly three hours until our return flight to the States. "Let's head back downtown and find somewhere to eat." I consulted the street sign and set off at a leisurely pace.

"Do they have any specialties here?" Erik asked as we once again threaded our way through the throngs of native islanders and tourists.

"Like what? You mean, as in food?"

"Yeah. You know, like something they're famous for?"

We separated to make room for an old man pedaling an ancient bicycle down the middle of the sidewalk. "Turtle, I think. I seem to remember turtle burgers on the menu when I was here."

"Turtle burgers? What're they like?"

"Green," I said and laughed at his grunt of disgust. "There's always conch," I added and waited for him to ask. "It's the little snail-thing that lives inside those big, beautiful shells you see everywhere. The ones you hold up to your ear to listen to the ocean?"

"I'm afraid to ask what they do with them."

"Conch chowder, conch fritters, conch stew . . ."

We settled for an exotic mushroom-and-pepperoni at the local Pizza Hut. I managed only a couple of slices, sitting back as Erik demolished the rest. I paid the check, and we strolled outside, enjoying the cool breeze along the waterfront.

"You met Darnay here, didn't you?" he asked, casually, as if the answer didn't matter.

I glanced sideways at him and kept walking. "Yes. He kept me from getting run over by a truck. Literally."

"Where did he go? I mean, a few days ago. Do you really have no idea, or are you just holding off the Judge and Red?"

We reached the end of the small harbor, and I checked my watch. "We need to find a cab and get out to the airport." I made a production out of scanning the street in both directions, and suddenly a beautifully maintained, late-sixties Chevrolet coupe made a U-turn and pulled up alongside us.

"Are you needing a taxi, my lady?"

I leaned in to check the license hanging around the young man's neck. "How much to the airport?" I asked.

He named a sum I knew to be within the acceptable range, and I let him open the rear door for me. Erik hesitated on the sidewalk. "What? Come on, or we're going to miss our flight."

"You're sure? I mean, about this being a taxi?"

"Absolutely. Let's go."

Reluctantly he joined me in the immaculate back seat, its original vinyl upholstery cracked but clean. Liberal use had been made of some sort of new-car-smell spray.

We rode in silence except for repeated blasts on the horn as the young man negotiated the snarl of traffic in the narrow streets of George Town until Erik turned to me, a pained expression on his face. "I'm really sorry. About . . . you know, prying back there. It's none of my business."

I glanced toward the front seat where the driver's thin shoulders undulated to the beat of reggae music blaring from the radio. I shrugged. "Don't worry about it. If I had an answer, I'd be happy to share it."

"It had to be something to do with his work. I refuse to believe he just bailed out on you because . . ." He shot a look at the driver and lowered his voice. "Because of your troubles. He just doesn't seem like that kind of guy."

I desperately wanted to change the subject. "I guess we'll just have to wait until he decides to get in touch." I patted Erik's arm. "Don't worry about it. And don't worry about me. You know, Neddie tells me I attract these kinds of situations to myself." I laughed. "And Red once called me a disaster magnet."

Erik nodded. "They could be right. But if we plan on getting this inquiry agency off the ground, that's not necessarily a bad thing, is it?" His eyes sparkled.

"Paranoia as a marketing tool. I'll have to give it some thought."

We maintained the lightened mood through the wait in the noisy, crowded terminal and the long flight into darkness. Erik fell asleep not long after we changed planes in Miami, and I managed to get through several chapters of the mystery novel without my mind wandering back into my own predicament. We'd been successful at retrieving the documents without incident, and in a few hours they'd be secure in Red's possession. The DNA test should be back within a couple of days. I firmly believed they'd exonerate me in spite of Erik's fears someone might falsify the results. My father and Law Merriweather were working on a plan to get the shotgun someone had planted under my deck into the hands of the authorities without implicating me or compromising the investigation into the body on the beach.

All in all, considering everything that had happened in the past ten days, my position could have been a lot worse. I closed my eyes and managed a few minutes' sleep before the stirring in the cabin around us told me we were approaching Savannah. I smiled as Erik stretched and yawned, happy to have had his company. The plane glided in smoothly and executed a sharp left turn. We gathered our things and trooped after the rest of the shuffling passengers through the jetway into the bright glare of the terminal.

And straight into the waiting arms of Detective Ben Wyler.

At nearly midnight all the cafés ringing the small atrium lobby were shuttered, so we settled onto one of the many park benches strewn around the waiting area. Erik had barely managed a civil handshake when I'd performed introductions.

"What do you want, Detective?" I asked, dropping the tote bag onto the floor at my feet.

"To find out what the hell you're up to, Mrs. Tanner." His tone sounded more questioning than nasty.

I shrugged. "I had some business to take care of."

Wyler cocked his head in Erik's direction. "And he's what? Your bodyguard?"

"Why on earth would you think I need one?" When he didn't reply, I added, "Erik is my partner. And my friend."

"Partner in what? This cockamamie detective agency you've been playing at with your father? None of you have a license. I could haul you all in—"

"Actually, you can't do a damn thing," I snapped, the lateness of the hour and the return of his confrontational style sweeping away any inclination I might have had to keep our exchange civil. "We're sitting in Georgia, in case you don't remember crossing the river. You have zip in the way of jurisdiction here."

Wyler shook his head. "You'll eventually have to go back into Beaufort County, Mrs. Tanner. I'm a very patient man."

I felt a wave of weariness settle over me, and I picked up my bag and stood. "Do whatever you have to do, Detective. I'm tired and hungry, and I'm going home."

He made no move to follow as Erik and I exited the lobby, crossed the empty road in front of the terminal, and made our way down the steps of the curved, split stairway toward the parking garage. I forced myself not to look over my shoulder, but we retrieved the Thunderbird without incident and were on our way toward Hilton Head in a matter of minutes.

"What was that all about?" Erik asked as we sped north on the interstate.

"Beats the hell out of me. Maybe he just wanted to make sure I actually came back."

"Don't you find it a little scary he knew the flight we'd be on?"

I glanced at him scrunched down in the bucket seat. In the soft glow of the dash lights, I could see his face creased in a frown. "I'm sure they have access to flight records. Even if they don't, I bet they have someone who could tease the information out of the airline's computer. I'm sure whoever they have isn't even remotely in your league, but still . . ."

My attempt to lighten his mood fell flat. "I don't like it," he said.

"I'm more interested in how he found out we'd left," I replied, and Erik sat up straighter.

"You're right! Do you think he was having you followed?"

I shrugged. "I have no idea. Anyway, what does it matter? There's no way he has any idea what we were up to in George Town."

"Good thing there won't be any indication of where the FedEx package is being sent from," Erik said. "Maybe I'd better call Red and make sure he's there at the station to intercept it first thing tomorrow." He pulled his cell phone from his pocket and dialed.

I tuned out the one-sided conversation and thought again about his question. How *had* Wyler known we'd left the country? Only the Judge, Red, Law Merriweather, and Lavinia had been privy to our plans. There was absolutely nothing which could convince me any one of them had betrayed me to the cops. Could Wyler have been keeping an eye on us? It seemed the most logical explanation.

"Red wasn't too happy about the phone call at one in the morning, but he's alerted." Erik's voice cut across my useless speculations. "He said he'll be at the station from ten on tomorrow. I think we've got it covered." He glanced across the dim interior. "Don't worry. Wyler won't get his hands on it."

"Good."

We left the interstate and whizzed along an eerily deserted Route 278 through the commercial sprawl which had forced the destruction of once vast stands of pines and oaks. As we neared the approach to the twin bridges onto the island, the low rumbling in my stomach became insistent.

"You hungry?" I asked.

"Dying," came the reply, accompanied by a short bark of laughter.

"I think Wendy's is open late," I said and banished from my mind all thoughts of anything more complex than whether or not to order fries with my double cheeseburger.

"Not again," I mumbled as my hand groped for the ringing telephone beside the bed. The slit I managed to force through my sleep-encrusted eyelids revealed not even a glimmer of dawn peeping through the drapes. I fumbled the receiver toward the vicinity of my lips and grunted, "What?" into the mouthpiece.

"Bay! Oh, thank you, Lord."

The voice didn't register at first. I propped myself up on one elbow and tried to force myself to focus.

"Bay? For God's sake, answer me!"

In a flash, my head cleared, and my heart rate accelerated to a pounding race. I flung back the covers and dropped my feet onto the floor. "Lavinia? What's the matter?"

"He's gone," she wailed. "Your father's gone!"

Chapter Twenty-Eight

A SCREAM ERUPTED FROM MY THROAT, THEN A FIST BATtering against my bedroom door stunned me into silence.

"Bay! What's going on? What's the matter?" More pounding. "Bay!"

Erik Whiteside burst into the room, and I had barely enough presence of mind to jerk the rumpled sheet around my breasts before he was looming over me.

"What is it?" His frantic brown eyes took in the telephone dangling uselessly from my hand, and he snatched it up. "Hello? Who is this?"

I watched the look of horror rise across his face as he listened, then his voice, soft and calming, washed over me. "It's okay. He's not dead."

I couldn't grasp it. *Not dead? What did he mean, not dead?* "Gone," I mumbled, repeating Lavinia's devastating cry, "your father's gone."

"Listen, stay by the phone. I'll call you right back." I heard Erik's words, but their meaning failed to register until I realized he was once again speaking into the receiver. "I know, I know. But you have to stay calm." A pause. "We'll be there as soon as we can." Again the silence. "What? No, we won't. I promise. Lavinia, you have to trust me on this. Just wait until we get there. And don't touch anything. I know it's hard, but we're on our way." Erik looked directly into my eyes, and I saw pain there, but resolve as well. I felt myself breathe for what seemed the first time in hours. "Okay. Good. You have to hold on, Lavinia. Just hold on."

He replaced the phone on its cradle and dropped down beside me on the bed. "Listen now, okay?"

I felt his hand hover just over my bowed head as if he thought stroking my hair might soothe me. Instead, he reached for my trembling fingers and clasped them tightly in his own.

"The Judge has been kidnapped."

My head snapped up as if it had been jerked by an invisible line. "Kidnapped? That's crazy! Lavinia said . . ." I drew in another shaky breath. "That's what she meant by *gone*?" I almost choked on the relief I felt, swallowing hard against the bubble of hysterical laughter I felt pushing against my lips. "Kidnapped? Who? Why?"

Erik tightened his grip on my hands. "They left a note."

I raised my eyes and found his own dark with fear and . . . something else, something he seemed desperate to conceal. Pity?

"It's them, isn't it?" I didn't need to see his answering nod. "They want the papers." I pulled my hands free and hugged myself, the shivers which wracked me having nothing to do with the cold or my own nakedness. "My fault, my fault." I pounded my thigh viciously with my right fist. "Stupid, stupid, stupid! Who did I think I was dealing with? They killed Rob! They murdered Hadley Bolles! And Miss Minnie." A sound—half sob, half mocking laughter—escaped past my crumbling defenses. "And now Daddy." I raised my streaming eyes to the dim outline of Erik's face, my voice rising on a tide of panic that erupted into a scream. "They're going to kill my father!"

His hands gripped my shoulders and shook me roughly. "Bay! Knock it off!" The force of it rattled me to my core, my head flopping around on my neck as if I were a rag doll. The harsh sound of his voice jerked me back to reality, and I gulped and fell quiet.

"I'm sorry, I'm sorry." Erik's hand rested gently against my skin, stroking my cheek, silently seeking forgiveness. "But we have to go. You have to get yourself together. Lavinia needs us."

I don't remember dressing or tumbling into the Expedition for the race through the waning darkness toward Presqu'isle. I rolled down the window and chain-smoked, my bleary eyes fastened on the glowing green numbers of the digital clock on the wide dashboard. I could feel Erik's glance dart sideways at me every so often, but neither of us spoke. A faint blush of pearly dawn touched the placid expanse of the Beaufort River as we sped across the bridge. I flipped another cigarette butt and followed its glowing end as it arced out into the gray mist rising from the water.

"What did the note say again?" I asked, surprising myself by the steadiness of my voice.

"I only know what Lavinia said." Erik ran a hand over his face and shook his head as if to clear it. "Don't contact the police, stay by the phone, and await further instructions." He stared straight ahead.

"And the papers?"

He turned to glance at my profile. "Not mentioned specifically. But the note said the ransom wouldn't involve money."

I nodded. "Well, that's it. Game, set, and match."

"Don't say that! As soon as we get there, we'll call Red. He'll know what—"

"No! No police!"

"Bay, Red wouldn't come into this as a cop. He's your brother-in-law. He has a right—"

"No, Erik. Absolutely not. We'll let him deliver the papers just like we planned, and we'll take it from there."

Erik ran a hand through his hair and shook his head. "We're going to need his help."

"For what? What good would having Red involved do us? You think we're going to bargain with these bastards for my father's life?" I shook my head as if Erik were a backward child. "Don't you get it? My little scheme has blown right up in my face. It's over."

We drove on in silence while the sky around us gradually lightened.

The soft morning glow filtered through the moss-draped limbs of the ancient oaks as we bumped down the rutted lane and pulled finally into the semicircular drive. Erik shut off the ignition and grabbed my arm as I reached for the door handle. I turned to face him.

"We're going to get him back," he said with a conviction I wanted desperately to believe.

"I'll be okay," I said, swallowing hard. "No matter what."

I almost meant it.

I could hear the rattle of pans in the kitchen as we came through the front door. The calm which had settled over me during the past few minutes evaporated in an instant, and I broke into a run. Lavinia spun around from the stove as I threw myself into her waiting arms.

"Child, child," she murmured over and over, her warm brown hands stroking my back just as they had so often in years gone by. "Hush now, hush. It's gonna be fine. Everything's gonna be just fine now."

I snuffled and stepped back, amazed at the strength of this woman who had taught me the meaning of the word. I managed a watery smile. "I'm sorry."

"Nothing for you to be sorry about, honey." She looked over my shoulder and said, "Good morning, Erik. Thank you for bringing Bay."

He crossed the room in two long strides and gathered Lavinia's slender frame to his chest. Surprisingly, she leaned into him without protest. "We'll find the Judge," I heard him whisper against her gray curls.

I don't know how long the three of us stood there, our arms wrapped around each other, before I finally disengaged myself. "Where's the note?"

Lavinia winced. "In . . . your father's room. That's where . . . that's how they got in without me hearin' them. If I hadn't been restless, come down early, I might not have realized until . . ." She squared her shoulders. "Come with me."

We entered the Judge's study almost on tiptoe, as if he might still be stretched out on the bed asleep. The innocuous-looking document lay propped against the pillow. It appeared to be standard white printer paper with the message in twelve-point caps, the font Times New Roman. It could have come from any word-processing program on any computer in the world.

> NO POLICE OR FBI. YOU WILL BE CONTACTED WITH FURTHER INSTRUCTIONS. RANSOM WILL NOT REQUIRE CASH. DAUGHTER MUST BE AVAILABLE THIS LOCATION. COMPLY AND THE JUDGE WILL BE WELL CARED FOR.

"They're very literate," I said. " 'Comply and the Judge will be well cared for.' It's not your typical 'pay up or he dies' kind of ransom note."

Erik flinched at my bluntness, but Lavinia nodded. "I think it's a good sign, don't you?" She twisted a crumpled hanky around in her hands.

I nodded and let my gaze wander around the inside of my father's room. Everything looked normal. Not surprisingly, there were no signs of a struggle. A nearly eighty-year-old man debilitated by a series of small strokes couldn't have put up much resistance.

"We shouldn't touch anything," Erik warned as I crossed to the ramp.

The door leading out to the back verandah stood open. "They came in through here," I said. Erik moved up next to me as I pointed to the scratches on the shiny brass door plate surrounding the lock and knob. "It wouldn't have taken them more than a few minutes . . ."

I tried to push the images away, but they rushed across my mind's eye like a movie on fast-forward. Easily overpowered, the Judge would have been whisked away in no time, his wheelchair providing easy transportation. I'd noticed its absence the moment I stepped into the room. "I told him to install an alarm system," I said to no one in particular.

"Your father had no fear of burglars," Lavinia murmured softly from the center of the room where she stood looking lost, her fingers still working at the scrap of fabric. "He always said they were welcome to anything they wanted." She made no move to wipe away the tears slipping silently down her cheeks. "I don't believe he thought anyone in this county would have the gall to rob the house of Judge Talbot Simpson. But he never said what to do if . . . if . . ."

I felt Erik lay a hand gently on my arm, and I turned back toward the doorway.

"There's blood," he said softly, pointing unobtrusively to a few scattered drops on the sill. He used his elbow to edge the door farther open and nodded toward the wood floor of the verandah. "Not much," he added quickly as I gasped. "I wouldn't attach any great significance to it. One of them may have nicked himself on the corner of a table or something."

"I wonder how they got him down the stairs in his wheelchair." I gazed out across the sloping lawn down to the short dock. The strengthening sun cast the whole scene in a golden glow. "Maybe they came by boat. I don't see any tracks in the grass where they might have pulled a car in back here."

Erik let the door swing closed, and we moved back into the study, my gaze straying to the silent telephone on the stand next to the empty bed. Several tissues streaked with blood littered the tabletop, and a glass half-filled with water stood forlornly amidst the usual clutter. It took me a moment to realize what was missing.

"Have you checked his medications?" I asked, and Lavinia gasped.

"Dear Lord, I never thought of that! And the blood!" She whirled and darted into the bathroom with its gleaming white tile and shiny chrome grab bars placed strategically to allow my father the maximum mobility and privacy despite his nearly useless legs and left arm.

I heard her flinging open cabinet doors, then her voice, sharp with fear.

"They've taken it all!"

"Wait," I said, rushing to intercept her as she emerged from the bathroom, "that's a good thing, right? I mean, if they took his pills with them, they intend to keep him alive."

It made perfect sense to me, but Lavinia was already shaking her head. "You don't understand. They can't give him the Coumadin, the blood thinner."

"I don't get it," I said, and she whirled on me, all her anger, frustration, and worry erupting at once.

"Of course you don't get it! When have you ever paid the least attention to your father's health? *I* see he takes his medicine. *I* get the doctor here when his blood pressure shoots up, or he's had one too many of those disgusting cigars. I take care of everything, you ungrateful child!"

We stood staring at each other, Lavinia's chest heaving in righteous indignation and fear. The fragile control she'd maintained since Erik had calmed her down on the telephone had finally snapped, and I would not have been surprised had she thrown herself at me. I stood defenseless, hands hanging uselessly at my sides. If she had pummeled me with her fists, I would have taken it without resistance.

Because she was right.

Only a few days before I had fought an anxiety attack at the mere idea of assuming responsibility for my father's care. I had seen myself withering, what tiny glimmer of youth remained to me shriveling under the constant tending and vigilance he required.

"That's not—" Erik began, but I cut him off.

"You're absolutely right, Lavinia," I said. "I haven't wanted to know. I've let you shoulder the entire burden of his illness and felt nothing but profound relief. I've been cowardly and selfish, and I'm sorry for that. But right now you need to tell me about this drug he's not supposed to take."

I saw the remorse for her outburst creep into her eyes, but I shook my head, and she drew a long breath. "He hasn't been feeling well lately. Maybe you noticed he hasn't been eating?"

I nodded. I remembered the hacking cough, too. "How long has this been going on?"

"A few days. I called Dr. Coffin, and he said it was probably some sort of flu bug. Lots of it going around this summer. But then I told him about the nosebleeds, and he didn't like the sound of that."

"Nosebleeds?" I asked, and she nodded. "Serious ones?"

"No, not that I thought, but the doctor said for me to take your father off the blood thinner for a while."

I still didn't understand the significance and said so.

"If they keep giving him the Coumadin and don't feed him properly, he could start bleeding, maybe even internally. There'll be nothing to cause it to clot." The control she'd fought so hard to maintain slipped, and her next words came out in a high, thin moan. "He could bleed to death, and no one would even know it was happening!"

I glanced away as Erik took Lavinia's elbow and gently guided her toward one of the wing chairs. She suddenly looked old and frail. I moved back toward the verandah, and stared at the watery drops of blood. My eyes followed their progression across the weathered boards and down the steps.

"We have to find him." I didn't realize I'd spoken out loud until I felt Erik's arm tighten around my shoulders.

"We will. I promise," he whispered, his breath soft against my hair.

The ringing telephone sounded like an explosion in the still morning air.

Chapter Twenty-Nine

"What are you doing there so early?" Red's voice sounded only mildly curious.

I'd grabbed the phone on the second ring, my heart thudding in my chest. I had to force the breath from my lungs in order to speak.

"Couldn't sleep," I managed to croak. "Did you get the papers?"

"Got 'em right here in my hand. They came about ten minutes ago. Let me speak to the Judge a minute."

I coughed to give myself some time to formulate a lie. "He's, uh, getting cleaned up right now. Lavinia's helping him get dressed."

"Really? He's usually up and made fifteen phone calls by now," my brother-in-law said. "Well, I'll just bring the package on over then. We have a lot to discuss. Will you contact Mr. Merriweather?"

Panic threatened to overwhelm me. "No! I mean, yes, I'll call Law. But why don't I come there and pick up the papers?"

I could see Erik shaking his head, but I didn't know what else to do. What if the kidnappers were watching the house? They had no way of knowing Red would be delivering the very thing they'd snatched my father to get. If he came in a cruiser it could be the Judge's death warrant.

"Bay, what's the matter with you? We all agreed I should bring the package there so we could go through everything together." I heard the note of suspicion creep into his voice. "Is something wrong?"

"No, of course not." I couldn't think. "You're right. Come ahead. We'll be waiting for you."

The minute I hung up, Erik said, "You shouldn't have argued with him. He's going to suspect something."

I pushed past him and strode down the hallway into the kitchen. "It doesn't matter. We have to have that package. Once he brings it, I'll get rid of him somehow."

We reassembled around the worn oak table in the kitchen where Lavinia busied herself with setting a pot of coffee to percolating. With quivering fingers, I lit a cigarette.

"Now what?" Erik's voice dropped into the gloomy silence like a knife clattering against a plate, and I jumped.

"Now we wait."

I exhaled and watched the ripple of soft yellow light dance across the ceiling. Outside the mullioned windows the world drifted on, heedless of the drama playing itself out in the deceptively bright, airy kitchen. How many tragedies this old mansion must have witnessed, I thought, my eyes following the drift of smoke as it spiraled upward, disappearing into the slow, rhythmic beat of the fan.

Births and deaths, births and deaths . . .

When the doorbell finally rang, the tension had become almost unbearable. I shot out of my chair and down the hallway before the first notes had died away.

Red stood on the verandah, the innocuous-looking package tucked under his arm. I almost collapsed with relief when I looked past him to the Bronco pulled up in the drive. *No police car!* And my brother-in-law wore rumpled shorts and a polo shirt instead of his crisp uniform. Maybe this could work. My mind whirled, and the decision seemed to make itself.

"Come on in," I said, stepping aside.

He stopped a few feet into the entry as I closed and locked the door behind him. Erik and Lavinia stood framed in the doorway to the kitchen. Red glanced over his shoulder at me, a slightly quizzical look on his face, before moving ahead of me down the hall. I patted the pocket of my shorts and followed.

The moment he stepped into the kitchen, I could sense a change in the atmosphere. Red had been a cop for a long time, and he knew immediately something was wrong. He tossed the FedEx envelope onto the table and whirled to face me.

"What's going on here? Where's the Judge?"

I met his eyes with a steady gaze. "Sit down, Red."

To give him credit, he didn't interrupt much once I got into the details.

"We need to get a forensics team in here," he said after he'd taken a tour of the Judge's study and we'd returned to the kitchen.

Red had no crime-scene equipment with him, so he'd picked up the ransom note with a pair of tweezers and sealed it in a simple Ziploc bag Lavinia had brought him. It lay on the table between us.

"How many ways can I say no?" I poured tea into the sturdy mug in front of me.

"What makes you think you're entitled to make those kinds of decisions?"

"What makes you think you are?"

"Bay," Erik began, but I shook my head.

"No! You're not here as a cop, Red. You're part of this family, and I'm not denying we need your support. And your expertise. But the note said no—"

"Jesus, woman!" he erupted before I could finish the sentence. "You're the great cop show expert. And you've probably read every mystery novel ever written. They always say no police. And do you want to know what the statistics are? Not in that fictionalized stuff you're so addicted to, but in real life?"

"No, and I don't give a damn!" I yelled, but again he ignored me.

"When the FBI gets involved, sixty-seven percent of kidnappings end in recovery of the victim unharmed. Sixty-seven percent! That's—"

"Don't play numbers games with me! Two out of three, that's what you're saying. What about the other third, huh? How do they come back? Dead? Or not at all?"

"Bay, for God's sake!"

I jerked my head around at Erik's voice and followed his eyes to where Lavinia stood at the sink, her shoulders slumped.

"I'm sorry," I said, resisting the urge to go to her, "but we all need to face the facts if this is going to work."

"That's just my point." I watched Red make a conscious effort to speak calmly. "The facts are you have a better chance of getting your father back if you let me get the pros in on this. Now."

The ringing of the telephone froze us all in place.

The voice was muffled, as if the caller had wrapped a towel around the mouthpiece.

"You have one chance to get this right. Come alone. Bring the documents. All of them. If you hold any back or try to make copies, we'll know. We get the papers, you get the old man."

"Where? When?"

"Later. Stay by your cell phone, and don't leave the house. And no cops."

"Fine. Agreed. When . . . ?"

"No questions. We'll call."

"Wait! Listen! About my father's meds, don't give . . ." I was talking to a dial tone.

I clutched the phone against my chest and looked up to find Erik and Lavinia staring at me intently. Red lifted his eyes from his watch. "Not even thirty seconds. They know what they're doing. We wouldn't have had time for a trace even if we'd had the equipment hooked up." He pried the receiver from my locked fingers and replaced it gently in the cradle. "What did they say?" He pulled a notebook from his pocket, pen poised above it.

I repeated the kidnapper's end of the conversation. A handful of words really, no more than fifty or so. How strange such simple combinations of sounds could hold such profound meaning, I thought. Life or death. Wild jubilation or . . .

"Bay! Stay with me." Red's voice cut across my useless speculation. "Man or woman? Young, old?"

I shook my head. "No way to tell. The mouthpiece was covered with something. If I had to guess, I'd say a man, younger, but I'm not certain."

"Accent of any kind?"

I thought about it for a moment. "Maybe. Something . . ." I let my voice trail off. "I just don't know."

He glanced down at his notes. "No indication of when the next call will come?"

"I told you everything!" I snapped.

"Okay, take it easy." Red tucked the notebook back in his pocket and reached out to pat my hand. His voice seemed to come from far away, and I had to force my mind to focus on his words. "We have some decisions to make."

I slumped back into my chair and lit a cigarette. "No, Red, we don't. We've got the papers, and I deliver them wherever they instruct me to. It's really quite simple."

"Just listen—"

"No!" The single word rang through the room like a shot. The three of us turned as one toward Lavinia, her eyes blazing from her pinched brown face, the dish towel she'd been using twisted nearly into a rope between her clenched fists.

"No," she said again, more softly. "Bay is right. She's going to do exactly what they tell her. No more, no less. If you or Erik can't agree to that, then just stay out of it." She dropped the towel onto the counter and moved to stand behind my chair, her strong fingers digging into the knotted muscles across my shoulders. "But don't interfere with us." I could hear the steel of her resolve, see it reflected in the eyes of the men she held riveted in her gaze. "If you do, and anything happens to Tally, I swear you'll live to regret it."

For a long moment no one spoke. Then Red nodded, but Lavinia needed more.

"Promise me," she said.

I winced as she tightened her hold on my damaged shoulder.

They stared at each other. Again it was Red who dropped his eyes, and again he bobbed his head.

"Say it."

"I promise," he mumbled, and I could almost feel the anxiety seep out of the air.

"More coffee anyone?" she asked in her everyday voice, and Erik nodded. Lavinia released me and turned to lift the pot and refill his cup. "Bay? Tea?"

I shook my head.

It might have been an ordinary morning at Presqu'isle except for the empty place where my father's wheelchair should have sat, the absence of his gruff, querulous voice an almost tangible hole in the fabric of the life of the old house. I thought about what I would do if he didn't come back. I glanced up to find Lavinia's eyes studying my face, her own unreadable through the steam rising from the cup she lifted to her lips.

I'll give the house to her, I thought, *lock, stock, and barrel. No one will ever love it or care for it like she does.* She frowned and turned away, as if she had been reading my mind.

My gaze wandered to the FedEx envelope now resting innocently on the kitchen counter, and I wondered if it had been my decisions which had led us to this point. Maybe if I had been smarter back then, if I had taken other roads, my father would be sitting here complaining . . .

Out of the corner of my eye I saw Red's hand slide toward his pants pocket, and I knew immediately he'd been checking for his cell phone. He stood and stretched, working his neck around as if trying to loosen a kink.

"I think I'll take a look around outside," he said, turning for the doorway. "See if there's anything out there to tell me how they got in and out so fast."

I looked into his face, and what I saw there made my stomach drop into my feet.

"No! You're going to use your cell phone to get a message to the feds." His gaze fell away, and I grabbed his arm. "Look at me, goddammit! You gave us your word!"

I watched the war rage behind his eyes: my brother-in-law, my friend, locked in anguished combat with the cop. I had no idea which one would vanquish the other, but I had no time to wait for the outcome of the contest. I slipped my hand into my own pocket and locked my fingers around the grip of the Seecamp. Before he could make a move toward the doorway, I had the miniature handgun pointed at his heart. Behind me I heard Lavinia gasp.

"Don't be ridiculous," Red snapped, his arm automatically reaching out toward the pistol. "You know I don't have any choice in this. The only chance we have is to get the sheriff and the FBI in here as soon as possible." We stared at each other, his arm outstretched toward me. "Come on, Bay. You know you're not going to shoot me with that little popgun."

I leaned back out of his reach. "Sit down, Red. Lavinia, get some clothesline from the pantry."

"Bay, for Christ's sake, don't be a fool! The only chance your father has is to let us—"

"Shut up, Red," I said, surprising myself with the icy calm that seemed to have settled over me. "Sit down. Now."

His eyes never left mine as he assessed my willingness to do as I'd threatened. Of course I wouldn't kill him. We both knew that. But he finally sensed I would hurt him, render him incapable of interfering if he forced me to. For an eternity we held each other's unwavering gaze before he tipped his head to me in a gesture of capitulation and lowered himself slowly into the chair.

Erik stared at me with an expression I couldn't read.

"Well? You in or out?" I asked, my voice much steadier than I felt.

When he nodded, I said, "Then help Lavinia."

Red jerked as Erik slipped the clothesline around his hands. "Bay, this is crazy! You're signing his death—"

"And if he doesn't shut up," I said matter-of-factly, "gag him."

By the time the second call came, I had more than once thought about turning the gun on myself. The strain of waiting had stretched my ability to deal with it almost beyond bearing.

There had been other interruptions throughout the interminable hours, but Lavinia had dealt with them calmly and firmly. She informed everyone who rang that my father was unwell, nothing serious, and would be back in touch in a couple of days. She brewed endless pots of coffee and kept a steady stream of food flowing from her stove to the table. Law Merriweather called twice, and twice I took the phone to tell him the package had yet to arrive.

I'd untied Red so he could join us in picking at lunch, and afterward Erik had escorted him to the bathroom. While they were gone, I'd taken a walk out to the dock and pitched his cell phone into the Sound.

When I returned, Red watched me through blazing eyes. "I hope you know what the hell you're doing," was all he said.

I couldn't argue with that. But I also couldn't let doubt interfere with what I knew had to be done.

As the day wore on, my head seemed to be filled with memories of my father. He had been a source of irritation to me ever since I'd charged into adulthood. Mentor, beloved teacher, childhood idol—once upon a time he'd been the center of my world. During those endless hours of waiting, I tried to remember when all that had changed. Of course, he would have loved it if I had followed completely in his footsteps, but my college applications were submitted long before the Citadel had been forced to open its doors, if not its heart, to women. But the University of South Carolina in Columbia was close. I came home frequently those first two years, my social life pretty much nonexistent as I strove to live up to his expectations of me. I hadn't minded, not really. The young men I encountered all seemed so shallow, so . . . *unworthy* when stacked against my handsome, brilliant father.

Neddie probably would have jabbered about Oedipus or some such psychological claptrap, but I knew that had not been my hidden agenda. I simply wanted to please my father, to make him proud of me. With my mother, I had failed miserably to come up to scratch, my womanly skills hopelessly lacking and likely to remain so. But things were different with the Judge. There the intellect I had inherited from him counted for everything. He didn't give a damn if I couldn't cut the crusts off dainty cucumber sandwiches without mashing them in the process. I could quote Shakespeare and Milton and Descartes and Oliver Wendell Holmes. I could stand toe-to-toe with him and debate the lack of merit of the most recent Supreme Court decision or congressional mandate. Our arguments were heated but without rancor.

I lived to see the light of pride glowing in those wise gray eyes.

Then I had done the unthinkable. I'd forsaken the law and the hope he'd long cherished of the state's first father-daughter firm. In a fit of pique, he pulled the plug on my tuition, and I was forced to scramble for scholarships. My choice of Northwestern represented my wish to put as much real estate as I could between me and the carping, hostile man who had once been my "daddy."

"Bay?"

I turned from my study of the well-tended window boxes, their herbs wilting in the heat of late afternoon, to find Lavinia staring intently at me. "What?" I asked.

"Are you all right?"

"No. Are you?"

"Why haven't they called?" She twisted another of her handkerchiefs between her knotted brown fingers.

I cupped her elbow and guided her back to the table, where Erik studied a game of solitaire spread out in front of him and Red stared out into space. I pulled out a chair for Lavinia and lowered her into it.

"My guess is they're waiting until dark. I'm also pretty sure they're watching the house. I would be, if I were them. It's just a good thing Red didn't come in his cruiser. If we're lucky they didn't recognize him."

Red glanced up at the mention of his name. He glowered across the table at me, then lowered his eyes to his lap.

He would be a long time forgiving me for the gun. And the rope.

"Anyway," I said, turning back to Lavinia, "they must be pretty sure I have the documents in my possession." I shrugged. "They'll want to be certain we're sticking to the instructions, not calling in reinforcements. They could even be monitoring the sheriff's office, checking for unusual activity."

Red's snort of derision had cut across my monologue, and I felt my face begin to redden, more from anger than embarrassment. "Go ahead and laugh, Tanner. You've got dirty cops in your little fraternity, let's not forget about that. Maybe they don't need to monitor your office. Maybe your pal Wyler just checks in periodically with his real bosses."

Red glared at me, his eyes blazing in what I almost thought might be hatred. The strength of his emotion stunned me, and I was the first to drop my gaze.

Dear God, how will I ever mend this? I thought, then kicked my fear of losing Red's friendship to the back of my mind. I'd worry about that tomorrow. We had to get my father back alive. Nothing else mattered.

The sky had just given up its last brilliant yellows, fading into the rose and violet of twilight, when the cell phone chirped in my hand.

Chapter Thirty

I DON'T REMEMBER NOW WHY I TUCKED THE PACK OF cigarettes and lighter into one of the breast pockets of the blue oxford cloth shirt. I'd thrown it on as a sort of jacket over my skimpy tank top before bolting out the door of Presqu'isle. I'd taken the steps from the verandah two at a time, the plastic bag containing my father's ransom and the keys to the Expedition swinging wildly from one hand while in the other I clutched the cell phone like a lifeline.

The instructions had been clear and concise, the entire one-sided conversation lasting less than a minute. I'd fired up the powerful engine and cut the wheel hard left. I heard gravel from the driveway rattle against metal as I gunned the car across the pristine grass of the front lawn and onto the rutted dirt lane. I'd ignored the pinging red light reminding me to fasten my shoulder harness, and twice my head smacked into the thin padding of the roof as the car bounced in and out of deep potholes.

I had less than ten minutes to make it to the checkpoint.

I barreled across Route 21 onto Resurrection Road, completely ignoring the stop sign after a quick twist of my head showed the highway to be clear. I flipped on the bright lights and kept my eyes glued to the left side seeking the old track leading down to a long-abandoned boat dock. I vaguely remembered its existence from my childhood, but its entrance had long since grown over with the wild hawthorn and kudzu which reclaimed any patch of open ground left untended for even a few weeks.

But someone had been busy, I realized, as the slight break in the endless tangle of dark undergrowth whizzed by, and I slammed on the brakes. The Expedition jerked to a stop. I threw it into reverse then back to drive and whipped into the opening created by the recent and haphazard application of a scythe. Again I felt my head bounce off the roof as I pulled the big Ford through the bushes and low-lying, stunted trees until I felt the nearly impenetrable wall close behind me.

I cut the engine and waited, as I'd been instructed. I wiped the long sleeve of my shirt across the sweat streaming into my eyes and checked my watch. One minute to spare. I stared at the cell phone, willing it to ring.

It had been a good thing, I thought, my breathing finally quieting in the still, humid darkness, that my father's captors had given me no time to think. They knew their time limit would necessitate my getting underway immediately. Even so, as we raced around finding a plastic bag large enough to hold all the documents, Red had fired orders at me.

"Untie me and let me go with you! I'll hide in the back of Erik's car. The rear seats fold down, and we can throw a blanket over me, and—"

"No!" I'd screamed as Lavinia and I carefully slipped the Grayton's Race articles of incorporation, lists of officers, bank statements, and every last piece of paper I'd stolen from them a year ago into the oversized bag she used for freezing vegetables. "Make sure it's watertight," the muffled voice had said.

"He may have a point." Erik sounded calm and reasonable in contrast to Red's frenzied shouting.

"No, no, and no! They said to come alone, and that's exactly what I'm going to do."

"I agree with Bay." Lavinia's soft voice made us all stop and look at her. "Think about it, Red. What if it were one of your children? Or Sarah? What would you do? Leave it to outsiders or insist on handling things yourself?"

The question, delivered in her calm, measured voice, had quieted my brother-in-law. Erik handed over the keys, and he and Lavinia followed me to the door. She hugged me for one long, sweet moment.

"Bring him home safe," she whispered into my ear. "And be careful, child," she said aloud and stepped back.

"Hang on one sec," Erik said as I'd turned to bolt out the door. "Give me your cell."

"Can't. No time."

In a move so swift I didn't see it coming, he wrenched the small phone out of my hand.

"Erik, for God's sake!" I screamed, grabbing for the one thing connecting me to my father's only hope of survival.

He pushed several keys, then handed it back.

"What did you do?" I demanded, my heart pounding in fear.

"Nothing. Don't worry, it'll work fine. Get going."

The warmth and confidence of his smile stayed with me as I flew down the steps.

Only two notes erupted from the cell phone before I snatched it up and pressed the green button. "I'm here."

"I know that. Get out of the car. Leave the keys in the ignition and put the package on the hood."

I shoved open the heavy door, startled and slightly disoriented by the sudden burst of light in the near blackness of the wall of trees. I slipped to the ground and debated whether or not to leave the door ajar. In an instant I decided I'd be too much of a target standing silhouetted there in the wash of the interior lights, and I pushed it closed. I kept the phone pressed tightly to my ear as I slid the plastic-encased documents onto the wide black hood.

"Excellent. Now move around to the front of the vehicle."

That sounded like cop-speak. I strained for some hint of where he—or they—might be hiding, but it was impossible. They had to be using night vision goggles. There was no other way anyone could see more than a step or two in front of his face. I tripped on a tangle of roots and righted myself as I felt my way along the fender and around to the grille of the Expedition.

"Set the phone on the ground. Then take off your shirt and turn your pockets inside out. Arms out and turn slowly in a complete circle. When you've finished, pick up the phone."

I'd anticipated this. I'd debated for hours whether or not to try to conceal the little Seecamp pistol somewhere on my person or in the car and had discarded the idea as too risky. Chances were I wasn't going to get close enough for the limited range of the gun to do me any good. I also saw no point in pissing off these people upon whom my father's life depended. I'd banked on their being professionals who had no wish to kill just for the enjoyment of it. Every instinct told me if I just played by the rules, they'd do the same.

I followed their instructions to the letter, laying the phone gingerly on the sandy vestige of what had once been a dirt road down to the water. I made a great show of removing the cigarettes. The lighter slipped from my sweaty hand, but I let it fall. I turned out both pockets of my khaki shorts, then slipped out of the shirt and tossed it, too, onto the ground. Arms straight out from my sides, I did a slow pirouette, desperately ignoring the swarms of gnats suddenly buzzing around my naked skin. When I'd completed the circle, I bent over and retrieved the phone.

"Well done," the sexless voice said. "Now get the package off the hood. Keep the line open and start walking straight ahead. Follow the road."

I swatted at the tiny insects thirsting for my blood. "Can I put my shirt back on? The bugs . . ."

He—or she—paused for a long moment. "All right," the voice finally said, "but hurry it up."

I bent to feel around in front of me, my hand lighting on the shirt. As I gathered the fabric into my hands I felt the small, hard cylinder of the disposable lighter under my fingers. With no clear plan in mind, I scooped it up along with my shirt. After sliding my arms into the sleeves, I raised my hands to pull the matted, sweaty hair off my neck and managed to let the lighter slip from my fingers back into my breast pocket. I waited, but heard no muffled demand to drop it.

The small act of defiance buoyed me. I grabbed the plastic bag and began walking.

With no light to guide my footsteps, I felt disoriented, but soon I could sense the change in the texture of the ground underfoot whenever I wandered off the rutted path. I knew there had to be a moon, but its glow never penetrated the thick canopy of vine-choked trees and towering bushes. Though I kept the cell phone pressed tightly against my left ear, I heard nothing, not even an unguarded breath, as I plodded on into the blackness. For a while I tried counting my steps in order to get some idea of how far I'd traveled from the car, but the split in my concentration sent me stumbling into the thickets crowding up against the narrow track, and I soon gave it up. With both hands occupied, I had to let the gnats have their way, and the skin on my exposed wrists and neck burned with the viciousness of their attacks.

I smelled the water a few steps before the voice commanded me to stop. Ahead I could see no break in the undergrowth, but my guide instructed me to angle my steps to the right. I complied, tripping a few times, before I finally broke through the choking blackness and stumbled out onto the beach. Overhead a few wispy clouds drifted past a sliver of moon, and gentle waves washed over the narrow strip of sand. Across the way, the lights of Hilton Head blotted out the stars.

I'd expected a boat, maybe even something as small as a dinghy. All the admonitions about making sure the papers were sealed in something watertight seemed to point to that. But the beach lay empty, silent except for the sibilant *sshussh* of the breakers and the occasional *plop* as the brisk breeze sent a pine cone toppling onto the sand. The old dock had crumbled into the dark water, one lone piling the only evidence it had ever existed.

"Where are you?" I said into the cell phone, the first time I'd initiated contact.

"Shut up. Just stand there until I tell you to move."

My throat tightened in anger, but again I followed orders. I longed to bathe my itching skin in the cool water, but I held my ground.

He must have come up the beach because I never heard a footfall until he spoke from behind and to my left. "Good evening, Mrs. Tanner. Nice night for a stroll, don't you think?"

I whirled and came face to face with Carter Anderson.

Chapter Thirty-one

It took only a second for the shock of seeing him alive to morph into anger.

"You miserable little bastard!" I shouted. "Where's my father?"

I dropped both the cell phone and the bag and lunged for him, jerking to a stop when he raised the automatic pistol and pointed it at my face.

"Pick up the package, Mrs. Tanner." His hair had been restored to its natural color, and the thin moonlight glinted off the sleek black cap as well as off the shiny metal of his weapon. "I said, pick it up!" he roared, waving the gun and taking a step toward me.

I leaned over to retrieve the bag, my eyes never leaving his face. "Take it," I said, thrusting the sand-encrusted package at him. "Take it and tell me where my father is."

"All in good time. I need to enjoy this moment." Again he used the gun to gesture at me. "Move back away from the water and sit down."

I took a couple of steps away from the foaming tide line and dropped onto my knees. If the opportunity came to take on this hellish child, I wanted to be able to move quickly. Stupid as well as arrogant, he let me get away with it. I roundly cursed myself for leaving the Seecamp tucked in my handbag back at Presqu'isle. Had I known I would be this close . . . that my opponent would turn out to be this boy . . .

"You sure did give it a good run, lady."

"I'm so glad I could provide your simple mind with a little entertainment."

He grunted and squatted cross-legged on the sand. Another stupid move. I just might have a prayer of taking him.

"You're awful damn cocky for somebody looking at the wrong end of a gun, you know that?" He shook his head, and his white teeth gleamed against the deep olive of his skin. "I like that about you, I really do." Before I could formulate any sort of reply, his voice lowered. "But you killed my father, so you have to die. Grandfather says that's the way things work in our world."

"That would be your mother's father. Juan Luis Hermano." I could see my knowledge had thrown him. He wanted to be the one taunting me with things he thought I'd be desperate to know. "I hear tell even Castro couldn't stand the sight of him. Threw him out with the rest of the Cuban garbage."

"You know nothing!" He spat the words at me. "My grandfather is an honorable man. And once I have avenged my father's killing, I will be one as well."

In his agitation, Cart Anderson's voice had fallen into the sing-song rhythm of the Spanish he'd no doubt heard spoken all around him as he grew up in Miami. It made him sound like the child he really was.

I lowered my voice, groping for words that might reach him. "Cart, listen to me. This is crazy! I didn't kill your father. It was an accident, just like I told you that first day. The propane tank—"

"And you left him to die! My *abuelo,* he has told me! How you left him there to suffer so you could blackmail my family with these papers!" His voice crackled with righteous indignation.

"It's not true! I was only trying to protect *my* family. I told them, I told their lawyer I'd never release the papers so long as they left us alone." I could feel the thin thread of my control slipping away. "Why couldn't you do that? Why couldn't you just leave us alone?"

"Shut up, you stupid bitch! You lie!"

"Listen, Cart, I'm not lying." I forced my voice into a soft, soothing cadence. "There was a man who knew all about it, who could have told you I kept my word. Hadley Bolles. Your grandfather had him killed. Just a couple of days ago."

I wished I could see his face more clearly so I could judge whether or not my attempt at reasoning with him had any hope of success. But shifting clouds hid the moon except for brief flashes swallowed up in the blackness of the island night.

"You lie!" he repeated, jumping to his feet.

I tensed my legs, my hands loose at my sides, ready to react to whatever came. "No, Cart, I'm not. I'm telling you the truth. I did not kill your father. He tried to kill *me*."

"Liar!" he roared, the gun waving wildly in his hand.

"No, Cart. Your father tried to shoot me. That's what set off the explosion." When he didn't scream back at me, I lowered my voice still further, calming, soothing. "And I didn't blackmail anyone, except to keep them from harming me and my family. You've got a phone. Call your grandfather and ask him."

"No, you are lying. It is my duty to avenge my father. My *abuelo* has told me. Then I will be a man."

Despite the strength of his words, his voice had begun to waver. He was, after all, still a child, a boy bereft of any kind of guidance except from his drug-smuggling grandfather. I sensed his confusion, his hesitation, and I used it. In one fluid motion I scooped up a handful of the fine, loose sand and flung it at his head. I saw his hands fly to his face, the gun tumbling onto the beach, and I lunged for it a moment before he recovered. I snatched it up and rolled away from the boy's flailing arms, coming to rest a few feet away. I pushed myself onto my knees and leveled the automatic at his chest.

"Get down!" I screamed, all the fear and rage of the last interminable hours erupting in a rush. "On your face, hands on top of your head! Do it!" I forced myself to hold my grip steady as the boy slowly lowered himself to the ground.

"My eyes—" he began, but I was having none of it.

"You've got three seconds before I start shooting."

I saw him lift his pale, trembling hands and lock them behind his head. I pushed myself to my feet and moved a few steps closer. "Where's my father?"

"I don't know," he whimpered.

"What do you mean, you don't know?" I screamed at him

"I swear to God I don't know where they took him! Please don't kill me!"

And in that moment my whirling brain stopped long enough to recognize the impossibility that this whole scenario—the faked disappearance, the planted evidence, Miss Minnie and the faceless body, my father's abduction—had been engineered by this one teenaged boy. I jumped back, my head whipping around, certain now his accomplices wouldn't be far away.

My mind fastened on that one word, *abduction*. They might have the Judge, but I had the *jefe's* grandson. A trade. If only there was enough time . . . I used my feet to feel around until the toe of one shoe brushed up against my discarded cell phone. Eyes never leaving the boy lying facedown in front of me, I picked it up and tried to blow away the sand encrusting the face. I could barely see the light from the keypad, but I prayed my fingers would find the proper numbers. My ear was met with absolute silence. Maybe a dead spot or more probably the sand. I jammed it in my pocket.

"Get up!" I yelled at the boy. "Keep your hands on top of your head."

I watched him struggle to comply, staggering a little in the loose sand. While he stood, wobbling on legs weak with fear, I risked a glance down the beach, trying to get my bearings. If I had it right, we weren't too far from the winding trail leading up to the back of Fort Fremont. If we headed that way, I'd be better able to keep my prisoner under control than if we tried to renegotiate the thick wall of brush I'd just struggled through.

"Move!" I ordered the boy, jerking my head in the direction I wanted him to go.

"You won't kill me," Cart Anderson said in one last burst of bravado. "You're just a woman."

I had to give him credit for guts. "My father is out there, possibly bleeding to death while I stand here debating with you." I didn't have to fake the dead, determined tone of my voice. "If you get in my way or slow me down, I'll shoot you in a New York second, you little son of a bitch. Now move it!"

He whirled without another word and set off in a stumbling gait down the beach.

I had just reached over to pick up the discarded package of papers when I felt the cold steel of the muzzle pressed up against my neck. My breath died in my throat.

"Drop the gun, Mrs. Tanner."

I thought about it for a split second, then let the automatic trickle from my fingers onto the sand.

"Step away from it. Slowly."

"Hey! What . . . ?" I heard Cart Anderson call from down the beach, then the steady slap of his sneakers on the sand as he trotted back toward us.

"Farther," the voice said, and I knew who it was. It gave me little satisfaction to have my own and Gabby Henson's suspicions confirmed on a dark, deserted beach with a gun aimed at the back of my head.

I moved a few feet away, and I sensed him reach down and retrieve the automatic moments before the boy hurried up. Without instruction, I put my hands on top of my head and slowly turned around.

"Good evening, Detective Wyler. I wish I could say I'm surprised to see you."

"I must admit I was somewhat taken aback to find you in possession of the gun."

"She tricked me," Cart Anderson whined. "But I wasn't worried. I knew Grandfather would come through."

A spill of moonlight touched the detective's lopsided face. I didn't understand the sardonic smile that played across his lips or the look he shot at the triumphant boy beside him.

"Right," he said, and I wondered just how long he had been lurking in the thick undergrowth observing the struggle on the beach.

Cart stuck out his hand. "Give me my gun. I'm going to whack her right now." All his brash courage seemed to have returned with the arrival of his partner.

To my surprise Wyler tucked the pistol into the waistband of his trousers. "I don't think so, son. It's time for the men to take over this enterprise. Hermano should have his head examined for sending a kid to take care of things."

"My grandfather—"

"Yeah, I know, he'll kill me for insulting his heir and protégé. I'll take my chances." His eyes never leaving the boy's, he bent over and picked up the plastic bag from the ground, then gestured with the barrel of the gun. "I believe you were about to take a little walk. Let's go." I could hear the smile in his voice as he added, "You can take your hands down, Mrs. Tanner. I have a feeling you've shot your wad for tonight."

Cart Anderson and I kept our distance from each other as we plodded through the loose sand in front of the former New York detective. A thousand questions raced through my head, not the least of which was why Wyler hadn't just let the kid shoot me. If kidnapping the Judge had been intended to lure me out into the open with the stolen documents, the plan had worked admirably. My thin hope that I was dealing with professionals had been dashed the moment Geoffrey Anderson's son stepped out of the dark. It was not, as I had been telling myself, a simple case of trading the papers for the Judge. This was about vengeance and *machismo,* about a boy proving his manhood. An eye for an eye. My father for his.

"You don't need to kill him," I said over my shoulder, Detective Ben Wyler merely a thin gray image against the blacker night.

"Just walk, Mrs. Tanner," came his reply.

I glanced at the young man trudging along beside me, his face hidden in the shadows of the vines and branches trailing from the stunted trees clinging to the edge of the shore.

"You haven't done anything yet you can't put right," I whispered. He ignored me. I thought about his mother's insistence, even going so far as to make it a condition of her will, that her only son should not be left in the custody of her own father. How she must have longed to send him far from the life she'd grown up in.

"Do you think this is what your mother would have wanted for you?" I said softly.

"Shut your mouth about my mother!" the boy yelled, his shout followed quickly by Wyler's terse command for both of us to can it.

A few yards later Wyler called a halt, peered around us into the underbrush, and muttered softly, "Good." He urged us forward again, this time up the almost invisible dirt path which wound its way from the water to the back side of Fort Fremont, and I wondered how an outsider knew so much about our local backwoods.

The vine- and ivy-covered fort loomed before us, much of its concrete expanse hidden behind undulating earthworks meant to help protect it from an attack by sea that never came. I let my eyes drift to the single chimney of Miss Minnie's rambling cottage, just discernible through the swaying boughs of the pines. We followed the winding path, the boy moving ahead of me, until we emerged finally into the dusty clearing at the front of the crumbling building. Cart stopped dead, and I nearly crashed into his back before I, too, halted to stare in amazement at the white Ford Crown Victoria with the black decals and the blue-and-red light bar squatting silent and empty among the trees.

I thought I heard Wyler mutter, "Shit!" under his breath.

"What are you doin' here?"

We all whirled at the disembodied voice that seemed to float out from the depths of the old fort like ghost-words on the still night air. I watched in dismay as Deputy Lonnie Daggett, in faded jeans and dirt-streaked T-shirt, ducked his head and stepped out into the clearing.

"This wasn't the plan, Wyler," he said, moving farther out into the scant moonlight. He shot a quick look over his shoulder and lowered his voice. "Why the hell'd you bring her up here?"

I whipped my head around to confront the calm, unreadable face of the detective.

"You know, Bay, at one point they were actually hoping you might do the dirty work for them," Wyler said, his eyes flicking briefly in my direction. "All the strain of the accusations on top of your boyfriend bailing out on you. Woulda made life simpler all the way around. And no repercussions." He nodded wisely, as if passing comment on a promising student's efforts. "Not bad, really. I think they set the stage rather nicely considering they were improvising most of the way."

I had only a second to register his use of *they* rather than *we* before Lonnie Daggett's voice cut across the night.

"Way I heard it, you weren't supposed to be in on this end of things at all, *De*-tective." He shifted his weight, rising a little on the balls of his feet. "Why don't you just tuck that pea-shooter back in your pocket and head on outta here." He tossed a look back over his shoulder. "Me and the kid got everything under control."

"Is my father in there?" It suddenly seemed the perfect place for them to have stashed him, deserted and close by with little chance of their being disturbed, especially with a police cruiser parked out front. "Daddy?" I shouted, lunging toward the dark opening. "Daddy!"

I felt young Cart grab for my arm, but I jerked it away. As if in slow motion I watched the deputy's hand slide toward his holster, his fingers tightening as they found the grip of his sidearm and jerked it free. A small, cold voice inside my head whispered, *This is it,* as I gathered my strength to launch myself at the only barrier between me and my father.

But suddenly Wyler's free hand smashed against my shoulder. I felt myself leave my feet, my body tossed aside as if I weighed no more than a leaf. Then the world exploded in a deafening roar as I felt the white-hot heat of the bullet skim by my head, and Lonnie Daggett collapsed in a pool of blood streaming from a gaping hole in the center of his chest.

For a moment I lay there, stunned, my ears refusing to function, my mind unable to grasp the fact I wasn't dead. I saw the deputy writhing on the ground, saw his mouth agape in an agonized scream, but none of it registered. As if in a dream, I turned my head to find Ben Wyler also down, one hand clasped to his thigh, blood oozing through his fingers.

High Noon, some detached part of my brain observed, *Gunfight at the OK Corral,* and I found myself suppressing a hysterical giggle.

I slapped my hands against my ears and heard a faint popping before I scrambled to my feet and stumbled toward the opening of the old fort. Something flashed in front of me, and I realized it was the boy. Faintly I heard Wyler call my name, but I ignored him, vaulting over the wounded deputy and throwing myself into the darkness.

Chapter Thirty-Two

I skidded to a halt just inside the doorway, willing my eyes to adjust quickly. I had no idea if the boy had picked up one of the fallen guns. Ahead, the inky blackness swallowed whatever thin light might have drifted in from the clearing. I clapped my hands to my ears once more and sighed gratefully as the sound of running feet and dislodged pebbles finally registered.

I waited, trying to gauge his direction, but the noise suddenly ceased. I strained for any indication of my father's presence but heard nothing. I had no idea what had happened outside the cavernous fort, why Wyler and Daggett had been shooting at each other. Useless speculation. Without conscious thought, my hand dipped into the pocket of my shirt and pulled out the slim lighter.

I risked a quick flare of light to get my bearings, then let the flame die. I had one distinct advantage over my adversary: my childhood memory knew the inside of this place like a well-loved playroom. I rested my hand against the left wall and stepped cautiously into the gloom.

We were in the section which had been intended as quarters for the soldiers. Several small rooms led off this central hallway. I forced myself to conjure up the layout. Nothing would have changed since Bitsy and I had run shrieking down this same corridor, imaginary Spanish cutthroats hard on our heels. I remembered a large shaft, open to the battlement above, through which stored ammunition could be hoisted up to resupply the big cannons that once stood in massive gun emplacements carved out of the stone. A second passageway cut off at right angles connecting this part of the rabbit warren of windowless rooms with a nearly identical one on the opposite side.

My groping hand suddenly slid into empty space, and I stopped, straining for any telltale sound. I held the lighter in front of me, my thumb on the tiny lever. I drew a steadying breath, then in a tense parody of every TV cop show I'd ever seen, I whipped my body into the opening, flicking on the light as I moved.

Empty.

I waited for some reaction from my quarry, for the *zing* of a bullet moments before it struck, but all was silence. I turned and stepped across the passage, repeating my darting glance illuminated by a few seconds of light. Again nothing.

I worked my way down the corridor, my fear growing exponentially with every empty room. He had to be there! That furtive look Daggett cast over his shoulder had to mean something. Why else would he be at the fort? What else could he be guarding?

A rattle of stones behind me and to my right sent me whirling back toward the entrance. I caught a brief flash of a white sneaker disappearing into the connecting passageway, and I sprinted after it, all thought of stealth gone. As I skidded around the corner, I thought I heard voices drifting in from outside, but I forced myself to ignore them. At the intersection with the next main hallway, I paused to listen, my chest heaving. The footfalls, more measured now, moved left, deeper into the heart of the maze. I spared a moment to wonder if Cart Anderson knew where he was going, would lead me to my father, or if he was just running blindly in fear and desperation. Again I placed my hand against the wall and moved forward.

This time I sensed the opening before my hand fell into it, and I stopped just short of the low, narrow doorway. It was lighter there, and I realized I must be close to the ammunition shaft, its top open to the moonlit sky. I held my breath, almost certain I could hear muffled wheezing through the foot-thick walls. I walked backwards, cautiously, again using the wall to guide me. I stepped around the corner and hunkered down. Using my free hand as a shield I flicked on the lighter, holding it close to the ground.

In the center of the corridor, away from my own precise footprints a few inches from the wall, I saw others, more than one to judge by the disturbance in the loose, dusty soil. And something else, something that made my heart sing and falter at the same time: tire tracks, narrow and closely spaced. My father's wheelchair! I clicked the lighter again and risked a quick glance down the hallway. The trail ended at the first opening.

I propped my back against the rough concrete and considered my options. I had only moments to decide. Outside lay two wounded cops, armed, and not on the side of the angels, although Wyler's actions continued to puzzle me. Ahead lay a seventeen-year-old boy, no doubt confused and frightened, but potentially deadly nonetheless. He could be armed. Or he could be cowering in a corner whimpering like a puppy. No way to know.

The one thing I did know was that my father was almost certainly inside that room. No doubt as confused and frightened as the boy, but also possibly bleeding to death from a medication meant to save him. What choice did I really have?

I tucked the lighter back into my pocket and dropped down on all fours. I swallowed the fear and crept around the corner, my eyes on the yawning emptiness of the doorway ahead. I concentrated on avoiding any noise that might betray my approach. The plan was simple. If Cart Anderson had a gun, he'd be aiming at the middle of the space, expecting a standing adversary. Coming in low might give me a few seconds' advantage. Or not. A small, insistent voice told me I had no idea what the hell I was doing, that I was just as likely to get us both killed as effect any kind of rescue. I ordered it to shut up as I silently rocked back onto my haunches, took a quick breath, and rolled through the door.

The only sound to greet me was a muted rustling somewhere on the left and a soft grunt as my leg connected with the footrest on my father's wheelchair. My eyes swept the room. It was tiny, barely ten feet square. Though my eyes couldn't penetrate to the farthest corners, I knew immediately there was nowhere for Cart Anderson to hide.

I scrambled to my knees and flung myself at my father's still form. "Daddy? Are you okay? Daddy!"

I tried desperately to quell the trembling of my own hands as they sought his chest. I nearly fainted with the relief of finding his heart beating, slowly but rhythmically. He mumbled something then, as if talking in his sleep, and I let my head fall across his lap. Drugged, but alive. "Thank you, God," I murmured, my fingers unconsciously folding together in a child's simple attitude of prayer. For a moment the source of their stickiness didn't register. Then I gasped, fumbling the lighter out of my pocket and finally coaxing it to blaze.

The entire front of my father's shirt was caked in blood. A slow stream leaked from his nose and dribbled across his chin.

"Sweet Jesus," I stammered, kneeling there in the dirt. My hand quivered, and the light flickered and died.

His body slumped, limp and unresponsive. I had to get him out of there. I groped through his pants pockets and pulled out a neatly folded handkerchief. The thick linen refused to be torn. I wasn't sure if tilting his head back would cause him to choke, but I knew I had to get the blood loss under control. I packed two corners of the hanky loosely in both sides of his nose. I tucked the lighter in my pants pocket and stripped off my shirt, wadding it into a ball and wedging it under his chin. If I went slowly and didn't jostle him . . . Or maybe I should leave him long enough to run for help. I twisted my head toward the doorway, the indecision an agony almost beyond bearing. I felt the hot tears dripping onto my cheeks as I knelt there in the dust, my father's head cradled in my hands.

The dying echoes of a voice, calling my name, made my head snap up a moment before I heard the soft rattle and felt the weight of something heavy slither across the backs of my legs.

Both of us froze, the snake and I. I bit down on the scream rising from my chest, my panicked brain ordering my body to be still, but it had its own agenda. I could feel the fear trembling down my arms and across my shoulders. I clenched the muscles in my calves to keep them from quivering, but I knew I couldn't hold the tension for long.

"Vinnie?" My father's voice shattered the stillness, and I twitched involuntarily. I felt the snake shift its weight, and the vibrations of its rattle intensified. A soft haze drifted across my vision . . .

"Just stand still." A large, muscular hand clutches my shoulder, forcing me to stop. Through the heavy wool of my winter jacket I feel his strength and assurance flow through me. "He's more afraid of us than we are of him."

"I don't think so, Daddy," I say, my eyes riveted on the long, sinuous body slithering by just inches from my red rubber boots.

The afternoon is unusually cold and overcast, even for the last of December. Two more days and I have to go back to school. Over on the other side of the woods I can hear Hootie and Beulah baying on the scent.

"He's just trying to get home, out of the cold," my father says. "We sort of stepped onto his driveway, and he's a little put out with us. If we just give him a minute, he'll be on his way."

"Why don't you shoot him, Daddy?" I ask, my eyes darting to the shotgun broken over his right arm.

I feel the hand tighten on my shoulder. "Never shoot anything you don't intend to eat," he says sternly, "unless you have no choice, unless it's his life or yours. Other creatures besides us have a right to exist. Remember that, princess, okay? Bay? Can you hear me? Bay?"

"Yes, Daddy," I said out loud at almost the same instant I realized it had not been my dream-father who'd spoken but someone behind me, near the doorway.

It took every ounce of willpower I had to ignore my gut instinct to turn in that direction. The weight had not lifted from the backs of my legs.

"Bay, it's me! Where are you?"

I saw the glow of a powerful flashlight reflected off the old stone walls.

"Red," I called softly but got no response. I had no idea how the rattler would react to loud noises. Or light. I sucked in a breath. "Red." Louder this time, and I heard him gasp and slide to a stop just outside the door.

"Put out the light," I said as calmly and succinctly as I could.

"What—?"

"Snake," I said, again speaking slowly and precisely. "Across my legs."

I breathed when I saw the darkness swallow us up again.

"The Judge?"

"Here. Bleeding, but alive." Again I felt the snake shift. He seemed to be moving in a straight line, not coiling for a strike, but I had no idea how long that would last. "Gun?" I asked.

Red had caught on to the shorthand immediately. "Yes," he said. "Moving?"

"Left to right. Slowly."

I felt the quality of the blackness change as Red stepped into the doorway. The snake twitched.

"Got him. Rattler. Big one."

I heard a muted, metallic noise, a slide being drawn back or maybe a hammer being cocked. I couldn't tell.

"Red—"

"Close your eyes and hold your breath," he said calmly. "Do it now."

I sucked in a mouthful of air, ready to plead with him to wait, but I was too late.

A brilliant wash of light flared a second before the reverberations of the shot threatened to deafen me again. The snake's body jumped, the tail with its hardened rattles slapping against my bare arm as a warm, wet spray splattered across my cheek, and I slumped across my father's lap.

Chapter Thirty-Three

THE SHERIFF TAPPED ME TO FILL IN FOR MORGAN BEcause of Judge Newhall," Ben Wyler said, resting his crutches against the side of the fireplace and lowering himself into the wing chair in the Judge's study. "Figured that would give me a good excuse to keep tabs on her."

Against the advice of every doctor who'd poked and prodded him during his three days in the hospital, my father refused to stay in bed. Wrapped in his comfortable old maroon robe, he held court from his worn recliner, smoke from a smoldering cigar being sucked into the updraft of the ceiling fan. Lavinia had fussed at him and finally thrown up her hands in exasperation and stalked from the room.

"Why you?" he asked in response to the detective's statement.

"Ginny—the judge, that is—we knew each other. Had some history." He smiled in that sardonic way I was getting used to and added, "Back in the city."

I itched to ask if he meant *knew* in the biblical sense, but I held my tongue.

"So they used Detective Morgan's leave of absence to set up a sting," my father said, and the detective nodded. "What put them on to her?"

Wyler smiled. "Lots of things. Her reputation up in New York, for one. Then she got herself appointed to fill out the term when Woodrow Carnes had his coronary."

My father nodded. "I remember that. Lots of us around town couldn't figure out why they skipped over other more . . . *entrenched* candidates."

Wyler and I exchanged a look. He seemed relaxed and just a little buzzed from the combination of pain medication and watered-down bourbon, and I found his slightly off-center face almost attractive.

"Beats me. I'd guess all the money she spread around during the last election didn't hurt. At any rate, it didn't take long for someone to notice that drug defendants seemed to be getting off on obscure technicalities pretty regularly in her court."

I pulled my feet up onto the wide cushion of the window seat and wrapped my arms around my knees.

Wyler continued. "There'd been rumors, back in New York, that she might have been on the pad, but she resigned before any real investigation got underway. Retired for her health, or so she said. Others thought differently, that maybe someone had a vested interest in seeing her settle in down here."

The Judge cleared his throat. "A few rumors flyin' around about you as well, Detective."

Wyler's jaw tightened, and his hand moved to the general location of the bullet wound in his left thigh, absently stroking the outline of the bulky bandage visible beneath the leg of his trousers. "I was exonerated of all charges," he said stiffly. "I could have had my old job back any time I wanted it."

My father smiled, and some of the tension went out of Wyler's shoulders. "I know. But instead you took a quite sizeable settlement in lieu of suing their pants off and headed south." He paused, then favored us with one of his snorts of laughter. "Close your mouth, Detective. I may not have the resources of the New York Police Department, but the ones I do have are generally proficient. We're not quite the little hick town you first took us for, are we?"

Ben Wyler relaxed back into his chair. "No sir, you're not" Again he stroked his injured leg. "As I've learned to my considerable discomfort."

The mood in the sun-drenched room sobered. "So lay it out for me," my father said. "How did my daughter get caught up in all this?" He cast a glance in my direction.

Part of me felt strangely detached from the whole scene, almost as if it were a play or the denouement of some television drama. I'd been so consumed during the past few days in dealing with doctors and hospitals, with Lavinia's near collapse at the sight of my father's blood-soaked form as they unloaded his gurney from the ambulance, I'd had little time for speculation. For two weeks I had fought and schemed to get to the truth. Now, when the answers sat less than ten feet away, it all seemed vaguely anticlimactic. My father was safe. Nothing else seemed important. Nevertheless, I swung my feet back onto the floor and forced myself to pay attention.

"Best we can figure, Hermano sent his grandson out to seek revenge for Anderson's death. And to try and shake your daughter loose of those documents she had stashed. That was the catalyst. The rest?" Wyler shrugged. "I think they just took advantage of the breaks that kept coming their way, anything they could use to jam up Mrs. Tanner."

"Bay," I said. "Considering you've pawed through my underwear and taken a bullet for me, I think we can move on to a first-name relationship."

Wyler smiled. "Bay it is. Anyway, they planned to use Judge Newhall to keep the pressure on. Just their bad luck I was the one she was dealing with."

"So you convinced her you could be had for the right price?" I asked.

"Something like that. It didn't take much convincing, what with our prior history."

"What does the boy have to say?" my father asked.

Ben Wyler shook his head. "Not much. The Atlanta lawyer Mrs. Anderson hired for him is sharp. He's perfectly willing to let Cart give up his grandfather's operation, but the kid's keeping his mouth shut about his own actions. He's going to get tried as an adult, so any homicide charges could put him on death row. I can already smell a deal simmering."

Red had told me they'd found Cart Anderson cowering in one of the rooms deep inside the maze of the abandoned fort. He'd also explained how Erik had switched my cell phone to "location" mode. Once Red had convinced my partner to untie him, he'd set the cops to tracking me, although the intermittent reception on the island had nearly caused them to lose me several times. The cavalry had arrived only minutes too late to prevent the shootout in which both Wyler and Lonnie Daggett were injured.

When they'd finally cornered the boy, dirty and hopelessly lost, he'd offered no resistance to the officers. His bravado on the beach had been replaced by tearful remorse and an insistence he'd been an unwilling pawn of his powerful grandfather. Cleaned up and presented in a sympathetic light by the recent loss of both his parents, he had a good chance of getting a jury to buy it.

"So he never intended to move in with his Anderson grandparents? They actually sent the boy up here to get me?"

"That was the plan. You were a loose end. Hermano didn't like having the potential threat of those documents hanging over his head. The way the kid tells it, he was just supposed to follow you around, see if there might be an opening for an 'accident,' " Wyler said.

I crossed the room, pulled my cigarettes from my bag, and shook the last Marlboro out of the crumpled pack. I stared at it a moment before tossing it into the empty fireplace. I drew a deep breath and turned at my father's grunt of surprise. "Time to get back on the straight and narrow," I said, and he snorted again.

"So whose idea was it to stage that little scenario out at the fort? With the empty car and the blood drops in the front seat?"

Wyler sipped at his diluted drink and continued as I settled back onto the window seat. "After your boyfriend roughed him up, the kid reported back to his grandfather. You have to give the old man credit. He saw the possibilities right away. He told the kid to hook up with one of the cartel's dealers in the area and set some sort of scene to make it look as if he'd met with foul play, then keep out of sight and wait to see what happened. They picked Fort Fremont because they'd used it as a storefront for their drug dealing before."

Wyler's talk of trouble at the abandoned fort reminded me of Gabby Henson and the incident reports she'd copied for me. I'd been unbelievably rude to her when she'd called my cell that horrible night. Pacing the waiting room at the hospital while the doctors worked frantically to staunch my father's blood loss, I'd screamed at her to leave me alone, and surprisingly she had. But I owed her an exclusive, and I intended to keep that promise.

"Did he ever stop at his grandmother's in Beaufort?" I asked, remembering with a pang the confused longing in Millicent Anderson's eyes as she'd stood at the top of her curving staircase and pleaded with me to find her grandson.

"Nope, or so he says. Claims he grabbed some fast food and went straight out to the meet. The little moron's a user, so he couldn't resist toking up a few with his grandfather's flunky. Cart says it was this other guy's idea to cut their fingers and dribble some blood around the seats, make things look more realistic, but who knows?"

I absently massaged my left shoulder. "And you bought it."

Wyler shrugged again. "Hey, your brother-in-law caught the call. Once he ran the plate, he didn't have much choice. Especially with the blood. And your extracurricular activities earlier in the day."

My eyes narrowed as I stared at the detective.

"You have to admit you made a helluva good suspect." He paused, and his voice lost its lighthearted tone. "All the evidence pointed to you—and your boyfriend. You really can't blame Sergeant Tanner for pursuing the lead."

"But you knew it wasn't my blood. Or Darnay's."

"No, I didn't know that. Not at first. Of course, once I got the search warrant, things started to look different."

"Why?" I asked.

"Because I never asked for one. I didn't even push right away for the DNA swabs and blood tests on the two of you, not until we had a lot more evidence. But suddenly there you were, marching into the station to make a donation."

"So if you didn't order the search warrant, who did?"

My father pulled a clean handkerchief from the pocket of his robe and swiped it across his nose. I watched to make certain it didn't come away streaked with blood. He caught me studying him and smiled, holding the pristine piece of linen up for my inspection before tucking it back in his pocket.

"Judge Ginny," Wyler said, ignoring the interplay between my father and me. "That's what first set off the alarm bells, at least for me. You know as well as I do it's almost unheard of for a judge to initiate a warrant in a case like this. Made me wonder what her agenda really was." He paused and downed the last of his drink.

"Bought off by the Florida boys?" the Judge asked.

"Bought and paid for, just as we figured." Wyler stretched out his damaged leg and winced a little as he resettled it. "Setting up Bay to take the fall for a bogus murder was just a little side job she was happy to perform."

"And what about Lonnie Daggett?" I asked. "How did he get caught up in this whole thing?"

"I can answer that."

We all swiveled at the sound of Red's voice from the doorway. So engrossed had we been in Detective Ben Wyler's revelations, none of us had registered my brother-in-law's arrival. Behind him, Lavinia hovered, her face more careworn than I'd seen it in a long time. She followed Red into the room, pulled an afghan from the back of the vacant wing chair, and tucked it around my father's legs.

"Too cold in here," she muttered, gathering up empty glasses and taking custody of the ashtray and its smoldering contents of half-burned tobacco and coils of gray ash.

She turned to stare at each of us in turn. "And the next person who gives this man a cigar is gonna have me to answer to! And let me tell you, it won't be pretty!"

She marched from the room, and I could hear her muttering to herself as she stomped down the hallway toward the kitchen.

Red lowered himself into the wing chair and crossed his legs. Obviously off duty, he wore faded green shorts and his Marine Corps T-shirt.

"Sergeant," Wyler said, acknowledging Red with a brief nod.

"Detective," he answered just as curtly.

"Nice to see you, Redmond," my father said. "You have information on this Daggett boy?"

"Not much to tell really. I finally got the captain to fill me in. Daggett was under suspicion along with his brother, who, as you know, had already been bounced off the force. Both of them seemed to have way too much cash for what they were makin', and we'd had a run of drug evidence disappear on busts. Caught Tommy red-handed, but the jury was still out on Lonnie." He scratched at a spot behind his right knee. "Guess someone got to him, too."

"He's not talking?" I asked.

"Can't." He glanced sideways at Wyler. "He died about an hour ago without ever regaining consciousness."

It seemed as if the air temperature had dropped twenty degrees. No one spoke. I listened to the steady beat of the old grandfather clock as it measured out the inevitable cadence of time moving on.

"I'm sorry to hear that," Wyler finally said. He reached for his crutches and pulled himself to his feet. He hitched them underneath his arms and locked his long, slender fingers around the handgrips. "They'll be wanting to talk with me."

"I'm grateful, Detective," my father said, and Wyler balanced himself on his good leg in order to clasp the Judge's outstretched hand. For a long moment they held each other's eyes.

"My pleasure, Your Honor," the detective said, finally disengaging his hand. "Sergeant," he added over his shoulder, "I appreciate you bringing me the news. I'll see you around the office."

Red remained silent as I stepped behind my father's chair. "I'll walk you out," I said, slipping in front of Wyler.

I held open the heavy front door, then walked ahead while he negotiated the steps, the muscles in his forearms rippling under the strain of carrying his entire weight. At the bottom he paused to catch his breath.

"Sure you're okay to drive?" I asked. I stood with one hand curled around the finial on the railing post, studying this enigmatic man.

Wyler squinted in the blazing sun and deliberately misinterpreted my question. "Takes me a while to get in the damn car, but once I'm in there I'm fine."

I drew a deep breath and asked, "Do they know who killed Miss Minnie?" It seemed to me, in all the rush to ferret out the crooked cops and judges and take down the drug cartel, the death of the old black woman had been pushed to the bottom of the priority list.

Ben Wyler's face tightened into a grimace. "No, and I'm not holding out much hope of ever finding out for certain. My money's on Anderson and his drug dealer pal, although the kid is claiming he knows nothing about it. If he sticks to that story, there's not a whole hell of a lot we can do. The stolen shotgun is what clinches it for me, but we never found any useable prints, so . . ." He hitched the crutches up and leaned forward. "However it turns out, it wasn't your fault. You and your boyfriend just happened to be in the wrong place at the wrong time."

His absolution did little to lessen my feelings of loss, but I smiled my thanks anyway.

Wyler smiled back. "You know, it's funny. Just because these guys haven't gotten caught and have managed to make a pile of money, we give them way too much credit. Criminals—even big-time operators like Hermano—are usually dumber than dirt." He shook his head. "It was strictly amateur hour right from the beginning, but things just seemed to keep falling their way. Your blood type in the car, your public fight with the boy, showing up at the old lady's house. Judge Newhall knew from her bosses that Lonnie Daggett could be had with a little extra cash, and he kept her informed about the investigation. She in turn was passing the information along to the boys in Miami. The old man was directing both her and the kid, trying to take advantage of every break that came their way. But then they got greedy. Blowing away Cart's drug connection with the old lady's gun and then planting it under your porch was strictly overkill."

"Did Lonnie Daggett shoot the boy?"

He shrugged. "What do you think?"

"My money's on Daggett. I know it's probably naïve, but I have a hard time wrapping my head around Cart Anderson as a cold-blooded murderer."

"Just a sucker for a pretty face, huh? Well, don't let him fool you. Kid's got a juvie record as long as your arm."

"Still . . ."

"Hey, what can I say? Unless we get Anderson to cop to it, both the dealer's and the old lady's deaths are gonna end up in the cold case files."

The afternoon breeze ruffled his hair and carried the cries of the gulls to us from across the Sound.

After a while, I said, "I really played right into their hands, didn't I? By getting the documents out of the bank."

"I have to admit that one had me going for a while," Wyler said, "you taking off like that. I began to wonder if maybe I'd pegged the whole thing wrong, and you really were involved somehow."

"We all thought we were being so damned clever. I couldn't have guaranteed my father's kidnapping any better if I'd been in on the plans."

"Not so. It took me by surprise, too. I had to do some scrambling to get myself invited into the game in time. But they had a lot of options open. Like I said, they were really playing it by ear. They just kept reacting as the situation unfolded. If it hadn't been that, they would have found some other way." He shook his head. "I don't think you realize the enormous egos of men like Hermano. You crossed him and won. He would have come after you no matter how long it took. Or how many bodies."

There didn't seem to be much more to say, and we stood in awkward silence for a few moments. Even though the sun had slid behind the trees, the heat still shimmered in waves across the gravel of the drive.

"Well," Detective Ben Wyler said, "I guess I'd better get to the office."

"Will there be trouble? About Daggett's shooting?"

He shifted his weight on the crutches. "I don't think so, but there's bound to be an inquiry."

I watched as he maneuvered himself around toward his unmarked cruiser. "I could be a character witness," I offered, and his genuine laugh brought an answering smile to my face.

"That could be a two-edged sword," he said.

I followed him down the walk and pulled open the driver's door. He tossed the crutches onto the seat beside him and gingerly swung his legs in.

"Thank you," I said as he turned the key in the ignition.

"My pleasure, ma'am," he replied in that same mocking drawl he'd used once before.

I stood watching as the car moved slowly down the drive and into the rutted lane before I turned back to flop down onto the bottom step.

I don't know how much later Red found me there. He came slowly down the stairs and settled in beside me.

"Ready for some good news?" he asked.

"That would be a nice change."

"I already told your father. The FBI picked up Hermano trying to make a run for it in his private jet. He's been arraigned on a federal warrant—racketeering, money-laundering, murder-for-hire, the whole enchilada. Corralled about a dozen of his closest friends as well."

I turned to look into his eyes. "For real?"

Red grinned. "Yup. Someone must have convinced the boy and Judge Newhall they'd be better off in a federal pen than out on the street where Hermano's goons could get to them. They named names, and they're both going to testify. Word is none of them will be seeing the outside for a few decades at least. The documents you brought back will just be extra nails in their coffins." He patted my shoulder. "I think we can chalk this one up as a win for the good guys."

I thought about all that had been sacrificed—the time, the resources, the lives ruined and lost—to take these bastards off the streets, and I wondered if it had been worth it. Rob had died fighting them. Geoff Anderson and Hadley Bolles and Lonnie Daggett had been victims of their own greed; Miss Minnie, simply a casualty of the seemingly endless war. Who knew how many others? But in the long run, would it make a damned bit of difference? Juan Luis Hermano was out of business. Who would swoop in to fill the vacuum?

Someone. You can be damned sure of that, I thought, shaking my head. *Still . . .*

"What?" Red asked, his hand still resting on my shoulder. "I thought you'd be pleased."

I turned to him and forced a smile. "I am. Really." The idea popped into my head from out of nowhere. *It's time.* "When do you have to be back on duty?" I asked.

He looked puzzled. "I've got the next two days off. Why?"

I rose and took his hand, pulling him to his feet. "I want to take a trip," I said. "Will you go with me?"

Without asking a single question, he nodded.

Chapter Thirty-Four

Red picked me up at the beach house a little after eight the next morning. After returning home the previous evening, I'd left a message for Erik, who had gone back to Charlotte to wind up his affairs. He'd be on the island for good by the first of the week. I'd also made Lavinia swear she'd call me on the cell if there was the slightest deterioration in my father's condition.

The letter from Darnay had been waiting for me amid a stack of bills and circulars Dolores had left piled on the side table in the entry. For a long time I'd simply held it in my hands, staring at the foreign stamps and my former lover's bold, decisive handwriting. Then I'd carried it out to the deck, settled myself on the chaise, and eased it open . . .

We took the Thunderbird. I put the top down and turned my face toward the warmth of the early morning sun shimmering out of a cloudless sky. Red drove, and I relaxed into the soft leather, which seemed to wrap itself around me like a comforting shawl.

"You okay?" my brother-in-law asked after several miles of silence.

"Fine. Getting better by the minute."

"You're a strange one, Bay Tanner," he said with a shake of his head.

A few wisps of light brown hair escaped the baseball cap pulled low on his forehead against the breeze whipping into the open car.

I pushed myself up a little straighter. "Why do you say that?"

"Why the decision to make this . . . pilgrimage all of a sudden?"

I shrugged. "It seemed like time. I've been a coward."

His snort did justice to one of the Judge's. "That's the last thing anybody would call you. Most women who've been through everything you have would be blubbering in a corner by now. Or maybe locked in a rubber room."

"I'm sure there's a compliment in there somewhere." I studied his profile for a moment. "I take it you've forgiven me?"

"What's to forgive? Oh, you mean that threatening me with a loaded gun and tying me to a chair thing?" I winced, and he actually laughed. "Water over the dam. I might have done the same thing in your place."

We lapsed again into comfortable silence as Red slowed past the turnoff for I-95 and took a left toward Hardeeville, then turned north on 321. We'd decided on the back way, a leisurely drive through the beauty of the South Carolina summer along narrow, winding roads. We had no schedule to keep.

I must have dozed a little. Somewhere south of Barnwell, Red had to brake hard, and the movement jerked me awake. "What?" I asked.

"Nothing. Just a truck making an unexpected right with no turn signal."

"You ought to give him a ticket."

"Too nice a day," he said with an answering smile. "Besides I left my badge at home."

For the next couple of miles I watched the light playing across the hood of the car as we passed under overhanging branches from the towering trees that crowded the roadside. A couple of times I felt Red's eyes dart in my direction. Finally, I said again, "What?"

"What do you mean?" he asked.

"You keep looking at me."

"You're a beautiful woman. I can't look at you?"

"Something's on your mind. Spill it."

He sighed and shook his head. "I hate to spoil things."

"Then don't."

His face grew somber. "It's about Alain Darnay."

I could feel my whole body stiffen at the mention of his name.

"I know you don't want to talk about it, but I have to know, Bay."

"Why?"

"For a lot of reasons. And don't pretend you don't know what most of them are."

His hand rested on the gearshift in the console, and I could see his fingers clenching and unclenching against the leather knob.

"Is this an official inquiry? I thought you left your badge at home." I adjusted the shoulder harness and stared straight ahead.

"Is he coming back? To the States? That's really all I need to know." I could hear the anger rising in his voice. "Or are you going back to Europe?"

I drew a long breath and forced myself to speak calmly. "No and no. It's over."

Red slowed behind an old tractor pulling a wobbly, wooden flatbed trailer and gave me a look. "Seems I've heard that song before."

"Look," I snapped, whirling to face him, "if you're gonna get snotty about it, just go to hell. But take my word for it, this is it."

He gunned the engine and pulled around the tractor. The young boy perched high on the seat whistled and waved as we roared past. "I wish I could believe that," he said when we'd settled back into the right-hand lane.

"I don't give a flying damn if you believe it or not." I drew a calming breath and lowered my tone. "I had a lot of time to think about things while I was hanging out all those hours in the waiting room of the hospital. You know Lavinia never went home? Not once in those first couple of days when it was touch-and-go, not even to change clothes. I had to bring her stuff from Presqu'isle."

"I know. I heard they had to pry her away from his bedside just to change the IV."

I nodded. "That's how it's supposed to be."

"How what's supposed to be?"

I ducked my head and mumbled into my chest. "Love," I said softly.

The word hovered on the currents wafting in on the warm breeze. Neither of us spoke for a long time.

I raised my eyes and looked across at my brother-in-law. "I've had a letter. From Alain." When Red didn't reply, I hurried on. "They wanted him out of there, didn't want him compromised by being tangled up in a kidnapping investigation. And he went. Just like that. He expects me to understand."

"And do you?"

I shrugged. "In a way. It's just that he can't give up his job. He tried, but it's no good. Darnay's not cut out for being an organizer, an administrator in a suit and tie. He's an undercover cop. It's what he does."

"Maybe—" Red began, but I shook my head.

"No," I said, "no maybes. He made his decision." I swallowed back the tears. "And I made mine."

The whistling of the wind was all that disturbed the quiet for a long time after I finished speaking. I watched Red's fingers relax their death grip on the gearshift lever and his shoulders lose their stiffness.

It seemed forever before he finally said, "And you're okay with that?"

I fought back the pain and forced myself to nod. "I will be."

We stopped for an early lunch at a little diner the other side of Aiken, then got back on the road. The sky had been clouding over the more we moved north until, by the time we rolled into the little college town of Newberry, we could hear the low rumbling of thunder across the hills. We pulled in at a gas station and put the top up, raising the windows against the swirling wind that was flinging roadside litter in little eddies against the car.

"Want to go someplace until the storm passes?" Red asked, but I shook my head.

"It doesn't matter," I answered, and he moved back onto the street.

We eased past the serenity of the college, its venerable old brick buildings and meandering walkways empty of chattering students for the summer. Lightning flashed off in the distance as Red wove through the narrow streets and eventually back out of town again.

"Hasn't changed much." I turned at his voice, soft and tinged with nostalgia. "I used to love it here when I was a kid."

I nodded. Though it had been years since I'd set foot in the picturesque little community with its restored opera house and marvelous antebellum mansions, I, too, felt the tug of familiarity, the peaceful comfort of a place remembered with fondness.

The storm broke just as we pulled through the wide wrought-iron gates. Red apparently knew the way, for he never hesitated as he followed the winding driveway through the wooded acreage. Finally he coasted to a stop and turned in the seat to face me.

"Are you going to wait until the rain lets up?"

I shook my head. "I won't melt."

"Want me to go with you?"

"Not yet. Just give me a few minutes, okay?"

"Sure." My brother-in-law squeezed my arm as I lifted the twist of green tissue paper from the back seat and slid out of the car. "Straight ahead. Inside that little fence."

The white stone shimmered against the sheets of rain. My hair hung in soggy strings, plastered to my face and neck, and I pushed it out of my eyes. I gazed at the inscription, stooping to run my fingers across the letters etched deeply in the marble:

ROBERT JAMES TANNER
BELOVED SON, BROTHER, AND HUSBAND

"Sorry I didn't make it sooner, sweetheart," I whispered.

I knelt on the soggy ground which I knew held nothing of the man I'd loved for so many years, neither his bones nor his spirit.

"I think I'm going to be all right now. I think I can let it be over."

I unwrapped the tissue and placed the single white rose at the base of the memorial stone. My tears had all been spent long ago, and it was rain I wiped from my streaming face. I felt Red move up behind me, his hands coming to rest on my sodden shoulders. I rose and leaned back against his chest as his arms encircled me.

"Okay?" he asked, his breath warm against the side of my cheek.

"Okay," I said, smiling through the raindrops.